Call Each River Jordan

Call Each River Jordan

Owen Parry

wm

WILLIAM MORROW
75 YEARS OF PUBLISHING
An Imprint of HarperCollins*Publishers*

CALL EACH RIVER JORDAN. Copyright © 2001 by Owen Parry.
All rights reserved. Printed in the United States of America.
No part of this book may be used or reproduced in any manner
whatsoever without written permission except in the case of brief
quotations embodied in critical articles and reviews.
For information address HarperCollins Publishers Inc.,
10 East 53rd Street, New York, NY 10022.

HarperCollins books may be purchased for educational,
business, or sales promotional use. For information please write:
Special Markets Department, HarperCollins Publishers Inc.,
10 East 53rd Street, New York, NY 10022.

FIRST EDITION

Designed by Fearn Cutler de Vicq

Printed on acid-free paper

Library of Congress Cataloging-in-Publication Data has been
applied for.

ISBN 0-06-018638-0

01 02 03 04 05 RRD 10 9 8 7 6 5 4 3 2 1

For Katherine,
my believer

John Brown's body lies a-mold'ring in the grave,

His soul is marching on. . . .

—Union anthem

Call Each River Jordan

one

I remember the burning men. Wounded, and caught like the damned at the reckoning. In brush and bramble lit by battle's sparks. They cried for help or death, for wives and mothers. Some begged God's mercy, while their fellows cursed. They smelled sweet. It is a scent no man forgets, once it has filled his nose. The fragrance of the pyre. The flames crept up and over stranded souls. Turning men into a twist of fire. Wild hands withered black. Uniforms burn quicker than the flesh, but hair blazes. Boys wore crowns of flame. That day I understood the pain of martyrs.

They burned in a poor-struck land, above a river. I have known many rivers. And many burnings. The heathen roasts the living wife along with her dead master. And when they burned the niggers dead of cholera, in great piles, you would have thought the heavens scorched with sugar. The Hindoo and the Musselman burned, and here and there a Christian gone astray. A rancid sweetness will connote the damned. It clings.

That muddy river made me think of India. But this was in America, and now, and white men burned.

I saw them in the smoke but yards away each time I shouldered up to aim and shoot. Those hit in the legs crawled on their elbows, but could not get beyond the spreading flames. Some raised themselves enough to catch a ball. I fired and bent to load and heard their screams.

A man beside me rose to make a rescue. I yanked him down.

Another boy in blue, torn by the cries, ran out to help. Ignoring my command. He fell to no effect, and burned himself. In that storm of lead and hate and heat. I gave them the devil then, the lads I had gathered from the ruins of a dozen regiments, and hoped they heard me through the crash of battle. I shouted that their duty was to fight, and damn the rest.

Thus I became a judge of life and death. For battle has to do with here and now, and I would waste no life where no hope lay. That is the soldier in me, a dreadful thing. I shall need much forgiveness. But let that bide.

The men in gray and rags rushed on and fell. Embers of spent wadding spread the fires. The damned in Hell will sound like burning boys. Our boys and theirs. For that is war. There was no succor, and death gleaned those who stood in the wrath of the day. If I shrieked in your ear in your safe parlor, it would mean little, for no art tells the agony of such. My words are shreds of nothing. Those men between the lines died hard and lonely. As lonely as Christ. I had heard screams before, of course, of brown men and of wounded friends in scarlet or in khaki, but never knew a chorus such as this. Dozens burned alive. Dozens and tens of dozens. A multitude. Crying.

And that was Shiloh.

.   .   .

THEY COULD NOT BUDGE US so they brought up guns. I heard the horses first, the whinnies of the teams. Then came the harsh commands and grump of muzzles, the sharp report of powder packed and lit. I could not see the cannon for the smoke. But branches broke and fell about our legs, and splinters killed. I thought I heard the bark of Whitworths in battery, recalling sepoys maddened with rebellion.

In all my years of marching, fear marched with me. But there is a fear that vanquishes itself, and makes of man a brutal, killing beast.

The cannoneers lowered their aim. Blasting through our feeble scraps of cover.

We were a pack of shrunken regiments, of companies pared down to ten and less. I knew no names, and pennants there were none. Any flag raised up fell back again. Men lay close, almost atop one another, dying by strangers. I worked my rifle like a common soldier.

The Rebels used the trees. Feeling for a gap beyond our flank. And they would find one. For never was a battle more confused. A broken army fought a breaking one. All combat is a boiling stew of chaos. But this fight was disordered through and through.

I should have been away from all such doings, as safe as this, our fragile life, allows. I meant to disembark five miles downriver, at General Grant's headquarters. I was no longer called to fields of battle. Not since my misfortune at Bull Run. No, I had come upon a criminal matter, at Washington's alarm. Twas murder of a sort so sensitive that telegraphic code would not suffice to tell the half of what I needed to know. They only said it was an urgent crime that might disturb the nation and our cause.

Dear God, what crime is greater than a war?

The steamboat that carried me docked at the breakfast hour. Below a town set on the eastern bluff. A high, white house shone above a cloud of tents. That would be headquarters, and no question. For generals do not like to sleep in shanties. But the mansion was no happy place that morning.

Staff men on the bluff stared south and pointed. Ignoring my vessel's arrival, with its whistle, bulk and smoke. I had heard guns along the Tennessee and knew a scrap had gotten underway. I was dismayed, for this was on a Sunday, and that was brazen insult to the Lord. But now I saw the matter was not planned.

Oh, not by us.

Upon the mansion's sloping lawn, an officer too stout to be less than a colonel cursed to astound. Profanity may be weakness, but his oaths roared above the grumbling boilers, above the splashing wheels and creak of ropes. You would have heard that fellow in a battle, but now his wind was wasted on his peers. A signals man waved madly from a roof.

I took my Colt and left my bag and jumped into a smaller boat just parting. Heading toward the fight. That is where an officer must go, see. No matter what his task on other days. I had naught else but purse and pocket Testament, a thing of solace indispensable, and last the orders folded in my pocket. I leaned upon my cane, skin all a-prickle, nose toward the clapping of the guns.

The gentlemen aboard paid me no mind, for I am not impressive at a glance. And they had other matters on their minds.

"There's going to be hell to pay," an unshaven major declared, repeating it over and over. "There's just going to be *hell* to pay . . ."

I half thought they would paddle with their hands. To reach the field of death a little sooner. They were distraught and heedless, if well-meaning. Surprise is hard in war, and good men fail.

It took me back, unwilling, to the Mutiny, and desperate days when time was scarce as powder. Urgent and shocked, we marched on bloody Delhi. Slogging through hot nights, because the sun killed white men in a hurry. With sepoys and sowars grim to our front, and cholera in our baggage. I remembered Molloy singing, to mask the groans of sick men in the wagons, and the corpses blue by morning, and black before we got them in their graves. I was a sergeant then, and should have shut him up to show respect. For there were officers among the sick. But I was hard, and hummed along myself. Our jokes grew cruel. We were glad of the fight when it come, and showed the poor buggers no mercy. When they tried to surrender, we gave them our steel, and washed the Subzeeh Mundee with their blood. Of course, we kept their holy men for hanging. Whenever we had rope.

Memory is the curse of Cain and soldiers.

They called our destination Pittsburg Landing. But no name tells the shame of what we found. We washed down the cool of the river, with the current brown and quick and spiked with branches.

Blossoms pinked the bluffs. The sun was up all lovely, I remember, as befits a proper April Sunday. But nature is a harlot in her beauty.

Have you ever seen a side of beef all maggots? A crawling thing, fit to turn the gut? That was our welcome on the riverbank.

The western shoreline festered. With cowards. Thousands had sought refuge by the water. They crammed the little space below the bluff. A shameful swarm of blue they made, speckled with the red of undergarments and shirts billowing like flags of surrender. Runaways and skulkers to a man. Cringing in the mud. Never had I seen such a filthy quitting. Even natives fight to save themselves.

Bull Run was a triumph by compare.

It looked as if our army had dissolved. Yet cannon sounded thick beyond the landing. A fight there was, a real one, some miles distant.

We put in to shouts of disaster and warnings of enemy legions. Our generals were dead, deserters cried, and the Rebels took no prisoners. But that was tosh. Americans had no stomach for a massacre, and I prayed they never would gain one. Surrendering was honored, more or less. The meanness comes when skins have different colors. Then men will kill and think it worth the sweat.

The sailor folk raised axes, clubs and pistols to keep our boat from being overrun. Men, half-naked, splashed into the river. As if it were the Jordan. A few swam out in the muddy stream, then disappeared, unable to cross over. Men begged and offered gold to come on board. A lieutenant colonel, splashing in an eddy, wailed that his brother was a Congress fellow, insisting that his life must be protected. He offered up his watch-chain, then the watch.

Now I have seen fear, and felt it, but there is no greater danger for an army than panic. No plague spreads so fast, or kills so surely. In battle, he survives who stands and fights. The man who runs will be cut down and slain. But we are not creatures of sense, and cannot be told. That is why a soldier must be trained. For running is the impulse of our hearts.

That day they ran, the good men after bad. I felt the shock and wonder of my boatmates, for they were young and green as Gwent themselves. Bleating like lambs in their newness. Well, they would learn what war was soon enough.

I jumped down in the muck and started marching. Limping up the bluff, with cane and pistol, an angry little man whose back was up. But misery loves company, there is true. More than one man clutched me by the arm, swearing, "Major, they'll kill you dead, if'n you go up there . . . sure as the devil, they'll kill you dead." To hear them tell it all was lost that morning. With no hope of redemption on the field. But I had been a sergeant and knew better. And now I was a major full of hopes. No battle is lost as long as one man stands.

And I was shamed. For I had taken this Union to my heart. More fully than we should love mortal things. I loved its promise of a better life, its goodness to the man who strived, its fairness and its hope, if yet imperfect. Our country took me in when I had fallen, and though I hated war I knew my debt. And there was pride mixed in, the pride of man. I am no gentleman when it comes to losing. Oh, I was hot.

A thousand cowards make a mournful sound. In Bible verse they call it lamentation. It is ignoble, and desperate, and rude to the ear. They might have been the ravished folk of Egypt, those fellows gathered witless by the bank.

Rifles lost and even shoes abandoned. Playing cards and papers strewn about. Pipes cast down. All trampled underfoot. Clean new greenback dollars sailed the breeze and frightened men ignored the dancing money. The earth stank of defeat and bad latrines.

The men behind the bluff had turned to cattle. A single company of Rebels might have taken them all. And not one would have lifted a finger to save himself. Now, you will say, "That is a lie, and foolish. A thousand will not give way to a hundred." But you have not seen men as I have seen them. Paralyzed by terror, cripple-souled.

A man with half his teeth laughed as I went. "They'll gobble that little pecker right up," he said. Those hiding in the ditch beside him laughed. One even hurled a stone and struck my back. Men in their shame are desperate, little things.

You would have thought the day was lost, indeed. Streams of men flowed back toward the river, as if the season rained them on the earth. Oh, how they ran. But I am an old bayonet and a veteran of John Company's fusses, and I listened past their wailing and complaints. The sound of guns and musketry come mighty over the land. For each who fled, at least one stood and fought. There was a battle not yet lost entire.

Men do not see when they are full of fear. They stumbled into me. As if I were but air. Blocked, they stared. Amazed to find themselves in human contact. Then they dropped their eyes and shook and fled. Men and boys. An officer in a uniform of beauty, a captain with a golden sash, ran off. Pursued by devils. And when the officers run, you cannot expect the other ranks to stand. God forgive me, I almost shot him down upon the spot.

But I would have killing enough.

A battery of ours charged through the runaways, shouts and hooves and whips and wheels and dust. Chains chimed under the carriages, and a dangling bucket banged. The gunners rode *toward* the fray, God bless them. Running down the stragglers in their path. Twas the first bit of sense I encountered. And though I had hard memories of caissons, my heart filled with a malice near to joy. I cheered the cannon on and followed after.

I walked a sorry mile to find the battle, bad leg sore but willing. My cane gored Southron earth beneath the dust. Tents ranked neat stood empty but for looters, hard men dumping bags and chests and field desks. Stealing from their comrades without shame. Even in a battle you hear glass break. It is the pitch, soprano, sharp and thin. Letters strewn about dishonored sweethearts, laying bare the secret thoughts of wives. A cook stood over his kettle with a rifle, as if his troops had just stepped off to drill and he must feed them all on their return. Bugle calls broke off before they finished, and drums beat contrary orders. April flies, oblivious, swarmed and balled.

Closing on the fight my hopes were bolstered. Regiments in order hastened up, jingling as they tramped across the fields. Aroused from rearward camps, they surged expectant, pointed on by officers with swords. Voices strained to command, and blue caps lifted while men wiped their sweat. Couriers galloped in between the groves. Lieutenants with red stripes upon their trousers searched out strong positions for their guns, crashing through the brush on nervous horses. The wounded limped along, those who could walk, helped by comrades glad to quit the line.

I saw few dead at first. Just those torn ragged by an errant shell, or bled to death of wounds as they strained rearward. They lay beside the roads and in the fields. In daunting stillness.

A sutler's wagon, looted, filled a ditch. With naughty pictures scattered in the weeds amid discarded bottles of camp remedies.

And vexed I was with fears for my old friend, Dr. Mick Tyrone, who served somewhere upon that wretched field. Good it is to have friends near in battle, where you can feel their shoulders against yours. Then you imagine that you will protect them, as they will you. But the friend in another regiment, the comrade out of sight, excites your worry.

A boy with a rifle as big as himself approached me.

"Major," he begged, "d'you know where the 11th Ioway's gone to? D'you know the 11th Ioway? You seen 'em?" A child he was, afraid to be caught truant.

I did not know and told him that. But then I thought me better.

"Come along, lad," I said. "We'll find a fight, if not your regiment."

And so I began to do what I long should have been doing. Rallying those who would heed me. Grabbing boys and turning them around. Snatching rifles from the dust and weeds and slapping them into their hands. Shaming them with looks as much as words. Not all were skulkers, see. Many were but confused. Left by their leaders, scattered from their comrades.

"Damn you," I said to a sergeant, for I was one who valued every stripe. "Damn you, get up and help me, man." Ready I was to drag him by the beard. But he got up himself, come to his senses.

Some who listened died for it that day. Leaving wives and children hard bereft. That is the soldier's lot. All those who slight the soldier do not know what he endures while they are safe at home. Why did they follow? I had a major's shoulderboards. And a sergeant's growl. Men only want their orders spoken clear.

I pointed into the weeds. "Take up those cartridge boxes," I told my growing band. For I judged by the sound we would need them. "And get you plenty of caps."

All a soldier wanted could be gathered along that road, thrown down by men who thought to quit the war. "You. *You!*" I seized an ancient musket from a private and thrust a fine new rifle in his arms. "That'll do a proper damage," I told him.

Some began to join our ranks unbidden. One boy ran across a fresh, green field. No one wants to be alone in battle, and men rally to those who show a little pluck.

Of course, there was no order to our march. A grunting mob in uniform we were. But they followed me, full thirty of them now. Some even started in to brag and swagger, mocking those who would not go beside us.

I had put up my Colt and got a rifle. U.S.-issue, fine but for the dust. I must have looked a sight, laden down with cartridge leathers and the long weapon, limping along on my cane. But those boys and men saw naught but my mask of confidence, a sergeant's trick learned fighting the Pushtoon, when confidence was all that got you through. A major had it easy by compare to the bloody young man I had been.

Bullets stung the air. I tried to sense where we were needed most, but gained no feeling for the battle's shape. Ahead of us loomed thunder and obscurity.

A riderless horse careened from a grove, seeking sunlight. Animals run from the fighting, see, unless they have been special-bred for viscounts.

"Over there," I bellowed. "Into the trees." I did not lead but drove them from behind, a sergeant still in soul and skills and bearing. I did not want to see them run again. Oh, two tried. But I smacked them proper with a length of cane. And nearly lost my balance in the doing, for I was loaded like a native bearer. I cursed the slackers, wounding decent English.

Set down like this, all reeks of sense and knowledge. But I was not a thinking man that day. In battle, men survive who learn to act. Thinkers perish, or, at best, they fail. They hesitate, and die. No, I had not the selfhood ink pretends, but was a beast trained by a master's hand. Forever a creature of the regiment I was, though I had long hoped elsewhere. I was, again, the boy in the scarlet coat, streaming with the gore of Chillianwala, and grinning at the slaughter and the triumph. That was Britannia's legacy to me, brought to my new land as a fateful cargo.

I was not myself upon that field, see. Not the Abel Jones I had constructed across the years I wore no uniform. Not the man I prayed that I might be as I approached the age of thirty-four. Not the loving husband and father, the dutiful Methodist clerk. I fell down. And Jones the Killer rose up like a ghost, bloody as the Kashmir Gate at Delhi.

But let that bide.

Suddenly, we were in it. I pushed forward. The lad beside me wriggled like a caught snake, then tumbled bloody. The scrub wood tangled our feet in roots and briars, tripping us with haversacks and blankets thrown away, with weapons lost and staring corpses. Officers shouted to be heard above the volleys, but their voices only blurred. It was a realm of rifles, with no guns wheeled between the trees as yet, though cannonades resounded on our flanks. Ahead, blue backs stood and knelt and crouched, while officers went rushing to and fro. Men fell.

I marked the weakest portion of the line.

"Over there," I ordered. Pointing with my hand and then my rifle. I knew that those remaining would stay by me, the way a soldier knows but can't explain. I did my best to lead them true and decent.

And now my cane would have to be discarded, although I feared my leg would not hold up. I needed both hands for the rifle, see, and thought to use the weapon as my crutch. Still, I felt a twinge amid the fury, for we have little sense of proper order. My stick was but another scrap of wood. Yet it had been a gift of Christian kindness, carved by honest hands in old New York. I had to let it go, but felt a grief. Well, men lost more that day than Abel Jones. A moment later, I had aimed and shot.

I put my rough platoon in place, back in the trees where we were screened by brambles. We would be hard to see, though not protected. Nor were our enemies set out on display. The Rebels came in rushes, darting out of the smoke. Game those fellows were, but poorly led. Their officers did not know how to mass, or how to make the left support the right. A proper sergeant might have put them straight. But this was not a war of regulars. Now and then, we caught a glimpse of lines, and once a braided fellow waved his cap, riding on a black and prancing horse. But most of it was deadly hide-and-seek.

The lads had been taught to stand and shoot, as all the manuals tell you, but that just made them targets. I had them crouch wherever there was cover. Though not before another soldier fell. A rotted log was all we had to shield us, yet that was more than our charging enemies had. Briars tangled them, and smoke grabbed their flags.

The Rebels thinned away. As if they had been ghosts. A pool of quiet spread before us, while battle roared and screamed on either flank. The boys kept firing till I made them stop.

"Reload, and hold your fire," I commanded. "Look you, lads. Set your cartridge boxes up beside you. And wait for them to come, for come they will."

Well I knew what such a silence meant. A fresh regiment, perhaps a new brigade, was forming to fall upon us. I scrambled over to the officer nearest, a colonel with his arm in a bloody sling, whose men were pouring fire into nothing. I tried to warn him what was bound to happen, but he only looked down at me, as if I were one of the malingerers under the bluff, and told me to get away. When the attack came, his line was pierced, and only the arrival of a fresh regiment restored our front. The colonel fell at his post.

By then I was back with my lads, giving what encouragement I could. ·

The Rebels charged screaming and howling, half an army, half a heathen tribe. Unmatched flags swept over a field. That meant we faced two regiments, at least. But we, too, had grown stronger. Soldiers looking for their units had wandered into our line and joined it. Orphaned companies wedged in to shore up battered regiments. We barely had space to load.

"Hold your fire," I said. "Hold your fire . . . and aim low when you aim."

Not all paid me heed, for fear was on them. But the stronger among them coiled. I could feel the fierceness in them then. Waiting to spring loose. It is a sense of power that should disgrace us.

I waited until the enemy was snared in the brush and bodies, close enough for us to mark their faces, their eagerness and fury and their dread. Then I screamed, *"Fire,"* in a voice gone raw.

A dozen dropped at once before our front. The suddenness stunned their comrades, and they wavered. I ordered the boys to reload and fire at will. That was when they pierced us on the right, where the colonel had dismissed me, but a tide of blue poured through the trees in time. I aimed and shot, more useful thus than barking.

We fired, and they fell, and they fell, and we fired.

Still, we were ordered back. Somewhere, the line had failed. We lost more lads withdrawing than while holding. I saw the bafflement of men who had fought well but must give up the ground for which they bled. Some cursed in spite, while others wept with rage. Myself, I had forgotten my bothered leg, as men will overlook dreadful wounds and keep fighting. There is a wild energy that sweeps you, an opiate to pain and spur to deeds. The devil overtakes us in a battle and fills us with a mockery of joy. You feel that you were never more alive.

The Rebels cheered behind us, but they paused. Their leaders were as new to this as ours and did not know enough to drive us hard.

Oh, we were motley. Sloven. Reloading left our faces black as miners, with powder acrid on our swollen tongues. Trees and smoke consumed troops by the hundreds. The sun was blotted and the heavens stained.

We came into a meadow of green shoots, and I began to understand the ground. The way a veteran suddenly knows a thing. It was no place to make your numbers tell or to sweep grandly round a hanging flank. The landscape broke the battle into fragments and made it but a brawl of split brigades. The ground was queer and crippled brave attacks. Twas as if the Lord had dropped a cloak, its folds become ravines or swales or ridges. Rhymeless stands of trees fringed poor men's fields. It was a sorry place, though it was warm. I late had felt the rawness of New York. Here all was buds and sprouting leaves. And death.

A fellow got up fine cantered abroad, followed by a brace of staff men.

"That's General Prentiss," one of the lads behind me called, but I knew of none such. And I was one for letting generals be.

You feel the want of water quick enough. When you are drinking smoke and shouting orders. The heat of battle multiplies the sun, and when you are in the thing the smoke wraps you hot and drains you dry as the Balooch deserts. The thirst, too, made me think of India. I longed to call out for my good, old *bhisti,* with his bag of lovely water and his grin.

I had not planned for battles in my travels, and had brought no equipment save my Colt. I had no water bottle or canteen. So I tugged vessels free of the dead, and had the boys still with me do the same. Scruples fade amid slaughter. And heat will drop a soldier like a bullet.

But there is right and wrong, even in battle. I caught a boy stripping clothing from a corpse. Now taking up cartridges or water is a matter of need, and only practical, but looting must not be permitted. It is a matter of discipline, as much as it is of morals. For the army that grabs dissolves.

I recognized the lad as one of mine, a boy whom I had gathered off the road. He had unruly hair, as I remember. But no one was well-combed that bloody day.

I gave him a whack with the stock of my rifle. The barrel scalded my hands.

"You'll leave the dead alone," I told him. "Come along."

The boy responded by tugging at the corpse's legs again.

I slapped him hard. And then he looked at me.

"I just want his trousers," he pleaded, with a pitiful look in his eyes. "I done shat mine through."

A bullet caught him where his cheekbone bulged. Teeth and brains and blood splashed passing men.

I marched off with a fierce, determined limp. For he who stops to think will think too long.

.   .   .

WE FOUGHT FOR HOURS. In another wood. Ears stunned. Ringing. Aching. The right ear always worse. As if our heads had grown lopsided. And swollen. With the shooting shoulder bruised by the rifle's kick. Parsing ammunition. Searching bodies for more.

Breathing men's burst guts. Gunpowder scours your nostrils, see. And gives you all the cesspit stink of war. We gagged and fired, eyes to the front. Afraid to look around us or behind. Terrified by the jamming of a barrel. Without the wanted time for proper action. Ripping weapons from the slop of corpses. Even those unscathed were splashed with blood. I had to wipe a boy's pulp from my face and slap his innards from my tunic's breast.

That is how we fought. And that is where the wounded burned alive.

Though I would be a Christian man, I strayed far from all righteousness that day. In war a man becomes a raging beast, hating those whom he will never know. And there is pleasure in killing, when the hatred is upon you. That is a secret that soldiers keep from those who keep a gentler watch at home. I would have slain the Rebels by the hundreds, with no thought that each was a man like me. I would tell you that I hate war, and I do, but what I truly mean is something other: I hate what war has taught me of myself.

At times I fear Christ threw himself away.

But that is looking back. That day I fought, and hated with my soul. Fellows who have never tasted battle make up fancies that ennoble us. Scribblers would have us full of thoughts of country, dreaming of wives and home and high ideals, of causes, flags and fidelity. But that is what you think of in your tent, if you are one who thinks of things at all. A warm meal matters more than any motto, and shelter from the rain is cause enough. Battle has its reasons, but they do not fit our words. Heroes are but men of timely impulse. We only want to live.

Tell me of glory, and I will tell you of boys burned alive at Shiloh.

.   .   .

ANTS. First I remember the burning men, and then I recall the ants. I lay in the dust of Adam, and hurt bloomed in my ear. The pain swelled up each time I pulled the trigger. I know that I reached for a cartridge and saw it was covered with ants. Copper in color they were. Then I saw that my hand was laden, too, and my sleeve swarmed. And then I felt the bites along my body, for I had stretched myself upon a nest. Each creature fights the battles of its kind. I will give Mr. Darwin that, though nothing more. I felt a hundred bites like stings of shrapnel.

They saved me, the ants did. I rolled off in a panic. Just as a Rebel brought his rifle down. He would have crushed my skull.

I shocked him with the quickness I could muster. Jolted by sudden terror, I rose before his weapon pulled back up and jabbed the nip of my gunstock in his ribs. He staggered with a grunt.

He was a creature of the poorest fields. Of stunted cobs and shallow furrows. Thin-faced, hair long and filthy, beard stained yellow-orange as if with sulfur. His cap was gone, his uniform torn. But his eyes shone full of lightning. His skin was red and ruined. But not those eyes. I will recall them till the day I die. They were black. Eyes alive as any man's, and desperate to stay among the living.

Tough he was, but not trained. He judged me less a man, due to my stature. It killed him, that mistake. For I was brought up on the bayonet, and fought with emptied rifle many a day. And when our blades broke off we clubbed our foe. I knew my tools.

He lunged for me and I slipped to the side. Bad leg or no, I had the old skills yet. He stumbled, driven forward by his weight. Greased with sweat, I parried as he passed me. Then my rifle's stock swung to his skull. And he went down.

In poems and ballads wounded men are spared. But fallen men may rise to fight again. Gasping, I pulped his brains with one fierce blow. Then I looked around. Ready for the next man, bloody-minded. When no one took his place, I knelt and loaded, stiff of leg but charged beyond the pain. For I had learned to load formed up in square or bent behind low walls of Punjab mud.

Mingled and mangled we were. But coats of blue surrounded me again. Steady in the trees behind a farm road. We gulped the smoke and stink, lungs desperate. Awaiting the next Rebel try.

Our enemies paused again. The battle carried on in other fields. But where we stood the cost had been too high. I hoped that we had stopped them in our front.

That is when they massed the guns against us, more than they had brought to bear all day. The smoke thinned and we watched as they unlimbered, across a field and stretched into the trees. Gun upon gun. Some began to fire right away. Seeking the range.

The fellows to our left pulled off the line. Rifle fire had sounded to our rear, trapping us as quarry for their guns. And so I had to choose. Stand beside our comrades, or withdraw.

Round shot shattered trees, piercing men with splinters fierce as bullets. Then shells burst near us. I felt the change come over every man, as if the cauldron around us had gone chill. Our lines would not withstand their dozen batteries. Nor would our hearts.

"Come on, you buggers," I called, for I was vicious. I yanked at collars and kicked with my good leg, nearly toppling over. "Come on, or you'll go to Hell and deserve it. Come *on*, lads . . . follow after . . ."

A goodly dozen obeyed me. We plunged back into the wood, with me hobbling in the lead. The Rebel infantry dashed at the flanks again, and action roared to the rear. I knew that they were trying to close a circle. A man could smell surrender in the air.

And I would *not* surrender. Not Abel Jones. Perhaps it was a curse on me from India, where those who quit were tortured, like as not, and always killed before their comrades reached them. This was not India, no, and skins were white. But I was in that rage of self-possession that guides the veteran soldier like a star. And I would not give up to any man. I am hard-headed, judge me as you may.

We were not the only ones withdrawing. Tattered regiments

made a rolling fight. Behind us, cannon opened by the dozen. Their ranging done, death rode on every shot. The woods burned, and the army howled like a beast.

"This way, lads. Over here."

I had lost several men to the confusion. Some outran me, for I was not quick. A rifle makes an awkward sort of cane. Yet on we went. The Rebels swarmed around to bag their prey. We paused by planted flags and joined the volleys. But no line lasted long. Sugar in water we were, and nothing more. With our own troops firing wildly, and regiments wrecked in the crossfire. Soon there was no order left at all.

Braced on my gun's stock, I shouted commands. Whether or not a body was left to listen. My words had the value of gibberish, and perhaps not a whit more sense. A handsome fellow on the eve of manhood leapt across my path just like a deer. Laughing. Twas not a laugh of joy or any health. The boy was Bedlam mad. Shrieking with laughter. He had a prophet's eyes and woman's hands.

We fled. And turned to fire. And fled again. The best men had the spunk of cornered beasts. Through burning tents and ruined camps we went. Clots of wounded, gathered then forgotten, lay defenseless in the battle's path. Some tried to join the fight, while others begged us to carry them away. Men crawled, dragging entrails or a useless limb. The lucky ones lay still with eyes of wonder, numb because the pain had not yet struck.

In a meadow a downed horse quivered. It kicked and twisted, trying to bite the pain of guts spilled out like flour from a sack. I do not like horses, but pitied that animal. Its eyes were stunned and might have been a man's. Yet, even with a rifle ready loaded, I would not waste my lead upon the beast. Nor did he merit one shot from my pistol. Every round was meant for killing men. That was but sense and discipline, see.

Our decency is thinner than a reed. I left the creature shrieking on the ground.

We were a sorry pack, a mass disordered. The few lads left

beside me blurred into a collision of regiments. Both ours and theirs. Men fought hand to hand, and I drew out my Colt, which I had saved for such a spot as this.

I think I shouted orders out of habit, but know that I pressed on. A shabby, limping thing, if truth be told. But a Welshman is tenacious, when you spin him up. I plunged through the mêlée, clearing a path with my pistol. Every shot went into a man close enough to embrace me. I screamed out curses I had thought forgotten, and called to comrades dead on distant fields. I, too, was mad. With the old, familiar madness. My last round took an officer in the chest, a stately fellow following his sword. He looked amazed that anything could harm him. I whipped him across the snout with the pistol's barrel and sent him sprawling. I think he died of astonishment.

Then we were safe. Twas sudden, as the ways of battle are. But our safety was a thing to be closely measured. A bloody pack of us had gotten through, and not too soon. Behind us, the firing faltered, and bugles sounded the sorriest of calls.

The regiments that stayed behind were finished. Surrendered. I closed my eyes in sorrow at the thought. For I would not have the day go lost. Too much had passed to end up in defeat, too much blood, too much hating, too much of mortal pride.

Four boys remained of those who had gone with me. I did not give them any time to think. I made them hunt up cartridge, cap and water, and two replaced the rifles they had lost. I watched them as I put away my Colt. For soldiers must be kept occupied, their reason dampened down by constant labors. When I was sure the lads were steady, I joined their search myself, scanning for dead officers who might possess the cap and ball I needed.

I found a spare canteen and splashed my face. The clotted gore mixed powder, grit and flies. My hat had gone astray upon the field. Sounds come to me ringing through a chamber. My leg ached, and my shoulder was a bother. Elsewhere, I was torn and scratched, but whole. The worst part was the bites left by the ants. It was a miracle, on such a day.

I should have knelt and prayed my richest thanks. But I was too ashamed to face the Lord. The Testament weighed heavy in my pocket. We are but creatures steeped in lust and blood, and saints are few and short-lived in our midst.

Where I stood now the battle held its breath, though fighting carried on to left and right. Still, there was something different in the noise, a thing I could not name but recognized. The rage was off, the fight was on the wane. For that day, at least. The enemy had used up their main strength. And we had held them, by the grace of God.

My leg hurt with a vengeance now that the scrap was done.

I married us to the end of an Illinois regiment, where we might be of some last use, if men were needed. But the wind was gone out of the Rebels, as sure as the devil was grinning.

As evening settled over the field, a ragged line of blue firmed on good ground. *Our* cannon massed now. We had been driven back, and badly, and could not count the day a victory. But we had not been vanquished, either. And rumors spread that we had reinforcements, that Buell had come himself with all his men. The Rebels had a last go at our left. But that was where Sam Grant had set his guns. Aching to reach the river and a triumph, the Rebels were too late and far too few. I listened to the sound of distant fighting, wary of attacks on our own front. But the long day was done. Twas only that the living could not grasp it. Each man stood bewildered by his fortune. And none of us would think about tomorrow. The day still held us in its wicked straps.

The flank assault broke off, and we saw naught but phantoms in the gloaming, and all we could hear were the wounded. Crying out in sorrow and delirium.

I read once that old Wellington, describing Waterloo, said the battle was "a near-run thing." And so was Shiloh. Had the Rebels had a strong reserve, they might have flung us in the Tennessee. But they did not, and fact is fact, and history does not give us second chances. In later years, the thing was much debated, but Abel kept his peace, for done is done.

I had no peace that eve, though. I was an addled man, stinking of powder and the blood of others, with my leg a wicked annoyance. It was always the same after a fight, when my rage was gone. A shaking come over me. Twas then I felt the fear penned up inside. And thought of wife and child, and saw my folly. I soon was as useless as those runaways, the men who fled to safety by the river.

I spoke to the boys I had led in a fragile voice:

"It is all right now. Go you and find your regiments. Your friends will want you by them."

After that I sat against a tree, sick at the beast that Abel Jones remained. I rubbed my leg and scratched the ant bites that had saved my life. How dare I call myself a Christian man? Then I recalled again that it was Sunday, but still I could not find a word to pray.

When darkness fit the land, the rain fell on us.

.   .   .

I HELPED AS BEST I COULD to cull the suffering. Lashed by rain as cold as the sun had been hot. I have known wounded men, shot in the jaw or throat, who drowned in a drizzle. I limped and bent and crawled to bring them in. But do not think the deed was Christian charity. It was my way of keeping off the devil.

I had come in pursuit of some queer murder, of which I had not yet heard the details. And found myself a murderer among many. That is war, see. Murder. And even if the murder's cause is justice, the thing is murder still. I wish to God that I could see the Right. Perhaps the generation after us will find a better way to settle things between them. But I fear otherwise. Cain dwells in every single living man.

Let that bide. Every man has sorrows, and when we speak too much we tell too little. I worked until I was a ruined thing, soaked through and aching, with my fingers as cramped as my leg. Perhaps I should have tried to find headquarters, for Washington believed my task so urgent that I had not been granted time for counsel, but sent to General Grant straight from New York and a sad affair of Irishmen and spirits. The telegraph had chased me along the railroad, then leapt ahead along the great Ohio, where clerks stood at the landings waving papers, and trailed me up the swollen Tennessee. The President himself had gripped the matter.

But what could be so urgent after this? And Grant would be somewhere upon the field, if he were any general at all. I would not find him now, in the rain and the dark. Even if I could, the man had more pressing matters before him than greeting a jumped-up clerk sent down from Washington. Let the battle end and settle, then I would seek him out. And time would solve the riddles of the day.

I found no shelter, but I spied a fire. Some men had torn dry boards from a wagon's belly, then cocked the rig half back against a tree, leaving a bit of cover for their flames. The fire was a trembling little thing, but soldiers by the hundred crowded round. Too far away to get the heat, I squeezed me down between a pair of strangers. They muttered, but made room, and I stretched out my leg. The little flame, unfelt, still seemed a comfort. Like a farmhouse lamp glimpsed through the snow.

The rain poured down, and none of us had waterproofs. All had been left behind in spoiled camps. That night was long and cold. Upon the field, hogs ate the dead and dying. We were too tired and selfish to shoot many. They squealed and grunted, happy at their feast. Lightning lit their bulk, but men ignored them. He will not understand who was not there. The rain beats down and you move not a muscle.

Our gunboats threw great shells across the night. Bombarding the wilderness, where our enemies shivered. The shells put me in mind of shrieking souls, hurled down from Heaven after one brief glimpse.

Men spoke. In voices native to our fields, and in the accents of a dozen lands. One insisted, "Grant was drunk, I'll betcha. They say he ain't been sober in his life." Another answered back indignantly, "*Das ist 'ne reine Lüge.* You are lying. I see him *mittags,* riding on his horse." "McClernand's the man for me," a fellow offered. "He looks like a general oughta look, all right. That Grant's no good. Nor Billy Sherman, neither." A fire-lit banty took up the refrain, "Bob's your uncle, 'e's a queer one, Sherman. 'E's got 'abits, that one. And . . . and preddylictions!" A shadow brogued, "The devil take the lot o' them, for the general never was born what had no sense." Not a few drenched men shared that conviction. But others cited Donelson, and Belmont, holding Grant aloft against all comers, while damning braggarts who had joined up late. A whisper reminisced of Garibaldi. And one voice bid five dollars for a dram. The others laughed and called the poor soul "Paddy," although his voice was Scots as Glasgow soot.

Twas no affair of fists, such disagreement, but only soldiers rubbing in their balm. Those who argued shared their bits of hardtack, pleased to have their tongues still in their heads. If one voice blamed the war on damned slave-owners, another cursed the African as cause. A young voice claimed we had to save the Union. The fellow wet beside him cursed him down, then cursed the day that he had volunteered. In the end, all governments were damned, and politicians and officers, and those who stayed at home and would not fight. They hated the war, and hated those not in it, and bunched more closely for the slightest warmth.

Now, you will say, "Jones should have intervened. He should have shown his rank and set them straight. Such talk is but one misstep short of mutiny." But you do not know soldiers, I can tell. Even the most admirable complain. It is their only freedom. Words are but the way we spill our pain, and pain is one thing soldiers have in plenty. It is a lonely business, truth be told.

No one slept. Not with the sleep that heals and makes you ready. We drowsed in the mud and shivered, and longed for the day to return. Despite the horrors that the light might bring. For memory is short when misery is upon us. Even the dirtiest cottage seemed fine in the memory, and those who had a home were sick and silent. Not far away, fresh regiments trudged by, countermarching to abrupt commands. And we had not delivered all the wounded hidden by the darkness of that night. You heard that plain.

A boy leaned on my shoulder, feigning sleep. I think he only wanted human warmth.

In the morning, the sun shone diamond-white behind the haze. We went on the attack. The Rebels held at first, but the lifeblood had drained out of them. I do not slight their valor. But we had the numbers now, and the energy that comes from going forward. I could not long keep pace with healthy legs and fell out of the advance. Relieved, if truth be told. For I had drunk my fill of the wine of war, and had no lust to taste the cup again. Not in that moment. Nor would I look too far into the future. Sufficient unto the day it was, that Abel Jones no longer was required. I thought I had become myself again, and promised I would study war no more.

But the mist cleared and a spectacle stretched before me, quickening my heart. Whether I wished my heart quickened by such matters or no. Long blue lines swept forward in good order, flags aloft above retaken fields. The 75th at Badli-ki-Serai was no more stirring to a soldier's soul. A part of me yearned to fall back in beside them, God forgive the weakness of my will. I almost took off at a child's run. So much for resolutions in this world. I wondered when my ghosts would be put down, when I might be a peaceful man and decent. I longed for grace, but felt the devil's claws. Only love is vivid as a war.

And that was Shiloh. Oh, they kept scrapping well into the evening. But all had been decided before noon. The rest was spite.

That field of death was one of birth, as well. It made the army that would conquer Vicksburg, then march down from Atlanta to the sea. But all that lay beyond time's bloody river, and I have got a different tale to tell.

So let that bide.

two

I found Mick at his work that afternoon. Standing in the door-yard of a cabin, where early lilacs bloomed. Just above the bluff that hid the river. I spotted him from afar. Blood-soaked and hat-less he was, with that scowling sliver of face and his hard black hair. I knew his leanness and the way he moved, the way you always recognize a friend. Drenched in blood, he remained a man of edges.

I would have run, despite my bothered leg. But hundreds of the wounded blocked my path, some curled on blankets, others dropped in the mud. All quivering, beneath the churning sky. We would have rain again, and a cold night behind it. Steel has pierced my skin more than once and I can tell you: Lying there gives a man a whiff of eternity.

Hospital tents stood pitched behind the shanty, too few for the wounded of a single regiment. But it is the sounds that linger in my mind. Perhaps because I like a proper hymn and this was supplication in the raw. They hummed like bees, that swarm of broken boys. Until the saw bit flesh. Then you heard the naked voice of Man.

I cannot seem to get me free of blood.

Grim and careful, I marched across that field. Men begged for help, but I had none to give. Not even water, for all the streams ran foul. I muttered lies to get me by their pleading. That is what my pride had tumbled down to: A man who lied to dying boys to get himself past their misery.

"It won't be a moment," I told them. "You're hardly scratched. It's nothing."

I only want to be a Christian man, and find I am a Judas to my kind.

He did not see me coming, good old Mick. Nettled he was by an ivory jut of bone. His apron was soaked like a threepenny butcher's. Sleeves rolled high, his arms were slimed with gore. He sighed and dragged a wrist across his forehead, leaving blood to mingle with his sweat. Then he marked me.

You would have thought poor Mick had seen a ghost. He believed me still in the New York countryside, see. And I was hardly cleaner than my friend. I had the muck of battle streaked upon me. Bareheaded, I leaned upon a stick to help me go. I must have looked a wounded sort myself.

"*Abel?*" he said, mouth unsteady and eyes in a gale. "You . . . you're not . . ."

"I'm fit and fine, Mick, fit and fine. And trust you are yourself?"

His face repented emotion. Wintry eyes glared at the world.

"Well, if you're 'fit and fine,' " he said, "get over here. Hold this fellow down until I finish." He glanced at his two orderlies, a sallow, sorry, weary-looking pair. "*Hold* him, damn you."

"I didn't mean to interrupt . . ." I began.

Mick flicked a clot of man-meat from his fingers. It fell short of a pile of severed limbs. "Later, bucko. Save your explanations." Then he flared up. "Hold him *down,* I said."

And that was my reunion with Mick Tyrone.

.   .   .

"MICK," I SAID, "there is a thing I would ask you."

We sat upon the bluff, amid human smells. Twas night. There had been rain, then hail, but now a swarm of torches lit the landing and sparks shot from the funnels of the boats. Tramping down the planks, troops filed ashore. Crates and kegs and sacks flew hand to hand where Negroes had been pressed into our service. Wounded men filled up departing decks. Whistles warned of comings and of goings, while in midstream the gunboats floated black. Wet through, we sat between the dead and the living.

Mick's pipe quaked in his hand, for he had worked until his muscles quit and his knife grew so unsteady it did harm. He should have been asleep, but wanted his smoke first. Perhaps he feared his dreams.

I had lit the pipe, for he could not do it. Now I do not take tobacco, anymore than I would alcohol. But we must be prepared to help a friend. The brief taste took me back to younger days, when I was as wild as the world.

A stevedore complained in words all filth, and a teamster's whip drove mules. The darkies started a chant, but soon were silenced. Beyond the river's glut the night ran endless.

"Well," Mick said, "what's on your mind, laddybuck?" His voice was sour. For he wished to be at his duty and spurned the weakness that had made him rest.

I knew him, see, and would not let him wound me. Twas only that Mick found our poor world wanting, and raged at it. He had no religion, only the hope of mortal things, and it told on him. A Socialist and atheist, he longed for men to act like perfect Christians.

"Have you . . . heard no whispers about murder? Have there been no rumors of such like? Anything queer at all, Mick? I ask in confidence. Have you heard naught of murder?"

He laughed. Twas so familiar. The lone crack of a syllable. A sentry might have thought it was a gunshot. He drew on his pipe and the glare revealed his face. Twas a ravaged thing.

Smoke poured from him. A furnace in the Merthyr mills he was. "And what would you call all this, man? Christmas in Dublin?" He lowered his pipe and the world darkened again. "Murder, indeed. What is it, bucko? Has another spoiled brat got himself killed, then? Who is it this time? And where's this one from? Another fine, old family, would it be?" He laughed again, the loneliest of souls. Harking back to matters best forgotten. Wicked scheming, and a murdered boy. "Sure, and whoever he is, he's more important than the cheap meat I've been hacking at these two days. Or they wouldn't be sending you scurrying down to see us."

"I do not think it like the Fowler matter. Although I cannot tell you that for certain, Mick. I only thought you might have got some knowledge. Look you. A man in your position hears things."

"Well, I don't know what you're gabbing about. Unless it's some farmboy cut up by his regimental gambler. And I doubt they'd send you down for the likes of that. No, the wealthy will have their due, and it doesn't take an Irishman to see it. The rest of us are only good for their slaughters." He held out his pipe as he might extend a pistol. In a shaking hand. His voice grew loud and ever more unsteady. "They're bastards. Every one of them. Davis. Lincoln. Your bloody Queen of England. What's the difference? Tell me that, if you can. They're naught but bloody bastards. Every one . . ."

Then he broke to pieces, strong old Mick.

I laid my hand upon my buttie's knee, for touch was wanted. "There is good. It will all come right, you wait and see. Sorry I am for my bothering you, Mick. It will all come right when you are rested."

He shuddered. "None of it will ever be all right." Twisting round with one last flame of anger, he asked me, "How can it be? How can it be all right? It's damned to Hell and hopeless, every bit of it." And then the hearty fellow started sobbing. For war was still unnatural to him.

.　　.　　.

THE NEXT MORNING, a Tuesday, I said good-bye to Mick for the sake of duty. He had toughened again and talked of a proper field hospital as he hacked at shattered arms and rotting legs. I do not know how surgeons bear the stink.

Although I felt that I must be superfluous now, I had to report my presence to headquarters. I had been sent to General Grant himself, although I doubted he would have leisure to see me. Doubtless, he had plenty on his hands, for the wake of a battle requires severe accounting. Even Washington's interests must have changed, given the carnage. What crime could matter after such a battle? Still, I would pay a visit to the general's staff and report my coming, for duty is duty. And the truth is that I wanted busy employment. Still dazzled I was by the ease with which I had abandoned my resolve and gone back to killing. Too, there was my longing after justice. For all my sins, I do believe in that. Mayhaps it would not signify to a general, but each small bit of justice counts to me. Even in a war.

We must each do the little bit we can.

I squeezed aboard a dispatch boat headed downriver to Savannah, the little headquarters town with the high, white house. Thrice I had been told that Grant had gone back to put things in order. High generals must write to explain the blood.

Filthy as a beggar boy I was. Still hatless, too, with a stick to serve as a cane. Left behind, my bag was surely lost, while the uniform I wore was ruined and wretched. Besides my Colt, I had my pocket Testament. Otherwise, I was desolate as a grub.

Still, my condition was come to honorably, and that was more than many men could say after Shiloh.

We moored below the headquarters, beside a groaning hospital boat, and I limped up the bluff, annoyed by flies. The comings and goings were constant: enlisted men all sweat and officers tired of returning salutes, with Negroes buckled under heavy loads. Even here, your nose filled with men's wounds and burial parties marched the dusty streets. A detail raised a telegraphic wire.

As I climbed the road, a red-haired general descended, heading for the river with an aide. He had a just-familiar face set bitter and fury trailed him. His aide said something I could not catch. The general coughed and gestured, disdainfully, with a bandaged hand. A zealot that one looked. You saw the skull beneath the layers of skin. I saluted, but the fellow just ignored me.

Now that the scrap was over, the headquarters guards were alert. They did not like the look of Abel Jones, for I am not a man grand in appearance at the best of times and I was slopped then shriveled by the sun. I presented my orders. Pages smeared by sweat and blood and rain.

Discomfited, a private called his sergeant, who rose and stepped reluctant from the shade. The sergeant looked at the paper, considered me, then scratched his Kerry bottom. He was unshaven. A proper army would have had his stripes.

Wary and unsure, he fetched a captain, a thing no honest sergeant would have done. The captain squinted as he tried to read. Young, he looked me up and down, from hatless head to shoes cleaned off with grass. My trousers were torn and the stick that served as my cane had begun to split. Finally, his gaze settled upon my remaining shoulder board. The other badge of rank had been sliced away and left back in the brambles.

I will admit I did not look much of an officer. And the captain was a clean fellow, as those set near a staff are like to be.

"Major . . . this . . . these papers aren't in order. I can't let you pass." He glanced around, uncertain of the world. "You'd best move on now."

Twas cool in the river morning, although the sun had floated up the sky. But I was hot in temper, for the battle had left my spirits in disorder.

"How 'not in order'?" I asked, as calmly as I could manage.

He twisted up his mouth, then loosened it again. "Well, I can't even read 'em. Looks like you went swimming in the mud with 'em. I can't properly—"

"I have not been swimming, Captain. Not in the mud nor elsewhere. And I only wish to report, see. For there is my duty, just as your duty is here."

"Well, I can't let you pass. Not if I can't read your papers. Anyhow, you shouldn't come around headquarters all dirty like that."

I struggled to hold my voice steady. For I knew the lad was not a proper captain. Most like he was a politician's son, playing dressup on the edge of war. Nor did he seem a vicious sort. He did as he was told by stronger men—at times a little less, but never more.

"Look you, Captain. I have come from Washington. It is a long way. And I am sent to report to General Grant. I believe I am expected. Or was expected. Only call a member of the staff, if you please, and we will see the matter through together."

"Sure, and I wouldn't do that, sir," the sergeant put in. "For don't he have the black look of a newspaper fellow? There's not one of them's a gentleman, the way they go sneaking about. Worse than priests, they are. You bother the high folk with them likes and out we'll all go on the pickets. Sure as there's hoors in the laundries."

"That's right, Cap'n," a private added, with a great spit of tobacco juice. "That runt ain't no major. Just you look at him. He can't even walk right. He like to took that uniform off some dead fella."

"Maybe he's a Confederate assassin," another offered idly.

Now I know that each man is a thinking creature, and the intellect is not the least of our gifts from the Lord. But private soldiers must not think too much. You see what happens. And officers must draw their proper boundaries. Rarely had I seen such a lack of discipline. Or encountered such a want of respect.

I fear I grew intemperate.

"Captain, I have been sent here at the behest of none other than—"

An officer with a Presbyterian face and the devil's eyes paused in his passing. "What's all this damned fuss, Morton? You're supposed to keep things quiet."

"Sorry, sir," the captain said, jumping to attention. His posture took on a child's exaggeration. The sergeant drifted back into the shade and the soldiers found interests elsewhere. "This fella claims he's come to see General Grant himself. All he's got are these smeared-up papers. If you look—"

The staff man ripped them from the captain's hands. As if he barely had the time to blink. Lean as a famine year, that one. And short of humor he looked, to put it kindly.

The fellow could not read my papers, either. I fear the fight was hard on the written word. He tossed the ruined sheets toward my chest.

"Who the hell do you think you are?" He judged me by my size and ruined uniform. And, doubtless, by the uncleanliness of my person. I must have shed an odor of some potency, for I wore a battle and the hospital yard. I had tried to wash, but the wells and streams were corrupted. And few men like to bathe beside a corpse.

Oh, what can shame a Methodist like dirt?

"I am Major Abel Jones, officer of U.S. Volunteers and—"

His face changed and the devil plunged toward me. "Jones? You're *Jones*? Good God, man, where have you been? We thought you were killed . . . captured . . ."

"Things wanted doing, see. I did not think—"

He thrust out his hand. "Rawlins. John Rawlins. Christ almighty, you're a sorry sight. Come in, man, come in." Then he bethought himself and turned to the captain. "Morton! Run down to the landing. Catch General Sherman. Swim after him, if you have to. Tell him the man from Washington's here. Don't just stand there, you ass. *Run.*"

As we approached the clean and lovely house, Rawlins said, "We've got an ugly business on our hands."

.   .   .

HE DID NOT LOOK a proper general. You might have thought him master of a freight yard, and not of a grand one, either. You never would have picked him from a crowd. He had an artless beard and weathered skin. His hair was neither brown nor red, but ginger, reminding me of undernourished Scotsmen. Average in form, he seemed at first a small man, with no least hint of pride upon his face.

He met me in his shirtsleeves and his waistcoat, plain blue frock behind him on a chair. Limping himself he come, and his collar points were frayed above his necktie. The battle's strain lay on him like a veil. When he shook my hand, I felt old calluses.

Now, you will say, "A general must be fine for inspiration." But I will tell you: There is more to leading men than splendid show. I will admit that I was disappointed, though only at first sight and not for long. For I still tended to a British measure and had expected someone grand myself. But if Grant wore no braid, he wore no bluster. He was a calm and steady man, and quiet.

Now "Grant" is Scots, of course. But hold your judgement. That simple uniform of his was not a miser's. No, he proved to be a generous man. Too generous to some in later years. But let that bide. The only stinginess he showed me lay in words. The man could not use two when one sufficed. Now we Welsh are a high and noble people, but I will give you that we like to talk. Grant thought first, then said what needed saying. And then he said no more but let things rest.

The first thing that he told me was:

"You stink."

I began to tumble apologies, but he pointed me to a chair.

"Battle smell, if I'm a judge."

"Some help seemed wanted, sir. I did pitch in."

He nodded, face gone heavy.

"The Rebels were properly beaten," I continued. "In the end."

"Tell General Halleck that when he gets here." Casualty lists ghosted through his eyes. "What's wrong with your leg?"

"A minor matter," I told him. "And an old one. It does not interfere with my duties. And your leg, sir?"

He grunted. "Horse fell. With me on him. Some weeks back." He tasted the memory and grimaced. "It's fixing up. Smoke?" He offered up a pouch of black cigars.

"I do not take tobacco, sir. But thank you."

He lit his weed and took a seat behind a littered desk. A staff fellow knocked and piled another sheaf of papers in front of the general, then left without a word. Grant gave the reports a glance and dismissed them for the moment. Examining his cigar with a jeweler's attention, he said, "Folks send me these by the case since we took Donelson. Craziest thing. Like to be the death of a fellow."

I watched his hands. He was no man of leisure, and he and I both seemed out of our element, for our interview took place in a gentleman's study. It was the sort of room I admit I covet, for books are lovely things to have and hold. And who would not wish himself a room for quiet reflection? Yet I was not born to such grand possessions and neither, it appeared, was Grant. We come rough-carved, the two of us.

Though colorful as a ball gown, the house kept a deathly quiet. As if it could not wait for us to leave, so that the maid might sweep away our traces. The staff work was conducted in the tents in the yard, I soon learned, but still this was a headquarters after a great battle. A veteran expects a certain fuss. I did not know two generals were dying up the stairs.

"Do me a kindness, Jones?"

"Sir?"

"Take off that coat. Mr. Cherry's a Union man, but the ladies of the house have other sympathies. No need to offend them, should they appear. They're good people. Hospitable, if a little wrongheaded."

I took my tunic off, but most reluctant. My shirt was beastly foul.

Grant stood up and opened a window wide. Puffing till he smoked just like a dragon.

"How much they tell you in Washington?"

Before I could begin the door swung wide. The red-haired general with the bandaged hand swept in. Without ceremony, he tossed his hat upon a polished table.

"Grant," he said, by way of greeting his superior. He covered a cough with his bad paw.

"Cump. This is Major Jones. From Washington. Major . . . General Sherman." I had risen out of respect, but Grant said, "Sit down. Both of you."

Sherman hardly acknowledged me. Dropping into a chair, he stretched out his legs. Impatiently, his spurs scratched at the floor. With his fiery hair, he put me in mind of a gamecock.

He looked me over, with pink-veined eyes. And set a skeptic's mask upon his face. Sherman was a neater man than Grant, though no parader, and I felt his scrutiny harden into disdain.

Grant seemed not to notice, though I sensed he saw full well, and Sherman took his cue. He lit up a cheroot from his own pocket, awkward with the bad hand and the match. The tobacco only made him cough the worse. I began to fear consumption, lean as he was.

Grant sat back down and fixed me with a stare. The sun poured through the window thick as honey.

We sat in silence, but for a fly that found me. And Sherman's occasional cough. It grew so quiet I could hear their lips pucker on their cigars.

I understood that I was being judged. On deeper matters now than my appearance.

After a stale of moments, Sherman's restlessness sparked again. "Well, tell him, Grant."

Grant nodded, but could not be made to go at another's pace. He looked at me doubly hard then. Now something had been chewing Abel Jones, an odd resemblance that I could not place. Suddenly, I had it. Twas in Grant's eyes. All sorrowful they were. As though he saw things he wished he might not. Though colored elsewhere, I had seen those eyes before. On Mr. Lincoln.

"First things first," Grant said at last, leaning on his elbows like a schoolboy. "Jones, what do you think of the Negro?"

. . .

"I THINK he is a man, like other men."
Grant cupped his chin and his beard crisped under his fingers. Sherman leaned forward.

"What about slavery?" Grant asked, shifting again and fitting his cigar back to his mouth.

"I would see no man a slave," I said. "It isn't Christian."

Sherman seemed about to leave his seat. "You think a nigger's equal to a white man?"

"No, sir," I said. "Not as a rule. Though some may be as good as any other."

"Count yourself an abolitionist?" Grant asked.

I did not understand this string of questions. Surely I had not come all this way to talk about the worthiness of Negroes. Yet, these men were superior in rank, and might put any queries that they would. I tried to answer honestly. But thoughts and words are not a perfect fit.

"I have never viewed myself as such, sir. Though my dear wife has leanings in that way. And . . . and I will tell you, the more I see into the matter, the more I think such people have a point." I thought of my troubles in the New York snows, and of those who had stood by me. "I have known black fellows as proper as anyone. Good and brave and decent." I looked at Sherman, for he seemed the harder nut to me. "Look you. If you please, sir. Even if the African is born with lesser faculties . . . still, he is a man, like you and me. But let that bide, sir. It is only that I would not have a man in chains. Not any man, see. Were it my choice to make."

"But it's *not* your choice. Is it, Jones?" Sherman asked. His voice had something of the naked blade.

"No, sir. That it is not. But—"

"Good." He looked at Grant. "At least he understands that much."

But Grant had not yet finished.

"Jones . . . if it *were* up to you. Would you fight a war . . . a war like this . . . to free the Negro?"

"No," I said. It was a ready answer. For I would not choose any war at all. I soldiered from a sense of obligation, to neighbor boys then to a country. I wished the black man free and left to himself, but not at such an awful price in slaughter.

Sherman met Grant's eyes and said:

"He'll do."

.   .   .

"FIFTEEN GROWN MEN, hanging from the trees," Grant said, with those remorseful eyes upon me full. "Hands and ankles bound. Eleven women slaughtered in the bushes—eleven, wasn't it, Cump?"

Sherman nodded. "And fourteen children. Total of forty."

"Runaway slaves," Grant continued. "Murdered not half a dozen miles from our lines."

"Thought it was a nigger orchard, with all of them hanging there," Sherman said with another cough. "Irregulars found them. Scouts who do some work for my division. Since the cavalry isn't worth a damn." He threw a teasing look at Grant. "When I can even scare up any of those dog-robbers. Anyway, they found them the day after my boys set up camp above the landing. Rode out to have a look myself. Weren't fresh, I'll tell you that. Three, four days dead. Animals had been at them."

"The men were hung, the women and children butchered," Grant repeated. And he was a man who did not say things twice. "Just a cold-blooded massacre, and a disgrace."

Sherman, whose anger seemed as close a companion as his cough, straightened his back and squared his narrow shoulders. It was a gesture more daunting than a fist. "Most pitiful damned thing I ever saw. Just pitiful. Wouldn't take a nigger-lover to vomit over a sight like that." He stiffened even more as he remembered. "Their brats were chopped up. Like a drunken butcher had been at them." Most men reveal their anger on their lips, but his shone through bloodshot eyes. "And one of the women, a young one . . . high yellow, they call them in Louisiana . . . had been disrobed. Disrobed and disfigured." His voice became a growl. "Disfigured in hideous ways . . ." Suddenly, he turned those eyes on me. "But I leave that to your imagination, Major."

And yet, he could not live up to his promise. The memory of what he had seen pressed more words from him. As if he hoped to spit out what he had witnessed and be done with it.

"The girl was a bloody mess," Sherman went on. "Lot of blood in a human carcass. And the African has more blood in him than a white man. Regulates his temperature in the heat, that's why you can work him in the cotton." He shook his head, slow as a funeral march. "God, I still see that girl."

The light had crawled the floor to the day's meridian. Beyond the window, down the hill, a steamboat scuffed the dock. Its whistle shook the glass. Out in the warm, soldiers spiced the day's routine with laughter.

The generals before me sat in silence. Pondering. Grant followed one cigar with another, but Sherman had settled. Like a storm rained out.

I cleared my throat, for I must put my questions. Before the little time allowed me fled. Once a staff man's head pokes in with a "pressing matter," all your remaining business goes undone, for generals are prisoners of the clock.

"And that," I asked, "is why I have been sent here? Because these forty Negroes have been murdered?"

The truth is that their tale chilled me deep in the belly, for I know more of massacres than I like. Careful I was to keep my voice restrained, though, for great folk do not need our small emotions.

Both men looked up, and both began to speak. Then Sherman paused and let Grant take the lead.

"No," Grant said. He sat enshrouded by tobacco fumes. "Not exactly. You must have been well on your way when they killed this batch." He glanced at Sherman, briefly locking eyes. "The first two massacres go back about a month."

.   .   .

"LEW WALLACE'S SLOWPOKES found the first bunch," Sherman said. His lungs did seem a bother to him. "Maybe a dozen of them, all males that time. We didn't think much of it. That was well north of here, the army was still moving. Few weeks later, we turned up nineteen or twenty more. Hard to tell exactly how many, the way they were cut to pieces. That was just downriver. My boys found that pack, too." He grimaced, with a glance at his superior. "That's when General Halleck was contacted. He passed the matter along to Washington. Isn't that right, Grant?" His withering eyes cut back to me. "Every time we find another massacre, it's bigger. Somebody's waving a bloody rag in our faces. And God only knows what it's about."

Oh, yes, I thought of India again. And of a hundred things that I had seen, only to wish I had not. The Mutiny had begun with brown barbarity. It ended with the white man worse than a savage. It is a dreadful thing for a man to say of himself, but I believe I was less shocked than either of the generals.

Less shocked I was, but likely more alarmed. By selfish fears. I had no wish to see my past revived beyond the sorry business of the battle.

"Perhaps," I said, "the Confederates are killing runaway slaves they catch as they retreat? As vengeance for their losses? It would not be the first time men misplaced their senses in a war, see."

"Nonsense," Sherman said. "That's the damned thing. I've lived with the men of the South. Served with them. Taught their sons.

Oh, they can be sonsofbitches, and stiff-necked bastards, all right. But this doesn't make sense." He carved his mouth into a bitter smile and scraped his throat clear. "They'll hang a nigger now and then. To set an example. But they'd no more butcher 'em wholesale than they'd shoot their farm animals. The African's valuable property. And forty of 'em that last time. Figure the money involved. Say, the fifteen men at eight-hundred to a thousand dollars a head, maybe an average price of six or seven hundred for the women . . . of course, prices are down with the war . . ."

Grant put in, "It may be the work of Southron renegades. The cracker sort, low breds. They're good haters. And they don't much like a black hide." He looked at the man with one less star on his shoulder boards. "General Sherman's been dealing with the gentry of the Southland. My experience has been a little farther down the pole."

I was befuddled. "By your leave, sir. It sounds a pitiful matter, but I do not see my role in this. Not if it is a Confederate affair. Although I find our Union's concern for these Negroes admirable . . ."

Sherman laughed out loud, though Grant did not.

"Oh, we're concerned," Sherman said, once his mirth and coughing subsided. "We're concerned to hell and high water."

"You understand," Grant interjected, "that all this is told to you in trust, Major."

"The hell now," Sherman drove on, "I'm no friend of the institution of slavery. Understand that, Major. It's filthy and foolish, and you can't refine it. Corrupts good men. I've seen it. But this business isn't about these runaway slaves."

Twas thus I went from befuddled to bewildered.

"Look here, Jones," Grant said. "This war's bad enough. And we're still a sight from finishing it. Hard enough to do, even without more abolitionist howling. Myself, I'd be glad to do away with slavery, if all I had to do was clap my hands. But even my own wife has other sentiments. And this war is not being waged to free the

Negro. We're fighting to preserve the Union. Slavery can wither on its own. It can't endure in a modern age. But that's not our business. First, bind up the country. Then see what comes."

He rustled his fingers over his beard again, hands uneasy in between cigars. "If the men and boys of this army thought they were down here fighting to free the black man, half of them would desert tomorrow and call the war one big swindle. Other half might be glad of it, but we can't fight with fifty percent. As it is, we're flooded with runaway darkies looking for protection. Blocking up the roads, stealing provisions. Clinging to the army like leeches. And they're still private property under the law and have to be treated as such."

Grant fit a new cigar between his teeth and did not wait to light it, but sucked so hard the wind whistled through his teeth. "As it is, I've got officers and men hiding runaways until they can smuggle them north. Others are only too glad to round up every Negro in sight and turn them over to anybody who shows up with a pair of shackles. Even claiming reward money, some of them. Make it the official policy of our government to offer protection to escaped slaves, and military operations would grind to a halt." He glanced at his subordinate. "Isn't that right, Cump?"

"First win the war," Sherman said. "Then worry about the Negro."

"We've kept these . . . occurrences . . . quiet," Grant went on, "though it's getting harder. Can't have something like this splashed across every newspaper in the North. The abolition crowd would get the upper hand back East, and the administration could be pushed into declaring against slavery. Then we'd lose half the states between the Ohio and the Missouri. Maybe all of them. The sentiment for war wouldn't hold together. Just ask Sherman's brother up in Congress. This country is not ready to fight on behalf of the Negro." He grunted. "It may never be."

"The killings have to be stopped," Sherman said in a January voice. "Before the newspapermen find out about them." He made a face as if served a rat on a plate. "I'd hang the ink-stained bastards, if I could. I'd rather see them strung up than some poor niggers."

Grant stirred the papers on the desk, but could not find the item that he sought. He muttered and shook his head, then lifted his pale eyes. "I sent a note through the lines to General Johnston. Over a week ago now." A shadow swept across Grant's face. "I suspect he had other things on his mind, if he even received it. Died on the field, the first day, if the prisoners are telling it right. Good soldier. Now he's gone. In any case, I haven't had a reply from him, or from his successor. Who, I believe, would be General Beauregard. Unless Bragg supersedes him."

"If Southron renegades are behind this," Sherman said, "it's in the Confederacy's own interests to stop them. Protect their property. Their reputations. They've got to see that."

"Indeed," I said, for I had been thinking, "there is the property issue. But there is a greater thing they must put to themselves, see. They will not want their image tarnished abroad. With their efforts to draw England into the war beside them. The Anti-Slavery Society in Britain would make much of such doings, were tales of Negro massacres to appear. Richmond would lose the sympathy of all Europe."

Grant and Sherman stared at one another. Surprised, they were. Twas clear they had not thought so far as foreign repercussions. But those were diplomatic matters, the stuff of Washington intrigues and plots up in New York and icy Canada, as I had learned through not a little pain. These men were fighters on the war's frontier and could not bother their heads with distant niceties.

"Damn it, that's a point that'll stick," Sherman said. "If I know Beauregard. Rather be a European himself, that puffball."

I trust I did not show it to the generals, but I was vexed. I wanted no part of massacres, no matter their cause or consequence. But we must do our part when we are called, and speak what we think is true when speech is wanted. The man who flees his duty has no worth. We must have faith and push through, even though we might well wish us elsewhere.

Grant sat back and sighed as men will do when they must summarize. "For all we know, it could be runaways killing each other. Plenty of them on the loose, and I suspect some of them are savage enough and crazy enough to do anything. But if I had to bet, I'd put my money on some sort of backwater white no-goods. They hate the Negro with a passion. Saw it in Missouri, where the feelings don't run half as strong as here. Thing is, it's got to be stopped. Whoever's doing it. The guilty parties must be identified and punished. But quietly." He looked to where I sat in amber shadows. "It appears Washington understands that."

"Whoever did it has to hang," Sherman said. "Even if they're white. Give 'em a hard lesson. But keep it out of sight."

"It's difficult enough," Grant said, "not to start hating your enemy. After such battles. Incidents like these . . . give those prone to hatred more excuse."

"The South has to be punished for this war," Sherman added with a hack. "But within reason. We have to remain soldiers, and not become vandals. Can't stoke the abolitionist fire. It's just waiting to burn out of control as it is. Too much hatred, and the breach with the South won't close for a hundred years."

Grant stood up and limped the little way to the window. Holding his still-unlit cigar, he stared into the day.

"Jones," he said, standing in a lovely flush of sun and speaking to the distance, "I want you to contact the Confederates. In person. As my emissary, provided with a safe conduct. And I want you on your way before General Halleck arrives." He turned his shoulders, then shifted his injured leg so he might face me. The sunlight drew his outline. "He's a brilliant man, General Halleck. Perhaps the greatest soldier of our age. But he's cautious, and I'm not sure we have much time. I want you to go immediately. I'll take the licking, if there's one to be served."

I noted Sherman made no comment on General Halleck. But then he come of a political family, according to those newspapers he hated. Such men do not antagonize the great. Now, you will say, "We read in those same papers that Sherman acted the madman the autumn before. And you say he was temperate, Abel Jones?" But I will tell you: Madness is like courage, taking a different course in every man. And madness is a measure of the times.

"I will not have the war lost because a couple dozen runaway slaves got themselves hung," Grant said suddenly and firmly. As if he needed to justify his actions to an invisible presence. Then he mused for a moment, uncomfortable with the need to say so much. Softening his voice, he drew on that wry smile. "You're not to let the Rebels know that, of course. Present them with the business as a crime, and a shameful one. Play that England card you talked about. That's a hard, black ace." He stepped toward me then, despite my stench. "Find the guilty, Jones, whatever it takes. And clear the way for us to win this war."

.   .   .

Now, I was still new to detection matters, with but two affairs behind me. Unless you count that time in India when Molloy made off with the regimental silver. Yet, I had got a brace of lessons solid, and knew where to begin, if not where to finish. I was not fully master of my heart, but I kept my wits about me.

I looked at Grant, then Sherman, and back again. "Well, sir, I am ready. Though I would not mind a wash and a change of uniform."

"Rawlins can see to that," Grant said, and seemed about to summon the man.

But I pressed on. "And before I go to parlay with the Rebels, I would see things done in proper order."

"How's that?" Sherman asked, ever impatient. His bandaged hand had come up.

"I would see the spot where these murders happened," I said. "For there is no place to begin like the beginning."

Sherman regarded me with failing confidence. "The first murders must've been sixty miles north of here. Fifty, anyway. You'd lose days."

"There is sorry I am," I said. "I was not clear in my words, sir. The place where last you found them was my meaning. The site of this killing of forty. That may do."

But Sherman was a stubborn fellow, sure that he was right. "There's nothing there, man. I had them buried." Then a shocked look dressed his bone-hard face. "You . . . don't mean to dig them up? Good God . . ."

"No need of such doings, sir. Not yet, at least. But I would see the place and do things proper."

"And just what good would that do?" Excited, his lungs took a wracking.

Grant set his words between ours. For he knew when to set a business straight. "Cump, get him out there and let him have his look. We know our business. If Washington sent him all the way down here, he probably knows his."

Sherman came around instantly. Not as a dog to his master's command, but as a man who trusts another's judgement. A loyal man, no lackey. He nodded. "I'll have Lott and his pack take him out. They know their way, and aren't like to forget it. The way Lott carries on about freeing the niggers."

He turned to me. "That's Micah Lott," he said, with a twist of the lips. "Calls himself 'Captain Lott,' though I've never seen the commission. Odd bird. Bible banger. Too damned radical to have any man-to-man sense. But he knows his scouting business. Has a dozen or so men who ride with him. Most of them from these parts, Union loyalists. Abolitionists with fire in their bellies and too much preaching between the ears. They're the ones found the last bunch of niggers."

He shifted his attention back to Grant. "They can take him south from there. Cut over to the Corinth road. Give him a white flag to carry so the Rebels can see him coming. Lott will know how far to take him and when to turn him loose."

"All right?" Grant asked me. "We'll get you out to the site of the killings, then on the way to Beauregard or whoever's in charge down there now. Without getting you shot, I trust." A trace of wit crossed his lips. "I do worry that the Confederate pickets might be a little edgy after the events of the last few days. I hope we won't need to trouble Washington for a replacement for you, Major."

I let him have his joke, for truth be told, I read it as a mark of confidence and not of fear. Grant had a lovely sense of humor that few saw, although I only got to know it later.

Sherman stood up, clipping his chair with a spur and shifting the phlegm in his lungs. "I'll be off then, Grant. Round up Lott and his pack. God knows where they are at the moment." He shook his head and wheezed. "Don't I wish that we had one regiment of decent cavalry?"

"I'll send the major along. As soon as his papers are drafted. And once we have him scrubbed sufficiently clean for the delicate nostrils of our Southron friends. Send Rawlins in, would you, Cump?"

Sherman picked up his hat, waved his bandaged hand in a half salute, and was gone.

Grant looked at me and shook his head again. He did seem worn. "Been a soldier, haven't you, Jones? I mean a real one."

"I have served under the colors, sir."

"British army?"

"Indian service, sir."

An odd light touched Grant's eyes. Rendering them luminous as a cat's.

"If I may ask, sir," I said, "how did you know? That I had served?"

I thought he would make mention of my bearing, for I am vain enough to keep my rigor.

"The handle of your pistol," he told me. "And the holster, for that matter. You're filthy as a river rat. But your weapon's clean as a silver dinner fork. Only a man who's fought would give his first attention to his arms that way." He stepped toward me, curiosity quick in those eyes. "Have a look at that cannon of yours?"

I drew my Colt and passed it to him, though reluctantly. I am ever embarrassed by the inscription my Pottsville boys put on it in farewell. Siney the Jeweler's son did the work and did it lovely, fine with filigree. I wept to hear of his death at Seven Pines. But the loss was yet to come, so let that bide.

Grant turned the pistol over in his hands. "Captain Abel Jones," he read aloud, "Hero of Bull Run."

"It is a terrible exaggeration, sir. I only did my duty, and that poorly."

"Well, somebody thought it made sense." He handed the revolver back to me by the barrel.

"I saw General Sherman at Bull Run," I said, to turn the subject. "He was a colonel then. His brigade formed up in square as it withdrew."

Grant laughed, though not imprudently. "Well, that'd be just like old Cump. Should've mentioned it to him. Got a rise out of him. Say 'Bull Run' around him and he gets wild as a mad skunk." He passed a hand across his beard, measuring his smile. But he kept his eyes upon me, pale and steady. "You must've been in the thick of things down at the landing, too. You smell worse than my father's tan-yard—and I always thought nothing could stink worse than that."

At this odd recollection, his eyes lost their confidence. His gaze turned vague and lowered to the floor. An ancient, wounded look possesssed his features.

"Your father was a tanner, sir?" I asked him. Only because it seemed I should say something. I have no skill in social repartee. My words come even slower than my thoughts when most I need them. It is a hard fate for a Welshman, for talk is our cakes and ale.

Grant nodded. "I never could abide the tanning business. Blood and death, and nothing but. Anything but that, I told myself. Still can't stand the sight of beef, unless it's black as cinders."

"I have worked in a tannery myself, sir," I said, for want of greater wisdom. "As a boy, see. A dreadful place it was." Oh, I remembered. The day the Reverend Mr. Griffiths sent me packing from his doors and all that I held dear, an orphan set to an apprenticeship amid the hides and bristles, the blood and stench and cauldrons. How I loved my little bit of schooling and wept to leave my books and Mr. Hughes. And worse to leave my shining Mary Myfanwy. But let that bide.

Of a sudden, Grant stepped closer, almost the way a friend will when sharing a confidence. "Your father a tanner, too?"

"No, sir. He preached a chapel. And did it lovely, I am told. But the cholera took him and my mother, God rest them. A high-church gentleman took me in, but he found me a disappointment. Twas him put me out to the tannery."

And then I added something else, although it had no place, for it was a trivial, silly and personal matter. But Grant had the gift of making others speak.

"More than anything," I said, "I feared the yard horse. When I did not finish my work to satisfaction, I was locked in a stall with the creature. It had a wicked temper with a boy. And I was small, see. Since that day I do not favor horses."

Grant smiled, bemused. I never sensed unkindness in the man. He knew the pain of those whose life turns downward.

"Well, we're different there, Jones. Sometimes I think a horse is an animal of a higher order than the average specimen of mankind." He laid his arm across my filthy shoulder. I smelled tobacco on his clothes and breath. "We've got the tan-yard in common, though. And the cholera." I felt his muscles clinch ever so slightly. "Worst days of my life were crossing Panama with the 4th Infantry. On the way to California. Worse than the tan-yard by a country mile. Cholera hit us. They left me behind to look after the sick and the women and children." He shook his head. With a slowness near despair. "I was troubled for a time after that."

The door opened. Rawlins, the hard and humorless fellow, stepped in. Grant dropped his arm away and hunted through his pockets for a smoke.

"John," the general said to his aide, "see that Major Jones here has an opportunity to make himself presentable as our emissary. Scare him up a fresh uniform, would you? And get him a hot bath. Two, if necessary. I have a message to write. Then we'll send him back upriver to Sherman."

Rawlins mumbled, as if such tasks were beneath him, complaining of the want of uniforms in the battle's wake. But Grant was unconcerned. He stretched out his hand and laid it upon my shoulder a last time.

"Good luck," he said. Then he bit a cigar's tip and added, "Strikes me that I never did get very far from that tan-yard."

three

*O*h, a wash is a lovely thing. A shame it is we cannot scrub our souls as we do our bodies. A tin tub in a tent set me up proper, and I grew almost jolly, soap in hand and all the world forgotten for the moment. I am, by nature, clean about my person, and wish that others were more fond of water, for careless habits lead us toward sin. I fear I was a terror to the Irish in my sergeanting days.

Two farmboys squeezed into uniforms assisted me, as if I were the Marquess of Bute himself. I was so foul they fetched fresh water twice, dumping it over me by the bucketful. Good lads they were, and not above a laugh, but they were green. When first I shed my rags, the taller of the two had marked my ant bites, for I had been scratching. Smirking, he asked me if I had the camp itch. Then my decline in dress revealed my campaign scars, livid as sins on doomsday. The poor boy stopped grinning and paled.

I am not proud of my irregularities, and keep me private when a fellow may. The scars of battle should be hid, for badges of shame they are, and not of pride. But in a camp few secrets last. Shaking out a just-delivered uniform, the tall boy said:

"Major, you look like you been rasslin' bobcats."

But I have wrestled men, and that is worse.

I bought a tin of oysters from a Hebrew. I would have rubbed the oil across my snout to mask the greater stink of death around me. But that would have been sloven and improper. I have always been sensitive to smells, see, and some are worse than others by a mile. The rotting human carcass tops them all. The air was poisoned. So the camphor reek of the new uniform pleased me, although it is a smell I much dislike, for it left no room in my nose for other scents.

The peddler sold all I needed. More soap, and a toothbrush. A clap-to razor, since whiskers are a vanity. A pen and ink, and paper. For I had to write to my darling and our little John, to tell them I was still among the living. I tried to write my Mary Myfanwy daily, but war corrupts our habits. Now I would be gone unto our enemies, and might not have the chance to write for a muchness. The sutler's prices startled me, and wasted pennies lead to a wasted life, yet I would have paid him thrice to write my lovely.

The writing had to be postponed until night, for my dispatches were ready and Rawlins burned to start me on my way. Ever a sour man he was, unobliging to all but Grant. But first there was a tussle about pay. Although I had a special authorization from the War Department, the clerk regarded me as he might a criminal. It is the constant temper of such fellows, who come to think the pay chest is their own. Rawlins had to bark at the man. Even then, the business proceeded slowly.

At last, I signed my chits and got my wages. I had been down to my secret service funds, which must not be applied to private use. My farewell from New York had come all sudden and my affairs were in disarray. I kept a tithe-worth of my pay for expenses, sending back the rest to dear old Pottsville, to Mr. Evans at the Miner's Bank. So my wife might draw to furnish her needs, while a portion could be put into railroad shares.

It cost me dear to send the sum along, but we must pay for safety and convenience. Bonded agents hovered by the pay tent, speaking German, Swedish, Norwegian and such, as well as queer varieties of English. Money could be sent from there to Pomerania, or off to County Mayo to be drunk up. Twas a commerce of vigor, the forwarding of monies. Of course, those fellows should have been in uniform, for healthy sorts they seemed and in their prime.

But business will not pause for war, and many's the man who covets the soldier's pay.

But let that bide.

Soon enough, I was back upon the river, with a young lieutenant detailed to guide me to Sherman. The day had clouded and the water sulked. Here and there, the banks had snagged a corpse. The earth stank mighty with the scent of dying, and black birds circled. But Abel Jones felt like a man reborn, scrubbed and decked out spotless, with a high kepi clapped to my head. The staff had even found me a pair of shoulder boards. Spotted they were, and I chose not to think on their origins. Fit precisely frock and pants did not, for I am short but broad across the chest. I fear I always want a bit of tailoring. Sleeves and trousers hung a trifle long, but I rolled them up and pinned them fast, intending to sit down and sew that night. Thread and needle are the soldier's friends.

We rode an emptied ambulance up from the dock. The teamster seemed glad of a healthy cargo. The wagon's canvas walls had been rolled high and we perched on a lip of boards behind the driver. I recognized the road that I had walked along that first, desperate morning of the fight. Now dawdling soldiers lingered at their chores, while others, urgent, squatted in the trees. The army had not learned to cook or clean. Still, this was but the old routine of camp, found everywhere that soldiers pitch their tents. If not for the stench and shattered groves, you might have missed the evidence of battle.

My escort had not been engaged in combat, but spent his time as an orderly in the rear. He did not know his way upon the field and seemed a silly choice to make a guide. The driver had to ask the way as we went, for he was not assigned to Sherman's division. Besides, the camps had been muddled by the fighting. We wandered through a fading afternoon. At first, the lieutenant's eyes shimmered to come so close to war at last, and he bothered me with questions from a schoolyard.

Until we turned a bend and saw a detail flinging Rebel corpses in a ditch. Our boys were buried proper, but communal pits were all the enemy got. Clods of shoveled earth slapped bloated bellies. Many of the dead had twisted up queer, as if tormented. Stiff legs angled skyward. Teeth were bared and eyes stared at the Judgement. Comrades blackened in each other's arms. Shovels sparked off rocks, and dirt fell in curtains. Swollen bowels exploded in a cannonade of stink. But the shock of death was gone and the soldiers on the burial party joked.

Do not imagine dignity in death. We rot, and will not rise. Not in the flesh.

We passed a scorched grove and a half-burned field. I saw white bones. But I refused to think more on the battle, ignoring the lieutenant's dismayed looks. I filled my mind with images of home, of wife and child and little joys we shared. I would have shut my eyes and held my nose, but that would have made me a poor example. Lieutenants are the army's softest clay. The boy beside me had all he could do to keep from puking down the side of the wagon.

He put me in mind of the son of an earl, a subaltern I knew in India. His red coat never sat well on parade, though Corporal Deane and I did what we could, and the newfangled khaki made him look a fool. The boy gave orders from his mouth, but never from his eyes, leaving me the duties and the discipline. He was ever writing letters in his tent, one a day at least to a lass named Jenny. I thought she was his sweetheart back in England, but later learned she was the poor boy's sister. He died in our camp by Peshawar, of nothing. The surgeon wrote him down dead of the flux.

Look you. Not all men are cut out for the army, and hard it is when parents press them in. Or when friends draw them on with wicked teasing. I conjured up Lieutenant Livingston, too, the lad in Washington, sick and sad and dead before his time. Suddenly, I swelled up with near-hatred toward the playroom soldier at my side. A stupid child who knew not what he had done. I would have liked to slap him and send him off to his mother.

A group of tattered horsemen passed us by, led by one dressed black as any preacher. And then we had arrived at Sherman's camp, amid tents lined up neat, though scorched and torn. I smelled great pots of beans and heard commands of drill from nearby fields, as companies were mended from the battle. The voices of the officers come hoarse, still raw from shouting in the noise and smoke.

General Grant had given me two letters. One would introduce me to the Rebels. The second was addressed to General Sherman. I was to give it him directly. But difficulties arose.

The general had taken to his bed.

An aide said it was asthma, which afflicted Sherman in the campaign's lulls. Now that was queer, although it explained his cough. Where I had served that ailment touched only the children who lived in the officers' bungalows or the offspring of high administrators. The sort whose mothers took them off to hill stations when the heat rose, little boys got up with ringlet curls and girls with drowsy eyes and beribboned waists. When lesser folk could not breathe we called it a wheeze. Unless blood come to the lips, which meant consumption. But high sorts want a different class of ailment to set them up above the common run.

I thought on these things while I waited. I had given the aide Grant's note to take in, see. It was the best that Abel Jones might do. I could not plough into a general's tent like some snooty Frenchman.

I sent the lieutenant back to the river and think he was afraid to go alone. No doubt he made a detour round the death pit. And likely found another for his trouble. I leaned against a tree by Sherman's tent, trying to read a verse or two of the Gospels. My Testament was stained, the text obscured in places. But I recalled most of the missing bits. I had just got me to Jerusalem when I heard a fit of coughing and bubbling phlegm. The aide come out a moment later, bilious and confused.

"The general wants to see you right now," he said. "Funny, he don't usually visit with nobody when he's like this." He stepped aside and told me, "Go on in."

I pocketed my Testament and poked my head inside the shut-up tent, getting a snoutful of stale air for a welcome. General Sherman sat on his cot, wearing trousers with his braces down and a red undergarment for a shirt. He looked as though too little skin had been stretched over too much skull, and he was sweating.

He glared my way and coughed, but it soon passed.

"Sit down there, Jones." He pointed to a camp chair with his bandaged hand. "And tell me something." His eyes were red as if plucked from a brazier.

I sat and said, "Yes, sir?"

"Grant sent me a note. He says you've got an iron declaring you the hero of Bull Run."

"Sir, I never would make such a claim, I only—"

"Just answer me this." His fierce eyes sought remembrance. "Are you the little fellow had that company high up on the ridge? The one who sent down the reply that there was no way in Hell you were going to retreat?"

Twas not a precise account. I never would have used a word like "Hell" under official circumstances. Not even to the colonel he had been at Bull Run, though many's the colonel could do with a splash of cold water. But well I recalled the day and our exchange. Twas only that a man must not presume. And I had not thought Sherman would remember. My role was minor, and the battle lost.

"I had a company then, sir. My boys put up a steady front. My boys it was who did the work, not me. Twas only that a battery come along—"

Sherman held up his wounded hand to hush me. "Damnedest thing I ever saw." He shook his head and let a little cough. "Just the damnedest thing. You and that little company standing up there, with the whole damned army running away on both sides of you . . ."

"*You* did not run, sir. Your brigade went off in good order."

Sherman grimaced, wheezing. "Damnedest thing . . ."

"Sir," I said, for I would change the subject, "if you have need of a doctor, there is a fine fellow of my acquaintance with the army, one Dr. Tyrone."

"Silent Mick?" Sherman asked. With an abrupt smile.

"I believe he has been called so, sir."

Sherman nodded and began to laugh, only to end up in a fit of gasping. Yet, ill or no, his humor had come up. When he got back to words, he said, "I'd be scared to go near the man. Tough as old boots. He's famous in this army, Mick Tyrone. Damned near good as Brinton. But one hard case. Cut a general's head off in a minute, if he doesn't get his way about his supplies."

"He is a lovely doctor, sir. He saved me from the typhoid."

Sherman waved all medicine away, and doctors, hospitals and hopes of cure. "Well, I suspect he's got his hands full, at the moment. Likely has a tired right arm by now. Listen, Jones, we've got to get about your business. Micah Lott's in camp." His mouth turned wry. "That 'Captain' Lott I told you about. He'll take you on your grand tour, then pass you south. But be careful. I've sent Sanger over to give him his orders. No skirmishing, or any kind of nonsense. Just get you out to the scene of the butchery, then slip you south to where you can approach the Confederate lines without getting your head blown off."

His cough swelled back and drew more sweat. "But watch him. You watch him. The man hates Southrons. Hates the South, Jones. Anything to do with slavery. He's fanatical." Sherman snorted at his thoughts. "Makes John Brown look like a parlor preacher drinking tea with the ladies." He paused to catch his breath again and seemed a fragile child. Narrow of form he was, like Mick Tyrone. "If I didn't need scouts so badly, I'd send him packing." He wiped his sweating forehead with a kerchief. "You rank him. Even if he does have a captain's patent from somewhere out in the territories. Keep him on course. You understand?"

"Yes, sir. I believe so, sir."

"And you'll just have to put up with his Bible-thumping." He raised an eyebrow. "You religious, Jones? You sounded a tad on the holy side back at Grant's shack."

I could not help but think about the fighting. And what a heathen creature I remained. But I told him, "I count myself a Christian, sir. And a Methodist."

Sherman twisted up his mouth again and his body tensed with his ailment. When he spoke, the words rode on a wheeze. "Well, you may not find Captain Lott's brand of Christianity everything you're used to. He's a touch on the severe side. Plenty of that out here, though. Country brings it out. Anyway, you just let it roll off your back. I'd send you out with an escort of regular cavalry, but they'd only get you killed."

"I see no need of cavalry, sir," I hastened to agree. I fear I have a horror of the equine.

Sherman made an ugly sound. Deep in his throat. "Your mission's important, Jones. I've been thinking about it. And about that business with England. Maybe this killing's even more important than we've got at yet. But, right now, we have to keep the lid on the pot. Before it boils over and makes one hell of a mess." He sucked in air and braced his hands on his knees. "Find out who killed those niggers."

At that, the coughing ripped down to his soul. His undergarment shirt darkened with sweat. I feared his lungs would come right out his mouth.

He gulped a potion from a medicine bottle, spilling some over his chin and onto his bandaged palm. He only choked the worse for the elixir. It was a hard thing, watching a general struggle. We are but sorry flesh, and the mighty are humbled. I wondered then if he was fit to lead.

What man can see beyond the present day's confusions?

Between his seizures, Sherman called for his aide. And sent me on my journey to the damned.

. . .

FROM ALL I HAD BEEN TOLD of Captain Lott, I thought his camp would be a tabernacle. Instead, I stumbled upon a wrestling match.

A crowd had gathered, lolling, sitting and leaning, where a black man and a white man clutched each other. Naked shoulders gleamed, and the opponents showed their teeth like vicious dogs. The white man was the taller of the two, all blond and sturdy. Thick, he looked to be a Swede or such. Muscled like a man who tills poor land. When the wrestlers broke apart, with a growl, the Swedish fellow straightened and gulped him a chestful of the air. I do believe he was six foot and six, and don't know how the Rebel bullets missed him. Stripped to the waist, his pale flesh bulged from his trousers, reddened where the Negro's hands had gripped.

The black man lacked his foe's commanding height. But he looked hard. With muscles thick as the ropes that fasten ships. Oiled to an Ethiopian hue, his shoulders would have yoked two fattened oxen. His neck was a siege gun's muzzle. But when he moved he showed a dervish grace. He was the one who pleased the eye, emanating a force words do not fit.

He pleased the eye and, somehow, made you fear.

The white man turned, slower and annoyed, while the black fellow pranced around him in a tease. Refusing the Swede's embrace with a mocking smile. The onlookers cursed the Negro, shouting for him to wrestle like a man. But the Moor went on with his jigging. Until the Swede seemed baffled as a cow. Then the Negro tightened up his circles, the way a tiger works around a camp. He stalked, and feinted with his mammoth hands.

Close up, you saw the Negro's thousand scars. He was acquainted with the cat-o'-nine-tails and with irons, that one. His back looked like a crocodile's pelt, the flesh a black-and-purple scape of callus, from the cord that held up his trousers to his skull. Men die from lesser beatings. And animals, as well.

My escort to Captain Lott, yet another lieutenant, edged us into the crowd with a look of excitement. I did not understand what I was seeing and thought the boy careless of his duty. But let that bide. The soldiers looking on were the troublesome sort. Betting men they were, who wanted blood. A vicious, baying pack of tarnished souls. No doubt, the loudest of the loud had cowered by the river Sunday morning. But the harm that comes to others has a savor, and men are ever ready to look on. Nor did I turn away myself, I confess.

The wrestlers smacked together.

The crowd was white, and race will cheer its own. Their voices backed the Swede, as muscles strained. Sweat darkened each man's trousers at the small of the back. The faces of the contestants grew ferocious, while the faces of the spectators went cruel. I do not think they would have stopped a killing.

The struggle kicked up clots of earth that were drying from mud to dust. The Negro's barefoot soles showed pink as mine. Twas odd, as if his blackness had worn off.

Neither man could break the other's stance. The spectators waved money, spitting and railing. If bulk were all, the Swede would have won with ease. But there is more to victory than size, as well I know. The Swede went bursting red and his chin slimed over. The Negro's eyes held steady as his grip. Four feet dug in, and four legs strained under rough cloth. You sensed no bit of muscle went unused.

Suddenly, the white man barked a curse.

Profanity helps no man. His grip failed. And his legs gave. The Negro swept him high into the air. It was incredible. The pink-fleshed giant might have been a rag.

The earth shook underfoot when the Swede come down. Oh, twas a slam.

The Moor dropped on the fellow like a tiger, artful in the use of every limb. And something cracked.

The Swede bellowed. A cry of sudden agony it was.

The crowd surged in, forged to a single creature. Roaring. Those who bet and lost would have revenge.

A pistol discharged. Its barrel flamed above the pack of heads. And motion ceased. The single muscle of the crowd relaxed, and men became their separate selves again, the way a company will after a battle.

Gamblers muttered in their disappointment, turning away from the Swede and the anxious comrades kneeling by his side, away from the Negro who had thwarted them all. The Moor bent over, gasping from his effort.

Twas then a voice come over us like thunder:

"Behold His work. Goliath is brought low."

. . .

"LIFT UP YOUR EYES and see His mighty work. Behold the angel of His vengeance. Chastised, spurned and humbled . . . lashed . . . every blow increased His servant's strength ten-fold . . ." The speaker waved a black slouch hat at Heaven. Erect and tall he was, hewn sharp by life. His long beard shook. "Jehovah is a God of fear and wonder!" He stepped closer to the Negro. "Raise up your swords against the plague of slavery, and surely you will triumph in His name. Leviticus, chapter twenty-six, verse thirty-two: 'And I will bring the land into desolation: and your enemies which dwell therein shall be astonished at it.' That land of desolation is the Southland, Brothers . . . great Babylon, who tried to make all nations drink of the wine of her fornication . . ."

Soldiers drifted off to other pastures, but a few remained to keep the ranter hot. I fear there was less reverence in them than a craving for a break in their camp routine.

A knot of spectators loosened itself and I saw the preacher full. Twas the fellow who had passed me on the road to Sherman's headquarters, leading his band of horsemen. It struck me, late, that this was Captain Lott. A coal-ash beard descended to his chest, extending a visage fiercer than a hawk's. His eyes lurked deep, but sparked when his voice swelled up. The man was rage made flesh. I knew the sort. The country parson brimming with damnation, who loves God's wrath and aims his wrath at love.

Truth be told, I like religion quiet. Unless there is a hymn sung fine and true. God does not hear us sooner when we shout.

Lott put on his hat and laid the hand thus freed on the Negro's shoulder. The preacher looked the elder by some decades, but strong enough to finish a scrap himself. His muscles were a workingman's, the sort life winds from hard and ill-paid labor.

"Tell me, Brothers," Captain Lott stormed on, "is any man among you such a heathen . . . that he has not received the Holy Word? Do you recall our Savior's loving promise . . . that the meek shall inherit the earth?" He clapped the Negro's back, spattering sweat. "Behold the meek raised up!"

"That nigger don't look all that meek to me," a sergeant said.

.   .   .

AND THAT IS HOW I come to Captain Lott. Or Reverend Lott, as he was sometimes called. Such he was, it seems, before the war.

Sherman's staff man was anxious to be gone, although he had enjoyed the wrestling session. He made his introductions and withdrew, promising a horse would be delivered for my use, although the battle had left a terrible want of the animals.

That is another story, the horse business. I do not like the beasts and ride reluctant. Infernal as the juggernaut they are. Monstrous. I would sooner face a Sindhi cobra twice my length as hold a set of reins. In all my wars I marched and got there fine. But legs are not sufficient for America. Here all will ride and have no interference. Americans are not fond of their feet and hate to walk as if it were a sin. They mount a horse to go across an alley. But let that bide.

"Welcome, Brother," Captain Lott declared. He tried on a smile, but his features did not like the fit. "It is pleasing to the Lord that His generals have seen the light. Though the wasted days will count against them. Sin must be pursued, the wicked chastised. Rip out evil by the roots," he said, and looked the man to do it. Bad skin gathered round his flaring eyes. "When innocents are slaughtered like the infants of Bethlehem, I hear the trumpet of the final days. Yes, Brother, the end of days is near upon us. The great day of His wrath is coming, when the sinner shall drown in a river of wormwood. That a Testament in your pocket?"

He was observant, I will give him that, and knew what soldiers carried and just where.

"That it is, sir," I told him.

He took me by the arm. His grip was strong. And then I noticed the fellow had a tattoo, like a sailor come out of China. Just behind his knuckles, seven blue stars curved toward his wrist.

"Twice welcome then, Brother," he told me. " 'Also thou shalt not oppress a stranger: for ye know the heart of a stranger, seeing ye were strangers in the land of Egypt.' Exodus twenty-three, verse nine." He looked me over. "Have faith. The lame shall walk. Come on and meet the brethren."

First, he introduced the Negro fellow. Twice my weight and twice my size he was. "Angel," Lott called him. We walked together toward a shattered grove, past picketed horses and into a clearing. Bright green grass, fresh thrusted, made a rug. The air was gray, but soft.

I smelled them first, as fragrant as perfume. And then I saw them, four fat hens on spits, dripping as they browned above the fire. Twas only after that I marked the men.

The hens were more appealing, I will tell you. But then I am a prisoner of my past, and like neat camps and uniforms and order. Captain Lott's detachment was irregular, composed of fellows dressed as their pleasure took them. Unshaven all, as if a beard were virtue, they wore their hair as scraggled as did the Rebels. Even a balding pate trailed a greasy fringe. They had the fierceness of Pushtoons armed for war, and the same watchful eyes. At ease here in their camp, they all wore pistols. And Bowie knives, as I believe they are called. Their shirts were patched, but all their boots were good. And their guns were clean.

Of course, I did not get the names of all. They come too fast, the nods and proffered hands. They made me welcome, I will give them that. To them, their leader, Lott, could do no wrong. One of them was even a Red Indian, the first such fellow who had crossed my path. His hair was sleeker than that of his comrades, long and straight and black, streaming with pink ribbons to his waist.

"Billy Wright," Captain Lott told me, "of the Choctaw nation." The Indian looked up from a saddle's repair. He did not rise or shake my hand, but only gave me a glance with solemn eyes. "Goes by 'Broke Stick,' most of the time," Lott went on. "The Lord has blessed him with a deep knowledge of this country, this wicked Egypt. A knowledge superior even to mine own."

We turned from the Indian and my host said, "I made Broke Stick's acquaintance back when I rode circuit, doing the Lord's work in Pharaoh's garden. Before the priests of Egypt drove me into the desert. He was one of the first to answer the call."

Now, I would not be a servant of my appetites, but the little tin of oysters had been all my noonday meal. And those hens smelled as lovely as the lilies of the field, if you will pardon the comparison. Twas all that I could do to keep my hands away and stop myself from ripping off a leg. I feared to pass them again.

I bantered with the men, though some were reticent. Country folk are often shy of words. They tallied one short of a dozen, until another fellow ambled in. He rose up from a draw like a corpse from a grave. Doubtless, he had been at private matters.

Lott changed. Forgetting me entirely. As if I had been swept from the face of the earth. The captain stood, black coat worn brown and beard mighty, raptly watching the last man's approach.

And then I saw the man was but a boy.

And then I saw a boy he would remain.

You knew at just a glimpse the lad was simple. His mouth hung open and his eyes roamed round. He wore a battered derby hat over dust-drab hair. Despite his outdoor life, his skin was pale. And blotched. All twitching leanness, he loped straight for Lott, calico shirt half tucked and trousers ragged. When he smiled, his left eye ticked.

A dozen strides away, he broke into a run. Stretching out his arms in a child's greeting.

Simple or not, the fellow wore a pistol. And a cutlass.

Lott embraced him, reeling from the collision. And I will tell you: In that moment, vengeance disappeared and hard words faded. The captain closed his eyes and love softened his face. The hand with the tattoo of stars stroked and patted the boy.

A minute passed before their hugs untangled.

"My son," Lott told me. "Major Jones, this is my only son, my Isaac." Where rage had been, a father's pride remained. He made me think of the Reverend Mr. Griffiths, whose daughter was that tyrant's only joy.

I looked at the boy, Isaac, and filled with pity.

Captain Lott could read a fellow plain. And he read me. But no harsh judgement passed his lips this time. He only said:

"The Lord has blessed my son with innocence. He knows no evil."

And yet, he had that gun and the dangling cutlass.

. . .

THE HENS MADE LOVELY EATING. Filling up the mouth with juice all hot. Broke Stick carved as clean as a Musselman slaughterer, and I was passed a portion equal to any. Remembering my wife's concern with manners, I tried not to be vulgar or to gobble. She does not nag, but chides from time to time. Still, I devoured that chicken with some haste.

Cakes of corn had been cooked in the ashes, a sort of bread that was all new to me. It chewed a little mealy, but made a welcome change from hardtack biscuit. A block of butter lay spread on a kerchief, strong of smell and specked, but rich to taste. It bettered up the cornbread to a fineness, once I got the nerve to help myself. For we must not be forward among strangers, nor take too much when other mouths must eat. But I will tell you: I could have gobbled up the lot myself, the hens, cornbread and butter, and the bones. I am a fellow grateful for his victuals. I even licked my fingers, I confess.

My manners, I fear, were not the worst in that company. Although the faults of others do not excuse our own deficiencies. Their great, fat knives were fork and spoon in one. But, to their credit, no man drew out whisky. If Captain Lott seemed otherwise intemperate, he had no toleration for the bottle.

"This is no common war, Brother," Lott said, as we chewed on. "It's a holy crusade." He pointed past my shoulder with a drumstick, showing me those blue stars on his hand again. The son beside him tracked the gesture's line. "And this is a crusading army. Oh, they don't know it yet. Man's lot is ignorance. We do not see His ways until the seals are opened. But they'll learn. Know that verse, 'Thrust in thy sharp sickle'? This army here's that sickle. And the South is the tainted harvest. Yes, Brother. The Southron is steeped in sin. He bears a thousand other sins, but none so black and deep as human bondage. Yonder, there's a chapel named in blasphemy. Slaver Methodists called it Shiloh, a name of peace and purity. Now it's no accident that this battle took place upon these fields, that the shadow of Armageddon fell upon us here. The Lord will not be mocked. He will have vengeance. He will not wait until Babylon is fallen." He looked at me, as sober as a clerk, and said, "The end of days is at hand. The signs are upon us."

I was not shocked or even much insulted by his comments about Methodists. For I had learned the hard way back in Washington that in the South some Wesleyans kept slaves. My uniform was cursed in a Georgetown chapel. But he troubled me with his talk of the end of days. Despite the warmth of the meal, I felt a chill. No man likes to think upon such things.

Lott put a remnant of yellow bread on his son's plate, then sat back against his saddle. The gray light had gone dreary as night approached. More rain would fall.

"I was driven from this land, Major Jones. Because I told them the Negro was not the son of Ham, but the true son of Abraham. Scorned, I went into the wilderness. Into Missouri. And Kansas. Where His fiery sword lay heavy on the land. I did His handiwork at the side of other righteous men. I claimed the great John Brown as my acquaintance, a herald sure as John the Baptist was."

He leaned sideways, elbow over the leather and beard brushing the earth. His son curled by him as a spaniel will, gnawing the last sweet flesh off a bone. "Now I have returned," Lott said. "And I come quickly. A tool of His judgement. Yes, Brother. When I returned I laid aside the Gospels. The Old Testament is what these Southrons need. That's the only God they understand."

Glancing around at his followers, some of whom had nudged up close to listen, Lott said, "We are few. But we are strong in the Lord. 'And ye shall chase your enemies, and they shall fall before you by the sword.' " He looked beyond us, beyond the splintered trees and resurgent green. Into the darkening wood. " 'And five of you shall chase an hundred, and an hundred of you shall put ten thousand to flight . . . and your enemies shall fall before you by the sword.' Leviticus, chapter twenty-six, verses seven and eight." He turned to me and grease shone in his beard. "Crave another cut of chicken, Major?"

.   .   .

TWAS THEN MY HORSE ARRIVED. I would have rathered have a bit more chicken.

A sergeant led him in, a German fellow. And clear it was the horse was other-minded. *"Verdammt noch mal, Du Teufel,"* the sergeant told the creature, which promptly kicked its hind legs in the air. *"Verstehst nur die Peitsche, nit?"*

Now I have learned a little of that language, and what I thought I understood was bad.

"Who *ist* Major Jones?" the fellow cried, as if he had to hasten to a latrine.

"That there's him." One of Lott's men pointed.

The sergeant brought the beast to me and I nearly backed into the fire. Its face was a devil's, long and vile and fierce. Yet, the others seemed to think the animal fine. They gathered around, commenting and cooing.

"That is one fine piece of horseflesh," a fellow said with a whistle. "Bet they stole him down outa Kentuck."

"Naw, that's a Tennessee horse. Look how he lifts them legs."

I would have sooner looked into a snake pit.

"You *ist* Major Jones?" the sergeant asked me.

"I am he," I admitted. Struggling to put up a valiant front.

The German held out the reins and the monster whinnied.

I forced myself to accept the leather straps. Now, I have been on horseback a pair of times. They did not turn out well. I had hoped—prayed—that an alternative form of transportation might present itself. Yet, I had known this moment had to come.

The horse loomed huge as a dragon.

Lott's men petted the creature as children do, avoiding only the range of its rear legs.

"Beautiful horth . . ." a hard man missing front teeth told his fellows. ". . . juth beautiful . . ."

Freed of the animal, the sergeant made his report. "The compliments of Cheneral Sherman, *Herr Major.* He sents on down to Sergeant Ike and tells him, 'Sergeant Ike, you knows them horses all *gut* and how many was kilt and not. You gif that major the fine, big horse. You do that, Sergeant Ike. You gif that man the best horse you got down there. Gif that man a horse fit for a cheneral, a horse what runs from them Rebels every which way.' And I do what the cheneral is telling me. *Jawohl,* I do. His name is Rascal. *Ach, Gott sei dank, ich bin diese Pferde los!"*

The fellow clipped a salute and disappeared.

Lott stroked the animal's forehead, where a white star blazed upon the reddish-brown. The captain's petting calmed the beast remarkably. Isaac, his son, caressed the animal's neck.

Lott told me, "It looks like General Sherman's appointed himself your guardian angel, Brother. Out in Kansas, I've known men to die over horses of less quality."

The fellows assumed I would try my mount while a bit of light remained. But I was not prepared for that ordeal. Morning would be time enough for misery. So I lied. Yes, lied. I told them that my leg had cropped a bother. At that, Lott had the Negro take the reins. Angel led the horse to where the other mounts were picketed, saying, "Come on, Rascal . . . you come on with Angel now . . ."

Obedient, the horse went at his heels. I sensed that men might follow Angel, too, despite his coloration. He had a certain quality that draws. We see it alike in the saint and the confidence man.

Now, you will say, "Jones, you were a soldier. Unbecoming it was to fear a horse." But I will tell you: Do not laugh too quickly in your pride. Every man on earth has got his fears, although they may be hidden half his life. When yours leap out before you, think of me.

I took me near the fire, dropped down, and wrote. And found my hand as shaky as my thoughts. Still, I filled four pages, then had to fold them up so I could sew. When I asked round, Broke Stick tossed me needle and thread, then bent back to his saddle-mending. He might have been a Scot, for all his silence. I think the Scots believe that words are money, see, and worry they will go poorer if they spend one. Perhaps they are related to Red Indians. The Highlanders I knew were wild enough. They made good soldiers when they were not drunk.

I was embarrassed to show them my unmentionables, though

they were new and clean. I always was a shy one, understand. First, I did my coat sleeves, then my trousers. At least I had the skill of sewing fast, although not half so well as my Mary Myfanwy. Back when I was a young buck in my regiment, no sergeant turned out finer on parade.

The night turned flannel dark, then preacher's black. The earth had stilled, except for a soldier's rumpus off in the tents. The world felt tired. Perhaps it truly was the end of days.

What if it was, and I was parted from my wife and child?

But that was nonsense. A weary man sees phantoms in his coffee.

Sufficient unto the day the labors thereof. Plenty there was for Abel Jones to think on, from horses to the massacre of forty. And I had much behind me to regret, from the banks of the Indus to the banks of the Tennessee. But let that bide. The time had come to sleep and gather strength.

Angel had brought me my saddle and the kit strapped behind it. General Sherman had equipped me well, indeed. From a white cloth to serve as a parley flag down to a blanket rolled in a rubber cape. From such, a soldier makes a warm cocoon, and keeps him dry in all but storms and floods.

I did not forget to search the ground for ants.

four

ad Noah been a touch less diligent, he might have spared me misery in plenty. I wish that he had left the horse behind. We rode out at the hint of dawn, when a man still senses more than he can see and the first birds call. Beyond our lines the air was lovely clean. But Eden itself would have been lost on me. I bounced along to shatter tooth and bone, reduced to constant dread of a four-legged beast.

The horse would run, and then the horse would slow. The horse would kick, and then the horse would canter. The other riders helped in his regulation, but Rascal was a creature aptly named. Remember that our Savior rode a donkey. It's Death that rides the pale horse in the Book. That tells a fellow something, if he's mindful.

My trials began before I reached the saddle. The creature whipped its tail across my face and knocked the tin of coffee from my hand. And then the devil swung its head to bite me, nipping at my bad leg then the good. The stirrups seemed a mile from the ground as I struggled to mount. They helped me up, did Angel and Broke Stick, while Lott's son held the horse and purred to calm him.

We rode through the softening dark. Soon my private circumstances ached. I dared not speak for fear I'd bite my tongue off. The fellows laughed. Quiet like, though, for we had passed into disputed territory.

Now, I will tell you: A Welshman will not show himself a quitter. I stayed on that horse's back and did not fall once. I may have looked a fool, but the prancing devil could not cast me down, although he knew more tricks than an Irish barrister.

Rascal snorted. Rippling his great body. I felt the shiver pass between my legs.

Captain Lott come back and rode beside me in the young light.

"It does look," he said in a low voice, "as if you're more familiar with the Gospels than the saddle, Brother."

And so all men should be. I gripped the reins as tightly as I could. No man of any sense would join the cavalry.

"Ho, steady now," Lott told my nickering bane. Then he turned his hawk's face back toward me. Below the wide brim of his hat, his gleaming eyes anticipated sunrise. "Can you feel it, Major? Is it creeping up and down your back?"

I knew not what he meant. All I felt was numbness in my nether parts.

"We're coming up on the place," he said, glancing about. "Not a mile off. Can you feel the sin? The wickedness? The guilt of those who laid their hands on innocents?"

I understood him then. But I could feel no change in our surroundings. Twas but the same trail through a poor man's world. The trees broke and we passed a derelict cabin, its yard home to a wagon without wheels, the axles braced on little piles of rocks. Broken implements lay strewn about, and the fence gaped. A balding path led under the sagging porch. But nothing stirred.

Except a halo of flies about my horse.

Woodland brooded on both sides of the path again. "How did you find them?" I asked. A hind hoof sparked a rock. "It must have been a startling sight, Captain Lott."

He looked away. The light snooped through the trees like scenting hounds.

"Wasn't hard to find them, Brother. They were meant to be found. All credit to the Lord, for He guides our every step. But those poor Negroes were strung up right where the trails crossed, for all the world to see. Hanging there heavy as sin. Though I am confident their souls rest in His bosom." Lott's pitch dropped to a growl. "Their nakedness was a mockery. A mockery of Adam, of His image. And the women . . . the children . . . all carved up like a heathen sacrifice . . ."

He soothed my horse again. "The Southron *is* a heathen, Major Jones. No matter what he pretends. No matter how smooth his tongue or polished his manner. I know, for I was born among his kind." He reined in his horse to stay by me. "Evil comes in many guises, even that of angels. Comely and fair was Lucifer, who betrayed his God. The Southron is Antichrist. And his armies are the legions of Antichrist. The end of days is near. The ears of the faithful hear the final trumpet."

I heard only hooves and the rustling of trailside brush clipped by our passage. The truth is that my thoughts were far away, where those we killed had skins of brown, not black. Not even a fitful horse could scatter the memories.

.   .   .

MOUNDS AND CROSSES marked the killing ground. There were not forty beds, but only six, their placement irregular. Negroes had not needed separate graves. No more than slaughtered villagers in Oudh.

I wondered how the dead had been divided for burial. Did the women and children sleep separate from the men? What of the married? Must they sleep forever in the arms of strangers? Was every mother with her rightful child? And father by son? Or had they been dropped in the closest hole, forever wed to strangers, indiscriminate? I recalled how callous we grew in India. Killing numbs you worse than any saddle. We mostly burned our victims to save time.

What did it even matter who lay where? Was that not empty sentiment? The flesh is but corruption and a shell.

Yet, I would lie forever by my wife, when my time comes. I cannot bear the thought of separation.

I had some minutes alone by the graves, see. While Lott dispatched his pickets and looked round. Alone, that is, but for a thousand ghosts.

I never turned my wrath on woman or child. Believe me. There was no shortage of others with a taste for such work. Not after we learned of Cawnpore. And, truth be told, some had the taste before. I was ready and willing to look away, though. Or to pass along the orders from above. Until that hot day when my young strength left me.

I will have a plenty to answer for. But let that bide.

When Lott returned, I had him show me exactly where they had hanged the men, and where the women and their young had lain. Demanding all the precision his memory could give, though some of the signs were evident. Their bark rubbed raw, branches recorded the scraping of the ropes. The brush had broken down where others fell. I found a shred of cloth, dotted and faded, dangling from a skein of briars. My back rebelled when I bent over to pluck it. I was stiff as drumhead justice from the ride. Fingering the strip, I almost felt the flesh it had clothed. Imagining the terror at the end.

I knew that terror. I had looked it in the face. And neither distance nor years had paled the memory.

Overconfident of the capability of my bad leg, I had left my cane strapped back of the saddle. Now my folly told. I labored awkwardly climbing down into a streambed. I had only thought to go a little way, see. But we are led along unexpected paths. Suddenly, I was not my own master. I went as if obedient to orders.

The wet earth gave as I descended, slopping my shoes and trouser bottoms. I nearly lost my balance. 'Twas hardly more than a ditch, but the cut was steep. The sort of hiding place that draws the fool. I imagined quaking children, and the killer's iron smile. But I found nothing.

I was not searching for a specific thing, see, but looking for anything that might turn up. Like a tramp at the dustbin.

"Looked to me like they rounded them up right quick," Lott said from the lip of the bank above me. Glimpsed from below, he towered. "No sign of a chase. Oh, a child or two tried to slip off and got killed back in the bushes. But it looked to me like those Negroes just gave up and surrendered. Maybe fooled into thinking they were only being led back into bondage, nothing worse waiting for them than a whipping. The tongues of false men always bear a promise, and the innocent believe." He crushed some tiny creature beneath his heel. "Maybe they knew their captors, Brother? Trusted them? Who knows what the slave-catchers told them? No doubt, Herod's men did likewise unto the children of Bethlehem, luring them out with sweet and wicked promises. Careful down there. Moccasins are out."

I clambered out of the gulley, ignoring a recitation of Bible verse he began. I fear I had no patience with sermons that morning. Far from true religion I was, and my mood was black as plague. Besides, I do not like my scripture barked. Over-use cheapens the Holy Word, and makes me wonder what men really mean.

"Did it appear they had been here long, Captain Lott?" I interrupted him. "Before the killing began? Did you find any campfire ashes?" I scanned and saw no scars amid the green, excepting the grave mounds. "Or concentrations of excrement, perhaps?"

He looked at me oddly. I am sure my methods struck him queer.

Lott's eyes set hard enough to silence the birds. Perhaps he felt my questions lacked in reverence. "Nothing like that," he said. "Nothing I noticed. Nothing at all. Only mortality, Brother. Mortality, and blood that cries for vengeance."

The members of Lott's band not riding picket stood about, uneasy, with carbines in their hands and horses near. They did not like the place, twas clear enough. And that made sense. For each would have his memory of the discovery, of human flesh made carrion. When animals go at a body, they take the soft bits first. It makes an ugly sight.

"How did you bury them, if I may ask? How did you choose who went into each pit? Proximity? Propriety?"

"We didn't bury them," Lott said, growing restless. "Sherman's men did that. We just prayed over them, then rode back in to report the sign we'd been given."

I paced the ground, wobbly as a drunkard without my cane. I picked up a stick to help me, but it was rotten and broke at the first pressure.

"They hanged the men first," I said suddenly, although I had not planned to share my thoughts.

Lott had a pistol ready in his hand. Pray as he might, he still relied on powder.

"And then they killed the women," I continued. "Although there may have been indecencies in between. They killed the children last. Except those who screamed and annoyed them."

Lott had paused some paces to my rear. I turned back toward him. For though I had not meant to speak at all, I craved an audience now.

"Have you . . . had a vision, brother?" he asked, fingering his pistol. "Do you see the sinful deed?"

Such as me will not be granted visions. Only memories.

"It is only a thing of logic," I lied. "The men must be finished first, for they are strongest. Their strength would surge up at the torment of their women and children. They could make difficulties, were one or more to break his bonds. Even tied up tight, they'll bite a nose off. Anything to protect their loved ones."

I paused before a rank of yellow flowers. I had not marked their loveliness before.

"So you kill the strongest first," I told him. "And keep the others bound and under guard. The women are killed next, for they would be unsettled and second strongest. There is a pattern to the thing, see. Most men will save the comeliest woman for last. Even if she is not ravished, they will kill her only when the rest are dead. Although a certain breed of man kills the beauty first."

The morning was not warm, but sweat had drenched me.

A breeze disturbed the petals at my toes. "Some children cry out, but most are cowed. They whimper, rather than scream. And then, it's the queerest thing, the way they settle to a common sound. It is a low noise, like a pulse. The youngest do not understand the doings, of course. Not in a manner they can fit to speech."

I took a desperate breath of the April air.

"It is clear how it was done, Captain Lott. Clear and regular. First, the men were done with. A few of the women pleaded for their husbands, but the mothers among them were more reserved than a fellow would expect. They hoped to save their children, see. Through good behavior. Imagining a charity not to be granted."

I turned to face Lott, recalling something else. "And then there is the numbness that comes over the women at the killing of their men. I left that out. That is a queer thing, too. Oh, some cry and collapse. But there is not the lasting noise you might expect. For violence shocks and stills the tongue." I smiled bitterly. "And never forget the power of hope. Each hopes that she will be the one preserved, the exception . . ."

White of face, Lott eyed me hard. As if I had conjured memories of his own. I have been told that Kansas was not pleasant.

He nodded. Slowly. "The end of days is upon us," he repeated. "His will be done." At that, he signaled to bring up our horses. "We'll double back and strike for the Corinth road."

.   .   .

THEY HIT US from both sides of the trail, shrieking like demons. Firing from their saddles and swarming over us. As if they had erupted from the earth.

I drew my Colt and thumbed the hammer back. Just in time to

shoot before I was shot. My round discharged into a fellow's face. And he tumbled. My horse shied and I grabbed onto its mane.

Three times our count I made them out to be. Although you cannot tell for sure in the wildness. A fellow in a checkered shirt fired close. Near enough to share his spittle. Had Rascal not bucked, the bullet would have slain me. I heard the crack and felt the throb of air. I shot, but missed the man as he surged by.

"Y'all come *on*," Angel shouted to me. "Gotta git." Galloping past, he leaned and smashed a Rebel's jaw with the butt of his revolver.

Then he was gone.

I am good on the ground. I know how to receive a cavalry attack. But I could not control the horse beneath me. I aimed for the chest of a fellow riding with a pistol in each hand. Riding for me and grinning.

Rascal shied and twisted. I missed, but so did my enemy.

Our horses tangled and our legs collided. With a great whack to my knee. The shock of it bent me double and my pistol stabbed into the fellow's thigh. I pulled the trigger. Just as the devil smacked my shoulder with the flat of his revolver.

His blood splashed over my trousers and covered his own.

The Rebel howled, recoiling. His mount peeled off from mine. Somehow, I kept my seat. I kicked my horse to goad him on after the others, but only lost the stirrups for my efforts.

Then Rascal reared up high, and I went down.

I struck the ground level, from head to hips, with my face toward the sky. Loud as a bass drum I hit. A great whacking thump it was. My wind fled in a gush. I must have lowered an inch, I drained so empty. The shock slammed my eyes shut.

Nothing on this earth is as swift as combat. When you are in such a mêlée. The affair lasted not a minute. No sooner had I reached the earth than all the shooting ceased. I heard complaints and curses. Men dismounted with a creak of leather, as hooves tapped to idleness. In the distance, horses raced away.

I opened my eyes and found two guns trained on me, a shotgun and a pistol like my own.

"Kill the sumbitch," a tin-thin voice said. "Shoot the sumbitch where he lies. The little sumbitch's the one killed Leakey. And put that bullet in McGilley's leg. The little sumbitch."

"Shoot him yourself," the fellow with the shotgun said. "I wouldn't waste the powder when we got rope."

I wished to speak, but had not found my voice. I had fallen hard.

Not far away I heard a voice I recognized. "Oh, no, oh, no, *Lord* no . . . pleath, no, *oh,* no. *Pleath* . . ."

"Git up, you sumbitch," the tin-voiced fellow said to me. He was so lean he hardly blocked the sun.

I struggled to rise. "Papers . . ." I got the word out.

"You jist git up."

"Oh, no, *oh, no* . . ."

I rose to my elbows and saw him then. Just at the start of the trees. They had captured the fellow who lacked his front teeth. The one who had praised my horse. Wounded now, he poured blood down his shirtfront. But it was not his wound that caused his dread.

Tin Voice kicked me hard, but I was transfixed. They already had a rope around the lisper's neck.

"Lord, *no,*" he cried a last time. Three Rebels pulled the rope that spanned the branch. His body rose in a frenzy. Legs kicked wildly, mad hands grabbed at the noose. Blood sprayed off his wound and men stepped back. When they drop you down, it snaps your neck. But when they haul you up, the end comes slowly. I watched his eyes bulge and his tongue swell darkling.

I understood I was to end the same. The thought clogged my heart with ice.

Tin Voice gave me the toe of his boot in the side, then in the buttocks. I scrambled up. The lisper's efforts dwindled down as all the air drained out of him. He jerked forward and back, in rhythm, spending his last fires. Desperate still to slip out of that noose. Imagining that he might yet survive. His fingers had dug between the rope and his neck, clawing the flesh and leaving crimson streaks.

He slackened and his hands fell to his sides. A man in a straw hat gave a snort of benediction. But the lisper would not die. He kicked again. At the end, we cling to life. With more tenacity than we bring to the living of it.

Except for those whose hands sustained the rope, the Rebels watched him die with folded arms. A few joked low and hard, but most looked on in calm satisfaction. One lit up a smoke.

"Don't them Yankees squirm?" a boy called from the clutch of horse-holders. His tone sought manhood and failed.

The lisper managed one last twist. Perhaps it was only a spasm. Then vulgar matters happened in his trousers, for hanging's indignities continue after death. They let him swing till slime dripped over his boots.

"Must've had him eggs for breakfast," a man in a straw hat said. "Downright ignorant, him stinking up like that."

The men who held the rope let go. The lisper dropped, ungainly. Bones snapped. I shuddered, feeling the pain myself.

I was afraid. With a degree of fear I had known but twice in my life. Once, when the Pushtoon got me down by Attock Fort. The time Molloy rescued me. And after Bull Run, when the surgeon tried to take my leg.

In books, men seek nobility in death and mount the gallows spouting perfect speeches. But there is nothing noble in the rope. I would not beg, I told myself, but I did not want to die. Not that my thoughts were ordered. My words come out of my mouth without reflection.

"I am an emissary," I protested. Trying to sound confident and bold, but only spluttering. "From General Grant. To your generals. I . . ."

A man sat back against a tree, with a belt around the thigh of his blood-soaked trousers. He had a pointed beard and a pallid face. "Jest git him hung."

You have heard speak of "pure hatred." Twas in that fellow's eyes.

Hands grasped and dragged me. Past the body of a fallen Rebel, straightened tidy. Another of Lott's men lay dead in the briars behind the Confederate corpse. A part of me could not believe what was happening. Yet, most of Abel Jones knew this was real.

"This is against the custom of war," I cried, looking about wildly for an officer. "I have a letter. I carry a letter. To your general, I'm sent to—"

They stripped the noose off the dead man's neck and pulled it over my head.

I found my mettle at the last. I would *not* die a coward.

How odd we humans are. Look you. Even faced with death, I thought of appearances and of the regard of strangers who would hang me. That is the truth of it, although I saw it elsewise in that moment. I could not bear for them to see me craven. There was no courage in me, only pride. And pride is a mortal sin.

"Then *damn* you," I said. "For damned you'll be for hanging those poor Negroes."

The noose bit.

A tall man pushed from the rear of the pack, revealing the shreds of a uniform. Broad he was, in every way, of face, at the shoulders and hips. The sort who could pull a plough as easily as guide it. I saw him clear, as you see all things at such moments. He had those cold gray eyes that frighten the Hindoo, all the brighter for his raw complexion and the sun-faded beard that framed it. He was not old at all, but his youth was dead, and his mouth had a savage set as he come on.

He raised his hand.

I thought its fall would bring my end. But it was a different signal he intended.

"Hold on, boys," he said. His voice was gruff as flat rocks

clapped together. "He'll keep a minute. Josh, you loose that rope, but don't take it off."

The fellow stepped toward me. His big hat was a farmer's brown, adorned with a loop of braid. The collar of his gray jacket was trimmed with yellow and stained where his neck bulged from it. He wore a captain's insignia. And a pair of stolen U.S. Cavalry britches.

He grabbed me by the tunic. Smelling of tobacco, labor and dogs.

"Who hung what niggers?"

"*You,*" I said. For I was up in a fury born of fear. "You and all these criminals of yours. You hung forty—no, you *killed* the forty. I don't recall how many were hung. But hang innocent men you did. The way you hang your prisoners of war. You slaughtered women and children." I looked around, spiteful of the very heavens, and noticed a fellow cradling his shattered jaw. "You're worse than savages."

The captain slapped me hard.

I would have struck him back, had his comrades not kept me in hand. Yet, a half-breath later, my terror returned, tormenting me with a vision of my wife, then of her and the child, left alone.

The feel of that rope will ever haunt me.

The captain began a tirade, from which I must extract the most offensive language. What remains is foul enough to scorch.

"You little shitworm," he said. "First off, no man riding with Micah Lott counts as no prisoner of war. No, he don't. Hear? And we know all about them niggers. You all come down here like turds on two legs, all full up with your dirty Yankee lies . . ." And so on. With every word I felt the scratch and grip of the rope. Twas wet with a dead man's sweat. And with mine, too.

When he stopped for breath, I spoke right up. I still had that much spunk. But the voice I heard no longer seemed my own. A giddy waver spoiled it, and made it seem a traitor to my will. I looked him in the eyes, though. Straight up into those steely eyes I looked. Smelling the tobacco and sourness on his breath.

"If you know everything about the massacre," I said, "who killed them, then? If not you and your rabble, who did it? We will learn the truth, see. And the guilty will pay twice over."

He raised his hand to strike again. This time it had balled to a fist. But he held it at his shoulder. Looking down at me with peerless hatred. His fellows tightened their grips on my arms, steadying me for his blow.

"Go ahead," I told him. "Oh, you're a powerful, brave man, a very lion. *If you didn't kill them, who did?*"

He lowered the fist to his side. Reluctantly. He seemed a man who would rather break a thing than try to understand it.

"I don't know who did it," he said. "But, by God, when we find out, we'll hang 'em every one. And we'll find out, all right. And put a rope to 'em like they was more of Micah Lott's murdering, black-damned—"

"That's why I'm here, see." I got the words out quickly. "To find the killers. Look you. There are letters in my pocket." I tried to free my arm, but strong men held me. "Look in my pocket, damn you. In the left one there. You'll find a letter from General Grant himself. I've been sent all the way down here from—"

"Hang your letters," he said and turned away. He stepped toward the man propped against the tree. The one I had shot in the thigh. "McGilley, how you doing there?"

"Tolerable, Cap'n. Like to see that fella kick, though. That sure would put a better spirit on me."

"Bone all right?"

The wounded Rebel looked down at his thigh. "Naw. That leg's a goner. Lucky I got two, ain't it?"

A pair of fellows laughed.

The officer stepped back toward me, with murder in his eyes and face and posture.

"For the love of God," I said. Of a sudden, weakness struck and my voice threatened to shame me. It is easy enough to be brave with comrades by you, see, but facing your end alone will test you proper. "Just read the letter in my pocket. It's from General Grant, it's—"

"Gabe, you get that letter out," the captain said abruptly. "And pass it here."

One of the men behind me loosened his grip and a hand prowled through my pockets like a rat in a commissary sack. He did not listen when I said, "The left one," and he took his time finding the document. As if he did not want it to be there.

The captain turned the letter over in his hands. Looking at it from one side then from the other. He looked at it from near and far away, holding it down, then raising it up to the light.

"Open it," I said. "Read it. It says I'm to cooperate with your authorities to identify the killers of the Negroes. *Read* it. *Break the seal*. Under the circumstances, I think we can—"

I thought his face had shown all possible hatred. But I was wrong.

"We're not schooled that way," he said. In a voice sharp as a dagger. "We don't have your Yankee habits." He glanced over my shoulder. And spoke as if the sentence caused him pain. "Take that rope off the little peckerwood."

The men did not obey immediately. "Aw, now, Buck . . . lookie what he done to—"

The captain plunged toward me and my captors. Stopping just short of boxing his own men's ears.

"*Do what you're told*," he shouted. "*This here's a damned army. Hear?*"

They loosened the rope and ripped it over my face, burning skin off my nose.

"I sure would like to see that sumbitch hang, Cap'n," the fellow I had wounded called from beneath his tree. His voice come wistful, not the least irate. "Make my leg feel better, it sure would. And to think of poor Jake a-laying there . . ."

"Later," the captain said. He paced the ground, holding the letter as if it might have fangs. "After we spy into things a little." Then he turned and stared straight back at me. "He'll hang just fine tomorrow, or the next day."

.　　.　　.

THEY KEPT ME IN A CAGE until my birthday. Ten nights it was, shut in a coop with my ankles fettered. They tossed me scraps and said I should be grateful. Nor might I have a bucket for my wastes.

I lived in filth and fear, veering between high hopes without foundation and despair. Was this a judgement on me for past sins? A retribution delayed, and crueler for the joys that I had learned through my wife and child, and the hope I had found in my faith? I wondered if we serve a vengeful Lord. And if some form of the rope awaits us all.

India haunted me, until I seemed to catch a glimpse of madness. Even if the Lord forgives, our memories do not. Of course, by day I am the soundest of men. I am as you are. But a part of us is alone in the best of nights.

My guards sat under a tree when the sky was fair, watching me through the gaps in the slats of my prison, but when it rained they leaned in the door of the barn. Their faces changed, but not their manners. Each man begrudged me life when his turn come to mind me.

A shanty governed the farm where I was held. I had a view of its rear across a sty. The windows were small and had no glass, and dogs went in and out the open door. A woman served as mistress of the manor. She did her chores in a slattern's rags and ignored me. She smoked a pipe in a shriveled mouth, but I do not think she was old. Whether the Rebels went off or come back, she hardly seemed to see them. She spoke to her hogs as she fed them, but not to the men. I never saw her smile.

Again, I thought of India. Of the day something froze inside me and I could not soldier more. They put me in a cell, then in a swill, and made me empty cesspits with the natives. I was not spared a Bible by the English. Now, at least, I had my Testament. I told myself I was not badly off. With my own waste piled in a corner and the floorboards swarming at night. And the rope still knotted.

I would not be broken, see. Resolved I was that the Rebels would shame me no further. A major must not beg, and a proper Welshman will not. Certainly not from the likes of my captors. Twas vanity and pride again, but perhaps there was a purpose. For anger makes our suffering easier to bear. The raging man feels little and sees less. And what man likes to sit and wait for death? Amid his own corruption? Perhaps my prideful nature was a blessing.

Oh, life is not as simple as we paint it when we're seated safe in chapel.

They told me we had crossed into Mississippi. It rained at first. Then every day seemed hotter than the last. The leg irons chafed. I sucked on bones and slept with crawling things, dreaming of my wife and son and home.

Most of the guards refused to talk, except the few who mocked me. Reminding me that the rope was tied and waiting. But they intrigued me, those Rebels. For I would know the reason why a clock ticks. Poor, they were as lean as any Pushtoons. And just as savage, though not near so clean. They dressed in shirts of cheap-spun cloth made up by country women. Their hats were random and their trousers patched. Long of beard, with hair unshorn, they did not value uniforms like city men. But weapons and horses were their silver and gold. Knives and pistols shone as they sat in their saddles, as easy when mounted as other men are on foot.

The officer, whose family name was Wylie, looked commanding on a horse's back, surrounded like a baronet by his hounds.

And the horse's back he sat on now was Rascal's.

I did not miss the horse, you understand. Still, I felt as though I'd lost my colors.

I felt far worse about my Colt. I did not know which of them had it, though twice guards joked about "The hero of Bull Run," asking if that meant I had run the fastest. That is how I knew at least one of them could read, see. Unless it was the woman, which I doubted. It grated on me to think of the pistol in an enemy's hands. For though I wished all swords might become plowshares, as a Christian must, the boys that gave me the Colt were good of heart.

I asked if I could wash and they guffawed. When I sang hymns, they howled along like dogs and asked if I was anxious for the rope. They mocked my voice. I only can conclude they were all heathens and despised religious anthems. For I am fine of throat, like all the Welsh.

And that reminds me: I must tell you of the Welshman. He kept his distance for several days, a nut-brown little man. But we are ever drawn toward our kind, if only for the sweetness of the talking. Now, I had no idea of his origins. For men of many lands are dark and small, and I did not hear a single whisper from him. Until one day when his comrades went off patrolling and left him in the shade to keep the watch. Of a sudden, he said:

"It is a pickle you are in, then."

How lovely kind it was to hear his tones! Oh, a Welshman has a handsome tongue in his head! Although I had no longing for Britannia, and loved America with all my might, I nearly wept to hear such music spoken!

"A Welshman is it?" I asked, got up all proper to my feet. I peered through the slats at the bright of the day and into the shadows cooling my compatriot. "And a Glamorgan man, if I have not misplaced my ears?"

He kept him to the shadows of the tree. "Cardiff and proud. But my mother come from your way."

"What way is that, pray tell?" I asked, a trifle huffed. For I am regular of speech and most American. My accent, if ever I did possess one, is gone sure as Glendower. I did not think that he could spot my birthplace. Not by my proper, modulated tones.

"Oh, Merthyr up and down. With your vowels all in the baritone."

As if a Cardiff accent was a prize!

"Well, I was Merthyr born, that I will give you."

He smoothed himself in victory and reclined. "It is a dreadful pickle you are in. I would not like to be where you are, see."

I did not like my habitat myself. But let that bide. I took a special care crafting my words:

"They do not see the crime of it, then?"

"Crime is it?"

"Well, hanging me is a crime, sure."

The lowborn Cardiff pick-head shook his skull. "I do not see it. Nooo, I do not see the crime there. Nooooo, sir."

"I'm a prisoner of war, man. No, not even that. I'm an emissary. Sent from one high general to another. Such don't hang."

He thought about that. "Oh, many a sort may hang, when there's a rope. Even an emmy-sary."

"It isn't proper."

"You shot Jake Leakey dead. And took the lovely leg off poor McGilley."

"That was fighting. It was the luck of battle, man."

He ruminated. "Still and all, one's dead. And the other is short of his walking instruments. And they are my butties, see. It is a great dilemma for a fellow. I would not wish to give offense to another Welshman, but what are wishes? Wishes are dust awaiting the broom. I think there is a hanging in your future."

A revelation struck me. Oh, the crawling Cardiff heathen.

"I know a thing. A thing about you, see."

"And what is that, then?" he asked, unaffected.

"That you can read. And likely write."

"Well, so can many."

"But when it come to my letter . . . with the noose around my neck . . . you did not tell them, did you?"

He shrugged. "One of them knows, and that is enough. I would not be differentiated, see. A fellow must not get himself differentiated. It is a terrible matter to be differentiated."

"But they would have *hanged* me. And you a Welshman, too. When all you had to do was read out the letter."

"I would have been horrible differentiated then. And forever presumed differentiated. For these fellows are not great ones for the learning. Irish blood, see. A fellow must never get himself differentiated."

"Look you," I said. "You do not want to be . . . to be differentiated. And I do not want to be hanged."

"There is true."

"But you would have let them hang me."

He nodded. "It is a war, see."

"But wars have *rules*."

"You rode with Micah Lott. They will not have it."

"He was my escort, and no more than that."

He shrugged. "A man is known by the company he keeps."

"And what is wrong with Captain Lott, then? Fierce he may be, but he is a solid, religious fellow."

"He is a killer, and a dirty one. And there is true. He is a killer and a bushwhacker. A bad sort, that one."

"It seems to me there are plenty of bad sorts, and I have met more than my share of them lately." I tried to keep my disgust within sensible bounds. "Why did you join them, anyway? Welshmen are not slavers. Not even Cardiff men."

"Well, I did not say I am for slavery, did I?"

"But you're fighting to defend it, man."

"Noooo. I am fighting by my butties. Beside the friends of mine who are my neighbors. There is simple. I do not see how slaves and Negroes figure."

He was a Cardiff man, as thick as oak. As thick as oak doubled and banded.

"And what, pray tell, is the name your father handed you in Cardiff?"

"Evans," he said. "It is not a common name."

. . .

YOU KNOW THAT IS NOT TRUE. Not that any Welshman is dishonest. That I do not mean. But Cardiff men are as vain as they are dull-witted, and, truth be told, they want nothing more dearly than to be "differentiated." Evanses are common as the raindrops. Wales drips with Evanses. Evanses fall from the eaves, they spill from the waterspouts. There is a very flood of Evanses, from the Wye to Caernarfon Bay. There are more Evanses in Wales than there are Frenchmen without morals. And that is a plenty, I am told.

This one was Dai Evans, settled in a Southron town that robbed the name of Oxford. He claimed they even had a university, though I was in a mood to disbelieve him. He had no evident bond to my roster of Evanses, but Evanses are shells upon the shore. And he was a Cardiff man, which implies an overseas influence, to put it delicately. Such are not always sound in their paternity. But let that bide.

We found a tie, though, on my dear wife's side. For the mother of the wife of this Dai Evans was a Protheroe, come down from Merthyr. Yet, the link was not so direct as that suggests. The woman was, by birth, an Abergavenny Protheroe, but married young to a Merthyr Williams, who died of an aggravation in the blood, after which she wed a Cardiff Rhys who come visiting. Now the Abergavenny Protheroes are, of course, related to the Protheroes of Ebbw Vale, who have matrimonial ties by way of the Davies family of Brecon to the Morrises of Tredegar who were originally out of the West, although that should not be held against them. For I will tell you straight: There are good men living west of

Gower, although they rarely attain the heights of achievement common to men of the Valleys. But to be short: A Morris of that Tredegar branch married an Aberdare Roberts, second cousin to my Mary Myfanwy's mother. Twas clear as day, once we figured it. I judged us wedlock cousins, at a tenth to twelfth remove.

And still the fellow would have seen me hanged.

"Oh, they are set to do it," he said to me one soft-complexioned morning. With his comrades snoring in house and barn and Captain Wylie gone off the day before. "They are set and waiting for the word."

The fellow should have been an undertaker, for all the dourness of him. Talking to curl the quiet he was, with never a joyful word. "And joke they do that the deed must be done by daylight. If you were hanged by night, they say, we two might be mistaken by our voices and *I* might see the sunrise from a tree. For we are not differentiated by the sound of us. It is a great teasing and mockery I have endured because of you, Abel Jones."

It was not true that we sounded a bit alike. His voice was Welsh as leeks. While I, in my maturity, by diligence in the study of elocution, have acquired a tone worthy of emulation by gentlemen and young persons alike. I have become a complete American, as anyone can tell.

I did not argue. For I had other matters on my mind that wanted ears to hear them. There is a human impulse to confide.

"This is my birthday," I told him. Across the yard, the woman come out and drew a bucket of water from the well. I craved the wet of it. "I am a man of thirty-four today, Dai Evans. This nineteenth day of April, in the year of our Lord, eighteen-hundred-and-sixty-two. Thirty-four I am."

"Well, that is ripe. May you have joy of it."

"It is no pleasant spot to spend a birthday."

"Better it is," he said, "than to be hanged."

"And they still do not see the crime in it?"

"Noooo. You rode with Lott. And all who do shall hang."

"But *why*, man? What's so bad about Lott? You said he was a
'killer.' All soldiers are killers in war. The better the soldier, the
worse. Who has he killed that makes him any different?"

"His wife, for one," Dai Evans said. "Before the war that was.
I have heard tell of it many times, for it is a great popular subject.
He was a preaching fellow up in Ripley. They found her in a barrel, covered in salt. With her head clean off. He should have
hanged, see. But he was gone in a twinkle. He took his son and
went. We heard he meant to liberate the Negro, but never thought
to see him back again. For there is talk in plenty in this world, but
fewer deeds." The fellow sighed. "Well, he will hang soon enough.
And deserve it. For he has killed good men. And women, too. They
say he was a terror out in Kansas. But such will not be tolerated
here. Lott has differentiated himself most awful, and his wife's
relations set a price on his head of five hundred dollars. Though
they are Scots and likely will not pay. But look you. It is not the
money that will hang him. Many's the man would kill him for the
sport."

Just then, Captain Wylie come trotting up the lane, in all the fine
of the morning. The hounds ran out to meet him, yapping gaily. But
as they closed the distance they went quiet, for a dog will read his
master's mood most clear.

I could feel the rage in Wylie before I could see one detail of his
face. He glowered, and he treated Rascal rough.

It was his wont to dismount by the fence post and take himself
directly to the house. But this time things went otherwise. He
dropped down from the horse and lashed the reins around a rail,
kicking at the dogs.

He ignored the men emerging to meet him and strode across the
yard toward my jail. No words describe our many shades of fear.

The door of the pen slapped back so hard it bounced. Wylie
reached inside and grabbed the first part of me he found available.
Twas the flap of my tunic, which I had not yet peeled off, for the
morning was still cool.

He dragged me into the yard. I could only stumble with my ankles chained. The light struck fierce.

"You blue-bellied sumbitch," he said. "You low-bred, snot-face bastard."

I tried to stand up proper like a sergeant. For such have better posture than the officers. And I would not be bullied in my final moments. Although I was not sure my resolve would last.

I thought, of course, that he had returned to hang me.

"General Beauregard wants to see you," he said, in a voice all spit. He could no longer look me in the eyes. The men had gathered round to see a hanging. Now they started in to curse and jeer. "I'm bound to deliver you to General Beauregard himself," the captain went on in a tone of enduring disbelief. His mouth pursed as if he had swallowed vinegar. "I should've hanged you straight off and got it done."

"Aw, hang him anyhow, Buck," one fellow said. "You kin tell the general we hung him while you was gone and it weren't your fault. I'll fetch a rope."

Wylie turned to face his men. More appeared from the house and barn each moment. They must have slept in piles.

"We ain't going to hang him," the officer said, sun-cured face made crimson by his anger. "Orders is orders. But I swear . . . by God, I do . . . I *swear* that if he ever comes my way again, he won't even need hanging." He glanced at little Dai Evans. "Ev, you water that damn horse of his and walk it a little. I'm going to eat some, then take him on into Corinth."

A Rebel dishevelled as a Hindoo holy man said, "Buck, you surely ain't going to give him back that horse, too? Are you?"

"It's his damn horse. It's nothing but a damn no-good Yankee horse, anyhow."

"And," I said, buttoning up my tunic and tugging my cuffs, "I will have my pistol, thank you."

The captain turned and stared, amazed. The men drew closer.

"You'll what?" Wylie asked.

"I'll have the pistol that you took from me. For it is mine and seized improperly."

"Hang him, for Christ-sakes, Buck. Old Borey won't miss him."

"I will not go without my pistol," I repeated, although my voice was not quite as steady as I might have wished it. "For it was seized against the rules of war."

Captain Wylie clenched his fists until they were hard as cannon-balls.

"It is not gloating I am," I said. "But fair is fair. You kept me in a pen and that was improper. I was no prisoner, but an emissary. Now you must return all that is mine."

A shabby creature drew a pistol, cocked the hammer back, and stepped toward me.

"Buck, why'unt you just look over yonder for a moment. The general couldn't complain none of an accident."

His fellow troopers murmured their agreement.

But the officer turned his rage on them instead of me. "This is an *ar*my, damn it, not some Memphis hoor-house. You'll follow orders. Every damn one of you. Just like I follow 'em. Any man don't like it, we can settle it here and be done." He glared from face to face.

"Aw, come on, Buck. Gabe didn't mean no harm."

"That's right. I was only fooling, Cap'n."

Wylie swung toward me again. He looked me up and down with frank disgust. "Truth is, boys, this here tiny little Yankee ain't worth the hanging. Just look at him. Now where's my breakfast? Ada broke out any ham this morning?"

A last brave, bitter voice said, "He killed McGilley, Buck, and it ain't—"

"Just let it go, boys," Wylie said resignedly. "Let it go. There's plenty Yankees left that need a killing. Ada? Ada, you got biscuits working? Where are you, woman?"

The woman, it turned out, was the officer's wife and the farm his own. He told me that as we rode into town. Not without some pride. There was strange, I will admit, but that is how these people are. His spirit toward me softened with the miles, for the Southron will mean to kill you one moment, then open his heart and his home to you the next. I do not say that we became all friendly. Only that he accepted what passed his way, the way he accepted the flies that dogged our horses.

It is a different world, the South, and a poor one for most. Although I could not see their stake in the war, these "crackers" were all for the fight. Perhaps they liked the change that war provides. Their lives seemed humdrum, otherwise, and hard. When the battle standard was raised, they rushed toward it. They are proud of what they view as manly skills and make a cause of any slight encountered. But that is the way of things, I suppose, from Ireland to far Kafiristan. The less a man possesses, the harder he fights for it. The rich man bends to fit the changing times. A poor man's bones are always at a discount.

But I must not stray too far.

Even after it was resolved that I would not be hanged, the Rebels offered me no common courtesies. I had a crust and a dipper of water for my meal, as usual, but might not even wash my face and hands. Evans stepped round and handed me my pistol, for the man who had claimed it was off in a terrible sulk. Twas Evans took my leg irons off, as well. Then he let me be while he saw to the horses. I could have run off, but to where?

Captain Wylie come out and took himself to the privy. Evans waited by the fence with our mounts. When I limped near, Rascal shook his head and snorted. It made a fellow wary. I thought they might at least have kept the horse. I could have used a proper walk just then.

Wylie strutted toward us, fixing his belt, and Evans whispered:

"Now you have had a fine birthday gift, Abel Jones. And there is good. For sad I would have been to see you hang. It is an end unworthy of a Welshman. And you a relation."

five

We traveled a threadbare country. Despite the succulent green, the soil felt poor and the husbandry negligent. Churned by an army's muddy retreat, then hardened by the sun, the roads would break the wagon wheel that chanced them. Our horses threw a regiment's dust, though we had slowed as the heat rose. Deep in a field, a woman steered a plough, twitching the inside line to work her mule. She paused and watched in silence as we passed.

It seemed a narrow place, this Mississippi, where men did not look past the near horizon. There were no grand plantations by the roadside, only shanties poor as Hindoo nooks. The men who cut these farms out of the forest had dragged their poverty along behind them. As if they feared to let it go.

The sun erased our shadows. The air brewed thick. I found my surroundings as foreign as India.

My fine new cap had gone lost in the skirmish that led to my ignominy, but my uniform was otherwise preserved, if meanly soiled. Wylie told me to remove my tunic so its blue would not draw fire. Truth be told, I was glad to be free of the wool. The shirt beneath was filthy, but it did not seem to matter greatly here. I laid the frock across the nose of my saddle. Then I thought me better and stuffed it under my rump. For there is not a great deal of beef on my hindquarters, if you will excuse my indelicacy, and I was bouncing up and down on bones.

I was not blindfolded, which surprised me. We passed the Rebel outposts with a nod. Once, at a barricade of logs, we stopped for a ladle of water. A sergeant touched the brim of his cap and said, "Regards to Ada, Buck. How's them dogs?"

"Passable, Clem," Wylie answered. "Ain't getting out much. War and all. Dog needs to run, if you want him keen."

"That's a fact." The sergeant considered my trousers. His eyes moved to the coat stuffed under my backside. "That little fella a Yankee, Buck?"

"More or less." Wylie slurped more water.

"Looks like he still got him a pistol."

Wylie handed back the dipper. "Ain't loaded. Best to the missus, Clem."

And we rode on.

As we were approaching Corinth, earthworks shouldered the road. Faces watched us from the parapets, but their curiosity never rose to a challenge. Jackets hid stacked rifles from the sun. Tents laced the groves and knotted every tree line that faced north. The heat pressed down on all. And this was April. I wondered what their summers must be like.

I smelled sickness in the camps. Wounded men in plenty there may have been, but it was the sourness of disease I caught in my nose. All fetid bowels and sweat it was, not the minty rotting of gangrene. I knew the reek from hot-weather campaigns in India, when more men fell to fevers than to jezails.

The Rebel encampments were uniform only in their slovenliness, and the soldiers looked slack. We passed unkempt fortifications and, by the batteries, gabions shaded idle cannoneers. I saw a defeated army. These Confederates could have been brushed aside, had our generals moved with dispatch. I pitied us such dereliction. I did not know that Grant was in disfavor, with General Halleck in personal command and creeping south by inches, schooled in caution. But I must cling to my story, so let that bide.

Wylie had done me a good turn unintended. His days of riding Rascal had tempered the beast. I could not like one shred of the experience, but riding had become less unpredictable. Do not imagine that the horse obeyed me. It merely kept to the pace of Wylie's mount. Still, that was progress.

We heard cheers up ahead. You would have thought a bastion had been carried, except that there were no shots. I turned to Wylie with a question spread over my face, but he had caught a scent and put his nose up, peering past the trees that blocked our view. Without a word, he teased his mount to a canter. Hastening toward a rise where the grove gave way.

Rascal hurried after, bruising my bruises.

From the knoll, we saw a disorderly crowd and heard the drumming of hooves. Rascal perked up like a wicked child. Of a sudden, the cheers resumed. Above the throng of heads and waving hats, a pack of riders rushed toward a post.

Twas a horse race. There is wicked. Men ride to the devil and money is wagered. Liquor is consumed. Profanity pursues both man and beast. Shameless women have been known to attend, though, to be fair, I saw none such on that particular day. But it is a constellation of depravity, the horse race, and a decent fellow wants none of it.

Wylie spanked his mount with his hat and went off at a gallop. Rascal asked no further encouragement, but shot along as if in a race himself. I held on for dear life and seemed forgotten.

I nearly pitched over headlong when we pulled up. I ended with my arms round Rascal's neck. Wylie had halted just at the rear of the crowd.

A race was done and money passed about. Beside me, Wylie stood up in his stirrups, searching the field.

Then he settled. Grinning. "Lord," he said to me, as if to an old friend, "I do love a horse race. Ain't nothing like a horse race."

Now, I have seen proper garrison tourneys, and that is a separate matter, conducted between officers on Indian service when the weather cools. A certain propriety is observed and there is a testing of skills applicable to the military. There is no squalor. Such events may be tolerated, if not condoned, by Christian men. I am even told that fine society is not above watching a race in England, although I suspect the tongues that tell of such affairs speak indulgently of the wealthy and debauched for selfish interests. But this was just a rabble at a fencerail. Gawking. Untoward stimulation had, I fear, made them intemperate.

Now, you will say: "I have been counting days, and this was a Saturday, and should not soldiers have a bout of leisure? You, yourself, have said their lives are hard." But I will tell you: The devil loves a Saturday afternoon, when drink and gambling have ruined many a youth. A man should use such hours for reflection. And though I did not wish the Rebels victory, the old soldier in me gets his powder up when he sees a hard-smacked army doing nothing when it should be fixing every cause of failure. Here, all was indulgence. Jugs of liquor bobbed from hand to hand. On the edge of the crowd, two men went to fisticuffs. Their language was as naked as their feet.

The next running paired but two riders. I could not help observing them as they come up, for I was at the mercy of my escort. The first fellow was a sooty, bearded sort, with that ropy look the Rebels often had. As he was hatless for the race, the sun caught the gleam of sweat where hair had quit him. His horse had a reddish tint akin to Rascal's.

And then I saw the other fellow. Young, almost frail, and made for a different world. He seemed as out of place as snowy virtue. A son of proper gentry he looked, of high folk bred to a taste. Clean-faced as a boy he was, but light brown hair flowed after him, long enough to whisk the collar of the whitest shirt south of Ohio. His sleeves billowed. And if his shirt was white, his horse was black. As black as coal before it leaves the mine.

The lad was fine as silver. With a polish to him. I could not see his features well, but knew he was not handsome. Not in the way that strikes the eye at once. No, he would have a look that unfolded with acquaintance, the look of character.

I knew all this, for I had seen such like in days gone by. Their families sent them out to India when the household could not afford a commission in a good regiment at home. Some became dissipated with phenomenal speed. But others rode alone into the frontier, learning things that threaten white men's souls, or kept their troops in line when others faltered and saved the day that rightly had been lost. They were the pinch of pepper sprinkled over the bully beef of our regiments, thrice as vivid as the common run of officers. Few survived long.

Lord knows, I do not favor aristocracies. I think America blessed for the lack. Like Mick Tyrone, I believe each man should be judged on his own virtues and accomplishments, not by an inherited purse or pedigree. Yet, I have admired a few highborn fellows. Grudgingly. One in a thousand, no more. For the typical young heir is not worth the breakfast he consumes. But look you. There is no rule that measures all of mankind. I have known honorable heathens and even decent Irishmen.

"Why, that's Drake Raines!" Wylie said. The recognition heightened his excitement. "No question who's going to win this here race. No, sir. Old Drake's the man to beat, from here to Natchez. Leastwise since Billy Barclay lost his legs at Donelson."

The horsemen drew up in front of a rogue with his arms spread wide. Pawing and ready their stallions were, and holy terrors the two of them. The crowd pressed against the fence, disregarding modesty and the heat. Men stood on tiptoe, each calling encouragement to his favorite.

I saw the lips move on the human gate. Both riders nodded down at him. The noise dropped to a hush and the black horse snorted.

The fellow dropped his arms.

The bearded man rode wildly, as if the hounds of Hell were on his tail. Whipping his horse most cruelly from the start. But the slight young man kept up the pace, smooth and even as waves in a sheltered bay. He rode just like those officers in India who kept a different mount for every sport. Nor did he touch his horse with spur or leather. He might have been out for a meadowy jaunt.

The cracker fellow's horse showed taller and broader. Seething rage, he gave it cruel encouragement. But the lad on the black was never an arm's length behind. You got no sense of gritted teeth from that one. Twas fury dueling with fineness in the sun.

Their sound faded to no more than a hint and their figures became small. Half a mile out, they rounded a lone tree. A blur of white and black floated beside a reddish smear, and a confusion of legs throbbed against a screen of dust. Quieted now, the crowd peered down the field, listening intently amid the swoop of flies and the heavy settling of the day.

The riders grew larger again. Hoofbeats drummed like regiments advancing. Of a sudden, the onlookers exploded. As if a spark had got into their powder. Jumping they were. Shouting and shrieking, complaining and cursing. Their lives might have been staked upon the outcome. Or their souls.

Beside me, Wylie rose up in his stirrups.

At first, my escort did not join the shouting, but only called to me, "You watch now, Yank. Now you'll see some real riding." Then, in a wink, he caught the fever himself and bellowed, "Come on, Drake. You show him how, boy. Feed him some dust, hear?"

I sensed the bearded man on the brown horse burning. If longing were speed, he was bound to win twice over.

Beside him, the lad with the billowing sleeves stayed easy. As if the outcome were a matter of indifference. Only as the goal neared did he alter his posture. With a smoothness fit for a fancy ball. His rump rose slightly and his shoulders lowered.

I will admit I felt a degree of excitement myself. The devil does not lure us with dullness.

Twas all decided in the last sliver of the course, hardly the range of a pistol shot. The young fellow gave his horse its first whipping with the reins and the black beast surged ahead. Horse and man flashed by us, with the cracker fellow vanquished clear as Johnny Seekh.

The pounding eased to a pattering up the field, and the young man reined his horse about, letting it pace toward the waiting crowd. The animal shone as if polished with oil and its huge eyes glittered. Foam dripped from its mouth. The horse seemed more excited than its master, who only set a mild look upon his face, mouth shaped into a pleasantness not quite a smile. The fellow's sleeves were slack now, sweated through, and his wet shirt clung to his chest. Had ladies been present, the display would have been unpardonable.

The bearded challenger had broken his gallop just past the finish, but he trotted far into the field before turning back toward the onlookers. As if covering a greater distance eased the fault of his loss.

"I won, all righty," a soldier near us declared, "but it weren't worth much. Can't never get no odds against that Raines."

Through all of this, no one but Wylie had taken the least notice of me. And the captain's attentions had been intermittent at best. Compared to a horse race, Yankees were a trivial matter. Indeed, it had been my impression that we were to hasten directly to General Beauregard's headquarters, but my escort had turned from the task without the least hesitation.

"Captain Wylie," I said to him, swiping at the flies that flocked to my horse, "should we not be going along now? Ten days have been lost already, see."

The Southron glanced at me. For a moment, he seemed to have forgotten who I was. Then he said:

"In a lick. I just want to say how-do to old Drake." He rose in the stirrups again, waving and calling, "Drake! Drake Raines!"

The lad had dismounted and was soothing his horse while admirers walloped him merrily on the back. When he heard Wylie's call, he turned, crisp as a Guardsman, and swept back his hair to better scan the crowd.

He smiled a grand smile.

Passing the reins to a well-wisher, the victor leapt the fence, expecting the crowd to clear a space for him. And it did. He smoothed through the pack, smiling generously now. And yet that smile seemed a sort of mask to me. It was not meant to keep the world at bay, but to hold some business in. Still, twas white and lovely, a smile to haunt the elder sister of the beauty on whom it was wasted.

Delayed a dozen times by congratulations, he finally reached the snouts of our mounts and stopped. Up close, you saw the muscles that had seemed a fragile thinness from afar.

"Buck Wylie, as I live and breathe."

His voice was soft as velvet, startling after the flinty tones I had come to associate with the Rebels.

With a creak of leather, Wylie dropped from the saddle. The fellows shook hands then clapped each other on the shoulder. Between smiles, each stared into the other's face. I know that look, see. It is born of war, appearing when old friends find each other alive and whole after a battle.

"Guess the Yankees couldn't catch you no more than Wid Loftus there," Wylie said.

"Nor you, Buck. Hear you've been catching plenty of them, though." At that, he turned his brown eyes up to me, showing me the exquisite plainness of his face, the bones as fine as Bohemia glass. His eyes mocked my squalor and he seemed about to speak, but he restrained himself. Manners, see. They don't reach to the eyes, but they temper the tongue.

"Taking this one to old Borey," Wylie explained. "Got himself a pass to speculate over that big nigger-killing."

At that, the fine young man forgot me entirely. "I heard about that. Over at headquarters. Somebody told me they were Billy's runaways."

Wylie nodded, and both men looked down. Darkened. My escort kicked a pebble, stirring the dust. "Damn this war. Been awful hard on Billy. Ain't it, though?"

"It has, Buck." The victor's eyes drifted.

"Seen him?"

"No."

"Got to see him," Wylie said.

"I don't know," the fine lad said, "that Billy wants to be seen."

"Know where he is?"

"Shady Grove. So I'm told."

"Tain't far. Maybe I'll get on down there." The flesh around Wylie's eyes tightened, adding a decade to his age. "And them niggers just run off? With him right there?"

The young man, Raines, shrugged. With a vast sadness. "Billy's chasing days are over, Buck. He probably wishes he could run off from himself."

"One of us got to go visit," Wylie said. I noted a hint of reproof. "You ought to go, Drake. You and him was like brothers. I was only good for hunting and liquoring and playing tomfool." He drew himself up and lowered his voice. "You got to forgive him now. The way he is."

The lad's mouth hooked. "I forgave him long ago." His voice assumed a false and jovial tone. "Come on now, Buck. You know an officer can't just ride off at his pleasure. I'll go see him. When I can. Maybe soon."

The day had gone dark as winter where they stood, although the sun glared round us, and words froze in their mouths. A fellow with a heart-shaped face patted the victor's back, ready to praise his riding. He sensed the chill and moved on with a mumble.

Wylie said, "Right warm for this early on. Might be a drought year coming."

"Hottest April I recall," the young man replied.

"Wasn't he a hunting man, though? You ever seen the like?"

"Sure haven't." The fair young man willed a change in himself, in the conversation, in the world. "And how's Mrs. Wylie? How's your Ada?"

Wylie grinned. "Passable. Getting tired of feeding up the boys, though. You know how women are, Drake."

"Well, Ada always seemed a fine one to me. Biscuits fine as spun gold."

"Drake? You ever think on that last morning we was all together? How that hard frost made a cramping sound when you walked over it? With them dogs running and Billy hooting like a damn fool down in the live oaks? Had us some good shooting that day." He shook his head and fussed at the earth with the toe of his boot. "Ain't it funny how shooting sounds so different to a body now?" His raised his eyes and they formed a plea. "You recall that morning, Drake?"

"Sure, I do." The fine lad, Raines, brushed back his hair again. He always did it with his left hand.

Wylie stared at the earth. "Aw, hell. Ain't no good talking. Is it?"

"Depends. There's pleasure in talking over certain things. Remembered pleasures. Old friendships. Other matters won't bear too many words."

"That's so, I guess. You always were a fine talker, Drake. Just like your daddy. Always worth a listen." Wylie laughed and there was a note of real glee in it, of an eagerness to flee a thousand miles from hopeless troubles. "I was feared you'd come back talking like a Yankee. With all that Yankee schooling between your ears. I wondered over that with your daddy once, when he come up for a shoot. Just before South Carolina went out, that was." He smiled, almost laughing again. "He said there wouldn't be nothing wrong with you a whupping wouldn't fix and that you weren't so big as he couldn't do the whupping himself. How's your daddy keeping, Drake?"

The young fellow smiled at the query. But I glimpsed a startling bitterness in his eyes. "Just fine. He's up in Richmond. Helping old Jeff run the war."

"He's a fine Southron gentleman, your daddy."

"He is that, Buck."

"Well, you see him, you pay my respects. Tell him, after this here war, those dogs'll be waiting for him. And for you, too, Drake."

"Thank you, Buck. I know he'll look forward to it."

"Drake? You go see Billy Barclay. And you tell him Buck Wylie says hello. Tell him I'm fixing to come visit."

"I'll do that. Word of honor."

I thought Raines would turn away at that. It would have been in the rhythm of things. But the young man paused. And raised a face as grave as a man bereaved.

"Buck? I don't want to be . . ."

"The hell, Drake. What's on your mind?"

"There's something . . . I need to ask you." His voice was quiet and duskier than any velvet now.

Wylie gave him a figuring look. Then said, "Drake, your daddy looked after us handsome when my pap died. A man don't like to be beholden, but your daddy made it easy as he could. He's a gentleman among gentlemen. Never played high and mighty. No more than you did. So you just name it. Anything you want, anything a body can do."

"It isn't like that," Raines said. He glanced at me, face too somber for a young fellow who had just won himself a horse race. A hundred times too somber. And he looked away again. "It involves a matter . . . that a gentleman has no right to raise."

"Aw, Drake. I never was no gentleman. Not like you and your folks. Nor Billy and his. And you'd be a gentleman no matter what you said or done."

"I heard that you saw them. Billy's runaways. That you and your boys slipped in and had a look before the Yankees put them in the ground."

Despite all he had promised a moment before, wariness tensed my escort's features. "I saw 'em. Wouldn't mind if I hadn't."

"Was the girl there?" he asked in a voice as fragile as china. "You know the one."

"There with them niggers, you mean?" Wylie spoke to delay, twas clear as light.

Raines nodded. "Was she there?"

My escort's face turned fit for a burial. "She was. It weren't easy to tell, for all the blood. The way they cut 'em up. But it was her, all right."

The fine young man tugged at the front of his shirt, separating the drenched cloth from his flesh. When he spoke again his voice was flat. Only those who have known loss would have recognized the sorrow in his tone.

"This war's been hard on Billy," he confirmed.

.   .   .

DUST CHALKED MY LIPS as we rode down the street, although there was no wind and little motion. Corinth was built of boards nailed up haphazard, a place of careless angles and few bricks. The commercial buildings had the look of widowers who have stopped tending their persons. Only the signs hung in advertisement and a few rare shutters had ever seen paint. Dust veiled the windows and all things green were banished. Nor do I recall any citizens abroad, except a pair of fractious boys. But memory is imperfect, and only the great things and the queer ones stay with us.

When I remember Corinth, it is always the dust that comes to mind. Fine as talcum powder, hazing the afternoon light. It was a summer dust, though this was early spring.

The dust is what I recall, and then the wounded.

They leaned on whittled crutches in the doorways, befuddled by missing limbs. Armless men tipped back on armless chairs. Deep-eyed, they watched the world go by in silence. Now and then, a fellow spat tobacco then sank back into the general stillness, a somnolence I did not associate with the white race.

A healthy fellow strutted by in boots, an officer scanning shop facades. The wounded watched him go with an indifference worse than hatred. They were broken, futureless things, those fellows. And these were the lucky ones. Two weeks after the battle, they were alive and free of fever.

I wondered how many were farmers. That is a hard life even for those with limbs intact.

I had never seen such a town before, so crowded and so desolate at once. Beside me, Wylie averted his eyes from the invalids. Only to blurt out, "They're just waiting on trains, Yank. They're going home, those boys. Old Jeff'll take care of them. They're just going home."

Yes. Home. To the wife who sees an armless stranger coming down the lane, hope and terror on his face. Home to children not yet skilled in pretense.

A locomotive huffed in place a block away, where tracks cut through the buildings. That engine was the only thing in the town that gleamed, catching the sun on its metals. It shone through the dust like a vision. Spewing little puffs of steam, with shimmers of heat off its boiler. As if it could not wait to leave.

As we drew near the station yard, I saw the men laid out. Another kind of wounded had been mustered, men who could not stand or even sit. They lay upon the earth, some few on blankets. Waiting to be moved deeper into their shrinking homeland.

Soldiers stripped to the waist shoved their comrades into freight wagons, laboring to a drowsy rhythm. They had the air of a punishment detail. Deserters, perhaps, recaptured and put to work. Whatever their sins, they needed supervision and had none that I could see. Little progress seemed to have been made in the loading, for the wounded lay waiting in hundreds in that yard. Dust crusted them, and the afternoon sun cooked all.

One decent fellow bobbed about the yard with a canteen. Watering the desert with a teaspoon.

Bandages listed every shade of pus and dried blood: green, yellow, brown, black. Crimson blotches marked reopened wounds. Complaints were low and few, though. Most of the men were too far gone, too weary, too listless. Here and there, a lad mouthed silent words, speaking to a phantom behind his eyelids. Suffering never has fit well into speech. Lips swelled and cracked. Skin reddened. Sweat gleamed on their faces, and their shreds of uniform showed great dark patches at the armpits, at chest and groin. The stench pierced.

A half dozen Negroes with shovels lolled by a fence. Waiting, I supposed, for men to die.

A boy began to writhe under the heat.

We are told to love our enemies. I cannot say I loved those men, for I did not. But I pitied them.

It shocked me when the music began to play. Rascal gave a start, but I was learning the business of the reins and I held him in.

I spotted the band as I settled the horse's prancing. Their brass instruments were mottled. Impressive at a glance, their shakos and silver facings faded under a stare. They stood ranked in a crescent, beside the station. Their master's arms waved handsomely in time, as if he were leading a concert in a park. He kept his back turned to the wounded men.

The band played "Dixie's Land."

six

*I*f cologne water won battles, General Pierre Gustave Toutant Beauregard would have won the war by himself. Hoarse as if from illness, his voice had a Frenchy taint. I am told his accent derives from New Orleans, a Sodom with infernal weather. His tongue slithered between a mustache pomaded to water-rat slickness and a little goaty beard.

The soft gray uniform he wore, collared and cuffed in braid, with two brilliant lines of buttons down the chest, was cut for a royal court, not a campaign. Grander than McClellan himself he was, with a sash trailing at his side and hair swept back with macassar. His face was that of an elegant rodent, though he moved like a cat got up to mischief. And Frenchy bred he might have been, but his eyes put me in mind of a cockney cheat.

All whispers of Welsh blood in him are groundless, or I'm the slaughtering Sultan of all the Turks. From the first instant, I found him the very summation of unpleasantness and suspected the fellow of improper habits. But it is not our lot to judge others, so I will not prejudice your opinion of him.

He met me in the parlor of a house and grimaced.

I was past the shame of being dirty. Twas the Rebels themselves who were at fault, so let the devils smell it and make faces. When you have been kept ten days in a cage, you either break to nothing or rear up. I was on my hind legs now, although those parts lacked a certain physical steadiness, thanks to my hours in the saddle and the lack of a cane. But I will tell you: Abel Jones was not the fellow for Frenchy nonsense that day. No, I was not. I was not arrogant or rude, you understand, for bad manners are unChristian. But I would not have nonsense, even from a high general. I kept my peace, though seething.

Beauregard puffed up his chest like a pigeon's and cocked back his head.

"You appear," he told me, rasping, "to have been incommoded. My apologies, sir." He glanced at Wylie, who still held me on an invisible tether, then returned his sniffy look to me. "My men are valiant, sir, valiant! But they are not always fully cognizant of war's courtesies. Rough men, sir, rough! But valiant *sans pareil!* We must allow for the conditions of the field, for the exigencies of campaign life. *C'est la vie militaire, monsieur, comprenez-vous?*"

"I was locked up for ten days," I said mildly. "In a dog pen or the like. Although I had my papers proper from General Grant."

At the mention of Grant's name, his fancy-man's face muddled up. Worse than it did at his first sight of me. But the fellow soon mastered himself. He stepped over to a small linen-decked table that bore a decanter and an array of tiny glasses. A silver utensil waited beside a cake and a stack of painted plates. Shining forks lay spread in a fan, sized to the fingers of maidens. I wondered if our interview had interrupted a gathering of ladies, for this did seem the finest house in the town and society will not pause for a war.

"A cordial, Major?" The general's eyes swept the room as he cleared his throat. Oh, grand he was. His aides, gussied up fine, eased their shoulders against the walls and door frames. Beauregard looked toward them, but did not really seem to see the fellows. They were but mirrors to reflect his glory.

I recalled the wounded in the sun, their burned lips, and the boy dying of a fit.

"I do believe we have reached the hour sufficient," Beauregard said, "for a small indulgence. Have we not, gentlemen? Have we not, *mes frères?*" Turning back to me with a sashay, he repeated, "A cordial, then?"

"And that would be a drink of an alcoholic nature, sir?"

He chuckled. "One hopes."

"I have taken the Pledge, sir. Thank you."

A new look come over his snout. As if an exotic creature had escaped from a menagerie and stood before him in all its unbelievable extravagance.

"The . . . *Tem*perance Pledge, sir? You speak of the Temperance pledge?" He looked bewildered. I might have been the king of the Hottentots, I struck him so queer.

He smoothed his feathers and tilted toward his audience of subordinates. "*Regardez, mes amis! Voilà! L'homme du nord! En parfait!* You see, gentlemen . . . our Northern . . . our Northern filials, let us say . . . are temperate fellows. Yes, gentlemen, they are temperate men in character. They lack our Southron heat, our fire. Our passion. They are creatures of sobriety, of desires restrained. But do not mock, gentlemen. No, do not mock! For they are steady. Steady fellows, these Yankee traders. Traders of diligence and competence, if . . . if unenlivened, if lacking a certain vivacity, *joie de vivre* . . ."

Cocking an eyebrow, he called, "*Sharl?*" A Negro sprang in from the corridor. "Charles," Beauregard continued, "*I* will have a cordial."

The general watched the amber liquid dribble. A single drop spotted the linen.

Accepting the glass, Beauregard sighed. "There is . . . a certain roughness in our ranks, Major. A devil-may-care boldness. '*L'audace,*' *en Français.* But it is all genuineness, *monsieur.* Southrons are sincere, sir, sincere! *Avec une sincérité infini! C'est vrai, c'est vrai.* Authentic fellows, *authentique,* the stuff of heroes."

He waved the glass and gave the air his perfume. He smelled, I fear, like a woman of unfortunate profession. "Ours is not *la vie manqué,* the life of hollow hypocrisy common in . . . in colder climes, let us say. I fear . . . that your letter . . . your letter, sir . . . as delivered by Captain Wylie . . . delivered promptly, sir, promptly, by this homespun cavalier . . . was misplaced by my staff until yesterday. We are fighters, sir, not clerks. Misplaced, you see. Under conditions of war. *C'est la guerre, monsieur.* Would you like a piece of cake?"

.   .   .

"SENT TO ME," he said, forking the yellow sweetness into his mouth, "by the incomparable ladies of Charleston. By rail, sir, they sent it by rail! I fear they admire me too much, the noble ladies of our Confederacy. Their accolades are too generous. Although I hear strangely little from the belles of Virginia . . . given my presence on the field of Manassas, one would think . . . but perhaps the mails have been interrupted. Interrupted mails would explain their neglect. Will you not, sir, join me in sampling this extravagant creation of the tender baker's art?"

I looked at the cake with longing, for I like a sweet. And I was hungry, too. But I would have starved before I went gobbling in front of that particular bunch of Rebels. Now, you will say, "His refusal was impolite. And if a fellow is hungry, he should swallow his pride and eat." But I will tell you: Ten days in a cage will make you sour. And I do not apologize for it.

"I thank you, sir. I am not hungry."

"No, no. Of course not. Northern abstemiousness. I understand it, sir. Respect it. Wary of . . . of corrupting pleasures, let us say. The Puritan heritage. *La vie puritaine.* 'Lead us not into temptation . . .' "

"I am sent upon a task, sir. And time has been lost. With respect, sir, should we not discuss the matter?"

All the staff fellows had been served and they went at their portions with vigor. Forgotten, Captain Wylie moved toward the remaining sliver of cake. But the general slid between him and the table.

"Ah, Wylie. Our rustic cavalier." The general cleared his throat again. "Indeed, indeed. Soon you'll be back with Bedford Forrest, no doubt. When he rises from his bed of honor. As rise he shall! For now, sir, you may go. Yes, go, sir, with my thanks. *Merci, merci.* Well done, *mon chevalier!* Off you go, sir! We will detain you no longer."

Wylie went, trailing bile. For even lions like to have a treat.

"Sir," I tried again, "should we not discuss the matter of the Negroes? These wicked murders, sir? There is concern—"

"*C'est terrible, n'est pas?*" the general cried. "*Une perversité!* A dreadful affair, dreadful! I understand General Grant's concern—is he steady these days, sir? Is he steady? A man afflicted by misfortune, sir, by misfortune, let us say. But his concern is only natural. The fault is his, of course. He was in command. We had withdrawn. Withdrawn, sir, in a strategic calculation. Grant's troops must bear the responsibility, sir. The scene of this bestiality . . . this monstrous behavior . . . lay within their jurisdiction. Thusly, they are responsible for good order, no matter the identity of the villains. This crime lies at the feet of the Federal authorities! The Federal authorities who have intruded themselves into our homeland, sir!"

"I understand, sir, that this matter occurred at a location between the armies. Between the lines. I do not see how it follows that General Grant is responsible."

"His forces were in the advance! We had withdrawn. It is a recognized rule of civilized warfare, *monsieur,* and I may cite de Saxe and Jomini, that the army in the advance must assume responsibility for good order upon its arrival."

"But the Union army had not arrived, sir. And the Negroes were murdered in the interval. Look you. Some days elapsed before the Africans were discovered by our scouts, judging by the condition of

the bodies. The logic of the situation, to say nothing of the prejudice, points toward Southron guilt. Begging your pardon, sir."

He had forked up a last bit of cake and a crumb stuck to his
mustache. His eyes widened and his chewing ceased. He lowered
the plate. And stiffened his posture.

"No Southron gentleman would soil his hands with such a
deed."

"Perhaps the killers were not gentlemen, then."

"And it is proven—proven, sir!—that the care with which the
Negro is treated by his benevolent masters defies criticism! The
Negro, sir, is a child, and is treated as such. Why, he is a member
of his owner's family! Guided by firm but merciful parents! By
parents concerned only with his welfare! He is indulged, sir! Why,
the little monkey is petted! The notion that . . . the very hint that
Southrons . . . certainly, that Southron soldiers . . . would . . .
would . . . it is *ne pas possible, monsieur!*"

I thought he would blow his cap then, for he was red as a
Ranee's ruby. His voice scraped. The crumb dropped from his mustache and fell on the Brussels carpet.

"Well," I said, "I do not know who killed them, and you do not
know who killed them, there is true. And speculation is an idle
business, sir. *But* think of the danger to your cause, were the matter
to go unresolved and the devils who did it unpunished. The outcry
in the Northern press would not be contained, see. Doubtless, it
would excite European sentiment. What would the great newspapers of London say? The English could not well support a cause
that slaughtered innocents. For they will have cotton, but not at
too great a cost to their self-regard. No, sir, they could not well support your Richmond then, if you were viewed as murdering innocent Africans right and left. Could they now? Not even the Frenchies
would do that, if anyone had an eye on them and they knew it. Begging your pardon, sir."

I looked at him all man-to-man and set our ranks aside.

Although my language remained impeccable in its respect for his position.

"I understand," I continued, "that your government means to have London's favor. But you will not have it if you are suspected of slaughtering slaves by the dozen."

The ruby face was gone, replaced by a sickbed paleness.

"Of course," I pushed on, amid the wary silence of that room, where every fork and glass had been set down, "if the truth come out and showed how it was renegades behind the deed, such might be punished and no damage done to honor and reputation. But what would the world think, if the Confederate commander right there by the doings refused to explore the matter? Oh, guilty he would look, sir. Even if he were not."

"I . . . you . . . I never said . . . never said we would not inquire . . ."

"And wouldn't the newspaper fellows make a great fibbing and fable of it?" I asked him. "Worse than the truth, they'd scribble it. Oh, I'd pity the man who turned up his nose at the business. A gentleman's name might be sullied forever, sir. Dirtied beyond all scrubbing."

"Of course, we shall look into things, Major! Of course! As General Grant has suggested! *Certainement!*" He posed again, most heroically. "Indeed, I had planned a thorough campaign of investigation myself and required no advice or encouragement from General Grant. Although you are welcome here, sir, welcome. Cooperation between foes is not without precedent. Indeed, it is not. *Entre nous,* I welcome it, sir. In the spirit of chivalry. And we have not been idle in the matter! No, it is only the vicissitudes of war, the demands of the day, that have restrained my hand. Were it not for our strategic maneuvering in the wake of the check inflicted upon your army at Pittsburg Landing, sir, the villains would already have been discovered and hanged. Hanged, sir, hanged!"

"Well," I said, with my bad leg a bother from riding all day and then standing, "that is good to hear, sir. For even in war, the murder of innocents must not be tolerated." I shifted my weight and caught a nose full of my own stink. I could have made good use of soap and water, I will tell you. Although I do not mean that perfumed soap of Beauregard's, for I would not be thought a fancy man. "I may begin my investigation, then? With your support, sir?"

Beauregard wheeled on a drooping cavalier.

"Is the Raines boy still in town? The senator's son? Young Drake? Is he still here? Lieutenant Raines?"

The staff man looked mutely at one of his companions, who stared at another fellow in turn.

"Begging your pardon, sir," I said to the general, "but I believe the fellow is here all proper. He was engaged in a horse race this afternoon."

.　　.　　.

I SHOULD NOT HAVE TOLD HIM THAT. It peeved him that I seemed to know more about his army than did his staff officers. The general looked at me first in surprise, then in calculation. That cockney, quick-fingered look it was. I could feel his mood decline, although his voice remained unchanged.

"Young Raines shall escort you, Major. He understands Yankee ways. Understands you people. Went north to school. Against his father's wishes, as I recall. *Ah, l'esprit du temps . . .* the youth of today have a will of their own. He attended one of your quaint little colleges. Harvard, I believe. Doesn't seem to have harmed him— why, for that matter, I understand Colonel Lee sent his own boy to the institution. *Gen*eral Lee, I beg your pardon. One forgets. Poor, old Lee! Best of families, excellent bloodlines . . . but the gallant fellow's aged, sir, past his prime. Lacking in *la vitesse,* let us say. Fine service in Mexico, in the old Army, but one hears from Richmond that Lee has . . . that he has slipped, sir, that he dotes! Why,

I'm told the soldiers have graced him with the appellation, 'the King of Spades!' " Beauregard fit a look of determined fairness over his face. "Still, he may well do us service as a quartermaster. Not everyone can share in battle's glory. We must look upon one another not as rivals, but as brothers in arms!"

He purposed a good-natured laugh that had no goodness in its nature, and his paladins attempted to laugh in turn. But the mood had been spoiled, as if the cake had been found mouldy in the mouth. "Then you know young Raines, Major? Am I to presume you are acquainted? From his Northern sojourn, perhaps?"

"No, sir. I only saw the horse race, see. But he is a great friend of Captain Wylie's."

Beauregard appeared confused for a moment. Then he nodded to himself and said, "Ah, yes. Yes, I see. Wylie. Wylie and Raines. *Noblesse oblige,* of course. That would explain it. Won the race, I suppose. Reputation, reputation. *Le chevalier parfait!* Perfect man to assist you, ideal. All doors will open to you, Major."

I thought of the willowy lad in the sweat-drenched shirt. With his voice all soft, but not puling and Frenchy like the general's. Our fates are strange, and surprise is our lot. I wondered what the lad would think of helping me. My horse had interested him more than I had myself. Still, he was an educated fellow and would be courteous, for manners are the very soul of learning. And I would do my part to get along. I wondered at the pairing, though, and if he would prove arrogant or mean.

And I wondered how these fellows ran an army. Sprawled about a parlor, with a war to be fought. And leaving those wounded men in the station yard. This seemed more a gentleman's club to me than a headquarters.

Suddenly, as if he had just awakened, a captain said, "General Beauregard, sir? What about that other Yankee fella, that Dr. Tyrone? You want him fetched?"

That startled me. I fair tumbled into speech. "Dr. Tyrone? Michael Tyrone?"

"A friend of yours, I am led to believe?" Beauregard said. "Yes, yes. Stroke of good fortune. Might not have found that letter of yours, had he not appeared with his demands. With demands, sir! As if he were the general! A brusque fellow, let us say . . . *indiscret* . . ."

"But what's Mick Tyrone doing here? I mean Dr. Tyrone. Begging your pardon, sir."

"You might have hanged, sir! Through no fault of ours, of course. We were ignorant of your existence, entirely ignorant. *We* would have borne no blame. But you must be thankful, sir, thankful! General Grant took an interest in you, a personal interest. As did far greater figures, I am led to believe. General Halleck himself sent the doctor along." Beauregard tilted his head and a strand of waxed hair broke from behind his ear. "Oh, at first, I failed to recognize him as a gentlemen. The Irish are so . . . so misleading at times. Not precisely . . . *distingué,* let us say. And he raged, sir! Raged! At me, sir! Demanding to know what we had done with you. When you yourself realize, *monsieur,* that we had done nothing with you at all. Nothing at all! I could not lay claim to the least knowledge of your existence. Our rustic cavalier . . . the letter . . . why attach importance . . ."

"Has he been sent to help me, then?" My heart soared at the prospect.

"Help you?" The general began to choke, but coughed his throat into order. "Help you, sir? Why that shall be the province of Lieutenant Raines! Has someone gone for Raines? No, Major. He was sent to *find* you. Why, he hardly seemed a gentleman. With his . . . his graceless demands, let us say. Insisted I produce you that instant. I hear he tore a rifle from a sentry's hands when he reached our lines. Lucky he wasn't shot, the rogue. Difficult people, the Irish, so difficult. Then, when he insisted on aiding our surgeons . . . on succoring our poor soldiers while awaiting your appearance . . . then, of course, one recognized a gentleman, however Northern and untutored his manners. A mortifying combination, the Yankee and the Irishman." He turned on one heel. "Has someone gone for Dr. Tyrone? Why can I excite no alacrity, gentlemen? Where's this Tyrone fellow?"

"At the hospital over to the hotel, most like," a colonel said. He had sunny hair, a sunny face, and handsome riding boots. "That fella's been cutting on folks day and night since he got here. And cussing like a sailor at anybody what comes near him."

That was, indeed, the Mick Tyrone I knew.

.   .   .

I WAS SCRUBBING MYSELF in a tent when Mick appeared. He embraced me. The Irish are an emotional lot.

"I thought you were dead and buried," he said. "Sure, I thought you were food for the worms."

When he released me, the print of my chest showed wet on his uniform. He was embarrassed by his outburst of affection, for I was not emboldened to reciprocate with like abandon, though glad I was to see him. There was a moment's awkwardness and his next words come out in shreds.

I did not mind the passion of his greeting, see. It showed the very soul of honest friendship. But proper folk do not hug their fellows so. Certainly not Methodists. And not when one of the two is half undressed.

I shook his hand heartily in recompense.

"I never thought to see you alive again, bucko," he went on, with his eyes unsteady and damp.

"Well, I am a bad penny and will turn up," I said. Oh, wasn't I glad to see him, though? Perhaps a better man than me would have hugged him back, despite the impropriety. But let that bide. I touched my own eyes with a cloth, for soap suds had annoyed them. "I hear you have made a great stir on my behalf, Mick. I thank you for it."

He gave his head a cock fit for the theater. The Irish think the world an endless stage. "And have you had a look at them, then? At these great Rebels? Oh, holy terrors they are, that's sure. The sort that can barely be got out of bed for their breakfast." He waved a hand at Heaven. "I've never seen such a grand careless-ness. And their medical treatment isn't fit for the veterinary service. Doctors, they call themselves. *Doctors!* Nothing but country butchers, the lot of them." He smoothed his anthracite hair. Ash had begun to stain his temples. "Well, you're none the worse for wear, by the looks of you. Where've you *been*, man?"

"In an animal pen, I think."

"You think?"

"The structure may have had another purpose. Unpleasant it was."

"Micah Lott told Sherman you'd been shot. That you were dead, and little doubt of it."

"Shot I have not been, Mick. Though I did fall off my horse, which proved to be an indiscretion. But I do not understand how you are come here? Though a welcome sight you are."

"Halleck sent me down. At Grant's urging. Halleck's a damned nuisance, by the way. Little Mac with a lesser tailor, and that's putting a ribbon on a pig. All puffed up like a schoolmaster proud of his Latin, with his bluster and bulging eyes." Mick pulled a face. "I'm not sure how you'd choose between him and this Beauregard. Oh, it's a grand war we have before us, laddybuck. With Grant shoved aside and fools in command North and South. And we know who's to pay the butcher's bill."

"Well, that is war, Mick. But I still do not see the thread of your involvement."

He sat himself down on a camp chair and I went from my scrub to my shaving.

"You said yourself that a man in my position hears things, Abel. I was treating one of Sherman's staff lads for a filthy, damned pox—by the way, don't go drinking the water here, for it'll kill you faster than a bullet, and pity us if we *do* take the fair city of Corinth from the Rebels. But this fellow of Sherman's . . . the blithest of morons he was. With a dreadful disease set to rot his meat and bones, though all a lark in the country it was to him. And he's wailing like Sheilah on wash day that his work is never done and now he's got to make a report to Halleck about an agent gone missing. And all to do with Micah Lott and murders it was, and with those that won't be disciplined according to high regulations. Then didn't I put together another pair of things I'd been hearing?"

Mick made a face as if he'd been splashed by a chamber pot. "I know what hopeless buggers the lot of them are, so I went to Grant myself to find out what was in the kettle. And Sherman had him riled with the business already. So it's off we go to Halleck, and doesn't the pop-eyed bastard treat Grant the way his lordship treats a bog boy? Why is he being bothered with the minor consideration of a missing major, by your leave? When the Rebels are all reinforced and mighty and poised for a counterattack at any moment? Oh, he's so crammed full of strategy it's dripping out his arse. A fine one he is, that Halleck. If it wasn't for Washington's inquiries, he wouldn't have budged till doomsday."

That invisible night-pot gave Mick another soaking. To know Mick is to understand the thousand degrees of disgust a man can express in the course of a day. For he is not a friend to things done poorly.

"No, you've got Sam Grant and a timely telegraph wire to thank for your deliverance, Abel. Your Mr. Nicolay in Washington spunked up at the hint of your loss. The wires must have been flaming, to tell you the least of it. You'd think they'd been fattening you up all year for the fair and Paddy made off with you. And didn't that bring Halleck's heels together? Then someone had to carry a message to the Rebels, and I told them I was the man to do it. For at least I'd recognize the body after the crows were done. So off I went, though not before lancing a great spurting boil on Halleck's backside, with him howling like an infant all the while."

"Well, there is good." I toweled my face, a new man. "For you have saved me a hanging, Mick. And I have never liked the thought of a rope."

His mood shifted again. Mick had a spirit that could not hold still. "And all because of your carelessness, bucko. For the needless risks you're taking, and you with a wife and a child. And that leg of yours a ruin already, and the traces of typhoid still in your eyes from December." He ran his eyes over me, for my promised garments had not yet been delivered. "And it looks like you're touched with the jaundice, for that matter."

Had Mick been a spitting man, he would have spit. "What's wrong with you, Abel? You've done your part and won't let others do theirs. Do you think you can win this war all by yourself? Is that what you're after?" He shook his head in disgust. "Hanging would have taught you a lesson. And here I am, taken away from my duties, when we've got a fine, new tent hospital set up grand in the open air, and the needfulness of sanitation pressed upon the medicals, at least. And I have to come traipsing after you through half the Confederacy, in all your glorious, thick-skulled Welshness. And next thing I know I'm in this sorry excuse for a town, hacking the legs off of Rebels who can't even keep their bowels shut for the length of an amputation. Oh, I'll tell you again, man, don't go drinking their water without giving it a long boil. And there's an end to it."

"It is good to see you, Mick."

"Oh, go on with you," he said, with that affected hardness of his. "You've been nothing but trouble since the day you first came bothering me."

.   .   .

"WELL," MICK SAID, "it's a small world, if not always a pleasant one. At least I've received a bit of good news from all this." He leaned forward, shifting in the canvas chair. "Do you recall a letter I wrote to you, when you were chasing your banshees all over the hills of New York? A letter in which I mentioned a Rebel officer wounded at Donelson? Both legs sawed out from under him and not so much as a whimper during the cutting?"

"The one who gave you the horse," I said, sitting down on a cot.

"Exactly." Mick gave me a nod. "Bravest man under the knife that ever I've seen. Or the stupidest. Anyway, I've learned that the fellow survived. The odds weren't with him, I'll tell you. It's almost enough to make a man believe in your holy miracles."

"Miracles happen every day, Mick. It is the only way we get along."

He dismissed that. "Oh, now I've let the bird out of the cage. Next he'll be singing to me about Jesus."

"Sing I will not. But I did pray night and day for my deliverance, Mick. And here we are."

He rolled his eyes. "I'm hardly the angel of the Lord, bucko."

"The Lord may choose what tools He will."

Poor old Mick held up his hands to stave me off. "Just let me tell you about my own handiwork, would you? For I'm spanking proud, and not ashamed to say it. At least not to you. I wasn't sure I could bring it off, you know. The rot was already on the poor lad. But damn me if he hasn't survived." Mick looked askance and dusk crept into the tent. "For all the good it'll do him, considering the parts he's missing."

He drew his fingers through his whiskers and a fly drifted off. "He was a curious one, though. I believe I wrote a good deal about him, didn't I? Could not get the fellow out of my mind. There are patients like that." He smiled darkly. "You'd think a man would remember the pretty girls, the ones he pulled through or didn't. But it's the odd cases that cling." Those gales stormed in his eyes again. "You know how I feel about all that Walter Scott nonsense, Abel. Yet . . . the boy seemed almost a figure out of a book, the truth be told. There was something grand, something . . . something frankly heroic about him. Except that in novels the heroes don't lose their legs. And their intimate parts, besides."

"He gave you a horse," I repeated. "A grand horse. The kind of horse that wants a proper rider."

Mick snorted. "And I'm hardly that. But what's the horse got to do with this?"

I shook my head. "It is not the horse, see. It is the fellow himself. His name is Barclay, is it not?"

"Well, you've got a memory on you, laddybuck."

"No, Mick. It is not memory. It is the fitting together of things. The name come up today. As you have said, it is a small world. This great lot of slaves who were murdered belonged to the fellow. And there is something else, besides, though I cannot grasp it yet. Something queer. And I am not certain it is heroic. But I was in no position to put questions."

Mick thought for a moment. "Well, if you run into him, give him my regards. And tell him . . . tell him that, after the war, he should see Dr. Smithson in New York City. I won't intrude further on his privacy. Just tell him to visit Dr. William McAdoo Smithson. The fellow's a real doctor, not a butcher like me. Can you remember the name? Smithson?"

"If I see him, I will tell him."

Mick leaned back a little, legs crossed and hands clasped over the high knee for balance. "Sometimes I wonder if I shouldn't have let the poor boy die."

Suddenly, he sat up. Slapping his hand to his breast. "Good Lord, I'm a sorry excuse for a friend. I'm forgetting your letters."

Letters? That is one of the beautiful words in our language.

He thrust his hand—scrubbed raw, it was—into his tunic and drew out a lovely pair of rectangles. Extending them to me.

It is impolite to examine letters in the presence of others. But I tore them open.

There were three missives, for one was folded in another. The first was from my Mary Myfanwy. To my surprise, it contained a communication from none other than Mr. Matthew Cawber, the great industrialist of Philadelphia whose acquaintance I had made in the course of the Fowler affair. The last come from dear Mrs. Schutzengel, my Washington landlady.

I looked at Mick, hesitating over the beautiful fineness of my sweetheart's penmanship. Oh, there was love in the loops, and dreams in the dots, and joy in the ink itself. A grand birthday it had turned out, after all.

"Go ahead and read them, would you?" Mick said. "You're slavering like a dog at the sight of his dinner."

I dare not compromise my darling's confidences. Suffice to say that she and young John were well and missed me. There was one matter I would need to ponder, though. I will tell you of that, for it is not a matter of intimacies, but of general relevance in these unsettled times. She asked me, did my love, if I might approve of her establishing herself as a dressmaker with the great Singer sewing machine I had sent her from New York?

Now her talent lay beyond dispute, for she was to cloth what one of these Michael Angelo fellows is to paint pots or marble. Although I do not imply that she has Latin vices, of course. Far from it. Yet, was it proper for my wife to go into business? What might our congregation think? And our neighbors? And the good people of Pottsville in all?

Twas not a matter of vanity, see. I would not make it an issue of pride. But a wife who works implies the husband is insufficient, and the regard of our fellows is not without value. Nor is commerce a fit domain for the female sensibility. A woman's province is the home, and isn't that a blessing? Our little John wanted constant care and minding. Who might provide it should his mother work?

Lastly, it saddened me to think of my Mary Myfanwy stitching her days away for pay, when she had been a governess to a high family and possessed a most grandiose education for a woman. My lass had a mind that wanted using. She was better than a piecework laborer. She was a creature of intelligence, far more so than the fellow she had condescended to marry. Though it shock you, I would sooner have placed her among the high professions than set her to work with her hands down in the trades. But such is not the lot of woman, for the female is not steady when dismayed. And the thought of her sewing tediously, of rich folk looking down on her and chastising her with complaints, oh, that gave me an itch that had nothing to do with ant bites or Confederate fleas.

Still, I would think on it. For I do not like to deny her. And perhaps a small endeavor would do no harm. There would be extra income, which never hurt a household. Even true love likes a prosperous hearth.

And then . . . what if I were lost? What if they had hanged me? That fear still ghosted in me, I will tell you. Oh, war is a great spoiler of dreams. I did not like to picture my wife as a dressmaking widow, but she had the skill to feed herself and John, if need there was. Might my strictures spill them into poverty? Because I spurned the making of a dress? Were my reservations naught but the sin of pride again?

She missed me, see. And wanted occupation in my absence. An empty house is heavy, and even a son will not replace a husband. Not if the marriage is sound.

Twas a hard decision. To sew, or not to sew?

Mick stepped out to have a smoke and my clothings had not come. So I read the note from Cawber next. Not that I valued him more than I did Hilda Schutzengel. But I was curious as to why such a grand fellow would write to me.

This 10th Day of March 1862

Dear Jones

Dont you take the cake you little bugger. A man gets a report of some new fellow nibbling at the railroad shares he is backing and he starts to wonder. Damn me if I didnt look into the matter myself. I visited that Pottsville of yours. Its a black enough place. I saw that fool Evans at the Miners Bank. He thought he wasnt going to tell me anything but he found out. I could of shit my pants when I found out YOU were the bugger buying into the railroad with me. I had you pegged as a smart customer. I wasnt wrong.

You must of gone sneaking around to learn what you did. But that is how it is done.

I put a scare into Evans to keep his yap shut. As for you I know you understand the value of a secret. The truth is you dont have enough shares to start any trouble and wont. So I was worried about nothing at all. You hold onto them. Buy more if you can. It is all right between you and me. This war is going to make the railroads. But arent you a sneaky devil. Next time tell me and I wont have to waste my time.

Maybe I like you because we are both sneaky fellows but honest. Drive a hard bargain but dont lie. Thats what I say.

I still shake my head about that Fowler commotion. They tried to keep it quiet but nothing is quiet from me. So I know what happened. You know how I feel about their society. They will do anything for money but what is decent and what a man deserves.

My offer stands. If you ever come to your senses and take off that silly soldier suit I will take you on as my private secretary and chief accountant. I cant trust the turd who works for me now to keep his mouth shut and that is the most important thing in business. So I am writing this myself. This whole country is in a state. But its a good state to make a profit in. So stop being a fool. Come work for Matt Cawber and if you dont end a rich man we will both die in the poor house. Cawber Iron & Steel is just the beginning. I bought that damned bank too. Just the way I said I would. Old Bates is nothing but a dirty bankrupt now and not just him. You should have heard Philadelphia howl.

Thats all. Its late. Olympia is not well. Its nothing I am sure. But I want to look in on her. Sometimes I sit there and watch her until the morning. I could sit longer too. There aint nothing like a good wife. And the children too. But mostly the wife. There is not one thing better. Not all the money in the world. I will take her abroad for her health if she dont improve and business will let me go. She is my treasure and I will tell that to anybody. But if they have eyes to see they already know.

Come to your senses Jones. Come to Philadelphia. And dont tell anybody else about the railroad shares. Or it will all be spoiled.

> *I am Sir*
> *Your earnest correspondent*
> *M Cawber*

He was not a proper educated fellow, Cawber, as you can tell. But he was a lion of business and the richest man I knew in those days. And his wife was, perhaps, the most beautiful woman I had ever seen. He was one of those fellows who draw others to them. But he would not draw me, of course. Not as long as the war required the services of honest men. And I am *not* sneaky. It is not a Welsh trait, no matter what the English will tell you. It is the English who think the truth is clay to be shaped to our wants.

Cawber meant well, though, and had been a great help to me in my duties, despite my insult to his person upon our first acquaintance. He was a great robust fellow, in flesh and spirit. And a good man, as I later learned with unforgettable clarity. In the meantime, he was headed for a rending sorrow. But that is another story. So let that bide.

·   ·   ·

I HAD JUST BEGUN to read dear Mrs. Schutzengel's letter when a shadow fell over me. I thought it was Mick come back from his smoke, so I only muttered and bent closer to the paper.

My visitor cleared his throat. In that exaggerated way that says, "Look here."

I looked there.

Good Lord.

He was not an especially tall man, but in width he beat the band. Now when you think of a fat fellow, you think of the sagging sort. He was none such. His belly protruded straight ahead, or even rose, as if an enormous cannonball was set to burst from his waistcoat. This was a gut of pride, defying even Mr. Newton's gravity. Oh, my visitor's beef rode high.

Just the oddest thing he looked. Above dainty, well-shod feet he wore old-fashioned buff trousers, tight at the ankles and grippy everywhere else. They expanded as they rose, until the vasty circumference of the fellow, tormenting inadequate cloth, made him look as though he might topple over. Yet, he stood erectly, back straight as a soldier's.

Up my eyes climbed and he narrowed again. His chest, though not insignificant, was smaller than his waist. His shoulders were narrower still. Shaped like a spinning top he was, of a size for a giant's plaything.

His head looked borrowed from another body. For his face was as long as a landlord's list of lies. His brows spiked bayonets of hair, but his pate shone like the moon. A wreath of chestnut hair wrapped round his skull, but it was the pink flesh up on top a fellow fixed on. It come near to a point, while the rest of his face broadened out to a shovel chin. His nose was a red, bristling exuberance and long mustachios dropped from it like the tusks of a walrus. If he didn't look queer, I'm the lost son of Lord Raglan.

He held a stack of folded clothes before him, supported by one hand, while the other paw held his derby hat at his side. With a slight bow, he said:

"Major Abel Jones, I does presume?"

English the fellow was. And from the lows of London by his accent.

I rose. "The very same, sir."

He extended the clothing. "Your garments, sir. Apologies for the delay. Small sizes in short supply, sir. Like most things these days. The best times are behind us, as me governor always said. You'll be wanting a hat, too, I expects." He leaned back the better to gauge me. "Just let us have a look and we'll fit you proper."

I reached into my pocket. For the Rebels had restored my purse unsullied. Money did not seem a great concern to them, though they had rued the return of my horse and revolver.

"How much, then?" I asked. Fearing the fellow would claim a dreadful amount, with me at his mercy. Sitting there all clean in my dirty drawers.

That took him aback. "Oh, no, sir. Money ain't wanted, thank you. All compliments of young Master Francis. You couldn't buy a proper rig-out for love nor money these days. His name opens doors, it does, our Master Francis."

An Englishman of low degree, he chopped the letter *H* away and smacked the vowel head-on, then clipped the *G* from the end of words to save his mouth the labor. As if the alphabet wanted a trim and he was the man to do it. Oh, why the Lord gave the English the language of Mr. Shakespeare is ever a bafflement! You might as well set beauty before the blind. Of course, it wants remembering that Stratford town is not so far from Wales. Perhaps the Bard of Avon had Welsh blood? I think it likely. That would explain his poetry, and richness, and generosity, and intelligence, and sense of justice, and the beauty of his doings, all in all.

"And who," I asked the fellow, "is Master Francis?" For we must beware the blandishments of our enemies. Beauregard himself had ordered that I wear the clothing of a simple citizen in place of my uniform. He said it would excite less danger and that he would give me a Frenchy document called a "lazy passy" to explain it all and keep me safe. I did not like the business. And now I was being made a present of my dress. Of course, it would be all right if I were expected to give the clothing back when matters were settled. But I could not accept tokens from the Confederates.

"Master Francis, sir? You'll be going along with him, I believes. But I've gone to confusing you, ain't I, sir? Begging your pardon, then. Master Francis would be Lieutenant Raines."

That crimped my snout. "I thought the fellow's Christian name was Drake?"

"Not exactly, sir, not exactly like. 'Francis Drake Raines' says his baptismals, sir, and all high church and proper they are, and a great deal more proper than some. There's them as calls him Drake, you see, but at home he's always been our Master Francis."

"And you, sir, are his commercial agent?"

"Oh, no, sir. I'm his gentleman's gentleman, as they puts it. Although I was in trade, sir. In olden times. In New Orleans that was. Before the yellow jack took the wife and the little ones and left me with embarrassments right and left. Funny you should mark it, sir. Most of 'em don't. But I sees as you're an observant one. Begging your pardon, sir, I always has found a Welshman sharp of eye."

I accepted the clothing and began to dress.

"Might you . . . turn around, sir?" I had to swap my undergarments, see.

"Oh, certainly, sir. Do things proper, I always says."

"And whom do I have the honor of addressing?"

"Name's Barnaby, sir. And Barnaby it's always been. Ain't never been changed on account of illegalities or such like. I'm born Barnaby and I'll die Barnaby, as sure as the Queen's in England."

I drew on the loveliest, softest cotton stockings in mankind's history. Or so they seemed to me. For they were clean.

"Well, Mr. Barnaby—or is that your Christian name, sir?"

"Oh, all's one, sir, all's one. It's Barnaby first and Barnaby last. Barnaby front and Barnaby back. I'm Barnaby Barnaby, sir. Like me governor before me."

Viewed from the rear, he blocked still more of the light. Twas evening and I fumbled through amber air.

"Well, Mr. Barnaby . . . if you will pardon me, sir . . . it's a curious thing to see you."

"Oh, I has a certain bulk, sir. There's a goodly prosperity to me. If that's your meaning, sir."

"No, no," I said, alarmed that he judged me the sort who would comment meanly on another's person. "I only meant that you're an Englishman. A white man, sir. I did not know the Southrons kept servants of their own race."

He turned his head without turning his body and I glimpsed his nose in profile. "Oh, they does and they don't, sir. Though mostly they don't. Young Master Francis, he's a more civilized sort, he is. Won't keep a Negro servant himself. Though his governor's dripping with 'em. Begging your pardon, sir."

The garments fit acceptably. Though their boldness would not have done for chapel. My trousers were a checkered brown, the waistcoat green and yellow. Only the frock was a decent black and fit for prayer and sobriety. The tie they gave me was but a long green ribbon and would not make the modest bow I liked.

"Mr. Barnaby? Please turn about again, sir. I have a question."

"About your dinner would that be, sir? Being's your a Welshie, you'll want a proper dinner, I expects. I could see to that for you, sir. Indeed, I could, sir. There's still victuals to be had, sir, for him what knows where to look. And Barnaby knows where to look for his victuals, sir." He positively jiggled at the prospect.

"Thank you, no, Mr. Barnaby. It's this ribbon affair. This necktie. In the North, I'm afraid . . ."

"Oh, that's all right, sir. Not to worry. The gentlemen all wears 'em down here, sir. Not just your gamblers and such. If you ties it in a great bow, sir, in a very great bow, and lets the ends go all droppy like, that's how they does it. It cuts a dash, sir."

I am not one to "cut a dash." But let that bide.

Twas then old Mick returned from his smoke. He squeezed past Mr. Barnaby, with a look of professional wonder at the fellow's girth. They were two fine ones, side by side. Mick as lean as a famine year, and Barnaby bursting with bounty. The latter made the John Bull in the weeklies look like a fasting Hindoo.

"You have the advantage of me, sir," Mick told the fellow. That was how he spoke in good society. And how he wrote, though his talk was plain to me. He did not recognize Barnaby as a serving fellow any more than I did.

"Barnaby, sir. At your service."

"Mick Tyrone." He thrust out his hand.

Barnaby backed away. With a bow. For serving fellows must not grip their betters.

"Mr. Barnaby," I explained, "is in service to a gentleman."

At that Mick reared up. "Too good to shake my hand, are you, sir?"

Barnaby straightened. Startled by the outburst. His thick brows climbed, his broad chin dropped, his grand nose swelled, and his belly thrust itself against the world.

Mick knew his doings, see. He grabbed the fellow's paw and gave it a shake. For he was a Socialist, and such do not hold with classifications among men. As soon as the gesture was done, he let go of the poor fellow's hand and turned to me.

Behind old Mick, Barnaby stared at his palm. As if inspecting for damage. "Most irregular," he muttered. "Something horrible irregular."

"Well, get your shoes on, Abel," Mick said. "A fellow can't even enjoy his pipe around these people. Some ass insists Beauregard wants to see the two of us. I think we're expected to feed with his lordship the general."

"Oh, ain't a good dinner a loveliness?" Barnaby cried, as if the words burst forth against his will.

"And didn't he make a great fuss about how we were to come at once?" Mick went on. "Not a moment to be lost, the fellow tells me. But didn't he have time enough to lead me into a shed and ask me to look over the damage the ladies of Memphis had recently done to his sword?" He shook his head at mankind, which he did with some frequency. "I suppose we'd best go along."

"Chops, gentlemen!" Barnaby declared joyously, with that same effect of helpless, blasting speech. "When Master Francis went in to report, I seen great chops, I did. Beautiful chops you'll be having, if Barnaby's fit to judge."

Yet, there was sorrow in that tantalized voice. For such as he, a serving man, might not join us at dinner. It is a curious world, see. Even in America. North or South, whose table makes room for all?

.　　.　　.

I TUCKED AWAY Mrs. Schutzengel's unread missive, saving its joy for a gentler hour, and we went, old Mick and I, to the house where General Beauregard had received me. The general had changed into an evening uniform, adorned with braid enough for the king of France. Beside him, young Lieutenant Raines, the horse-race fellow, stood in a sort of glow, distinct from the other officers who had gathered to cram their bellies. Nor was his radiance a trick of the gaslamps, for Corinth had not one. Oh, Raines was not handsome. Not the way we commonly think of handsome. But shining he was, a very flame of youth.

It pleased me that we would work together, and didn't I find that odd? For I am all suspicion of the high-born.

The lady of the house made a gracious hostess, with her husband smiling mildly at her side. Got up in a satin gown she was, though with the pleasant look of a settled wife. She even wore an emerald at her throat, suspended on a ribbon of black velvet. Oh, she seemed delighted at the hours before her, for candlelight brings back a woman's youth and company buoys her. Merry it was at her end of the table. But the husband wore a look of quiet concern. Women embrace the evening, see, but men think of the morning. The master of the house knew as well as I did that the Rebels would leave the town in the days to come, whether they put up a fight or just moved on. And then a hostile army would arrive.

Only the husband and I proved meager talkers. All the rest embraced a spiteless gaiety. Including Mick, for he is not all dour. They talked French, see, even young Raines, and that was how old Mick fell into the thick of it, for he liked to jabber in heathen tongues about things high and knowledgeable. Between our grand devourings, Beauregard and Mick volleyed talk across the plates and platters, filling the room with city names I recognized from books and newspapers. They conjured Europe to that country table, and our hostess gleamed like the emerald pendant she fingered.

You might have thought our country was at peace.

seven

J dreamed of a red-haired girl in a field of snow. She had her health again and smiled kindly. My heart soared.

A noise woke me. When you are an old soldier, whose life has depended on hearing the scuff of a pebble a second before the blade dropped for your neck, you do not think. You act.

Colt in hand, I started to roll off the cot. But strong fingers closed over mine, contesting the pistol, while a damp palm clasped my mouth. A man's weight pinned me down.

I smelled horse-sweat and leather.

"Friend, friend," a peculiar voice whispered.

Moonlight soaked my eyes, for I had left the flaps of the tent open for the freshness. Pale ribbons dangled from the intruder's hair.

Twas Broke Stick. Micah Lott's Red Indian. He lifted his frame from my person and took his hand from my mouth. But he kept his grip on my Colt a while longer.

"Quiet," he said. "No trouble."

"What the devil . . . what do you want?"

"No trouble. Reverend Lott, he watch. Every day. Pray for you. Satan all over. You look out."

I cocked up on my elbow. Ordering my thoughts. The Colt was mine again. "Well, if he's watching me, why did I sit in a pen for ten days? Waiting to hang? And why did he tell Sherman I was dead?"

"Big vengeance coming, brother." I saw the black gleam of his eyes in the moonlight. "You rise up from the dead. Like the Hoodoo man. Now you better pray. Every man better pray. Angel coming with the sword. Break the seal. Big vengeance coming."

"I didn't rise up from the dead. See here. What's Lott up to?"

He moved his head and the ribbons shimmered. "Reverend say beware that Anti-Christ. Big Reckon almost here. Earth run blood. You look out."

.   .   .

IT MIGHT HAVE BEEN ANOTHER DREAM, no more. The Indian left no sign. And I gleaned no sense from his ravings. Why would Lott send the fellow to me, through Confederate lines, to say what he had said? Had Broke Stick got the message muddled up? Or was he mad and acting on his own? And was Lott truly a wife-murderer? Or was that a Rebel lie, to ruin a goodly man opposed to slavery? Such defamations could not be put past a folk whose generals spoke French. Oh, it was all gone to slops in my brain by morning. There was no sense to it, see. A mystery is one thing, but lunacy another.

A shame it is I did not listen better. Many a life might have been spared. But we are as the deaf, until the Lord opens our ears.

I told no one of the Indian's coming. I did not say a word until the dying began, and the burning. But I must not go too swiftly, so let that bide.

I had other matters on my mind, see. For I was reading when Mick come into my tent. With the sun behind him and bugles brassing the day.

Twas Sunday morning.

Mick stopped short. "Don't you look a state, bucko? Is it the camp trots you've got, then? I warned you not to drink their filthy water."

I held out the letter. Not the one I had written for him to take back and send to my wife, but the one from dear Mrs. Schutzengel. I had read it by the light of a stinking candle before wrapping myself in my blanket. The news had so disturbed me that I nearly ran to find Mick in the darkness. I had paused, though, at the thought that a sentry might shoot me. And naught could be done until morning, anyway. But I had lain long awake, thinking on the matter. I had barely got to my sleep and my lovely dreaming when the Indian appeared to addle me worse.

Mick drew the camp chair to the front of the tent where the light was stronger. He nodded as he read. "Oh, that's good," he said. "Good for her. I hope she goes." He lifted his eyes to me, with the light on the side of his face. "Is that what you're so glum about? That your landlady's pondering a journey to London to visit *Herr* Marx? I think this international congress sounds like an interesting idea, if she can move him to it. And don't worry. Marx's philosophy isn't really dangerous. It's cold soup. Fourier's the man. Is that all that's bothering you?"

"No, Mick. It is not that. Read lower."

He scanned the lines. Suddenly, he stopped. As I knew he would. But instead of appearing aghast, he shot his solitary crack of a laugh at the morning. Officers washing at a trough turned round to stare at him.

"Oh, that's grand! That's wonderful news! It'll be the making of the fellow." He turned his face to me again. This time, the morning sun glanced off his hair. "But where's the bad news, Abel?" He ruffled the letter. "Have I missed a page?"

"You have read it. Think you, Mick. He'll ruin the girl, sure as the English will come for the rents."

"Oh, nonsense! I've no doubt Molloy will make her a fine husband." He curled a smile. "See to that, she will."

I slipped my thumbs behind the straps of my braces and took my position. "A fine husband, is it? There is foolish. He'll be the ruin of poor Annie Fitzgerald. Why . . . why, I know him to be the slave of a thousand vices. Of a thousand and more. Mick, I don't suppose there's any way you could go to Washington? Just long enough to talk sense to the girl?"

Mick laughed again. Twas more than a lone syllable this time. The fellow sounded absolutely jovial. "Well, you know I can't. And do you think I would if I could?" He shook his head in lengthening amusement. "You're too hard on Molloy, Abel. And that girl knows which end of the goose is which, I'll tell you that much." He gave me the fierce of those eyes of his. "And who are you to get up on a high horse, your lordship? When did a Welshman last walk on the water? Didn't you tell me your wife was the making of you?"

"Well, I was set to be made. Molloy is trouble."

Mick stood up and crossed his arms, with his Irish stubborns upon him. I thumbed out my braces till my trousers rode up and deviled me. Like two great roosters facing off we were.

"Oh, for pity's sake . . . is *that* your great Christian charity speaking, then? Is that all there is to your redemptions and mercies and promises of forgiveness? Are there to be no second chances, then, not even in America?" Mick conjured up a sound like a dog provoked. "And you have the gall to mock Socialism . . ."

"Molloy is trouble. He always has been trouble. And he always will be trouble."

Mick made a scolding face at me, as if I had delayed his revolution. "And didn't he save your life in India? Oh, didn't you get the brag up over that, bucko? And didn't you tell me, all puffed up and proud, how Molloy went running off to New York when you needed help with your ghosts and goblins? 'Leaving a prospering business behind him,' you said. 'A true friend.' And now listen to you."

"The business was a low saloon. And there is friendship and friendship. Annie Fitzgerald is a good girl, who deserves a decent, God-fearing husband, even if he is to be a Catholic. Molloy is trouble, I tell you."

"But he did save your life. Did he not?" Hard Mick bore down.

"And doesn't every man deserve a chance? Just tell me that. Doesn't every last man deserve a chance?"

I shuffled and rustled and growled and grumped. For the truth is I was shamed by Mick's remonstrance.

Look you. I saw that he was right. At least on the matter of chances. Twas only that he called my Welsh pride to account, see. I am a man who thinks he knows what's best. It is a fault of mine that wants a humbling. I was given to picturing Jimmy Molloy as the thief he had been when he stole the regiment's silver, and not as the man he might yet make of himself. Unworthy of my friends I was, and still less of our Savior, who saw more in a thief than Abel Jones.

I am too hard. I know it. And cold hearts are a curse upon this earth. Jimmy Molloy had come a mighty progress. And if he still had far to go, the same thing might be said of someone else.

"Well, he'll bear watching," I muttered, for my meanness would not go down in a single gulp. "And if he pains the girl, I'll teach him manners."

Mick laughed to wake Kate. The Irish know a fool when they behold one.

.   .   .

DEAR MRS. SCHUTZENGEL had written to tell me I was invited to the nuptials as a guest of honor, if I could but arrange my coming by. Of course, I had judged it a trick of Molloy's to lull me until he had his wicked way. And now I had to wonder if the fellow might not hold me in affection.

I do not understand why people like me, though glad of it I am, as you would be.

And Mick just stood there grinning, as if he could see through me like a window. What *was* the difference between Molloy and me? Oh, I had rigor. But Molloy had heart. I always had to give the fellow that, though his morals were never the best. Loyal he ever was, and brave as Mr. Shakespeare's noble Harry. Kind to women and children, and always merry. Nonetheless, I hoped Mrs. Schutzengel had not lent the fellow money.

Mick took the letter I had written to my Mary Myfanwy. Unsealed. For the Rebels must examine it for secrets. Thus I had to temper what I wrote. With my heart longing to pour out of the pen. Oh, wouldn't I have stuffed myself inside the very envelope to have a moment's look in my love's eyes?

I told her I was well and not to worry. And that she must be careful to make dresses only for respectable ladies, to insist upon deposits, and to keep strict accounts. I suggested she read aloud from the Gospels to little John. For though he might not understand a great deal, there is many a grown man who understands no more than a child.

And then we said goodbye. I was properly dressed, so I allowed myself a brief embrace of good old Mick. Nothing vulgar or low, you understand.

That rogue elephant Barnaby come swelling and swaying and rolling across the yard toward us, derby on his head and a great floppy slop of a hat in his hands for me. He bore a lacquered cane with a brass ball, too.

"Don't be a bigger fool than you can help," Mick told me. "For the likes of you are ever in short supply." He turned away most sharply then, and got on his horse and rode off. A patrol waited in the street to escort him northward. He touched at his eye as he went. Twas dust, most like.

"Smack of a morning, ain't it?" Barnaby asked, shielding me from the light with his mighty figure. "Are we all right, sir? Are we all right? Well, here's a handsome stick, in case you're wanting of one, and a topper to keep a gent's brains from off the boil. Finest quality. Feel the nap, sir. And the proper color for the summer season."

He thrust his cargo upon me, then reared back. As if he needed distance to get a clear look at a fellow.

"Are we all right, then, sir? Oh, you won't weep when you see the breakfast beefsteaks in the pan. Fit for a lord, by the sniff of them, fit for a very lord. Almost helped meself, though it ain't mannerly. Oh, there's nothing like a beefsteak in the morning, I always says, sir. Me governor would've et nothing else, if you let him, and he lived to be fifty. You'll be fine, sir. A proper beefsteak puts a fellow right."

.   .   .

I ANGERED BARNABY'S MASTER. We sat at table, lacking the general's presence, for he had sparred with the Madeira the night before. Officers came and went, eating with vigor. Lieutenant Raines was the only one who put down his knife and fork between bites.

The young fellow asked me how we would begin. I waited until we were alone, then told him.

"That's impossible, sir," he declared. He did not speak with Beauregard's bluster, but in a tone that covered steel with velvet.

"And why is it impossible, Lieutenant?"

"It's just impossible. And . . . unseemly."

"Is it now? And why would that be?"

"Billy—Captain Barclay—does not receive, sir. He has withdrawn from society."

"Well, I am not society, young man. You may be. But I am not. And we must go to this plantation of his."

It was plain that his eating was done. He stared at me, eyes a queer mix of anger and something akin to fear. An egg, unstaunched, bled gold over his plate.

"What earthly good would it do to bother Billy Barclay? Lord knows, he's suffered enough."

"I know he has had a terrible injury. But the Negroes were his property, were they not? The murdered Negroes?"

"Billy wouldn't know anything about their murders." He paled. "Sir . . . you're not suggesting . . ."

I finished chewing a crust I had spread with preserves. "I do not suggest anything, Lieutenant Raines. It is too early for suggestions. First we must learn a few things."

"What could you possibly learn at Shady Grove?"

"We must wait and see. Look you. I have been to the scene of the murders. And little enough I found. So now we must go backward. To where and when these slaves were yet alive. It is how the thing is done. We will not bother your Captain Barclay a moment longer than necessary."

In the distance, church bells rang. I wondered who would go.

"Billy won't see you." The young man's eyes were brown and big as a milkmaid's. "He won't see anybody."

"But will he not want to know who killed the Negroes?" I asked. "As they were his property?"

Raines turned toward the curtains and showed his profile. Light poured over a sideboard and flecked the china. The bells pealed on, and I wished that I were elsewhere.

"I don't know what he wants," the young man said. Moodily. "Nobody does. But he's suffered. More than any man should. He wants to be let alone, I do know that. That wish should be respected."

I finished a great wet rasher of bacon. The notion of a beef-steak in the morning is extravagant. No Methodist would succumb to such indulgence. Bacon will do for an early-rising Christian.

"Many will suffer," I said. "For that is war. And I will not insult your Captain Barclay, or annoy him beyond what is required. But visit him we will. To see what we may learn. Unless you wish to complain to General Beauregard?"

He sat full proud before me. Containing all the rage of youth at elders who will not see. If he lived ten years, he would be master of himself, revealing only what he chose to show the world. But he was young, and still unlearned in falsity.

"You will excuse me, sir," he said, folding his serviette. "I must look to my horse."

Well, I thought, best get it over now.

"A moment, please. Sit you down yet, Lieutenant."

He had begun to rise, but lowered himself again. He did not put the cloth back on his lap.

"Yesterday," I began, "I was not master of my situation. I had no choice but to overhear the words that passed between you and Captain Wylie after the race. Think you what you will, but I must ask you: Am I to understand a woman was involved in this affair? A woman among the slain, I mean. For whom one of you may have . . . harbored an affection?"

"I know nothing about a woman," he said quickly. "And you are immodest, sir." I had been wrong. His eyes had already begun to learn the knack of lying. "You *will* excuse me."

"Sit you down, Lieutenant. And listen. I am as fond of good manners as any man. For they save us many a hurt. But this is not a matter of society. It is about murder. About many murders. Forty, I am told. And your general has sanctioned this investigation. If you cannot support it, say so now. I will ask him to find another officer to accompany me. And the next time you lie to me"—how he winced at those words—"our relationship will end. I am sent to find the murderers of those Negroes, and that is what I will do, if do it I can. If such matters are beneath you, get you gone. Otherwise, we are going to this Shady Grove of Captain Barclay's."

"You don't understand," he said. In a weakened voice. The bells had stopped and the world fell burial still.

"That may be so. But I will do my best to correct the situation. And if you are the gentleman I think you are, you will help me. For crime unpunished dirties us all. Off to your stables now. And when we ride away, we will leave this talk behind us."

He rose. Jarred by my bluntness. His Northern schooling had

not prepared him for everything. He wanted to answer me, but hesitated between the possibilities jumbling in his mind.

His lips began to form a word, but I did not want him to say anything rash.

"We have had talk enough for now," I told him. "Go you and think on what I have said. For we must pull together. Or the doings are senseless."

Out he went with a grace few men possess, lifting his sword belt from the corner and sweeping it around his waist. Twas an odd business, see. I sensed he wanted to visit this Captain Barclay far more than I did, but had to be forced to the doing of it. That wanted consideration.

I sat alone, drinking an odd-tasting beverage that may or may not have been coffee, when Barnaby rumbled in.

"Sampled the beefsteak, sir? Lovely, ain't it?"

"Mr. Barnaby, if you please . . . what exactly am I drinking?"

He bent his bulk down and took himself a sniff. "Chicory, sir. A New Orleans speciality. The coffee bean's gone rare, it has. With the blockade, sir. But we makes do." He lowered his eyes. I could not tell if the fellow was downcast in spirits or if he was eyeing the breakfast leavings. "Begging your pardon, sir?"

"Yes?"

"I couldn't help overhearing your words, sir. Them what passed between you and Master Francis." The big fellow seemed profoundly discomfited. I was surprised. He had struck me as the sort born to an aplomb even the gallows would not disturb.

"And?"

"He's right, sir. Right as sugar in your tea."

"About what, Mr. Barnaby?"

The fellow's gaze dropped lower still. For the first time, his belly seemed to sag. Doleful eyes peered down his mighty nose.

"How as you don't understand of the matter, sir. It's all terrible complicated between Master William and Master Francis. He ain't disagreeable, Master Francis ain't, but it's all terrible complicated.

And that's what Barnaby B. Barnaby has to say, sir, and mum's the word hereafter."

He cleared his throat with the bark of a great polar animal. "Begging your pardon again, sir. But if you was to help yourself to another of them beefsteaks and leave it on your plate, sir . . . seeing as no one's about, sir, I might help meself to it all legitimate like."

I forked a slab of meat onto my plate.

"Oh, Barnaby's in your debt, sir," he cried. "Barnaby's in your debt! 'He's a proper gent,' I said to meself, the moment I laid me eyes on you, sir. Dirty drawers and Welshman notwithstanding."

As I left the room, I saw him provision his coat pocket with the beefsteak. Then he grasped a fistful of bacon to stuff on top of it.

After the performance of a few necessities and the collection of my documents from the general's clerk, we mounted our horses and rode through the busying day. I wished there were time for chapel, but there was not, and there's a pity.

The black pranced under Raines. Though plagued by flies as ever, Rascal seemed in gentle Sunday spirits. I kept my wits about me, though. And I pitied the poor creature upon whose saddle Barnaby enthroned himself. I do believe the horse's back sank by inches when the fellow got up.

As we left the town, the wounded men still lay in the rail yard.

.   .   .

FRANCIS DRAKE RAINES had the gentleman's art of restraint. While even gentlemen may have a temper and speak unguardedly in the heat of the moment, they do not let their anger rule their days. We had not ridden far when it became clear that my escort had accepted his situation. Indeed, now that the matter was resolved he seemed more anxious than me to reach our destination. His horse danced out in front.

Twas a handsome April morning, and Raines called, "This weather's more like it. That run of heat was out of season. Hard enough to get the planting in, with the men gone to the army." He pulled up his horse to wait for me and peered across a spread of greening fields.

"But don't the Negroes do most of the work?" I asked. Bobbing along on my backside. If you will excuse my bluntness.

He reined in close to me. The brim of my new hat flounced up and down, hiding his face from my eyes then revealing it again.

"On the plantations. Or the better farms. This is poor-white country, by and large. Man with even a handful of Negroes counts himself rich." A blue bird sailed across our path. "Lot of the acreage up here is cut for one man and a mule. Barely able to feed a family. There's tenantry, as well. It's a hard life." With a shake of the head, he continued, "You'll find good enough land in the bottoms. But the up-country doesn't give much return." He scanned the horizon. Fields, groves, low ridges. "Fair hunting, though."

Barnaby rode some lengths behind us, heedless of the dust, chewing his bacon.

We passed a country church, with tethered mules and buggies sparse in the yard. A sturdy voice complained of slack devotion, loud enough for passersby to hear. The road entered a stretch of forest and air fresh as rainwater chilled my skin. The horses slowed to drink where a stream snaked across our path. Raines let the animals ease their thirst, but not too much. Soon, he clucked at the black, and Rascal followed. Barnaby still lagged us on his bay.

"I had imagined the South otherwise," I said to pass the time. "I thought there would be houses grand as palaces. And fine plantations."

"Plenty of those, Major. Maybe not palaces. But fine enough houses." He thought for a moment. "Houses men dreamed into existence. Dreams in brick and painted boards. Down our way in Natchez. And on along the river toward Baton Rouge. Things run a good bit smaller up here."

"So I am not like to see any of these plantation mansions?"

"Oh, you'll see a few two-story houses. Nothing to be ashamed of. But the people up here aren't house-proud, as a rule. Most any roof will do." He thought for a moment. Judging what he might say. "You'll see half of a great house, though. A little more than half."

"And how is that, sir? The consequence of a fire?"

He laughed. The sound was small and dark, unlike him. "No. At least not the kind of fire you mean. I'm talking about Shady Grove. Billy's—Captain Barclay's—place. Would've been the grandest house north of the Big Black, had it been built to a finish."

"Financial difficulties?" I asked. "If that is not too indiscreet a question?"

Raines looked straight ahead. Into the depths of the forest. I felt the sudden change in him. He already had said more than he intended. Telling himself I had tricked him, he would blame me for his fault. That is how men are, see. Even the best of them.

"He was building it for his wife," Raines said in a flattened voice. "She is no longer with us."

He get-upped his horse and let it run ahead. The woods we passed through next smelled of decay.

·   ·   ·

SUNDAY THOUGH IT WAS, some worked their fields. Women, boys and mules, and slow-paced Negroes. Furrows ran askew by dreary cabins. Roofs and porches sagged. Arms as thin as spokes clutched broken fence slats, as silent children watched us ride along. The few Negroes abroad quickened their labors when they spotted us, and their glances measured our progress. Twas as if man and nature had agreed to a truce that suited neither party. It was a world let go. Or never grasped.

Even when the sun could climb no higher, the day remained pleasant. Barnaby kicked his martyred mount up beside us.

"Master Francis," he said, "begging your pardon, sir. But ain't the master hungry? A journey do work up an appetite."

"Next cabin, Mr. B." A sullen trace remained in the young man's voice.

But when we reached the next dwelling, I assumed my escort would continue past, for it appeared to be the residence of Negroes. Pickaninnies, as I believe they are called, yipped about the yard in carefree levity, and everywhere I looked disorder ruled. A goat, disdainful, wandered between the children, eyeing mismatched curtains blown out a window frame. Broken chairs sat on a broken porch. Just behind the shanty, a woman of imposing bulk bent over her washing, head got up in a turban like a Hindoo.

Raines guided his horse around and stopped by the railing. Where he could just see the woman, and she him. The wooly-headed angels ceased their revels and stared up at us. With huge eyes. They seemed astounded by the sight of Barnaby.

My escort leaned forward in his saddle, bracing himself on crossed arms. The woman spanked her hands dry then slapped them on her dress as she ambled along the side of the cabin toward us. Her physique had twice the magnificence of Hilda Schutzengel's, and that is a serious measure. She was, in fact, a good match for Barnaby himself. Although I do not mean that in an immodest sense.

Coming near, but not so close a horse could nip her across the fence, she set a doubtful look upon her face and canted her head. Her eyes examined Raines and his uniform with blunt suspicion.

"Anything good in the pot, auntie?" Raines asked. "We've got money to pay."

"Jingle money?" the woman replied in a deep alto. Almost a baritone, really. "Or just that fold-up money?"

"Jingle money. Now you tell me what's in the pot worth trading for."

"Ain't nothing in that pot, young marse. But I got fixings. Make up them cakes on the griddle, and plenty 'lasses. Buttermilk, too."

Raines smiled and swung out of the saddle, sliding neatly down. But the Negress did not budge.

"First you shows me that jingle money, white folks. I been et for nothing too many times."

My escort reached across the fence and showered coins into her hands. Her brown eyes widened. But only for a moment. Then she thrust the money into some deep ravine of cloth and womanhood and turned for the cabin.

"You water them high mules you got there," she called back, "then go wash to the well, young marse, and don't come pesting me till I'm ready to be pested. And I be the one tells when." She shoveled pawing children from her path, a kind leviathan. "And don't you go mussing my washing, cause you ain't paid for that."

"Yes, ma'am," Raines said, with a smile and a tip of his hat to her disappearing, though hardly diminishing, back.

Barnaby dropped from his mount with a thud. I tell you the poor horse sighed.

"I do love a small glass of buttermilk," he said, "but a small glass and no more." He slapped his girth and dust rose to the heavens. "I runs on the heavy side, if I ain't careful of my victuals."

I did not draw my new cane out of my blanket roll, for it would be a labor to replace it. And one result of my recent deprivations and the battle that come before had been to show me I could go a little stretch without a stick. I might never run nor walk with youthful grace. But I was growing accustomed to my leg and its bit of queerness. And my limp had not come shamefully. No, a stick was a great help, and would be all my life, most like, but twas not the necessity it had been in my first months of repair. Truth be told, the hours in the saddle had done more to hinder my stride than my bothered leg. My nether parts were in devilish torment.

The pickaninnies, chided by the matron, fetched water for our horses, pouring bucket after bucket into a hollowed log by the roadside. They kept their distance from Barnaby, though. As if he might pop several of them into his mouth.

I steeled myself to Rascal's care. With Raines watching me. Judging my worth by a measure that he knew.

A smell of frying lard rose from the cabin and we went around to the well. Removing our tunics, we splashed our faces and scrubbed our hands. Barnaby's dress was stained where the bacon had seeped through and the flies took to him like children to Christmas. But Raines did not seem to notice and I kept my eyes to myself.

"Lieutenant Raines," I said, in a voice held down, "I was taken by the . . . the firmness of our hostess . . ."

Raines laughed. Twas a soft sound once again. "The 'insolence,' you mean? That auntie's nobody's slave. She's a free Negro. Not that uncommon, though there's less of them up here. Go on down-river, they're even in trade. New Orleans"—he spoke it "Nollins," as did most of the Southrons, and it had taken me some time to make the connection—"is full of them."

"Beauties," Barnaby said, "beauties exotic and winsome."

"And such are tolerated, then?"

"Some more than others. I wouldn't want to mess with that mammy in there."

We sat on the porch and waited for our meal. I was assured by my escort that I would not want to go inside, let alone eat there. "Just look out that way, Major. Admire the landscape. You'll eat happier."

Eat happy we did. They were pancakes the woman made. Golden-brown orbs, haloed with syrup. The buttermilk was cool in the mouth.

The grand woman watched us. Hands on her hips. She refilled Barnaby's plate a number of times, till she finally put her foot down. Literally. She stamped the porch so hard I feared its collapse.

"That's the last heap you're getting, big white folks," she said to him. "Praise Jesus, I done seen a new thing this day. White man come to my door and eat him a whole field of buckwheat at one sitting. Just gobble down that whole field. And pay me with a penny."

"Do you think," my escort asked his servant, "you might last till dinner now, Mr. B.`?"

"By all means, Master Francis, by all means. I was only pulling her leg. In a manner of speaking, sir. Ready to go when the master is, that's old Barnaby. Might I inquire if the gentlemen are done with the buttermilk? Don't want to insult our gracious hostess by wasting. 'Thou shalt not waste,' like it says right there in the Good Book."

A wooden bucket sat half-full of buttermilk. The smell was rich and sweet.

"I'm about full up," Raines said. He glanced at me. "Major?"

"Full to bursting, Lieutenant. Delightfully full." I reached for my purse. "May I recompense your hospitality?"

He waved down the possibility, but said, "I'm sure Auntie wouldn't mind another small coin. As thanks for a splendid repast. What do you say, Auntie?"

She shook her great head and the little cloth ends of her turban fluttered. "I don't know about no splendid pasts, young marse. But Baby Jesus done said, 'Render unto that Caesar over there,' and Caesar's my menfolk's name. And I ain't talking no back-of-the-woods marrying, neither, but right there in the preaching ground. So I'm going to take all a Christian feel bliged to give. And Caesar hisself better not go holding out on this womanfolks, neither, or I'm going to go upside that nigger's head."

She held out her hand and I graced it with a dime.

"Capital!" Barnaby said. "A generous man never wears out his welcome." At that, he lifted the bucket of buttermilk and drank it dry. Neat as a duchess drinks sherry.

The woman wobbled inside, muttering, "I ain't never seen no white folks do like that, nor black folks, neither. That man must be one of them plagues on Egypt, how he do. Eat the buckwheat field and drink the cow! Lord, have mercy!"

We took our turns at the lesser cabin in back. It was unpleasant.

Barnaby went last. Raines and I waited by our horses. My escort petted his black, and spoke to it, but kept his eyes on the path Barnaby must take to rejoin us. The fellow's coming seemed long delayed.

Finally, Raines said, "Damnation," and leapt the fence. With that good meal in him. Marching he went, heading for the necessary house.

When he returned, he was still alone.

"Let's ride ahead," he told me. "Mr. B.'s fighting a war all of his own making. He'll catch up, all right."

.   .   .

"It's a few more hours of riding," Raines told me. "Up past Parker's Woods. We'll be there by settling time." He thought for a moment. "If Billy decides to let us settle."

It was a queer day for the young fellow. Although the sky was the hard blue of enamel, his moods were a field under broken, running clouds. Shadows swept past, darkening his spirit, then the sun returned to brighten all. I was just about to try another question on him, when he forestalled me:

"I suppose I'll have to tell you a little about Billy and me. So we don't turn embarrassment into mockery. Billy Barclay's a proud man, Major. I won't say it's been his downfall. But it's done him some harm. And I'd as soon not add to that harm."

"No harm is meant, Lieutenant. But the visit is—"

He waved a hand to quiet me. "Best not interrupt, sir. If you'll do me that kindness. These things are hard enough to put into words."

A wise man is ever ready to be silent.

"It goes back. My family's been here since the turn. Grandfather came out with Claiborne. Billy's father wandered in later, out of South Carolina. His father was a Walker man. Showed up around the time of the Chickasaw Cession. Thirty years back, almost exactly. Shady Grove's on old Choctaw ground, by the way." He reined back his horse. "Mr. Barclay bought about all there was to buy. Land was cheap for everybody, but a lot cheaper for Walker people. He was a younger son, I believe, making his way. But with enough money in his pocket to make a good start."

I caught the trace of a smile on his lips. "There was a conflict about a land parcel over in Lafayette. Folks calculated that Mr. Barclay and my daddy would get out the dueling pistols over it. Instead, they hit it off like princes. Local folks judged them all wrong, you see. Saw Billy's daddy as this brash Johnny-come-lately fellow. When he was a cultured man, a gentleman of surpassing fineness. And, of course, my daddy was Natchez born, with his big house already standing, so it was assumed that he must be a pillar in the grand arcade of civilization." Raines laughed to himself. "Truth is, he never valued a book in his life, and he only read the law cause my grandfather whipped him into it. You'd think Billy and I were swapped at birth, if Billy wasn't a good year the elder."

We sauntered along. The voices of the birds changed as the sun began its long decline. As if they sang by regiment it was, relieving one another at their posts. I rode, and listened, and let things go their way.

"Maybe there's something to the idea of 'rebellious youth,' " Raines said. "I was the one drawn to books. Couldn't get my fill as a child. Might've been sugar candy. And Billy . . . likely he's the smarter of the two of us. But he couldn't care less. Spent a couple of years at the state university, but it didn't amount to anything. Except some aggravation for the citizens of Oxford. No, he'd rather be out ranging with Buck Wylie than anything else in the world. Than almost anything else."

Raines gave his mount a pat. "Anyway, my father . . . my father and I differ on a number of matters, Major. Respectfully, of course. He is a great advocate of this war. Which I support, since Mr. Lincoln left us no alternative. Although I would not have wished it. But my father is a man of strong temperament. Of exceedingly strong temperament. Would not hear of me going north to college. Wanted to know why our own university wasn't good enough." He glanced toward me, but seemed to see only the past. "It was Billy's daddy stepped in and talked to him. And . . . that's a sensitive intervention down here, a family matter. It speaks well of their friendship, sir, that cards were not exchanged."

I whacked at a fly the size of a hummingbird.

"All that's by the by," Raines went on. "But Billy . . . I loved my books, but I looked up to Billy. He was better than all the heroes in all the books in the world. Always bigger, quicker. Sharper. Years back, Shady Grove was just a hunting camp got up by Mr. Barclay. Old man Wylie used to manage it. Couple of cabins, no more. Had to check under the bunks for cottonmouths. We used to come up in season. Riverboat to Memphis, then overland. There's a train now, bring you part of the way. And Billy wasn't twelve before he was outshooting grown men. Oh, I was fair enough, by a boy's measure. But Billy'd just about get out in front of the hounds. Loved to be in on the kill." He laughed again. "I was a disappointment, I suppose. For me, the joy lay in the bite of the frost, and that light that comes up the color of ice, and the warm feel of the dogs. The way they'd gather up around you, all steaming, and want you to tell them they'd done well. I liked the men-together feel right enough. Any boy would. But killing had no special appeal to me."

He took a drink of water from his canteen, looked around at his earth, and said, "Ever wonder, Major, how many more days like this we'll see? How the sky can be all that blue? As if the world had become so beautiful it couldn't do anything but break on apart? And the war no more than a paragraph in a newspaper . . ." I did not answer, for he did not want me to. When we ask such questions, our loneliness is impenetrable.

"Well, now, Billy," he went on. "We were the best of friends. More like brothers. Him the elder. Billy always went first. The only thing I could do almost as well as him was ride. I took to horses before I could walk, my father tells me. Billy might beat me out. But not by much. And not easily. Used to make him red-faced mad. But we were close. Neither of us had real brothers, understand. Although I have a younger sister, our Cordelia. For a while, there was some talk of Billy marrying her, but that horse didn't run. Before that, though. Nigh on ten years back . . . eight, anyway . . . we both lost our mothers to the yellow fever. Billy's mama was downriver on a visit when it took her. It just swept on up the river like a flood going the wrong way. We were all *en famille* at Wrexham, though my father talked of going north for the summer, on account of the contagion. My mother was one of the first to succumb in Natchez. Seemed so hard a thing then. After that, my daddy and Billy's daddy went to leaning on each other like never before. Neither remarried." He smiled warmly. "Although Mr. Barclay does make his regular visits to New Orleans."

He turned in his saddle, stretching his back. Looking at me. "You see? Like brothers. We were like brothers."

"What happened?" I asked. In my quiet voice.

I did not know if he would answer me. We rode a stretch with the question dragging between us. Then he said:

"Oh, what ever happens? I went off to Harvard. To that 'den of Yankee iniquity.' And . . . Billy married. Some time thereafter." I thought that might be the end of his confidences, but he added, "Marriage changes a man. Changes different men in different ways. It changed Billy in ways that . . . made our friendship cumbersome."

He removed his hat, a soft affair with a fluttering plume, and said, "There you have it. The story of Billy and me. Now he's a sporting man with no legs. And not much else that matters." He shuddered in a way that chilled the air. "How's he going to feel looking at me? With my two good legs and no good reasons for it?"

"War picks whom it will for its favors, Lieutenant. But perhaps the situation is otherwise, see. Perhaps your friend needs you now. Perhaps this is a time for mending matters. And it must have been a double blow he suffered, since his wife is 'no longer with us,' as you said."

"He was building Shady Grove for her," Raines said, in a voice reduced. "Emily couldn't tolerate the summers in Natchez. He was building the biggest, finest house he could, so she might be cooler up here in the hills. He would've fanned her himself, day and night. She was the great prize, you see. The ultimate victory. He would've done anything for her. Anything but what she needed done."

I longed to hear him tell me more. For I like a tale's unfolding. And, toward the end, I sensed that he had begun to speak truly at last. But we were interrupted.

A young Negress in a straw hat come down the road, skipping like a child on bare feet. At the sight of her, Raines cantered ahead. My own mount followed. With me holding on.

She stopped at his approach and put her fingers to her lips. Swaying where she stood. Her dress was a rag and she seemed all awry. The brim of her hat looked chewed.

Raines pulled up just short of her. "Paddycakes?" I heard him ask.

The girl smiled radiantly. As I drew closer, I saw the curiosity of her. Her form was much a woman's, if you will pardon my frankness, but her expression was that of a child.

The lieutenant spoke gently. "Paddycakes? Do you know who I am?"

She giggled. With wondrous merriment. "You'se Marse Drake. I knows. You'se Marse Drake." She thrust out her hand. "Chris'mas gif, Chris'mas gif . . ."

Raines leaned toward her. With a smile of greater warmth than ever I had seen on him. "Now, you know it isn't Christmas, Paddycakes. You know that right well. Don't you?"

She raised her hand still higher, the palm an empty desert. "Chris'mas gif . . ."

He chuckled. "Is that all I am to you, Paddycakes? A 'Chris'mas gif'? After all these years."

"Chris'mas gif."

He put a coin into her palm and closed her fingers over it. "Now you hold onto that. And you show it to Auntie Dee when you get home. She'll tell you what to do with it."

"Yes, Marse Drake. Marse Drake? You don't come no more."

"Man business," he said. "Now you tell me what you're doing way down here. You're a long way from your supper, girl. You been sleeping in the woods again?"

"Sometimes I does."

"Bear's going to get you. You need to stick closer, now you're growing. You know where you are right now?"

"Course I does, Marse Drake."

"You want to go home?"

She swayed, looking up with the eyes of a six-year-old coquette. "Maybe."

"Well, if you want to get home for your supper, you climb up here behind me. We're going that way." He reached down a hand to help her.

The girl hesitated. "Sometimes I doesn't go home no more."

"And why is that?" he asked, hand still on offer.

She lowered her gaze and the brim of her hat shadowed her face. "Cause Marse Billy so funny. He ain't got no walking legs no more. Make me laugh to see him. Uncle Samson, he say not to laugh. But Marse Billy so funny in that little cart without no walking legs."

"Come on," Raines said, in the gentlest voice on this earth, "get on up here and you can laugh at me instead. It's time to get for home."

.   .   .

HE MADE A GAME of the journey. He told her, "That nice fellow over there's a Yankee. You see him over there?"

She gawked at me. Astride behind the saddle. "Him's a Yankee?"

"That's right."

"He's near's little as Marse Billy, and Marse Billy ain't got no legs."

"No, no. He only looks on the short side because he's sitting on that great big horse. And you know why he traveled all the way down here from Yankee land?"

"Chris'mas gif?"

"No, girl. He traveled all the way down here because he wants to learn to ride like Marse Billy and me."

"Marse Billy ain't got no walking legs now. So he don't ride no horse. And Bridie say he got other parts took away, too. It a judgement, Bridie say. She say I ain't good, they goin' take away my fixings, too."

He ignored her. "You and me, we're going to give that Yankee fellow lessons in how to ride. See him just a-bouncing all over? He came all the way down here and said"—at this, the young man lowered his voice, as though impersonating a wild boar, and his tone bore no resemblance to mine own—"he said, 'Please, Lieutenant. I done saw you in that big horse race, and I got me a fine old horse, and I want to learn to ride him just like you do.' What do you think? Should we teach him?"

"Is he Marse Lincum?"

Raines laughed. "No, girl. Not unless they're fooling everybody west of the Tennessee. Now you hold on. And I'm going to show this fellow how to post himself right."

At that, the fellow began my instruction. I am not simple, see. I realized he had longed all that day to criticize my horsemanship, such as it was, but had found no gentlemanly approach. Now, by making it a game, he had softened the insult. And he was doing a good turn to both myself and the girl.

The girl laughed and laughed.

"All right, sir," Raines told me. "Now let's try it at a trot. Ready?"

Without receiving my reply, he get-upped the black. The horse charged and the girl's hat blew off.

She began to shriek.

Raines pulled up immediately, turning to her. Rascal stopped beside him.

"What is it?" the lieutenant asked. "What's the matter?"

"Her hat fell off," I said.

And then I saw her.

The loss of the hat revealed a misshapen head. It was the queerest thing. It looked as though her skull had been caved in above the ear. Her wooly mop of hair could not cover the damage and a kidney-shaped swale of livid flesh stretched down to her cheek. I would not have thought one with such an injury could live.

The girl screamed toward heaven, pounding her thighs with her fists.

"Hush up, now," Raines said, throwing a leg high over his mount's neck and dropping to the dust. "You hush. I'll fetch your covering."

She did not lower her voice until the straw hat sat on her head again. Then she whimpered down.

"You just sit right there," Raines told her. He stroked the black's neck. "Easy, boy. It's all right." Instead of mounting, he strode over to me.

"Got to fix those stirrups," he said. "Draw your feet out. Can you straighten that leg?" He glanced back down the road. "And where the damnation's Mr. B.?"

"What happened to her?" I asked.

He did not look up. "Accident," he said. And cinched my leathers with a savage force.

.   .   .

THE AFTERNOON SOURED in the wake of the outburst. After a few snappish comments, my riding lesson ended and silence possessed us. Perched behind my escort, the girl wore a cautious look. Reading his mood as an animal would. Twas clear young Raines no longer feared the world might break apart from too much beauty.

Again, I sensed how much I did not know. What had just happened that I failed to see?

I did not understand enough to fit any pieces together. I was not even sure which piece was which. I thought again of all that Raines had said. And tried to spot the holes words failed to fill. I kept coming back to the female question, and not because I have an indecent bent, you understand. It is only that women are often at the core of things.

Look you. This Captain Barclay had been married. And then bereaved before a house was finished. And he was young. The marriage had not been a long one. I wondered how the wife "no longer with us" had perished. There had been a reference the day before to a woman among the murdered Negroes. I tried to recall which of the two, Wylie or Raines, had said what. I needed their precise words. But my memory was not powerful enough to recapture them with the clarity I wanted. I thought I recalled Raines asking if "she" had been among the slain. And Wylie, though he hesitated, had understood exactly who "she" was. Surely, the wife would not have . . . could not have run off with her husband's slaves? And been murdered for it?

I fear my mind grew lurid with imaginings.

In the afternoon's maturity, we entered a forest. Just at that hour when the light turns into gold dust and the day's warmth rallies for its final stand. The countryside was hillier now and deep hollows anticipated the evening. By the side of the road, someone had decapitated a man-long snake. The horses shied and Paddy-cakes said:

"Moc'sin."

This was poor land, not worth the sweat to clear it. A meager skin of soil hid bones of rock. Yet, the undergrowth was a jungle. This Southland was a world of contradictions, of things closeted and unexpected. Again, I thought of many-layered India.

We passed a clearing with a shanty. A woman smoked a cob pipe on the porch. Her eyes had the steadiness of a serpent's and her cheeks were impossibly sunken. She looked as though she had not moved for ages. Wilderness had reclaimed the adjacent fields, and the woman had not even a dog for company. Human intrusion seemed fragile here. And, perhaps, unwanted.

Our journey led us deeper into the woods.

We were coming around a turn in the trail when the men with guns surrounded us.

eight

 _T_ hree men in tattered uniforms they were, two of gray and one blue. A fourth man positioned himself in the center of the road. His lurid attire looked robbed from a fancy man, and a top hat, askew, pressed down on his dirty hair. An officer's dress sword dangled from his hip. He would have seemed a fool but for the revolvers in his hands. The other fellows held long arms, a shotgun and two muskets.

Top Hat glared at Raines and said, "Thet feller moves his hand another inch, you shoot him dead, Jake." Then he spoke to the lieutenant directly. "Don't go touching thet gun, sonny. Won't help none, though it's like to do you harm."

I hoped Raines would be sensible. Rashness is not valor. I watched his hand as it wavered above his pistol. For my part, I made no move to defend myself, for my Colt had empty chambers. All things had been returned to me except cap and ball.

Carefully, Raines lifted his hand away from his holster.

"Thet's right, sonny," Top Hat said. "Thet's right. Lighten their loads for 'em, boys. Git them irons."

The fellow to my flank reached up and took my Colt. Rascal nickered.

Behind young Raines, the Negress made herself small. Watching us with the eyes of a cornered doe.

The bandit in blue grabbed the lieutenant's revolver and passed it off to his comrade. Then he stroked the girl along the thigh. No frightened creature could have matched her stillness.

"Christ amighty," Blue Coat said, "ain't she one ugly nigger bitch?" He raised his face to Raines. I saw only the back of his forage cap, but I knew the fellow was grinning. "Hell, boy. Dockyard hoor looks better than that there cunny."

Raines spoke to Top Hat. And to them all. "You men are all traitors to your country. In time of war—"

Top Hat cackled, followed by the others. "And what country would thet be, sonny? Damnation, we ought to jest set us up a country of our own right here, thet's what we ought to do." He smiled broadly, displaying ruined teeth. "Jake, you got a cotton to be president? Charlie? You got that senator look, boy. Yes, sir. The Republic of You and Me. One of you boys lift that girlie on down."

A gray-clad youth, the cleanest of the pack, grabbed the girl by the forearm and tugged her off the horse. As she tumbled, the hat left her head.

Paddycakes screamed. Plunging between our mounts.

The boy yanked her toward him and gave her a slap. But the girl fought back and shrieked.

He let her go. Abruptly.

"Lord Jesus," he said, "she got a great big dent in her head."

Paddycakes scrambled over to the fallen hat and pulled it on with both hands. Pulling it down as low on her brow as she could, stretching the straw. Then she cowered, eyes skittering from one face to another.

"Like as not she'll have another dent soon enough," Top Hat told us.

"For the love of God," Raines said. "You can see the girl's touched. She's simple."

"Ain't nothing wrong with simple," Top Hat said. "Some fellas kind a like 'em thet way. Though a crazy nigger's some ways low." He waved one of his pistols, first at Raines, then at me. "Now you two boys git down easy. You go first, little man. Thet's right. And we'll settle things up."

Behind me, a voice said, "I'm figuring as to how to cut a bullet in half. Cause I ain't about to waste no whole one on a midget."

Why I do not know, but I became aware of the birds again. The forest fair raged with them. Loud as a battle they were.

"Thet's right," Top Hat said when we had both dismounted. "Now step right up here. Fine horses you got there. Say thet much. Beholding to you both."

Two of the men moved up and nudged their gun barrels into our backs, while Top Hat shoved his pistols behind his belt. He started with Raines, testing each pocket, drawing out the lieutenant's purse then a fancy handkerchief.

"Well, ain't thet pretty." He shook the folds from the linen and wiped his nose. Grinning black-toothed at Raines. "I do thet right, sonny? Like a real gentleman?"

Then he patted the lieutenant's body for hidden treasures. And found one. He tore open Raines's shirt at the chest.

Gold flashed.

"*No,*" Raines cried. Jerking backward into a rifle's muzzle.

"Well, just you lookee there. A little gold heart. Your Sally Darlin' know you ride with a nigger gal up behind?"

I sensed Raines was about to commit an act of great folly. "*Master* yourself," I said in the most commanding voice I could muster. Twas that of an angry sergeant. "Control yourself, Lieutenant."

Raines understood me. He stood stiff as a grenadier while Top Hat ripped the locket from its chain.

When he got to me, the fellow tossed my Testament in the weeds, but paused over my purse. Examining the crisp green notes.

He looked at Blue Coat. "Hiram . . . what the hell?"

"Them's the new Federal dollars. I seen 'em around camp afore the battle."

"See thet?" Top Hat asked me. "Tain't no disunion here. We all united. Hiram fit over on the Yankee side til he come to his senses. And the boys here, well, they seed the light when it come out the other end." He smiled again. "Seems a fool thing to go killin' for nothing. Now don't it? When you got the choice of killin' for something you can put right in your pocket."

Finally, he drew out my papers from General Beauregard. He opened them to insure nothing of value was concealed within, then flicked them after my Testament.

"Now I ask you, gentlemen," he said, stepping back and straightening. "What does it profit a man to have money in his pocket? Well, I'm going to tell you. It makes for a right good time." He laughed. "Beholding to you both. Hiram, you walk these two friends of ours on down the hollow. Far enough to where ain't no traveler goin' to come by and disturb 'em. Charlie, you gather them horses up. Me and Jake got to look over this here nigger."

Again, Raines almost acted. But I closed my hand over his wrist.

"Thet's right," Top Hat said. "You boys behave. Go on now. And you be sure to think high thoughts. Yes, sir, you all just go walking on down there in the path of righteousness. Git now."

The fellow with the shotgun and the Union tunic prodded me in the side. "Move," he said. And I did. Drawing Raines along beside me. We went slowly. For there were briars just off the road. And the pain of the moment knows naught of the pain to come.

I felt Raines tense. I understood him, see. For these were doings of a sort I knew. The boy was trying to judge the right moment to turn on our captor. I prayed he would hesitate long enough to leave the business to me. For I feared he would move too soon and bring down the others upon us. To have any hope of success, we needed to be out of their range, two against one and not four against two.

Every stolen second was a treasure, every yard we covered a little miracle.

I listened to the footfalls and branch-breaking of the fellow behind me. Waiting for him to stumble or slip.

And if he did not? If the moment never came?

It would come. For I would make it come. The Welsh was up in me. And my old regimental rage, the methodical fury.

Sometimes I fear we do not change at heart, but only put on years like layers of clothing.

Behind us, the girl began to scream. It was a different sort of cry this time. Like the loudest of birds.

We blundered down an embankment. A welcome way it was, for now the earth would shield us from the fire of the men on the trail. Oh, they were sloven and did not know their trade.

One was off with the horses. Two were pawing the girl. How many rounds did our guard have for his shotgun? I had not seen a pistol on him. So we would have one weapon only between us. If one of us did not die in the taking of it. And the shotgun was good only at close range, while two of the others had rifles.

I feigned an even greater weakness in my leg than I felt. Our captor cursed and prodded me with his weapon. But I had drawn him too close for his own safety. I waited only for a slicking of mud, a mutter that signaled the slightest loss of balance or diverted attention. Ready to strike, I was.

Things happened otherwise.

.   .   .

SHOTS PIERCED THE QUIET. Up by the road.

Service in John Company's ranks and old India made a hard school. But you got your lessons for a lifetime.

In an instant, I had turned on my good leg and had the shotgun in my hands. Blue Coat stared down at me. Baffled by the celerity of fate. That look was only on his snout for a sliver of a moment. I clipped his jaw with the peak of the gunstock. You use the point, see, so a discharge is less likely. We could not spare the shotgun's load.

The bones of his face collapsed like an emptied sack. He staggered, clutching the damage. I swept the gun's butt back around and caught the side of his head with the other tip. It is the simplest motion, once you learn it.

Down he went, into a pile of moans. He must have been thick-skulled, for the second blow should have killed him.

I started up the embankment, shotgun in hand, when Raines reached out for it.

"I can go faster," he said.

He was right. Twas no time for postures of manliness. I let him have the shotgun. And looked back at the figure on the ground. A twisting, suffering creature.

I should have crushed his skull with a rock for safety. But the battle had gorged me with killing, and I had enough to atone for.

I judged the man. Still conscious, he saw me watching, but pretended he did not. Covering his eyes, he rolled over and groaned. He was a coward in the face of pain. As so many of us are. I knelt and patted him down as he squirmed, but found no other weapons. Blood stained my hands and I wiped it on his trousers. He did not even have the strength to beg.

The shooting above had ceased. It had lasted no longer than a proper roll of thunder. And I had not heard the shotgun fire. That worried me. But neither did I hear the bandits calling one to another, as such men do when they survive a fuss.

There was only the sound of the girl, her fear transformed to yet a new variety, and a boy's voice calling, "Oh, Lordie, oh, Lordie, help me up, help me git up . . ."

I sneaked up through the brambles. Barnaby was the first thing I saw, for he was hard to miss. I saw him before I spied our loitering horses. Then I marked the girl clinging to the Englishman's trunk of a leg.

And I saw Raines. Tearing at a corpse.

"Help me up . . . I cain't git up . . ." that boy's voice begged. "Sumpin's wrong, oh, Lordie, sumpin won't let me up."

As I neared the road, I saw the young fellow. "Charlie" I think they called him. His body lay as still as the grave, but his head jerked sidewards. He lay just in front of the horses. He had not led them far.

"There, there, missy," Barnaby said to the girl. "Bob's your uncle, but you're a brave lass. There, there." These comforts were his means of breaking free. He left her and walked up the road, a pistol in each hand.

He stopped above the young fellow. The boy quieted for a moment, then said, "Help me on up, mister. I didn't mean no harm. I cain't git up."

Barnaby shot him. Without the least expression on his face.

I was standing over Raines by then. He savaged Top Hat's pockets. The dead man's eyes were open and his tongue stuck out like a dog's. The last fellow lay nearby, face down, with deep stains spreading over the gray of his jacket.

When Raines found the locket, a gold heart the size of a dollar coin, all the tension fled his body. His shoulders sagged, and he sighed. Then he forced himself up and wandered to the side. Leaving it to me to recover our purses.

Up the road, Barnaby was dragging the boy's body off into the brush. Too proud to bolt, the horses stood with their rumps to us. Disgusted by our doings.

The lieutenant remembered himself then and went to lift the girl, cooing to her as to an infant.

"Mr. B. has your Colt," he told me. In a voice calmed almost to normalcy.

I fetched my papers from the weeds and found my Testament a little farther off. When I come back to the road, Raines gave me a cool, almost sly smile and said:

"You've been wondering all this time what earthly good Mr. B. could be to me or to anybody. Now haven't you?"

"Lieutenant Raines, I would not be so ungracious . . ."

The swollen fellow trudged down the road toward us, as if he had been forced on a Sunday stroll.

"Mr. B. fought seven duels, and killed three men who insulted his late wife," Raines told me. "He had a certain repute down in New Orleans." The young man gave his uniform a dusting. "Yes, sir. There's more to Mr. B. than meets the eye."

And that was saying a good deal.

.   .   .

"MR. B. TOLD ME your Colt wasn't loaded," Raines said. It was the first time he had spoken since we mounted. The forest and the dead lay miles behind us. We rode through softening light. Killing keeps good men from speech. Though fools and braggarts shout their brains away.

We had not killed all four of them. The fellow whose jaw I smashed made off. But I did not think him a danger. Three corpses were enough.

"When Captain Wylie restored my possessions," I said, "he did not think it good to return my ammunition."

Leaning against my escort's back, Paddycakes lolled and hummed. As if the recent danger had been a frolic.

"Well, that won't do." Raines let the leathers drop on his horse's neck and used both hands to unfasten the cartridge box from his belt. He pulled his mount in beside mine and held out the black rectangle. "Here. Take what you need." Our eyes met. "I rely on your honor as a gentleman."

The somber mood rode between us a little longer. Fear haunts every man who comes near death. It may take many forms, but it is there. Shadows stretched across our way and Mr. B. dropped back to nibble the secrets of his pocket. And then the girl sang out, in stainless joy:

> *Run, nigger, run,*
> *Pater-roller git you,*

Run, nigger, run,
It almost day . . .

Halfway through another verse, she broke off and asked, "Marse Drake? You fixing to take Marse Billy off?"

Raines twisted about in the saddle. "Now what makes you ask a silly thing like that?"

"Marse Billy, he gone so mean now. He so funny without his walking legs, but he don't laugh none. Just drink that old whisky and be mean all the time. Bridie say he ain't gettin' better, neither. She say he born mean, and now God done let all the mean loose in him. Times I'se scared, Marse Drake."

"Bridie's a fool," he answered. Without a great deal of conviction in his tone. Then he asked, "What's Uncle Samson say?"

She crooned for a moment, then said, "Uncle Samson say Bridie don't know nothing."

"Well, Uncle Samson's right. And what's Auntie Dee tell you?"

"Oh, she don't say nothing tall, Marse Drake. She just make that Hoodoo face when she mad."

"Auntie Dee's a good Christian woman. And what do you know about Hoodoo?"

The girl at the lip of womanhood became a six-year-old coquette again. "Oh, I knows what I knows. I knows lots, Marse Drake. Bridie got her a John the Conquer. She fixing to show me, if'n I cross her up with the silver."

"Bridie's a wicked woman," Raines said. "And you tell her I said that. You tell her she better say her prayers that the Yankees don't get her, cause they gobble up anybody who even whispers the word 'Hoodoo.' Cook 'em on a spit and swallow 'em down."

The girl glanced, balefully, in my direction.

A certain mirth played on my escort's lips. Then he added, in a voice of comical sternness, "You listen to me now, Paddycakes. You tell Bridie that Marse Drake said if he hears one more whisper about any Hoodoo, or Voodoo, or boo-hoo, for that matter, he's going to see to it that Old Marse Barclay swaps her back downriver where she came from. You hear? You tell her she won't be taking any more naps in the linens. She'll be out there in the fields bending her back till it stays crooked."

"Bridie say there ain't gone be no more bending of that back, Marse Drake. She say the Lincum gunboats coming, and the meek gone to 'herit."

The humor left the young man's mouth, replaced by furrows at the corner of his lips. This time his speech was authentically stern. "Well, you tell Bridie that Mr. Lincoln's gunboats need a river. And there isn't any river at Shady Grove. Or anywhere close. And they're sure not going to come up the creek. You tell her she better get to practicing on her meekness, or the only thing she's going to inherit is trouble."

The girl had an uncanny sense of his nature. She began to bawl.

"Oh, what's the matter, honey? I didn't mean to upset you now," Raines said. With all the metal gone from his tone. He sounded almost like an older brother. "It's just been a hard day all around, now hasn't it?"

"You'se mad at me, Marse Drake."

He thought for a moment before speaking. "No, Paddycakes. I'm not mad at you. Maybe I'm just mad at the world. Still and all, you tell that Bridie everything you can remember from what I said. Will you do that for me?"

"Yes, Marse Drake. Marse Drake?"

"Yes?"

"Them peoples back there? Them ones you kilt? They gone come back and be haunts under the Hoodoo power?"

"No. We killed them a special way. So they can't come back. And don't you go telling any fancy stories to that Bridie about what happened. You hear? You just tell her what I told you to tell her."

"Yes, Marse Drake. I ast you something?"

"What now, girl?"

"Is Miss Emily a haunt now?"

I caught the jolt. It passed through his entire body.

"No."

"But she gone, though."

"Yes."

"Bridie say Marse Billy talk to her in the night."

I had no living man beside me, for Raines was cut of marble.

"She say Marse Billy call out to Miss Emily, an when she don't come, he call out for Lucy, but she gone to Kingdom herselfs an—"

He fair lifted himself out of the saddle. For a moment, I feared he would strike the girl.

"You just tell that—"

He caught himself. Francis Drake Raines was a man who chose his enemies fairly, as I would learn. He settled down. But he kept his back to his companion now. Rigid as a hussar on parade. The girl curled up in fright. He understood that, too. As soon as he could trust his voice, he asked:

"Getting hungry, Paddycakes?"

"I'se always hungry."

"Me, too. Wonder what Auntie Dee has in the pot?"

"Marse Drake?" The girl eyed me warily as she spoke. "That Yankee you done fetched up really eat the Hoodoo peoples?"

Raines glanced at me. With an uncontrollable smile.

"Every last one," he said.

.　　.　　.

THE LAND CLEARED BEFORE US. But many of the fields had not been planted. Where high trees lined the road, my escort reined in his horse.

"Slip on down now," he told the girl. "You go on around back. And go straight to Auntie Dee, you hear?"

Paddycakes dropped, flat-footed, to the earth. Glancing up at me with lingering doubts.

Raines watched her run across the near field, then let his horse walk on. Behind us, Barnaby had closed to a half-dozen lengths. Sensing his supper, I supposed.

My escort spoke in the soft voice he used for the most serious matters. "Major? You handled yourself finely, sir. In the course of our difficulties back there. I'm not certain I've ever seen a man move so fast. No, that's not right. With such precision."

"Twas little enough, Lieutenant. That fellow may have been a soldier briefly, but he was not a proper one. He did not know his business."

"Well . . . I'm in your debt, sir."

"As I am in Mr. Barnaby's."

We turned from the road where a brace of pillars framed a gravel path.

"I'm afraid, Major . . . that my judgement was rash. I underestimated you." He said it with a boyish shyness. Wanting to apologize where nothing of the sort was necessary.

"And I'm afraid," I told him, "that this may prove a war of underestimations."

I sensed a change in the lieutenant, a quickening of the heart. Perhaps he had seen something I could not. Or perhaps a memory sparked. Our horses had drearied with the long ride, but Raines teased his to a canter. As though he were approaching his own home. I did my best to keep up with him.

Before the house appeared, he slowed again. Now it was as if our arrival must be delayed at any cost. We clopped along at a pace that was almost a sleep. Clearly, there was more to tell than he had seen fit to share. Men will tell you a great deal, hoping they will not have to tell you what matters.

I decided to try him again. Before we faced a half-built house and its shattered master.

"Lieutenant Raines?"

My voice seemed to surprise him. Calling him out of some deep revery.

"I may have been under a false assumption," I continued. "For I did not think you were a married man?"

"I'm not," he said. Matter-of-factly.

"The locket holds the image of a sweetheart then? Or a memento?" I had watched him put the gold heart into his pocket after he recovered it. The chain was broken and he buried his treasure deep, clutching it long in his fist before he could let it go.

The remaining light was pale and weak. Perhaps that accounted for the whiteness of his face. But not for the burning in his eyes when he looked at me.

"I must ask you, as a gentleman, sir, never to raise the matter again."

He did not wait for a reply, but kicked his spurs into the flanks of his horse. It was the first time I had seen him use them.

The black sprang to a gallop. Raines swept off his hat and loosed a wail to wake the ancient dead. I supposed it was a typical Southron greeting. Rascal nearly threw me, but I brought him around and kept him to a manageable trot. Well ahead of me, the young man began shouting. I could not make out a great many words, but caught, "Billy," a good-natured, "damn you"—if such a thing may be—and "whisky."

The path turned and I saw the house. It was not a grand manor after the English fashion. But it was big. With high columns like ancient Greece in an engraving. Yet, one wing was only a skeleton, a frame of weathered boards.

The house looked crippled, and I thought at once of its owner.

I saw him on his verandah, sitting like a statue in his rolling chair. Raines had stopped his horse short of the front steps and the two men considered each other in silence.

Barnaby come up beside me.

"Welcome to Shady Grove, sir," he said. "I does believe you'll find it jolly queer."

nine

*B*arnaby and I drew up to let the two lads have a good stare at each other. Beyond the long porch, the heavens flamed over the hills. You might have thought Jerusalem on fire. The fields and groves smoked in the low land around us, and the air was gray as gunpowder. Raines and his horse had become a silhouette etched in crimson, with Captain Barclay a white face and white hands in the evening shade.

Silence tested the gulf between the old friends, but if colors had voice, that twilight would have been a bloody howl. The maddened sunset was but an accident of nature, of course. Yet, I thought it spoke what words could not between young Raines and Barclay.

We are told in John's Gospel that Jesus "knew what was in man." That alone would make our Lord unique.

I believe there were fireflies.

The lieutenant's mount snorted and tossed its mane. It caught my eye but briefly, for Barclay was the center of this world. As surely as a king is the heart of his kingdom. His throne was a got-up contraption and his forearms rested on the rims of its wheels. Smaller wheels balanced the device in front. Where feet and legs should have been. As my sight found purchase, I marked his open-collar shirt and waistcoat. Such informality of dress should have softened his aspect, but did not. He looked a fierce one, high up on his porch. A king in a realm of darkness.

Cushions packed him in place. He sat in a tin pan.

Barclay was a bold-cut man, the sort who is as handsome at a distance as at arm's length. While Raines possessed those high-bred looks you must learn to like, Barclay struck you instantly with his beauty of countenance. And beauty it was, though with something brute about it. He would not think of others, but others would think of him. He had a look that wrenches women from content-ment, that fills them with confused anger. Until he turns to offer them one word, and wrecks their hearts. He reminded me of young Trenchard, a bad sort I had known. Yet, Trenchard was dark, and Barclay was fair as sunlight. Of course, I speak of his face and that alone. For his ruined body would no longer call to the women who might interest him.

He looked at Raines with a killer's eyes.

We might have sat there through the end of days, had Barnaby not taken matters in hand.

"That ham I smells, Master William? It do give a fellow an appetite, the smell of Shady Grove ham."

I was befuddled, for I smelled nothing of the sort. I smelled earth. And new grass.

The crippled captain glared at the man. For as long as it takes a bat to swoop past a lantern. Then he grinned. With impossible beauty.

"Well, Drake Goddamned Raines," he called, shifting his smile to his friend. "I didn't know if you forgot your way, or run off and joined the Yankees. Damn me to Hell, boy. Where you been hiding? And I see you still got that old fat man dragging after you."

Face graven with hospitality, the master of the manor turned to Barnaby. "Mr. B.? You come round to eat my smokehouse empty again? Swear to God, you're twice the size I recollect. Come up here to eat me out of house and home, I reckon."

"One don't want spoilage, Master William. 'The stocks must be renewed,' as me governor always said. And he lived to be fifty."

Barclay laughed. As though testing an old skill after letting it languish. Then he slapped his hands on the wheels of his chair and swung himself halfway around. Violet light engulfed the porch.

"Samson!" He shouted. "Uncle Samson! Company for dinner!"

.　　.　　.

RAINES LEAPT FROM HIS HORSE and dashed up the steps to shake his friend's hand. Barclay had difficulty sustaining his balance under the force of the onslaught and there was an awkward moment. But the invalid fellow made light of the matter, clapping Raines on the shoulder and praising the development of his strength.

"Army life agrees with you, Drake," Barclay said.

Barnaby and I dropped from our mounts in succession. Now I am not a tall fellow, as you know, and I have my sour leg. Getting down from the saddle was ever a trial. I struck the ground hard and felt the jolt right up my spine. With the flank of the horse in my face, I wondered if I would ever be free of discomfort again, or if the age of thirty-four meant I was past my prime.

A grand black fellow emerged from the house, got up as if off to the opera. The very patent of a gentleman he looked, but for the maroon of his skin. His posture was stately, his shoulders broad, and only the ash of his close-cropped hair reported declining strength. His face was a shadow in the shadows, but hinted the folds of flesh that come with cares. He might have been serving at Windsor Castle by the bearing of him, and it gave me a start to hear him speak when he greeted Captain Raines, for he had a better English than the lot of us.

"If I may take the liberty," the old darky said, "it is a pleasure to see you again, sir. It seems a long time."

"Too long," Raines told him. "How are you, Uncle Samson? How's Auntie Dee?"

"We are well, sir. Thank you, sir."

The old fellow bent, as if bowing, to confer with our host. I could not hear the words from the yard, but Raines gave a start at something. A moment thereafter, the Negro turned to Barnaby and me.

"Good evening, Mr. B. May I attend your horses, gentlemen?"

"Wouldn't hear of it! Not at all!" Barnaby answered. "Barnaby's the man for the horses, sir. Raised in the livery service, Barnaby B. Barnaby was. Practically born in a stable, like other fine sorts what preceded him."

With that, the titan led his mount across the gravel to the black Raines had left standing. Drawing the horses about, he shot me a look that was more than a hint to go with him.

We left them on the porch, the old friends and the Negro, in the fragrant air and failing light. As we rounded the unfinished wing of the house, a door slapped shut behind us.

"How the mighty are fallen," Barnaby said, with casual sorrow. A row of cabins, lifeless, stood pale against a grove. The roofline of a barn traced black. "It ain't proper when a lovely old fellow like Samson has to run the house and look after the horses, too. Must've all gone off, the rest of them. And not just them what got themselves killed, sir. No more sense than white men, some of them."

He swept a big arm from the barn to the darkening fields. "Oh, t'ain't the grandest of plantations, Major, not like what you sees downriver. But there was a dozen Negroes in the house before the war, and five times that in the fields. And that was only a start, it was. Master William had mighty plans, sir. Terrible mighty plans, he had." He shook his head between the spluttering horses. " 'This war ain't naught but a calamity,' Barnaby B. Barnaby says. Like to break the heart it is. Naught but a calamity, sir."

Rascal followed me with a goodly will, as if he sensed bed and board, and I feared him a measure the less now. Still, I felt blue. The slow clop of hooves made a lonely music that eve.

"War is always a calamity," I said.

"Right you are, sir, right you are. After a fashion, sir. For some wars do got more sense than others, it seems to Barnaby, though there's little enough sense in the best of 'em. And no sense at all in this one, as I sees it. Right you are there, sir, right you are."

Lilacs. I smelled the dream scent of lilacs, the perfume of young nights consumed in longing. It is a flower that always grips my heart. I thought of my love, my Mary, and wished the war away.

"Look you, Mr. Barnaby. There is a thing I do not understand here. You do not favor the war. Yet you follow the Rebel flag."

Barnaby stopped before an outbuilding and the smell of a crusted forge pierced the veil of lilac. The girthy fellow stared at me in wonder. With night crushing the last glow against the hilltops.

"I *don't,* sir. Nothing of the kind. I follows Master Francis, sir, not that fool Welshman Davis and his lot. Begging your pardon, sir. Master Francis wants some looking after, though he don't always see it himself."

"But . . . if I'm a judge, Mr. Barnaby . . . you have seen military service? In the past?"

His joviality returned at that, and we walked on. With the horses growing restive as the barn swelled. "Oh, Barnaby's et the Queen's beans, sir. Still tells in me bearing, I expects. The 69th Foot, sir. The good old 'Ups and Downs.' And I took to it, sir, for it's in me blood, it is. But the colonel was a meager man and said I cost too much to feed and how's he could have a rifle company for half the fare. And out I went. It was a terrible blow, sir, for I was young and a bit addled still, and I admired the profession of arms, I did. There's nothing like a uniform to give a fellow's corpus a trim line, sir. Deadly to the ladies, begging your pardon." The fellow stopped sharp at the open doors of the barn. "Bless me, sir, the stable's empty!"

It was not empty. I saw the heads of two mules and a gray in the faint light by the entrance. The lone horse nickered a welcome at us. Or perhaps it was greeting our mounts, grown weary of the company of its lessers. Beyond those front stalls, though, no shadows plowed the dark and we heard no sounds of life but whirling flies.

"It's enough to bring a tear to the eye," Barnaby said, bending to light a lantern. "A stable fit for a baronet, it was. All lovely with horses bred proper. Oh, how the mighty have fallen, sir, how the mighty have fallen!"

The prospect distressed the fellow terribly, which seemed uncharacteristic. He seemed a man who could sniff out roses in a lake of brimstone. But now he was cast down. Of course, it might have been the want of dinner.

He instructed me in horsing matters. First we slung down the saddlebags and bedrolls, then undid the saddles and spread the blankets over the boards to dry the sweat. He had to help me with Rascal's bit, for I remained too wary, but I recompensed the good fellow by bringing in buckets of water from the cistern, getting along nicely, if slowly, without my cane. Then I drew out the oats from the bin. Barnaby understood his fellow man and did not wound my pride by insisting he must help with the lugging. It was not laziness in him, I do not think, but the sense to know I would not be treated as a thing of diminished capacities. For when we tell ourselves we are defeated, we are.

Rascal behaved admirably, and I even found the courage to brush the beast down. His pelt shone in the lamplight and I nearly could see beauty in his form. He seemed to like the brushing, though perhaps it was only my scattering of the barn flies that gratified him, for they come over him thick as beggars at a Hindoo temple. Meanwhile, I queried Barnaby further. For I like the story of a man's life, when it is told without design or imposition.

"So, Mr. Barnaby . . . after your regimental days, twas off to America?"

He combed the dust from the mane of his master's horse. Delicate of touch the fellow was. "Not directly, sir, not directly. First I reacquainted meself with London town. For I was young, sir, and still a bit addled. And I had a certain flair for the city, I did, although I lacked an equal flair for work. But I was young, sir, young and foolish. Then me governor woke up dead one morning. Though he reached the ripe old age of fifty, which was four years older than his own governor, if all the counting was done true. And Mother had wandered off some time afore. Oh, I ain't one to gild the lily. We was poor, sir. And me brothers and sisters was dead from the start, for the close at the end of the alley weren't fit for a beast. So I thought to meself how the old fellow was always talking about his own governor, and about going to America. To New Orleans, to put a clear name on it. You see, sir, me governor's governor served with Wellington on the Peninsully. And then he took ship with Pakenham and enjoyed the battle of New Orleans, he did. Said it was a dreadful cock up, sir. Worse than a Spaniard would've done it. He said what if he had it all to do over, he'd go on the American side, if only for the want of sense on our own. A sin and a shame, he called it, sir. And his mate got et by an alligator when they was retreating."

Barnaby towered over the lantern. The barn could hardly contain the shadow he cast. "Still and all, he liked the air or something. Always talked of going back, he did, though I hardly remembers meself. Me own governor told me all about it, sir, for he said I weren't to forget our proud family history. Now I wouldn't put stock in everything I heard, sir, for the old boy liked his gin, but America come to seem like mother's milk to me. How me governor was always going on about it, though he'd never been and wasn't like to go. For he had a position, sir, in the livery of an inn, and such luck don't come knocking every day. But I was different, sir. Full of adventures, I was. I tried the livery yard, I did, but there was a dreadful row about the innkeeper's daughter. Oh, I was a rogue, sir, I admits it, and a girl of spirit likes a man with a certain abundance of physicality to him. Well, it come to me right thereafter how's a fellow ought to try what's new, once he bites the old and finds it bitter. So off I went to New Orleans. By way of Havana, sir. Almost stayed among the Spaniard, sir, for the ladies was an excite-

ment and I was young. But on I come in the end, for I had set a
goal, sir, and Barnaby B. Barnaby ain't the sort to fall short by an
inch."

"I hear New Orleans is a sinful place," I said.

"Oh, that it is, sir! It's lovely sinful, it is. Though I don't think
it's no more sinful than the next city. It's only how they are, sir. Displaying things what others hides away. They do take a great joy in
their sinning, sir. Why, your creole can stretch more enjoyment out
of a little sin than the rest of us gets from a big one. He don't just
gobble it up, but savors it like a cat toying with a mouse. But then
they're Catholics, the most of 'em, and get forgiven on a regular
schedule. I ain't Catholic meself, sir, but my little Marie was, and I
can see where it's got its inducements, the Roman Church does. If
ever I was to go back to spoiling perfectly good Sundays with that
sort of business, begging your pardon, sir, I just might tread the
Roman way meself."

The fellow was clearly benighted. I struggled for words that
would not give offense, but managed only to say, "You put little
stock in religion, sir?"

"Oh, I does and I don't. I do believe He's up there, sir. And
looking down and watching. Shaking His head, most like. But I
ain't convinced He's keeping score all day." He paused in his brushing, hands resting on the horse's back. "Here's how Barnaby sees it,
sir: If a fellow was a thoroughly bad lot, but went to sing his Sunday hymns most regular, would that save him, sir? And should it,
sir? What if a fellow lives proper and treats the next man decent
like, but don't go for his regular snore in a pew? Will the Good
Lord make a fellow like that to burn up in Hell, sir? I mean, it
makes it all seem like a bad grammar school, don't it? Where atten-
dance is all what matters, and the master's handy with the cane."
He switched the brush from one hand to the other and gave the
horse a long stroke. "Give me the man what acts right, sir. Not the
one what only makes a show of things. And I suspects the Lord
thinks much the same. Begging your pardon, sir."

It was a lax theology. Yet, after the battle I hardly seemed a model Christian to myself. I brushed the conversation along the way I brushed the horse. With dull and regular strokes.

"These Southron gentlemen seem much of your mind, Mr. Barnaby," I said. "Not great chapel-goers, from what little I've seen."

"Oh, no, sir. Religion's for the ladies, sir. Sport for the man, sir, sport for the man! Although they does appear for buryings. And births, when there ain't any guilty faces in the crowd. No objections to Christmas, though they finds Easter a bit glum. But them's the gentlemen I'm speaking of, sir. Your poor might wander in and out of church a bit more often. For they like a good fright of a sermon, sir. If there's no sporting matter on that particular Sunday. A horse or a blue-tick hound will trump a parson."

I brushed Rascal where he did not wish to be brushed. He gave a leap and kicked the wood, and I jumped back a yard. I still had a great deal to learn about horses.

Perhaps the Catholic faith was not entirely in error and the horse was sent to bend me to my penance. I wondered what John Wesley would have said of the notion. Can we ever reckon the wisdom of the Lord? Why did he make the horse? Of course, he made the serpent and the Frenchman, and no one knows how they fit His design.

"Keep the brush away from the dark parts," Barnaby told me. Finishing with his master's horse, he turned to groom his own.

"New Orleans has a French influence, I believe," I said. Meaning to turn the conversation away from his irreligion.

Barnaby sighed. "French, and Spanish, too. And there's Americans, and English come-latelies, and there I includes meself. You've got Africans running from Chinaman yellow to black as the devil's behind. And not a few queer mixings in between, sir. If you takes the meaning of it. Oh, it's a lovely place, New Orleans. An injurious climate for them what ain't robust. But lovely as Eden with gutters."

"You were there a long time, Mr. Barnaby?"

He sighed again, more deeply, and paused in his labors. "Not so long's I'd have liked. No, not half so long, sir." He made a face that forgot me and remembered. "I met me lovely Marie there, I did. Better than I deserved, she was. Better than any man deserved. Spanish blood, sir. All stirred up with the French. And other influences not to be spoken of, I always suspected. But I didn't care, sir. All's one, sir. And she was a lovely agglomeration. Sweet as a good cup of punch, sir. And give me two little ones, she did. I had a proper establishment in them days. Sold fittings to the gentlemen, sir, and the firm of Barnaby B. Barnaby was known from Mobile to Memphis! Then the fever rose, the yellow jack." He lowered his face behind the horse's neck. "Took all what mattered from me, sir. My Marie and the little ones both. I neglected me affairs after that, sir. Let things slide, I did. Let the clerk keep all the books and me never suspecting. Oh, never trust a clerk, sir. The fellow shot the moon to Hispaniola. Never thought I'd end a bankrupt, sir. A bankrupt and a widower. The last what I had went for the vault. For there's no proper burying down that way, but you got to put your loved ones above the ground if you values 'em. If old Master Raines hadn't taken pity on me—he'd always been a grand customer, sir, and a judge of cloth to shame a master tailor—if he hadn't taken in old Barnaby, I might have ended me days down in Gin Lane. Or worse."

He let me have a glimpse of his face, of his shining eyes. " 'Come up to Natchez,' he says to me, the old master. 'For you've lost your wife to the yellow jack just as I has. And you've lost your little ones,' says he, 'and I've a son wants manners put on him, and I'm hardly the man to do it. Come up to Wrexham,' he says, and I went and that was that. Oh, Master Francis was a lovely child, sir. And now he's a lovely man, ain't he?"

I thought of the war, and of what it did to lovely young men. Twas as if Barnaby read my thoughts.

"He'll come through fine," he said, "if Barnaby B. Barnaby has any say in the business."

The good fellow seemed overwrought, so I changed the subject. "That girl today. The young Negress . . ."

"Paddycakes?"

"Yes. Do you know what happened to her, Mr. Barnaby? That damage to her skull. It would appear to be a medical enigma."

He took a moment to answer, shutting his horse in a stall then stepping over to help me with mine. Standing close enough for me to smell the weight of the day on him, he looked into my eyes and said:

"Master William struck her with an iron. Some years ago, of course. When Shady Grove was still a hunting establishment, sir, before Miss Emily come and the big house was begun. A child he was, and hardly responsible. Done something displeasing to him, the girl did. The Lord knows what. Master William took a fireplace iron to her head. We were on a visit at the time. For the hunt, sir. A great uproar and commotion it was. No one thought the girl would live. And Master William wouldn't as much as say he was sorry. Not to the girl, I don't mean, for she didn't signify. But he wouldn't apologize to his own father for what he done. A difficult child he always was, sir. Not like my Master Francis."

Now it was my turn to stare into his face. It showed yellow in the lantern's light, as if memory, too, brought fevers.

"Frankly, Mr. Barnaby," I said in a voice of some bewilderment and not a little revulsion, "I'm surprised that you would tell me such a thing. It seems—"

"Like a family secret what wants keeping?" He laughed, but it was the first time I heard spite in the man's voice. He collected my brush from me. "Oh, you'll learn more, I expects, sir. Me governor always said, 'The first lie's never the last, so don't tell the first one and all's well.' "

He looked at me with more candor than the length of our acquaintance recommended. "Anyways, sir, Barnaby B. Barnaby ain't a bad judge of men. And you've got eyes in your head, as a fellow can see, and ears wide open behind 'em. I don't imagine you was sent down here by chance, sir. No, you're like meself, begging your pardon, sir. All suited to root things out. For other men think you less than you are and let down their guard. Wounds the feelings, sir, but it do help a fellow get by." He picked up the lantern. "Shall we go then, sir? You'll want a bit of a wash before your supper."

And we went out, saddlebags over our shoulders and blanket roll in my hand. Not halfway to the great house, I smelled the ripeness of a good kitchen at work. The fragrance was as lush in the nose as the sunset had been in the eyes.

"Auntie Dee's a splendid cook," Barnaby told me. "Eat like the Prince of Wales on holiday, you will."

After a few paces, the remark registered. "And you, Mr. Barnaby?"

"Oh, I'll eat even better, sir. For I'll be in the kitchen. Wouldn't be fitting for me to eat with the gentlemen. Master William wouldn't fancy it. Though Master Francis don't mind."

I could not reply. For his world was not mine. Just as, if the Confederates had their way, his country would not be mine. I had much to think on.

As we approached the lighted windows of the great house, he said, almost idly, "Sometimes I likes the Negro more than I does me own race, sir. Excepting Master Francis, of course. Knocks me down, it does, how your black fellow can laugh, sir. Whip him in the morning, and he'll laugh at the world that night. Finds his joys, he does. Where the likes of you and me wouldn't have sense to look." He paused. "I don't say he's as good as you or me, sir. Not on principle. But if suffering's the path to salvation, sir, if the church folk are right about that, then he's holier than priest or pope or parson. I'll take me leave here, sir. Have the lantern, for Barnaby knows his way. You'll want to go round by the front door."

I made my protestations, but he would not be dissuaded. When our hands touched at the lantern's handle, I saw his up-lit face and somber eyes. He lowered his voice:

"You find them what killed the Negroes. Find the guilty party, sir. It cries for justice till the stars could weep." He released the lantern. "There was better among them Africans than some what sits high at the table." He ruffled his shoulders and jigged up his belly and swallowed his earnestness down. "Begging your pardon, sir, but Barnaby B. Barnaby had to have his proper say. Mum's the word hereafter."

I detained him a moment longer, though I knew his supper called.

"May I ask, sir, what your middle initial stands for?"

"For 'Barnaby,' sir. After me governor's governor. Him what was a soldier. Anything else, sir?"

.   .   .

I BLEW OUT THE LANTERN and set it down, then opened the front door. And got a devil of a fright. A creature of surpassing ugliness, the size of a gnome, shot from a chair beside the staircase and darted down the hall. Female it was, judging by what little sense I could make of the dress and shape, and black as a burnt-up sausage. She was a ragged thing, worse than a tinker's widow, and bent. With matted hair like an Indian Sadoo fellow.

Vanishing, she left me in lamplit opulence. I am no judge of furnishings, as my Mary Myfanwy has given me to understand, but I have seen the private apartments of a ranee's palace before the boys of the regiment stripped them bare. Shady Grove had no such wealth as that, but wealth it had enough for any American.

Every item gave a sense of newness, of having been made, or at least bought, within the past few years. The furniture was dark and weighty, the tables topped with marble. In the room off to my right, blue-velvet couches and chairs sat on display, plush as a fancy man's promises. The lamps lit paintings of less than Christian subjects, and Orient carpets tricked the eye with color. Only the draperies seemed unfinished, for their heavy damask ends and tassled frills puddled over the floor in want of trimming. Though not as large, the place put me in mind of Mr. Cawber's Philadelphia mansion.

Before I could take in more, the high-dressed Negro fellow reappeared, stepping through a doorway at the end of the hall.

"Major Jones," he said, approaching me, "may I show you to your room, sir?" He looked me over, but his face did not betray the impression he received. Nodding gently at my saddlebags, he asked, "May I relieve you of your burden, sir?"

Before I knew it, he had the leather pouches in his hand.

"We have tried to anticipate your requirements, sir," he continued, "but if anything is found wanting, you have only to ring the bell." He smelled of toilet water like a white man. "The gentlemen will gather in the library in half an hour, sir. Just there, the second door along."

He positioned himself at the foot of the staircase and gestured, ever so slightly, for me to precede him.

I laid my hand on the banister and placed my cane, all set to climb. But I wanted to learn as much of the place as I could as swiftly as possible and I began with the Negro.

"You are Mr. Samson, I believe?"

"Simply 'Samson,' sir. The 'Mr.' is . . . superfluous."

"Samson, there was a woman waiting in the hall when I come in. A small woman, see. She rushed off. To alert you, I expect. Would she be this Aunt Dee I hear of?"

His brows climbed up in a startled look. Then a smile threatened his aplomb. "No, sir. That was Bridie. If she annoys you, you must tell me immediately, sir. But I am keeping you from your room, sir."

Perhaps he had to help out in the kitchen and wanted me off his hands. I went up as he wished, though I climbed more awkwardly than usual, for the long day's ride had stiffened my leg. I would have liked to ask him further questions, but was unsure of the propriety. Anyway, I was anxious enough for a wash, though it would have to be quick, with a proper scrub later. I did not want to keep my host or the supper waiting.

My clothing was khaki with dust, the very color of the gray-tan uniforms issued us the year before the Mutiny. I looked a disgrace next to the immaculate Negro and regretted not brushing myself off and giving my coat a good shake before coming inside.

The room in which I was to sleep was not so fancy as some I have seen since, but it was a handsome step up from the pen in which I recently had spent ten nights waiting to hang. The chamber was got up proper and dark, with a great canopy bed fit for a viscount. A table lamp and two candles under storm shades gave me light.

"Captain Barclay asks that you make yourself at home, sir. The water in the pitcher is fresh." I marked the blue and white wash-up set. Beside it lay a stack of Turkey towels. Samson touched a cord hanging from the ceiling by the bed. When he had my eye, he gave it a delicate tug and a faint tinkle answered. "The bell, sir. May I assist in any further way?"

I thanked the fellow and sent him along, then peeled down to my shirt and poured a basin of water. Oh, lovely it felt on my face. Lavender soap there was, and a brush for the clothing, and square-cut rags for the cleaning of shoes. The bed wanted someone to drop himself on it, I will tell you. But I did not indulge, not even for a minute, for reclining before the proper hour breeds sloth. A Christian man sits upright until bedtime.

I cannot tell you how fine it was to be in that room, though. Do not misunderstand me, I would not have traded the least corner of my bedroom back in Pottsville for all these Southron luxuries. But the fellow lies who claims to like no comforts.

I hurried along, for courtesy's sake. And supper was a not unpleasant thought. Kitchen smells twined up the stairs and slithered beneath the door.

In the event, I was the first to reach the library. Half of an hour in the South does not mean what it does in colder climes. I leaned upon my cane and took my bearings. Bookcases filled one wall and half of another. A fancy liquor jug and glasses sat on a table in the middle of the room, kept company by a sugar bowl and a brimming pitcher. The day's thirst was upon me and I nearly helped myself to a glass of the water. But gentlemen must wait for an invitation, and my Mary Myfanwy would not have me be rude.

I took me to the books instead.

The first shelves I glanced over contained works on agricultural matters and the law. Then I passed to books with Latin titles. Next come a row I took to be Greek by the queerness of the letters. Raines had described our host's father as a learned man and I wondered if these volumes were not his, although the mansion seemed to be the son's property. A family is complex as a contest of nations.

Then I spied the deviltry. Books in French they were. Now the tongue of the French is the easiest of heathen languages to recognize because they take perfectly good words and make a mess of them. For example, the first set of Frenchy books on which I fastened stood all in a row, bound in leather, with fancy gold imprinted on their spines. And what was the title of that line of massive volumes? *Histoire de ma vie.* Now it doesn't take a fancy education to figure out that this *histoire* is just the way your lust-befuddled Frenchman, agitated by his vices, molests the good word "history."

The young fellows had not yet appeared. And I fear I gave in to temptation. Look you. I have always wondered what a French book might be like. Twas only curiosity, see. And I assumed that any row of books with "history" in their title must be as moral a literary matter as a Frenchman would bother to print. So, with the house a great silence around me, I drew out a volume from the middle of the set.

The author appeared to be an aristocratic fellow, with one of those great long names they have. Jacques Casanova de Seingalt.

With a deep breath, I opened the covers and fanned through the pages.

The first illustration stopped me. If history it was, twas the history of Sodom. The unchastened moral disarray of the figures distressed me beyond words. Now I am an old bayonet and have seen the human figure disrobed, forgive my bluntness. But never did I view it in such postures. The very geometries alarmed me. So much that I stared at the plate for a long time.

"Glad to meet a Yankee with a taste for literature," a voice said at my elbow.

I swirled about in horror, slamming shut the book. Twas Captain Barclay in the doorway. Propped in his rolling chair. The book had so dismayed me that I had not heard him approach.

"I . . . French . . . wondered . . . never . . ."

"Used to be a favorite of mine," the invalid said, smiling and wheeling himself closer. The reek of ammonia pinched the air, despite his lavish use of cologne water. "Nowadays it just unsettles me."

"You are developing morally, sir."

His laugh smelled of whisky. I would hear his laugh again, but it was never so genuine as that howl.

Lieutenant Raines stepped in, dusted off and with his buttons polished. His hair was wetted down.

I thrust the book back into its place on the shelf. My embarrassment served me right, I saw, for meddling with French matters.

"The major and I were just discussing literature," Barclay said, as he spun his chair about. He glanced back toward me, winking.

ten

*R*aines positioned himself by the liquor.

"Fix you a toddy, Billy?"

"Look after the major here. A good book gives a man a thirst. Major? You take your whisky clean or dirty?"

"I have taken the Pledge, sir," I explained. "Though I would pour myself a glass of water and be glad of it."

My host's features tightened. Though confined to his rolling chair, he seemed to look down at me. "Sure now. To every man his humor. Isn't that right, Drake?"

"That's right, Billy," Raines said. He smiled, but wariness flickered in his eyes.

Barclay settled into a look of amusement. The way a fellow stops adjusting his hat once he finds the sit comfortable. His face gleamed. Had we faced an audience, all eyes would have been on him. Twas a sorrowful case, no question, of a man who might have been much. For he possessed the appeal that binds men to a fellow even as that fellow betrays them. He might have made a splendid politician.

But now he smelled of the body's baseness. Despite his generous use of scent, he reeked of waste and whisky.

"To the major, after his pleasure. But pour my poison neat." Our host eased his chair back over the Turkey carpet. His vision encompassed both of us, though his interest leaned my way.

"Drake here tells me you're looking to find out who killed my niggers. That a fact?"

My escort passed me a glass. Twas sized for spirits and would not quench a thirst.

"I am sent to look into the matter, Captain Barclay." Relieved I was that our talk had left those French matters behind.

He smirked at Raines, then gave a brief whistle. His pitch was not true.

"The Yankees sure do love our niggers," Barclay said. "Isn't that right? Love 'em till they get up real close. Then it's a different horse race." Raines handed him his whisky, with some care. Barclay paused to drink. "Those generals of yours looking for something nasty to spread over their newspapers up North? All about how we Southrons aren't content to whip the poor, suffering Negro, but like to kill them and chop them into pieces now and then?"

I thought of the simple girl with the battered skull.

"No, sir. It is the opposite, see. Washington wishes to put the matter to rest. Before there is more sensation. And more hatred."

Barclay coughed out a small, dismissive laugh. "No matter who wins this war, Major, we'll be hating each other a hundred years from now. Born to hate each other, and that's a fact. We're separate peoples. Always will be. Lincoln should've had the sense to let us go. To let us be. Could have saved us all this . . . all this . . . Drake, you draw me another one of these, would you?" He held out his emptied glass.

I sipped my water. Unwilling to be riled. For duty must not founder on our emotions. The curious thing was that his tone of voice carried no message of attack upon my person, but remained genteel. In contrast to his words.

"Do you have suspicions, Captain Barclay?"

"Suspicions?"

"As to who murdered your Negroes?"

He slumped a bit. Propping himself on his elbows, as if the only bones left him were in his arms. I tried not to look. For it was a troubling business. A young and handsome man plumped on his hips in a drain pan, with his trouser legs cut off and double-seamed. He did not even have a stump of thigh.

"No damned idea," he said. And out of all he said to me, I believed those three blunt words. His eyes strayed as he spoke and it gave him a lost, tormented look that had little to do with his injuries.

Abrupt as vengeance, he laughed. Looking at Raines, whose drink was hardly touched. "Damn me, Drake. You know what I was about to say?" He cackled again, all darkness. "I was about to say how, if I did have the least notion who killed those niggers, I'd shoot them down like I would a mad dog." He left a space for our thoughts while he put his glass to his lips. "I guess they'd have to come up to the porch and volunteer themselves to be shot. Isn't that right, now?"

He did not wait for an answer, but addressed me. "Major, I hope you find out who did it. Sure now. I hope you find them and hang them. Wish I could help. But I'm strained to figure it out myself. Don't see where there's any sense or profit in killing run-aways then cutting them up into little pieces. That true, by the way? That's what I'm told. Cut up into little bits. Butchered like hogs. The women . . ."

He shifted his weight. I thought how uncomfortable it must be for him in his pan.

"Hell, I don't even know why they run off," he continued. "Our niggers always had the best treatment anywhere around. You just ask old Drake here." A lock of fair hair draped the cripple's brow. "I don't for the life of me know why they run off," he repeated, in a tone that hinted reflection behind its bristle. "Some passing nigger fancy, I reckon. All stirred up by talk of freedom and other nonsense."

"If you don't mind, Captain Barclay," I said, "I would like to put a few questions to your remaining Negroes. Perhaps they know something."

"Sure now. Don't you think I've asked them?"

"Of course, sir. I did not mean to offend. But look you. Sometimes a body knows more than he sees that he knows. And must be coaxed to the knowledge of his knowing."

He looked at me with the eyes of a coiled snake. "Well, you ask anything you want. See where it gets you. They're nothing but dumb animals."

I noticed Samson standing in the door. The servant let the last words settle, then said, "Gentlemen, the table is prepared." He stepped aside to let us pass with the grace of a Hindoo prince.

But Barclay did not wheel toward the archway. Not yet. He rolled over to me and smiled affably. "Perhaps, Major, we should postpone further discussion of this business until the morning? To rescue what conviviality we may?"

"As you wish, sir."

Of a sudden, he held out his hand. "Sure now. I haven't even welcomed you properly." I took his hand, though I wondered at its deeds. The flesh was cold and damp, but his grip was crushing. "Drake told me he broke bread with a mutual acquaintance of ours. With Dr. Tyrone."

"I count the man a friend, sir. And, indeed, he gave me a message for—"

"I must beg your indulgence, Major. Never thought I'd willingly see another Yankee in this house. But you are welcome, sir. As a friend of Dr. Tyrone's. He saved . . . what life I have." He relaxed his hand, but his stare was as firm as his grip had been. "He's a brave man, your Dr. Tyrone."

"He has said the same of you, Captain. He said you were the most—"

He broke away and wheeled toward the door. "Mustn't keep Auntie Dee's fixings waiting any longer. Isn't that right, Samson?"

The tall Negro bowed an inch. "Indeed, sir."

"Captain Barclay," I called. "Before I forget the matter. Dr. Tyrone suggests you visit a Dr. Smithson. In New York. After the war."

Barclay looked back at me with eyes I could not read. "Do thank him for me. When you see him again. But it strikes me," he said, "that I've already met up with one doctor too many." His smile was a study in manners, but no more. "Now allow me to offer you what hospitality our reduced circumstances afford. You all come on now. Hear?"

.   .   .

THE SILVER SHONE in the light of the candles and lamps. Twas a banquet set out for three. At the end of a long table.

The smells were of supper in Paradise.

I paused on the threshold. For the truth was I had never sat at a place set out so grand. Now I have my proper manners, and know which hand should hold the knife and which the fork, but there is something daunting to one who has been poor when great wealth is spread before him. I feared I would do some foolish thing and lessen the regard of my companions. I felt . . . as though my place was back with Barnaby, in the kitchen. With my own kind. This was America, despite the war's disagreements, and such differences should not have mattered. But it is hard not to feel small in this life, and I do not mean the smallness of the body.

My host saw me looking at the silver, but did not understand my gaze. For he had been born to judge and would not comprehend the fear of judgement.

I would have liked a simpler supper, see.

"Samson insisted," my host said, gesturing toward a gleaming tureen. "Had to show you gentlemen proper Shady Grove hospitality. Isn't that right, Samson?"

The old fellow nodded serenely. "Indeed, sir."

Barclay grinned and wheeled himself to the head of the table. "Fact is, Samson's proud of that silver. Likes to show it off. Picked it out himself in New Orleans. Made sure it was all delivered in time for the wedding." He turned to Raines, still smiling. But, then, a skull is said to smile. "Samson wanted to put it all on display one last time before we bury it. Which we're like to have to do, unless old Beauregard finds his manhood and makes a fight of it. That perfumed dandy aiming to fight, Drake? He worth a damn with old Johnston gone?"

"I'm not in the general's confidence," Raines said, with a too-obvious glance in my direction.

"Oh, hell, Drake. The Yankees already got it figured out that Borey's no fighter. Though he's like to talk them to death, given the chance. Major Jones, you come on over here and sit on my right. You're the evening's guest of honor. In Dr. Tyrone's stead, say."

I stepped along a sideboard glittering with platters and their hoods. The polished metal showed me queer reflections. The way a tired mind will twist a fact. At my seat, I propped my cane on the next chair, ready to give both my bad leg and the good one a rest, for the day had been long and hard.

As I made to sit down I saw her. And kept to my feet in wonder.

Above an unlit hearth a portrait hung. The ceiling was high and it needed to be, for the painting was big as life and full in length. Twas of a woman, brown-haired, with pale skin. The artist put no roses on her cheeks, but gentler petals, orchids shaded pink. Slender she was, in her blue silk dress, and formidable in her beauty. Her eyes peered down in a challenge. Alert and thoughtful she looked. And properly demanding. The sort of woman who will fill the life of the man she chooses. If he has the courage to let her.

"My wife," Barclay said. I did not turn to look at him, for her aspect canceled manners. I wish the word "ravishing" were not a common adjective for beauties, for there is no word truer to describe her. "The former Emily Stone. Of Boston, Major. A *true* Yankee. Who condescended to marry Mr. William Barclay, late of

Natchez, and now in retirement at Shady Grove. Isn't that right, Drake?"

"Billy . . ."

I thought I understood his sorrow then. Twas greater than the loss of legs and other parts. I forced myself to look away from her, to sit me down and behave properly toward my host.

"My condolences, sir," I told him. "The loss must have come as a shock."

A succession of emotions shaped and reshaped his face. So swiftly that I could not fix one mood. Then he laughed out loud. Looking at Raines.

"Drake? What the hell and damnation you been telling him?" He snapped his head to me, eyes bright. But not merry. "Old Drake's been putting things delicately, I expect. Drake always likes to put things delicately. He's your true Southron gentleman." Barclay grunted. "What did he tell you, Major? Or what did he 'imply'? See, our Drake here likes to 'imply.' He finds plain telling a tad vulgar. I take it he 'implied' that Emily was dead?"

I was confused and could not recall my escort's words with certainty. "No longer with us" had been his phrase, if memory served me right. But the suggestion had been mortality. That had been clear.

"Samson? Pour me out some whisky. And fresh up Old Drake's glass there." My host straightened himself and took a fortifying breath. "Well, she's not dead. Take more than me and Mississippi to kill Emily. Isn't that right, Drake?" He tried to force himself back to jocularity. With a carved smile. "She left me. Went back to Boston. Didn't like the South, after all. And didn't much like me, either."

Raines leaned in. "Billy, you—"

"Be quiet, Drake. Hold your peace. This is my affair and I'm explaining something to the major. No, sir. My wife didn't like the way we did things. Came down here with all that claptrap in her head about the torments of the Negro. Didn't know a damned thing about it. And didn't like what she learned, because it wasn't what she expected. Wasn't all as clear and easy as it looked from Old North Church, I suppose." He took a drink of whisky that half drained his glass. He did not so much as grimace at the swallowing. "Sure now. Old Beauregard didn't fire the first shot at Sumter. The man's tardy. *Slow.* Emily's one Yankee didn't wait to be fired on. She shot first. Up and left long before Mississippi ratified the secession." He glanced at the splendor around us. "Nothing could hold her."

Now you will find it strange, but I was relieved to learn the last bit. For I had feared she left him after his injury, when he was no longer the man whom she had married. Men and women do ferocious things. Marriage is not only for our pleasure, though some think it so these days.

"What day is it, Drake?" he asked, turning so suddenly he almost lost his balance in his catch pan.

"It's Sunday, Billy."

"No. What day of the month? What month, for that matter? I lose track."

Raines thought. I knew the date, of course, but would not interfere as I had done with General Beauregard and his staff officers in the matter of Lieutenant Raines. When we seem to know too much we learn too little.

"I believe it's the twentieth of April," my escort said.

"April. April twentieth. Then she'll still be in Boston for a good while yet." He looked at me. "She'll go to Newport for the summer, though. With that steel-nosed family of hers. They go despite the New York people, Major. She's not a snob, you see. Not Emily. She has the Yankee democratic spirit." He drained another glass. "What about you, Major? Do you have the democratic spirit?"

"If you mean—"

"Do you have that Yankee democratic spirit to tell other men what's right and what's wrong? What they should do and what they shouldn't? To care more for some prettied up idea of the nigger than for the reality of a husband?" He smiled. And calmed. "But I forget myself. I'm being a poor host, and my father would not approve. Isn't that right, Drake?" He looked up at the portrait with the pure hatred that is a continuation of love. "Any more than Emily would approve." He chuckled. "Proper behavior is important, if society is to function. Not just appearances, though that contents most folks. No, sir, our behavior must be immaculate. And I have been keeping you gentlemen from your supper. Samson? Would you serve? I believe we're ready now."

.   .   .

I WAS CAREFUL OF MY TABLE MANNERS, although I ate with relish and had seconds. For in a war you never know the composition of your next meal, no matter the apparent safety of your surroundings. My host ate little, picking like a lady come for tea. But he drank steadily. It did not seem to impair him, but only put a harshness in his voice, as if the liquor stripped away its coating.

Ham there was, indeed, and chicken, too. Those meats played king and queen to a court of vegetables, and there were biscuits better than any I had eaten. Not what we Welsh call biscuits, mind, but puffing little breads you coat with butter.

At last I took my napkin from my neck, for I could eat no more. My belly was slapping full.

"Captain Barclay," I said to my host, "you keep a good kitchen, you do."

My host's lips flicked and failed to restore his smile. "Sure now. You hear that, Samson? You tell Auntie Dee she's pleased her another Yankee."

"Yes, sir."

"And fetch the French brandy. Clear this all away and get the brandy."

"Yes, sir."

"Samson?"

"Yes, sir?"

"You know what this Yankee major journeyed all the way down here for? All the way down here from Washington? You know what he's doing down here? He wants to know who went and killed our niggers. Ain't no business left the Yankees don't count as their business."

"Indeed, sir." The black fellow shifted plates of scraps to a silver tray. He reached for Barclay's. But my host leaned over his plate as if protecting it, balancing with his elbows on the tablecloth.

"What do you think about that, Samson? About Major Jones here? Prying into nigger killings and such things?"

"Shall I finish clearing, sir?"

Barclay looked up. With much the same expression he had loosed on the portrait. "Answer me, goddamn you. What do you think about this Yankee chasing after our dead niggers?"

"It's not my place to think about it, sir."

At that, Barclay smiled and sat back. The Negro captured the plate.

"Hear that now, Major? Samson's what you call a 'good nigger.' Finest nigger either side of the river, in my opinion. Understands which side his bread's buttered on. Doesn't go thinking he's a white man and getting himself all swelled up and confused. Do you, Uncle Samson?"

"No, sir."

Barclay leaned toward me, balancing himself on the edge of the table again. "Sure now. That's why Samson didn't run off when all the rest of them did. Or Auntie Dee. A smart nigger likes things just the way they are. Doesn't want trouble." He smiled his broadest smile of the evening. It was the first time he had showed an expanse of teeth and I saw they were not of the quality of his other features.

"Wasn't always that way, though. Was it, Uncle Samson? Now you just hold on a minute. Those dishes can wait. I'm trying to teach our guest something about the reality of things down here."

He twisted back to me. "See, Major, Samson wasn't always this well-behaved. No, sir. He was one bad-tempered buck nigger when he was young. Had a mouth on him. Always sneaking off for a lie-out. Stirring up the women in the quarters. Fancied himself a fighting man. Even caught him with a razor once, I hear tell. Yes, sir. Samson took some breaking."

His eyes were cold as stones on a winter's day. "Now you think about my daddy, and the grief that caused him. My daddy wasn't a whipping man. Not as a rule. No, sir. Hated to bring out the cat. He was more in the nigger-lover vein. Like Emily. Or young Drake here. Not that Drake loves a nigger the way she's meant to be loved." He slapped toward Raines, but his hand only clattered the table's remaining fixtures. "Couldn't even get that boy to go under the hill in Natchez, let alone down the hollow for a change of luck. Our young Galahad here." Barclay braced himself up straight, defying the gravity of the liquor. "My daddy wasn't a whipping man, but he sure whipped the hell out of Samson. And it did him a world of good. How many times you get yourself whipped, Uncle Samson?"

"I didn't count, sir."

Barclay laughed out loud. "See there? Nigger can't even count how many times he's been whipped. But he wants to run off." He smacked his hand down on the table and grimaced what was meant to be a smile. "And to where? You think he's going to be welcome up there in Boston when he shows up with ten thousand other niggers and twice that many shit-ass brats? Just run off and get himself killed is all he's good for. But not our Samson here. He got sense, for a nigger. Got it beat into him. Only way it takes hold. He knows which side his bread's buttered on. Samson, where's that brandy? I told you to fetch the brandy."

"Yes, sir," the Negro said, with his customary bow and no hint of emotion on his face.

"Well, you just go and—" Barclay's torso quivered and he winced. In seconds, the smell of excrement pierced the air.

With a look of rage, my host wheeled himself from the table. Banging into furniture along his way. A silver bowl, not empty, crashed to the floor.

"Samson," Barclay called. "Come here. I need you."

.   .   .

I WOULD HAVE LIKED TO SPREAD MY ARMS and clutch the night air to me. Sweet it was. And chill enough to fresh a fellow up and make his movements a pleasure. After the heaviness of the house, twas lovely as a swim in a river to wander the grounds.

I stopped and closed my eyes, drinking the dark sky down.

I had excused myself from the table before young Raines could start apologizing for his friend. I was sour and did not want to hear a word. I will not insist the Negro's emotions are as highly developed as our own, but Barclay's treatment of the old retainer had repelled me. The Negro is a man, and all men feel. I know we must allow for the weight of suffering on the next fellow's shoulders, and Barclay had endured much. Still, he seemed to me at least as great a producer of pain as he was a consumer of it, and I could not like him.

Nor would I grant him the plaint of too much drink. Alcohol is never an excuse. For drunkenness does not turn men to monsters. It only frees the monsters that we are.

My contrary mood come from more than my embarrassment at being caught with the French book, so do not think that I am shifting blame. And do not tell me that a crippled man must be indulged. We are all crippled, if we have lived at all. My leg is not the worst-shaped thing about me. The worst things are inside.

And what of you? I do not mean an insult. But are you free of scars? Who among us bears no imperfection? Would you abuse a wife or child or servant, blaming the deed on the pain of childhood spankings? Past sufferings do not excuse our vices. The war that matters is our daily life. Our cause must be to rise above our injuries. We must engage to keep our persons upright, and not blame Joseph when we, his brothers, fail.

Barclay seemed to me no more than a schoolyard bully off his luck, and I did not wonder that his wife had left him. I only wondered that such a woman as the one in that painting would have married him in the first place. But no young woman is wise, nor young man, either. I fear, though, that I was unfair to Raines. My ructious mood spilled over onto him, and he had done nothing.

But look you. Perhaps that was the problem. Raines had done nothing. He sat and let his old friend rant and rave.

I had left him in the dining room with the portrait of Barclay's wife.

Resuming my stroll, I stopped again almost immediately. Turning at a sound. It was the girl. Paddycakes. I saw her in the moonlight Heaven parsed us. Her eyes shone as if lamplit. Then she scrambled off into the garden, pale rags fading from view. Perhaps she had believed young Raines about the appetites of Yankees.

Was this war for them? Or was it for us? Was the Negro but another excuse to unleash the Devil in men? Did we fight to preserve the Union? Or to impose it on a land grown alien? Such questions were too large for me that night. And, yet, they gnawed, disguised as petty pains.

I heard another stirring in the undergrowth. Paddycakes, perhaps. Or an animal. The Southland was as rich in life as in hatred. The rustling ceased the moment I looked round.

I found a marble bench blue in the moonlight and sat me down, new cane at rest by my side. My eyes had learned the night well enough to trace neglected garden plots. As long and straight as graves they were, with their former beauty ruined. The trellises might have been a line of gallows.

No. That is morbid. Twas a place for soft hands to help flowers, the domain of Woman, who spites one rose and bids another flourish. I wondered if Barclay's wife had shaped this yard? His wife, or her desires? Or a young man's notions of a woman's wants?

I had a good muchness to ponder. To what degree was my interest in Shady Grove and its inhabitants no higher than a gossip's curiosity? Which hints had to do with murdered slaves? And which with private sorrows? Could the two matters be cleaved? Was I a seeker after truth, serving the cause of Justice? Or just a small man peeking in a window?

But we are flesh. My thoughts slipped from my duty, and soon I sat dreaming, homesick, of wife and son. The reverie summoned pity for young Barclay. Is there a harder fate than a loveless life? A man may do without his legs, but not without affection. We need someone to give to, that is the soul of it. My joy was at my hearth, in honest embraces and fatherly hopes for John. A simple meal with loved ones beats a feast shared with a king. I longed for Pottsville, for our small house and its certainties. It seemed to me there was no deeper happiness than to sit of an evening beside my Mary Myfanwy. With John asleep upstairs, as safe as life allows.

All is fragility. Love is robust, but our small lives are not. It does not take a war to break a heart. We smother like those flowers in the brambles. We are clipped back before we start to bloom.

I fear I come near weeping.

The night birds were not those I knew, nor were the smells that ghosted through the air. I was alone in a foreign place. Even in India, comrades had brushed my shoulder. Here I was alone. And I felt no courage. Only the fear of failure in my duty. Perhaps it is a soldier's way of thinking. Regretting choices made, but marching on.

I told myself that each small justice matters, but what mattered to me was far away that night.

I heard a snap behind me and I turned. The figure of a man stirred through the dark, blocking a window's light, then revealing it again. He strode toward me with a purpose.

Twas Samson. I rose. Such is my habit. Though I am told we must not rise for servants.

"Excuse me, sir," he said as he approached. "I regret any disturbance."

"Not at all," I said. For the disturbance had been within me, not without. How we are glad of another human presence when we feel glum.

"Captain Barclay regrets the haste of his withdrawal, sir, and wishes to know if you have any desires."

I had desires enough for a thousand men. But let that bide.

"No, sir. I thank you. As I do Captain Barclay."

I thought that would be all, just fancy courtesy. But the Negro did not seem of a mind to go.

"May I be bold, sir?" he said at last.

"Go on."

"Sir . . . Mr. B. describes you as a Christian. He believes you to be a good and trustworthy man, although your acquaintance has been short."

"Mr. Barnaby's a good fellow himself," I said.

"Yes, sir. A magnificent fellow, if I may be permitted the judgement. But . . . may I ask, sir . . . *are* you a Christian?"

Twas a question I took seriously, though posed by a Negro. I took a drink of air and gave it back. "I call myself a Methodist," I told him, "and would like to think myself a proper Christian. But there are times when I do find it hard."

"Yes, sir," the fellow said. The moon and the windows of the house were behind him and his face was a puddle of shadows around the wet glow of his eyes. "It *is* hard. Sometimes I think being a Christian is harder than being a slave, sir. The vineyard of the Lord is a harder row than any in a cotton field."

I agreed, but said nothing. I find it hard to speak of faith out loud, beyond the simplest affirmations. I can peel off a proverb now and then, but do not know the words to speak of souls. Perhaps that's why a Welshman loves a hymn. It lets him sing the faith he feels but cannot put in words to tell his neighbor. I wonder at the faith of those who chatter.

"I overheard, sir," Samson continued, "your conversation with Captain Barclay. Even the faithful servant cannot shut his ears. Do I understand that you wish to put certain questions? And that Captain Barclay has approved?"

"There is true."

"Perhaps you have a question for me now?"

I had so many questions I could not see a clear way to begin. An insect nipped my wrist and fled my slap.

"My questions . . . may be indelicate," I said.

"I have not enjoyed a delicate life, sir."

No. I supposed that he had not. Still, it is hard to ask certain things of a man. A Welshman is born with a healthy curiosity, but he is not mean.

"All right, then. When Captain Barclay questioned you during the dinner . . . he said you were too intelligent to run off. In fact, you did *not* run off with the others. Why not? And why didn't this Aunt Dee go? She is your wife, I take it?"

"She is my wife. To the degree such things are permitted. I believe she is my wife in the eyes of Heaven, sir."

"But why didn't you run off?"

Twas his turn to sigh. "Oh, we were tempted, Major. My Dee and I were tempted to go. Though my desire was perhaps the stronger. My wife's world is her kitchen, sir. She clings to what she knows. But who would not want to taste the air of freedom? Just once, before he dies? To stand on soil where no man has a right to call him to serve, or to whip him when he comes too slowly? To choose whom he should love . . ."

He shifted to face me directly. "Perhaps it will amuse you, sir. But I have always wanted to go into a shop and buy myself a book. With money of my own. Not to fetch one for a master. But to choose and pay and hold *my* book in *my* hands. I wanted to go

north, sir. To follow that selfish dream. But we couldn't bring ourselves to it."

"Why not, man?"

"Because of Captain Barclay, sir. We had almost made the decision to go with the others. Then Captain Barclay returned. With his
flesh so cruelly punished. He cannot do the simplest things for himself, sir. We could not abandon him."

"You feel affection for the man, then?" I know such things
occur. The beaten wife clings to the cruel husband, and the soldier
gives his life for men who despise him, laying his love at the feet of
thoughtless officers.

"No, sir. No affection, sir. It would be easier if we did. We
longed to escape. At least I did. And my wife had warmed to the
thought. But, after Captain Barclay returned, my Dee and I decided
we could not go. God has sent us that broken boy as our cross, and
it is our duty to carry him until the end. Had we gone with the others, sir, how could we have described ourselves as Christians?" I
thought I marked a gentling on his features, but the darkness might
have fooled me. "And you see what happened, sir? We did our
Christian duty, and lived. Had we fled it, we would have died with
the others. There are rewards on earth, as well as in Heaven, and
we have been blessed. And do not be too hard on Captain Barclay,
sir. He has suffered deeply," the slave said.

"And the others? Those who ran away? Was it a simple flight to
freedom, then?"

"Hardly simple, sir. But yes, if I take your meaning. They heard
the preaching and knew of the approach of your army. They
thought the time had come to seek their freedom."

" 'Preaching,' Samson? And what preaching would that be?"

"The Reverend Mr. Hitchens, sir. Mr. Will Hitchens. He has
erected a tabernacle in the wilderness. He is a Negro, sir, and once
was a slave. He went north, but heard the call and returned to us.
He is a lamp, sir, and our succor."

"And this Mr. Hitchens lures slaves from their masters?"

"Oh, no, sir. No luring is required."

"But he encourages Negroes to run away?"

"He encourages them to embrace the Word. To proclaim the Kingdom. To love one another." He drew himself back. "Perhaps that sounds common enough, sir. The Christian message un-adorned. But Mr. Hitchens is different. He has found Grace. The people go to him of their own accord. He would not take from Caesar what is Caesar's."

"Did the Negroes from Shady Grove go to him?"

"Yes, sir. I believe they did."

"And were massacred?"

"That has not been explained, sir. I'm certain the Reverend Mr. Hitchens would like to know what happened himself. Perhaps you will meet him."

"It seems unlikely."

"Much is unlikely, sir. Some say we have come to the end of days."

I dandled my cane. "I . . . have no wish to offend you, my good man," I said, more testily than I wished. "But I have heard a bit more about the 'end of days' than I care to. And though I would not call myself a well-read man, I have made my way through what books I could. It seems to me that many a man has preached this 'end of days,' from olden times until now. Whenever things go awry, see. In plague or war or what have you. Instead of rolling up their sleeves, they call for a messiah. It makes of Jesus no more than the world's mechanic." I did not want to tax the poor Negro's brain with complications, but I felt the need to have my say on this. "Now I will tell you, Samson: I think the Lord will come when he is ready, not before. And none of our wishing or worrying will hurry him. A man should just live proper, do his work, and not go bothering things."

"Yes, sir. Still, we never know when we may be called."

"There is true. But let that bide. I have another question."

"Perhaps we may be called in unusual ways," the Negro went

on, ignoring my attempt to close the matter. "I hear this Mr. Hitchens is a remarkable man, sir. If ever he calls you, perhaps you should go."

"Well, we will wait and see," I said to content him. "Now there is a delicate business I must put to you. Even more delicate than the first, perhaps."

"Yes, sir?"

"Who is Lucy? Or should I say, 'Who *was* Lucy?'"

Now, you will say: "We know who Lucy was. This Abel Jones is slower than a sinner at the chapel door. We have the matter figured out long since." But I will tell you: Some things must be said aloud to make them real.

The Negro did not answer me. I did not need the sun to see his struggles.

"I do not look for disloyalty," I told him, slapping away another fly. "But the matter must be made plain. If we are to find the murderers in this, I must understand who is who."

"Lucy was a slave, sir."

"Yes. A slave here at Shady Grove. And she was among those murdered."

"It has been so rumored, sir."

"Samson, I have no wish to torment you. So I will speak the thing out. You have only to stop me when I am wrong. Let us begin. This Lucy was a slave girl. Young. And pretty. Beautiful, perhaps. And she had . . . admirers, let us say. Captain Barclay had . . . let us say that he was close to her. And, perhaps, Lieutenant Raines as well."

The Negro recoiled. He literally jumped back. "Oh, no, sir. Not Master Francis, sir. He would never force himself upon—" He stopped himself.

"Lucy . . . bore no love toward Captain Barclay?"

Again, the servant hesitated.

"I see," I told him. For I did. "She did not love him. But he, in his pride, barely noticed. Or believed she loved him. Or didn't even care. You do not need to speak, if I am right. What was it, then? He believed she loved him, I would guess. For he is proud. On his part, he convinced himself that his passion was uncontrollable. Or that he need not control it. That it was acceptable to indulge it."

The Negro muttered. Twas not a denial.

"He did not even pause when he married, did he?" I continued. "Or not for long. And his wife discovered the . . . the liaison. Did she not? That is why she left. Oh, perhaps there were other matters, as well. But that tie of the flesh drove her decision. She left him because she would not share him. Because, whether from pride or morality or human decency, she would not have him in the bed of a slave and in her bed, as well. Forgive me. That was indelicately put. Is there anything you wish to say, Samson?"

His head moved faintly from side to side. "There is nothing I need say, sir."

"And she left him. This Emily Stone. Emily Barclay. And he redoubled his attentions to the slave girl. Perhaps enraged. Even violent. Vengeful. Then he went off to war, only to come back with a broken body and a worsened temper. Perhaps the girl feared him. Despite his physical impairments. Perhaps there is more to passion than a straightforward animal act? Perhaps that animal act was the easiest of it for her, and she feared what must come in its absence? I only speculate, now. And I have become vulgar, I know it. But I am not one of these high gentlemen, Samson. I am only a small man sent to get the truth."

"There is . . . something more, sir. I admire your grasp, sir. Indeed, I wonder at it. But there is something more."

"Yes?" For I was at the end of my piercing of the thing.

"Lucy was married, sir. Not in a church, of course, for Captain Barclay would never have permitted it. He would have whipped the man to death. But *we* love, too, sir. And Lucy and Jase loved deeply. They were married back in the grove, sir. As Christian as the matter could be arranged."

"By this Mr. Hitchens?"

"No, sir. The matter was settled before he came. And there is more still, although it likely does not bear upon your quest, sir. Lucy had an admirer. A terribly fierce fellow. Another Shady Grove slave, sir. He was unhappy when Lucy wed. We feared blood, sir. But he only disappeared. Then . . . then he returned, sir. Not six weeks ago. A changed man, sir. With a message of salvation. He led the slaves to Mr. Hitchens. And then, so rumor has it, to their deaths. The whisper is that all of them perished. Lucy, her husband, her admirer . . ." The Negro's voice ached of a sudden. "He meant to lead them north, sir, to your army. But it was not to be."

"Do you know who killed them, Samson?"

"No, sir."

"Do you have a suspicion?"

"No, sir."

"Back to Lucy. And her husband. And this admirer. Captain Barclay knew nothing of this?"

"Oh, no, sir. His reaction would have been intemperate."

"But how could he . . ."

"How could he fail to see, sir? Of course, you wonder. It's as difficult for you to understand as it was for Miss Emily. Yet you have touched upon it yourself. It is pride. And, perhaps, not a little fear. The masters know nothing of what occurs in the quarters. Because, sir, the masters do not wish to know. It is the great struggle of their lives, sir, to avoid any evidence of our humanity. It is their cross, and they bear it with their eyes closed, from cradle to grave."

"But you believe that Captain Barclay loved the girl? This Lucy? Whatever his violence or wickedness?"

"We cannot see into another's heart, sir. But it appeared he loved her. Even desperately, perhaps. It is a thing not unheard of in this country. Though it is not a thing of which men speak. Not without resorting to pistols."

"So Captain Barclay didn't love his wife?"

Samson gave another visible start. "I would not say that, sir. Indeed, he seemed to love Miss Emily as much as such a man might love anyone or anything. He almost seemed to worship her." He spread a black sleeve through a veil of darkness. "All this was for her, sir. The grandeur of Shady Grove. All for her. I do believe he loved Miss Emily. Although it can be difficult, sir, to distinguish love from pride of possession. But . . . don't you think a man can love two women? And slight neither in his heart?"

This time it was myself who did not answer.

"I believe he loved the two of them," Samson continued. "And now he has lost them both. And much else, besides." He was a man of splendid posture. But now his silhouette had slumped, as if a great weariness had come over him, and I glimpsed a sliver of window light over his shoulder. Twas from an upper story, for the house was going to bed.

"Will there be anything else, sir?" he asked.

"No. Thank you, Samson. You have been helpful."

"Then may I say good-night, sir?" He began to turn away, but stopped. "Sir? If I do not presume too much . . . should you have the opportunity to meet the Reverend Mr. Hitchens, I hope you will seize it. I fear there is still vengeance in my heart. I would like to see justice done in these murders. Mortal justice."

"You believe this Mr. Hitchens might be of assistance?"

"I cannot say with certainty, sir. I am a limited man. But Mr. Hitchens was the last to see our people alive."

"And how would I find this Mr. Hitchens? This preacher fellow?"

For the first time, Samson's voice took on a hint of insincerity. "I do not know, sir. But perhaps he will find you. Good night, sir."

"Samson? Just a moment. I do have a last requirement."

"Yes, sir?"

"Show me where Mr. Barnaby has his bed."

.　　.　　.

I FEARED that I would need to wake the fellow, but he was reading a book by candlelight. In a meager room at the back of the house. He looked too great for any bed, protuberant and vast, and the quilt he had drawn up seemed but a dishcloth upon him. The window was open, but the air reeked of digestion.

He had not risen at my knock, for he likely thought it was Samson. When I stepped in at his bidding he looked surprised, then embarrassed.

He marked his place with a ribbon and closed the book.

"Anything wrong, then, sir? Anything wrong? Old Barnaby's the man to put it right." With a struggle, he rolled himself onto the edge of the bed, where he paused to gather the strength to gain his feet. He looked gray and hard used in the wavering light.

"Please," I said, "don't rise, Mr. Barnaby. I have but a question or two." I looked toward a lonesome wooden chair.

"Take yourself a seat then, sir. Be so kind, sir. For a day like this one do weary a body, don't it?"

I sat down. Wondering how to broach a matter of enormous sensitivity. "Reading, then?" I said to start our talking.

"I does love a book, sir."

"You read a great deal, Mr. Barnaby? A great many books, then?"

"Oh, I does and I don't, sir. I mean, Barnaby B. Barnaby's a reading man, when he's let the time for it. But I knows what I likes to read and reads it over, for I like my books dependable, sir. Once a fellow's found a book what's good enough, I don't see why he needs to waste time on another. 'Stick to the tried and true,' me governor always said."

Referring to the Bible, that might have been an enviable sentiment. But the book he had in hand did not look holy.

"And what book have you found that is good enough to merit such devotion, Mr. Barnaby?"

"Oh, the adventures of Mr. Pickwick, sir. It's a jolly lark, sir. Makes me laugh, it do. Have you read it yourself, sir?"

"I believe that is a novel. Is it not?"

"Well, I believes it is, sir. For there's plentiful exaggeration in it. You'll never meet a fellow quite like Pickwick."

"A work of fiction, then?"

I suppose the tone of my voice betrayed my disappointment.

"You doesn't approve, sir?"

"Mr. Barnaby . . . I understand the virtues of Mr. Shakespeare. Although I do not mean upon the stage, sir, but taken as edifying reading and with the avoidance of unfit passages. We may even admire the beauties of poetry, although we must beware of moral laxity. But fiction, sir? Think you. It's nothing but lies! Stories made up! Why should we pay a fellow to do what a child would be chastised for doing? Then praise him for good measure?"

Barnaby appeared suitably dismayed at my counsel. "But . . . it's only that I likes it, sir. It makes me laugh. And the world do seem a bit short of laughter some days. It's . . . it's a comfort, sir. That's what a good book is, sir. A comfort!"

"For comfort we have the Gospels. But I do not wish to interfere with your pleasures, Mr. Barnaby. I have come on a matter of business."

"About the matter of the Negroes, sir?"

"Perhaps. I cannot say. For I have not got halfway through the matter. But I must put a set of questions to you. Not from idle curiosity, I hope. In the interests of truth, sir."

He looked at me dolefully. Perhaps it was my advice as to his reading. Or maybe he already saw far more than I knew. Perhaps he had been waiting up for me.

I decided to take the approach I had taken with Samson.

"I have no wish to embarrass you, Mr. Barnaby. Or to erode the trust between you and Lieutenant Raines. Perhaps it will be easier if *I* speak the matter out. And you may simply stop me when I am in error. Raise your hand or give me another sign, if you are uncomfortable with speech."

Twas better here than in that darkened garden. For the candle lit Barnaby's eyes, and eyes tell true.

"Now there is a scramble of things to be put together," I said. "Beginning with this Emily Stone of Boston. Or Emily Barclay. Lieutenant Raines attended this Harvard College, I believe? And Harvard College is in a situation near Boston, is it not?"

Barnaby nodded. Warily. For he saw immediately where I was going.

"And it was in those environs that your Master Francis met this Miss Stone. And fell in love with her. Intending to marry her. And he invited her to visit his family. Perhaps to persuade them, perhaps to persuade her. Perhaps she came at Christmas, in the coolness? Or was it in the summer's heat? No matter. She arrived and Captain Barclay, who was not yet a captain, of course, laid his eyes upon her. And she saw him. From that day on, young Raines could not compete. Not for a young girl's heart. Barclay stole her away. And married her."

The big man's face was scribbled full of sorrow. For he loved the young man whom he had in charge. Question what you might, but trust to that.

"Master William," he said, slowly, "has ever been jealous of Master Francis. He always took things from him when he could."

"But . . ." Now I was confused. ". . . I thought . . . it seems to me that Barclay was the elder, the stronger, the handsomer. Begging your pardon, Mr. Barnaby, perhaps young Raines has more intelligence, more of a leaning to the books . . . but I would have thought the jealousy would be the other way round."

Barnaby shook his head. "Jealousy got no more sense to it than love, sir. It's the queerest thing. Master Francis has a gentle heart, sir. The gentlest of hearts, he has. And true enough it is that Master William was the stronger, and the faster, and all such like. Still, Master William always wanted what little Master Francis had. And the more Master Francis prized the thing, the more Master William craved it. And there weren't nothing in his life that Master Francis wanted how's he wanted that girl, sir. He was a calf in love, sir. And Master William slaughtered him. Now I suppose Master William will be wanting Master Francis's legs." The fellow caught himself. "Begging your pardon, sir. That was terrible improper of me."

"But . . . in the end . . . the girl chose Captain Barclay. It was her decision, after all. She had her choice and made it."

"She did, sir. That she did. And perhaps it was a blessing. For there was deep cuttings in that one, sir. Deep cuttings. I ain't sure as how she wanted to be happy, sir. Though I'm speaking out of turn now. But there's women like that, and look out for 'em, says Barnaby B. Barnaby. And mum's the word hereafter."

"The young are foolish," I said.

His eyes found mine. "And are we so much the wiser, the likes of us, sir? Or is there only different kinds of foolishness, for different times of a man's life? Oh, sir, sometimes I wish life was a book, so's a fellow might close it when he needs a breather."

I looked at the broad-plank floor. And the chipped pot tucked beneath the bed.

"You've figured out a terrible lot, you have," Barnaby told me. "It's a right inspiration of the human mind, sir. Terrible clever. But . . . what has all this to do with the murdered Negroes?"

That was, indeed, the problem.

"Nothing, I'm afraid. I thought I saw a thing. But I fear I'm no more than a meddling gossip, Mr. Barnaby. We are easily led astray. You have my apologies."

He gave me a smile. "That's our lot, ain't it? Led astray for wanting to go straight."

I wondered if I wanted to go straight. Or if I was but a sorry little man, given to interfering.

I rose to go. "Sorry to have disturbed you, Mr. Barnaby."

"Barnaby don't mind, sir. It weren't like I was sleeping. For I never can drift off when old Sam Weller's on the page, sir. He's a corker, that Sam."

Just at the door, I thought of something else. Twas more of my low curiosity. But I am one for knowing all of a thing.

"What did Lieutenant Raines study at this Harvard, if I may ask?"

"Divinity, sir."

"Divinity?"

"Yes, sir."

That cast the fellow in another light. "He intends to take the cloth? After the war?"

"Oh, no, sir. He give that all up, he has. Ever since Miss Emily broke his heart. No, he's set his eyes on other pastures now, sir. He's got great ambitions, he does."

"To do what, if I may ask?" What could be a greater consolation or reward than the ministry?

Barnaby's face clouded with trepidation. But he was an honest fellow, and he told me:

"He wants to write books. Novels, sir. Like Mr. Dickens."

.   .   .

I WENT UP THE STAIRS with a candle of my own. Seeing naught but sorrow in the world. Twas on the landing I first heard the weeping.

Coming from above it was, from somewhere along the hall, the sound of a child crying. As I helped my bad leg up with my cane, the sobbing grew worse with each step. It was not loud, but it echoed in the great house. It almost could have been a mourning ghost. Surprised I was that no one but me seemed to hear it. For every door was shut and no one stirred.

I decided it must be the girl. Paddycakes. Maybe she was left to her devices by night as she was by day. A wounded, wandering creature, free to come and go, but never at rest. I felt the child must want some bit of comfort, so I scraped my way along the midnight hall, listening at each door.

The weeping seemed to come from the last room. At the very end of the hall.

I knocked. Ever so gently. Barely touching the wood with the tip of my cane.

No one answered, and the sobbing continued. As if my careful knock had gone unnoticed.

I tapped again.

The poor girl was a simple thing and might not have sufficient wit to answer. Or perhaps I had frightened her more.

I set the candle down and tried the door.

It was not locked. I pushed it open and put a foot just after.

The door swung into emptiness. Twas the unfinished wing of the house, a mere skeleton of beams. My heel was in pure air where the floor should have been.

Had my cane not found a lip of wood, I would have tumbled down. And broken half my bones, if not my neck.

I caught my balance, gasping, and saw the stars beyond the ribs of the roof. A sea of lights looked down from a velvet span. The stars are like our sun, they tell me, only farther off. They say it proves that Heaven can't exist. But Providence was with me in that instant. Twas a greater hand than mine that held me back.

I caught my breath and eased away from the abyss. Carefully. Releasing the latch, I let the door swing wide. Seething with sweat I was, and cold in the bowels. My hand shook on my cane.

And it was dark within, for the fresh air had blown out the candle. Twas brighter by thrice outside than it was in the hallway gloom, though a wash of starlight flowed back toward the stairs. As if a goodly spirit meant to lead me away from my doings.

But the sobbing come clear as could be now, off to my left. Calling from behind an adjacent door, in the finished wing.

I did not see how I could have made such an error. It was not like me, for I have good ears and a soldier's senses. Perhaps I had been addled by events. Or by my fears.

The house seemed eerie, and wrong. I would say haunted, except that I will not believe in such like. Still, I sensed it was an ill-starred place, and that its walls led men and women wrong.

Twas no place for the girl to be meandering, and we must look after those weaker than ourselves. That, too, is a duty. I put myself back in my proper order, and this time I knocked upon the proper door.

The sobbing broke off.

Perhaps, I thought, I had frightened the poor child worse. Still a bit unsteady, I went in.

Twas a closet the size of a room, crammed with women's gowns and other fancies. By the light from a silver candlestick, I saw Captain Barclay. He was rubbing a satin dress across his nakedness.

I never saw such terror on a face.

eleven

_T_hey came for me in the darkness before dawn. Hollering like children poorly raised. I may have been the first to wake. Once a soldier, all your life you jump from sleep when someone calls your name. I dressed me quick.

They called me "Major," and they called me "Brother." They shouted for me to come out and have a talk. They made no threats, but I belted on my Colt.

I did not start a candle but moved in the night gloom, testing the stairs with my cane as I went down. When voices hail us in darkness, he who bears a light will help their aim.

Samson beat me to the porch, half-dressed and bearing a lantern. From upstairs, Captain Barclay called his name, but the slave seemed not to hear. Then Raines stepped out, in trousers and a shirt.

Two of them there were, out past the hedge. They lolled in their saddles, faces ghostly vague. Songbirds chipped the silence. Calling daybreak.

"What do you want?" I shouted.

Behind me, Raines clicked back his pistol's hammer. He did not know his doings and stood too close to the lantern. His face was tense and fair. I feared the boy would not survive the war, for he was drawn to the light, and light brings death.

I kept my distance from the lantern's cast.

"You Jones? The praying Yankee?" a melodic voice inquired.

"I am Major Abel Jones, U.S. Volunteers, sir."

"Praise the Lord! You done been called to Beersheba, Brother. Rev Hitchens sent us to fetch you back, if you's the fella studying them murders."

"You can't go with those Negroes," Raines insisted. His voice was low and furious. Such anger is the way we mask our fear.

"Who are you?" I called. Wanting a moment to think.

When I looked at Samson, his eyes were on me, not on the intruders. The night before he had suggested that such an opportunity might come my way. But I had listened poorly, vain of my own concerns.

He had told me they would come and pressed me to go with them.

Stranded up in his bed, Captain Barclay cursed to fright the Devil. Raging at his incapability, at Samson's absence from his side, and at the world. Had he been by us, I am certain guns would have spoken.

"Well, now," the fellow with the musical voice said, "I'm Roland. I'm the talking man. This here ugly pilgrim's name of Cupid. Cupid's the deciding man. Us come to bring you to the preaching ground, if you wants to go. But ain't no trouble doing if you don't. This here ain't nothing but your grabbing chance, Brother. Us don't want no shooting trouble, and no talking trouble, neither."

"And why should I go with you?" I asked. "How do I know I can trust you?"

A huge form slipped back through the trees, fleet as a prowling Pushtoon. Twas Barnaby with a long-barreled gun. The Negroes did not see the fellow.

"Brother, you just gots to have the abiding faith. Rev Hitchens say he got the doing will to find them killing people, but not the doing means. If you got the doing means and the doing will, Rev hope to talk to you about that. I expects he's praying on it right now."

Barnaby had gotten behind them, face pale as a flower in the trees. His gun was up, waiting for his moment.

"I have to saddle my horse," I said.

"Your riding horse been saddled, Brother. Waiting on you in the barn."

"You *can't* go with them," Raines hissed, in a voice only Samson and I might hear. "I forbid it."

"Do you now?" I turned on him. He looked so pale and earnest in the lamplight. His pistol gleamed.

"And if either one of them makes a move, I'll have Mr. B. drop him," Raines continued.

"Well, I am going. For I will follow where this business goes. That is what I have been sent to do, and do it I will."

"You *can't* go, Jones."

"And why is that, Lieutenant?"

"You gave your word. To General Beauregard. You accepted me as your escort. You're here on the general's parole. You can't go anywhere without me."

There was true. I had forgot. A promise is a troubling thing at times. Made lightly, it may change the course of lives.

Twas Samson who spoke next. At risk and out of turn. Still ignoring his master's outraged calls.

"Forgive my interference, sir," he said to Raines, "but perhaps you could accompany the major? If your purpose is to discover the identity of the killers? I would not judge these Negroes to be harmful."

"For all we know, they might be the damned killers themselves," Raines said. "Renegades. Or outlaws."

Samson did not speak again. But I did. Twas clear to me all this had been arranged, that Samson knew these men, that word had been sent. I did not believe the servant meant us ill. And if my horse was saddled, he had done it.

I did a shameful thing, though in a good cause. I played upon this Southron sense of honor.

"Perhaps these fellows would take you along, as well? Unless . . . unless you are afraid, Lieutenant?"

He did not answer me. Beyond the lantern, his face clenched like a fist. Had we been on a battlefield that moment, he would have shot me without hesitation.

"Gentlemen," I called to the riders, "there is a problem, see. For I have made a pledge to do all things together with Lieutenant Raines here. I gave my word and cannot go without him. Might he come with us, then?"

The Negroes conferred. To the east, the raven night turned pigeon gray.

Roland, the one given to speech, cast a thinner silhouette than his companion. "He can come along on his riding horse. But not with that shooting gun of his. You can bring yours, that's all right, cause you got the Lincum manners on you. But he don't bring no Jeff Davis gun. And you both goes blindfold. All the way. Cause Beersheba's a keeping secret and ain't no white folks got the knowledge of the lying-out places or the preaching ground."

"That's outrageous," Raines said.

"Well, we can stay," I said. "And you may drink your old friend's whisky to your heart's content, Lieutenant. But chances lost may be chances lost forever. I leave it to you to see your duty."

He was a brave young man in a tottering world.

"Put up that cannon of yours, Mr. B.," he called in disgust. "And saddle up my horse while I get dressed."

.   .   .

ROBBED OF MY SIGHT by the blindfold, my balance failed me, too. I strained to brace off the stirrups, swaying like a boat caught in a monsoon. Our path turned from the road to a broken trail and my stomach heaved. I jerked and jolted, clutching the saddle where my groin pounded. I did not know if I would spurn my dinner first, or go tumbling at a lurch. The first would crack my pride, the second my skull.

We were off to a challenging start.

Then the Negroes spared me, sudden as grace. One of the fellows tugged at the knot he had made at the back of my head and the rag fell from my eyes.

Twas day. The sun was up, although its light fell soft. A big grin met my bewilderment, with a finger laid from lip to lip to quiet me.

They did not take the blindfold from poor Raines.

Deep in the woods, the stouter of my guides began to sing. Jordan was a far river to cross, but he was going over. He was unsightly, pockmarked and cut thick, but his voice belonged to an angel militant. The morning air chilled the flesh, but he warmed the glens with devotion. I did not know the hymn or I would have joined him.

Cupid. Twas sad the singer was cursed with such a name, for it was mockery. His form was low and his skin was pitch. He was the sort that cruel men draw upon to belittle the Negro, to tie him to the ape instead of man. Holding the reins of my escort's horse, he guided the beast with skill as the trail meandered. He had a confidence to his doings that matched the strength of his voice and the big dragoon pistol on his hip. But we live in a world of appearances, and he would never be judged quite as a man.

The other fellow, Roland, formed his opposite. No darker than milk coffee, he was sleek. Almost pretty, but for the bobbing smallness of his head, he looked the sort who will always reach the corner and slide around it out of trouble's grasp. His range of moods ran from a smile to a grin. Now and then, he shook his head at nothing.

We rode until the warmth come up, and then we rode some more. I thought I recognized a marsh by a brook as one we had passed earlier. An hour later, when we crossed the stream for the third time, I realized we were making circles for the benefit of Raines.

As if to keep my mind from too much mischief, Roland turned in the saddle.

"Brother Jones?" he said. "Folks ever explained to you how come Jesus was a Negro? They know about that up North there?"

The query took me aback. As it would you. Now I had no wish to offend the simple fellow, but could not let such blatant folly pass.

"I believe," I said gently but firmly, "that Jesus was born in the land of the Jews. So the Gospels tell us. And Jews are not Negroes."

He laughed and slapped his leg. "Who said they was? I only said how Jesus was a Negro. I can prove it, too."

"How's that, sir?" Alarmed I was by his ignorance, where reverence was due.

"Well, first proof *you* needs is how they got us Negroes over there in that land of the Jews. Just like here. Yes, sir, that's a true enough thing. Cause *some*body got to do the work so's the white folks don't starve. Who you think do the plowing and the picking while the rest of them folks is off phariseeing all the time? I expects there's Negroes just about everywhere there's eating folks."

I opened my mouth to protest, but got no chance.

"Next off," Roland said, "look how little Jesus got hisself born in a stable. Ain't no white folks put up with truck like that. And even afore that, Mary done gone to Joseph saying how she got a little baby coming. And Joseph *knows* how it ain't been none of his doings. *No,* sir. He done kept his hands off that sweet little gal, cause he been saving it all up for the big day. Then that Mary go telling him how the little baby come from the Holy Ghost. White man shoot her dead for saying a thing like that and making him a fool. Cause the white man ain't got no faith. Next thing, he going to get out them dooley pistols and start looking around for the blame person." Roland shook his head in mock despair. "No, sir, missy ain't going to get away with telling young marse no Holy

Ghost give her a chile. But the Negro got the faith. And even when he don't, he make the best of things."

"The verse implies that Joseph had doubts at first, but—"

"And you just *look* how Jesus done gone ever place on his walking feet. White man get him a riding horse, or least a mule. And the white man don't just go straying ever where. No, sir. If Jesus been a white man, he would of thinked on things a time, then he would of wrote him some letters, saying, 'Cousin Herod, I'm coming up your way and I'd be beholding to stay at your big house with you, and give them regards to Missus Herod from me,' and then he going to write 'Brother Pilate, I got me big business down there in Jerusalem, and I sure would like to rest myself a few days in that pretty house you gots in town, and you tell Missus Pilate hello from me and Cousin James.' But Jesus just went walking on his way, like he don't care a lick. He don't worry none. *No*, sir. Cause he know wherever he go some Auntie Mary or Auntie Martha going to feed him off the back porch."

"That's a fact," Cupid said over his shoulder.

"And study that old miracle over to Cana now. White man turn the water into wine, he going to want him a money payment. Ain't no white man turning no water into wine for free. *No, sir.* No more than he going to go healing folks for nothing. He gets around to healing, he going to get him a buggy and a big black bag and call hisself a doctor. And study that there Sermon on the Mount. If Jesus was white folks, he would of charged least a nickel to come in, like at the fair. And all that nointing with the precious oil on the feet. Jesus see the beauty of the thing, how it nothing but a kindness and meant all sweet. But white folks wouldn't hold still for them doings, cause they ain't going to waste nothing like that on no preacher's walking handles. They going to put that precious oil in the chest and lock it up. Same thing with that Mary Magdalene. White folks don't want no truck with that kind unless it's after dark and they thinks nobody looking. But she come up on Jesus and what that preaching man tell her? He say, 'Sister, everything all

right, cause I knows how you fell down under that great big temptation. I knows how the brothers done you wrong. You just gets up
now and dry them eyes, cause you be forgiven. You get on back
down them quarters and sin no more.' White folks set her in the
county jail she even step near a preacher man."

"Hah!" Cupid said. "Ain't that the jelly on the biscuit?"

"And study about them disciples. Jesus just done scooped 'em
up where he found 'em. He didn't care if they was high-borns. No,
sir. Just come up on 'em while they's fishing in the creek of Galilee.
But if Jesus was white folks, he would of started off asking all
about their families and if they's respectable and who's whose
cousin and how many acres they got. No, sir. Jesus done even
moved over and made space on the bench for a low nigger like
Judas who couldn't wait to go tattling to the white folks."

"That's a fact," Cupid said. "That Judas was one woofing nigger."

We paused at the stream we had passed several times and let the
horses drink. Raines sat upright, shut against a world he found dis-
jointed. Beneath the eye rag, his lips were locked and dry. Doubtless, he shared my moral alarm at this misapprehension of the
Gospels. Twas only pity constrained my tongue from scolding. The
Negroes are a simple, suffering folk, and we must not expect too
much of them.

"But all that ain't nothing," Roland picked back up. "*Big* proof,
that's what they done with Jesus when he come up to Jerusalem.
Stripped him down and whupped him. Cut him to the bone with
the cat-o'-nine-tails. And that Pilate didn't find no fault with Jesus,
cause that manchild ain't done nothing wrong to speak of. But the
town folks was in a mood. So they killed him anyhow, just like they
do any black man makes 'em feel unsettled."

Roland's constant smile had faded at last, for he had talked
himself deep into sorrow, as a child might do. He come-upped his
horse and we began riding again, always through the backwoods
and the glades. After a while, he said:

"Jesus done made him one great big mistake. *That* done killed him sure. Time he went turning over them money tables in the temple, that done sealed his fate. You can trouble white folks about a fair amount of things, but they gets serious you starts fooling with their money. Black man can go preaching all he wants, long's he watch what he say around the white man. Only a white-trash fool get riled if the preacher dip the brother and the sister in the river and sing, 'Hallelujah.' But money trouble set the white man to killing."

The day had come up warm and lovely, although the insects pestered us in the low ground.

"Is that what this Reverend Mr. Hitchens teaches you?" I asked in a wary tone.

"No, sir," Roland told me. "I done read my Gospels and them Acts of the Possums, and studied that out myself."

.   .   .

AT LAST WE TURNED from our circular trail onto an overgrown wagon path. We rode into sunlight so pure it stunned the eye. And there, at the edge of the next copse of trees, knelt Paddycakes. Setting a rabbit snare.

She straightened her back, lifting her hand to the brim of her battered hat. Then she got to her feet and raced toward us.

"Marse Drake?" she called. "Marse Drake?"

"Paddycakes?" he asked, just as she reached his stirrup and clung to it.

We stopped. With Roland and Cupid scanning the fields, hands on their pistols.

"Marse Drake, you got you a hurt?"

"No, Paddycakes."

"But you got a rag onto your head."

"It's a blindfold. We're playing a game."

She thought about that. "Can I play?"

"It's a man-folks game."

Her hat hid all but a sliver of face from me, for she had come to the opposite side of his horse. But now and then I saw her troubled eyes.

"Marse Drake, you told me how's there ain't no spooks and haunts."

"That's right, girl. Don't you go believing all that Hoodoo silliness."

"But I *seen* one."

"You didn't see any ghost."

"I *did*, Marse Drake. Last night I seen one. I was sleeping in the truck shed where I mostly sleeps now, and I seen him go floating by. I thought it was the Devil, cause of how quiet he be going and all, and I got up to see, cause Bridie say if you see the Devil and he don't see you and you spit behind his tail, he got to give you a wish. And I seen how he gone up on the side porch to peek in the window of Marse Billy's eating room. That's when I seen him by the light and knew he weren't nothing but a haunt and not no Devil, cause the Devil don't wear ribbons in his hair."

I did not say a word and we rode on.

.   .   .

WE PASSED A CABIN with a collapsed roof and entered a pine wood. Hares quicked in the brush. Where the track divided, the left fork climbed a ridge. We steered right, into the low ground. Marsh grass soon replaced the trees and the hooves of our mounts sucked mud. Cupid drew his pistol.

"Is there danger, then?" I asked. Twas incautious talk, for such a remark might have told Raines I could see while he could not.

Roland answered for his partner. "Lot of them serpents as tempted Eve down here. Cottonmouth moc'sins all over the place. Just keep an eye, brother."

I grew alert, but felt no special fear. For I have faced the cobra in the desert and know that men are worse.

My greatest concern was for our horses. I worried they would sink and stumble, for the going was difficult. A spray of water reached my face. It smelled.

But the ground firmed and the trees thickened again. Cupid slid his pistol back into its holster.

The track led through a maze of broken rocks. Barrows loomed to the sides, unearthly in their symmetry. In Wales, such mounds are said to be haunted by ancient spirits, though no man in his senses credits rumor. The ground narrowed to a shallow gorge and we rode one behind the other.

I sensed that we were watched. Old soldiers know.

The defile opened into a glen and a white-haired, bearded Negro tottered against us. One hand reached out, the other clutched a cane. Blind he was, with eyes like boiled egg whites. He plunged among our horses.

"That my boy?" he begged. "Anybody seen my boy?" His voice rose plaintive as a widow's wail.

"Nope," Roland said. "Not yet, Old Toby. I expects he'll be along when he's done sowing them oats."

The old man settled back, his face in ruins. I glimpsed a sagging woman by a cave.

After we had clopped a little distance, Roland told me, "Poor Old Toby. His boy up and went with the Shady Grove folks. With them what was killed."

Soon I saw the first signs of a settlement. Cabins of the crudest sort slumped in the trees. Those were the finest shelters. The rest were but open sheds and cribs, some lower than the pen that had confined me. Negroes quit their work at garden patches or bent their heads to swell from low-cut doors. Dusting their hands they come, drying them on aprons. Eyes upon us. If poverty is virtue, these were the just. For they were ragged as the sore-plagued beggar.

"Praise the Lord!" one turbaned woman cried. "That Mr. Lin-cum on that red-head horse?"

"Cupid done catched him a Rebel, too," a boy declared.

"Ain't no catching been done," Cupid said. "You step on back now. You all just get on back." At that, he reached over and snapped the blindfold off of Raines. The young man's hat went tumbling, but he caught it.

I wondered what Raines thought of the sight before him.

It was a sorry place, not fit for smugglers. Men were clothed in shirts that would not have done my wife for the scrubbing of floors. The women were covered, but dirty, and the children scratched at themselves. A dozen shacks and sheds. That was Beersheba.

A smiling man of medium height strode toward us, fixing his direction straight for me. He was not tall or visibly distinguished. Indeed, he might have seemed the drabbest of the Negroes in his old black suit and yellowed shirt, for the others had some color to their scraps. He wore a mighty smile, but so might a dishonest clerk.

A single thing set him apart. A gash began at his hairline, livid purple on his leather skin. It sliced down over his brow and caught his nose, gnarling its meat, then split the corner of his mouth. When the scar reached his jaw, it took a jagged turn to furrow his cheek. Now, I was an instructor of the bayonet, and I will tell you: a drunkard's knife did that. For any man close enough to make so long a slash should have stabbed instead. And sober men cut straight.

The scarred man spread his arms. As if he would embrace my horse and me.

"Welcome," he said, "to our city on a hill."

twelve

"We call this place Beersheba," the preacher told me as we walked together, "for there is a well, and the water is sweet." He smiled, splitting that great scar wider. Twas a crescent moon carved in his face. "Perhaps this seems a wilderness to you, Brother. But to us it is a garden."

We entered a spread of pines. Back in the settlement, in a lean-to granted us as quarters, Raines sulked like Achilles in his tent. Our meal of "pone" and fat soppings had not troubled him so much as the suspicion the Negroes felt of men in gray. Nor did they show respect. With straightened backs, they strutted past, watching from the corners of their eyes. They welcomed me, but spared no words for Raines. I pitied the boy. He was a stranger in a strange land, a land that he had long believed he knew. But let that bide.

"Careful by those rocks," the preacher warned me. "There's serpents in this garden."

He led me to a log upon a knoll and we sat down. The sun poured golden rivers through the trees.

"I did not see guards posted," I said to him.

He shook his head. "We're in the Lord's hands."

"But, surely, you have arms?"

"A few pistols," the preacher said. "Shotgun or two. The wild beasts bless our cookpot now and then."

"Look you. Given the murders . . ."

He smiled. "His will be done. Brother, if the Confederate army appeared before us, what good would a dozen times a dozen old guns do? I will have no killing in this place. No, sir. The sword in Peter's hand dismayed our Lord. That's written down." A bee hovered, inspecting the Negro as he might a flower, then floated away. "We have our prayers, Major. Our prayers, and the peace of the forest for our comfort." He raised his face to warm it in the light, clenching shut his eyes, as if the rays were splashing water. "Lord willing, your army will come on by soon enough. On that day, the children of Beersheba will be jubilant. Upon that day, Lord, upon that day . . ."

"Un*til* that day, Mr. Hitchens, I would judge your situation a dangerous one."

Setting his knees apart, he planted his hands on his thighs and swung his meaty face toward me. Brown eyes soft. "My life has been a running life, Brother. First, I ran after my freedom. Then I kept on running for my safety. In the wilderness of men, I chased after the things of this here world. Then the time come when I went running to try and catch the Lord in this place here or that one over yonder." He nodded, more to himself than to me. "Those of little faith go looking for Him outside themselves, but a true-faith man knows the Lord resides within. I had to study that for a time."

He raised his right hand a few inches, making a small gesture toward the settlement. "Our Beersheba is as close to Heaven as any other place. So I guess we'll just wait on what comes." His mouth stretched in a smile. "Maybe in the later days, this here war gone by, we'll go on out to one of those Western places, to good breathing land. Just like the childern of Israel. Build us a real city on a real hill. Just now though, with the whole world nothing but war and rumors of war, it strikes me that we might as well stay put."

Perhaps the fellow was right, after all. The Negroes who were slaughtered didn't 'stay put,' and their journey had not saved them. Maybe their sorry camp back in the woods would keep these others safe and sound. Still, his confidence left me uneasy.

"Well, it is your flock," I told him. "And I am a stranger, see. Though sorry I am for those who have been murdered."

He looked down. When his face expressed sorrow, it wrinkled in rising waves above his brow and in ripples that descended from cheekbone to jowl. The livid scar cut through the flows of skin.

"That is a powerful sorrow to bear," he said. "And blame is on my shoulders, a heavy blame." He brought his eyes to me again, as if I were fit to judge him. "Oh, they wanted to go on. They had the desire on them to go North. Their feet were just trampling to go. They were only stopping over here, breathing a little. Looking out on things. Hesiod, he had them all full of visions of milk and honey. If only they could reach Mr. Lincoln's army, they'd be over Jordan and into Paradise. Yes, sir, they wanted to go on. But I did not try to hold them, either. I had the worrying on me, for my dreams tell me things. More and more, I dream about the Day of Judgement. No, I didn't try to hold them."

He smiled wistfully. "See here, Brother. I can pour out the Lord's love for these folks. But I can't do that miracle of the loaves and fishes. There's precious little to fill their bellies. What there is comes pretty much from nighttime borrowing. You might call it stealing, if you was to look at it under the hard law. But these people . . ." His hand lifted again in that slight pointing gesture. ". . . they been stole from all their lives. The fruits of their labor have been stolen in their Babylonian captivity. They have wept cruelly by the waters of Babylon, crying for Zion. Crying for a justice foreign to idolatrous masters. Should this here land of Egypt begrudge food to a man whose wife was torn away from his bosom? To a mother whose child was sold off? I hope we'll be forgiven for borrowing a little mush-meal and trimmings now and then."

He took a deep breath. "That Hesiod was rearing up to go. He had them halfway to exultation about moving on up North. Jerusalem was just across the creek, and Heaven just a little wade beyond. And I couldn't keep on filling no forty extra bellies." He tapped his knee. " 'Forty's a Bible number,' I told myself. 'Maybe they're meant to go on. Maybe there's a hand held over them.' And they went. Those forty. And old Toby's boy with them."

I shifted, for the log was hard and my rump was sore from my travels. "Then forty-one went north?"

He nodded. "One and forty children of the Lord."

"You're certain? Forty-one?"

"Yes, sir. Forty came, and forty went. Forty-one, with Old Toby's boy stirred in."

I wanted his knowledge, not his speculations. At least not yet. So I did not make an issue of the difference of one. I had been told that forty had been murdered. Did that mean one survived? Or were the slaughtered bodies too hard to count precisely? In India, we would have tallied skulls.

Of course, one more or less might have no meaning.

"Tell me, sir, about this Hesiod fellow."

He groaned as if his body were a machine in want of oil. "Bought down out of Virginia by the Barclay family, I'm told. When they were growing that Shady Grove of theirs. Had him some blacksmithing skills. Yes, sir. And he swallowed up some learning somewhere, though not much more than a gulp or two. Ran away a time back. Can't say how long, for I was still wandering in the desert back then. Showed up here in Beersheba onto two months ago, heading back to that Shady Grove. Yes, sir. Good-looking man. Strong. Said he had the revelation and come on back to lead his people to freedom."

"He sounds a noble sort," I said. "Risking his own freedom by coming back for the others."

The preacher had begun to sag, as men will in the waning afternoon. A light of reddish-gold inflamed the trees. "I suppose. Yes, I suppose that's the truth of it. Surely, a brave man. But he troubled my heart. When he got to preaching. Oh, he had the talking power. Didn't have his Scripture all chapter and verse. Not that the Spirit can't move in the man of lesser knowledge, I'm not saying that. No, sir. That Hesiod could raise a soul up and cast it down again.

*Mer*cy. Called up my envy, too." His brows climbed to a higher frankness. "Preacher has the pride on him, too, Brother, try how he might to lay it to the side. And that Hesiod had the jumping rants. The Lord's hand was on that boy. Only when he talked holy, it always sounded hard. Come out more hellfire than heavenly light, the way he preached the Book."

He slumped still lower and cocked his head, chin down in his jowls. But his eye sparked. "See, Brother, these people . . ." The hand rose languidly and fell again. ". . . these people here done had their share of hellfire right here on earth. They don't need no hate talk. No, sir. I *know* that my Redeemer liveth. And He is love." He slapped his leg and smiled happily at the thought. "Remember that eleventh commandment? How it goes in *John?* Jesus told us to love each other. All the people have to do is get to loving each other and everything else is going to go right. Nothing but that at the heart of it. *There* is your balm in Gilead. Just you love other folks. Now, ain't that simple?" He shook his head. "These people here know plenty about hatred, and they don't need to know no more. Turn up here mad as red-eyed bears, some of them. All I aim to do is soften them down. Soften them down and wait."

"For our army?"

He nodded. "That, too."

The lowering rays gilded the preacher's face.

"Do you recall," I asked him, digging idly with my cane, "a woman with the runaways? The forty? A woman named Lucy?"

"Lucy?" He brightened, only to have his expression collapse into sorrow. "Surely. As beauteous as the Rose of Sharon. Fair and comely. Worthy of the Song of Solomon. Lovely as the daughters of Job. Husband was a good man, too. Upright. None of that shiftless, Hoodoo sort. Jase was not a hating man, either. Didn't mind a bit about the child. Loved it like it was his own."

"The child?"

"Surely. Sweetest little girl. Fair skin and those blue eyes. Couldn't of been his with eyes like that, or with that creamy color on her. Hardly dark enough to tell she had Negro blood. But you could see Jase didn't hold it against the child. Or the woman. No meanness in him. Though he looked like he could scrap, if he took a mind to." He sighed as if at Eden's loss. "All gone now. I pray for them, Brother. There's times His purpose truly passeth all understanding."

I wondered if any man in this Southland would ever tell me the entire truth. If any white man would, I mean to say.

"Mr. Hitchens?"

He grinned. It was a lovely change. "You want to call me 'Rev Will' like other folks, you do that, Brother. Or plain, old 'Will.' However you sit comfortable with it."

"Your people . . . the two who summoned me. This Roland and Cupid. They said you had something to tell me about the murders. About those who might have done it, perhaps?"

"Surely. Yes, sir. That's why I done brought you way out here away from folks. They're good Christians, most of them, but some get too curious for sense. Go listening like the Devil at the kitchen door. Just make worries out of a thing." Bracing his hands higher on his thighs, he drew himself up from his sag. Golden sweat licked his forehead. For a moment, he only looked at me, mouth open, pink tongue swollen. His riven face shone dark.

"I had a dream," he said. "Visited me three times, and three's a Holy number. I was called to share this dream. That's why I sent for you. I knew a body was coming, for I had the Sign, but I didn't know who. Then Samson sent word along. About your arrival. And I knew. Yes, sir, three times means the dream has to be passed on."

I could have stood and shouted a rebuke. All this fuss to pass along a dream? That lit my fuse, I will tell you.

Still, I behaved with restraint. For they are simple people, after all. I kept my seat, determined to listen, as I would to a well-meaning child. But now I regretted the time lost in my coming, and the possible danger to Raines. And I was disappointed, for I had hoped to find a swift solution. I wished to finish this business and go home. Or back to Washington, at least, to my waiting clerkship. I wanted no more blood, nor bloody leavings. And now some darky pestered me with nightmares.

"You . . . called me here to talk about a dream?"

"Yes, sir." He smiled, scar-cracked. "A vision. Come three times. Like Peter's denials."

"A vision."

"I dreamed about the horsemen," he said. "They were here to fulfill the prophecy."

"The horsemen?"

"From the *Book of Revelation.* I dread that book, Brother. Wish it had not been given to us. Though the Lord knows best." He nodded to himself. "This dream was a hard dream. The horsemen rode among the people, hewing them like the blades of grass. And of these, Death was the greatest. He rode a pale horse. I saw him clear as I see you right now."

The crudity of his beliefs, this primitive stock in omens, repelled me. Not that I lack faith in the Holy Writ, and we must take the dark texts with the bright. But forty murdered Negroes made no Apocalypse. I wanted facts, not country superstitions.

Oh, I was cross. For selfish is the man.

"I don't worry on it, though," the preacher went on. "I put my faith in Jesus. When the trumpet sounds, I will rise up. I've been forgiven. No matter how far a man falls, Jesus can reach on down and pick him up. I *will* rise, Brother."

At that, he slapped his legs and got to his feet.

"We should go on back," he told me. "Near time for evening meeting. The hour to praise the Lord. You're welcome to enter in among us, Brother. You, and that young soldier fellow, too."

.　　.　　.

RAINES SAT IN THE DUSK with the look of a prisoner. He had taken off his tunic and waistcoat in tribute to the heat and his shirt hung damp and heavy. I knew he was troubled by the place in which he found himself, and I was glad of it. For I wanted him looking one way while I struck from another.

Tired I was of all their genteel lies.

I sat me down beside the boy, but back a bit so I might watch his profile. The Negroes strolled toward the "preaching ground." Colorful in their rags they were. A few of them clutched books.

"There is good," I said. "When people go to meeting on a Monday."

My companion sniffed.

"Lieutenant Raines," I went on, "did you know of the child, or did you not?"

He swiveled his head on that fine neck. And I saw he had no inkling of my meaning.

"Let me tell you a thing, then," I continued. "And then you may tell me if there is more. Captain Barclay's wife, this Emily, did not leave him in a fit of vanity at his preference for—or shall we say, his unwillingness to break off his relations with—a slave woman. Strong enough she was to win that fight. And beautiful enough, too. As you know yourself, sir. Do not make faces. You are a better man than that. Hold your peace and let me finish. If I disgust you, let that be my lot. Only do not stain yourself with lying. Sit you there and listen."

He feared what I might tell him next. I saw that plain.

"No," I said, "twas when she found out Barclay had a child. By the slave woman. Lucy. He had a child by her and let it be counted a slave. That is what your Emily could not bear. That the man she loved would abandon his own flesh and blood to slavery. That is when the 'Northernness' come out, see. That is when she saw the gulf between them. And given Barclay's temper, who can say—"

"That's a *lie*," Raines said, a bit too late to convince. "Billy wouldn't have done that."

"But he did. He had a child, a little girl. Pale and blue-eyed she was."

"He would've taken any child—"

"Pale and blue-eyed the child was. Like him. And he found the infant of less worth than a horse or dog. But the mother, the slave woman, loved it. She took it with her when she ran away. With *her* husband, a man named Jase. The child died with them in the butchery."

Raines looked straight off, but I kept watch on his features. His face was tight as leather stretched and dried, and he smiled with a shrunken mouth.

"Now what do you have to tell me, Lieutenant Raines? To bring us closer to an understanding of these murders?"

"Billy didn't have anything to do with them. For the love of God, Jones . . ."

"I did not say he did, nor do I think so. But this is your world, not mine, and I cannot see in from outside."

"You seem to have done a fair job," he said bitterly.

"No. I only gather the threads that drop in front of me. And I know that this . . . drama . . . may have nothing to do with the massacre. But something there is in it that will not let me rest."

"And what's that, Major?" There was no great respect for rank or age in his voice.

I shook my head, though he could not see me. The gloaming deepened and the Negroes began to sing of going homeward.

"I do not know," I said. "It is like a burden on my back. A thing that others may see, while I cannot."

A smirk pruned his mouth. "You really don't know, do you?" He turned and looked at me then, leaning backward on an outstretched arm. "You don't even know who this 'Reverend' Hitchens is? Now do you?"

"He is a former slave. Who heard the Call."

Raines rolled his eyes. Then he glanced around us, insuring we were alone. And he leaned toward me. Twas the only time he spoke to me with undiluted venom.

"That's Martin's Will, old Colonel Martin's killer and a damned runaway. You go in any sheriff's office or government building, any railroad station or what have you between Mobile and St. Louis, and you'll see that face and that scar sketched on a wanted poster. He killed his master, then killed the men sent to bring him in. He's nothing but a murderer, a fugitive from justice. That's who's leading that little prayer-meeting over there. Martin's Will, a vicious killer. He's worse than Micah Lott."

I did not speak for a time, but listened to the Negroes as they sang. They were exuberant, but lacked the discipline that made a proper chorus. Above the trees, the sky spread pink and gray and indigo.

"Well," I said at last, "then there are two of us disappointed today." I recalled, or tried to recall, all that the preacher had said to me. About redemption, about rising from our sins.

Suddenly, I picked myself up. Leaning on my cane to reach my feet.

"I think I will go and have another look at the fellow," I said. "And pray a bit." I looked down at Raines, who raged in lovelorn youth. Twas not his old friend's guilt that chewed on him. I am enough of a man to understand that. It was the mention of Barclay's wife, the woman he had loved, and whom he loved still. "You are invited, too," I told him, "and might do well to join me. Prayer is a soothing matter."

He stared into the thickening darkness. "There is no God. There's only what men do. And what they fail to do."

Well, that was hard. But do not judge him unforgivingly. For he was young and crossed in love, and young men speak to wound the world that hurts them. If he survived the war, he would have time to put himself right.

I took me off toward the squalling Negroes, who were doing their best to get the Lord's attention.

.   .   .

THEIR WORSHIP WAS UNRULY. They never would have done for proper Methodists. We may display emotion through a hymn, but do not gad about. Or interrupt a parson with shouts and calls. We know our place, see.

The Negroes raised their faces to the sky. As if expecting fiery revelations. Torches fixed in the sod lit the meeting, but the flames were no more agitated than the members of the congregation. The shadows cast were huge and wild. I might have been amongst an African tribe. Even Baptists show less agitation.

"That's *right*," Mr. Hitchens called, "let the Spirit *come*, Brothers and Sisters. Just let it pour on *down*. Open up your hearts and let Him *in*. I take my text from Luke, chapter ten, verse twenty-four: 'For I tell you, that many prophets and kings have desired to see those things which ye see, and have not seen them; and to hear those things which ye hear, and have not heard them.' " His voice was near-majestic in the grove. "And I *know* what I have seen, Brothers and Sisters. And now I'm going to *tell* you what I've seen."

"Tell it, Brother."

"I have seen what men see with their eyes. Hah! That ain't nothing."

"Testify!"

"The eye is but the servant of temptation. Hah!"

"Ain't that the truth?"

"Man sees with his eye, he takes to grabbing. Says, 'Gimme that, I want me some right now.' And where's that lead?"

"I hear you talking, Brother."

"It leads to *sin*. Hah! And sin leads to damnation."

"Lord have mercy!"

"Don't you trust that eye that got the sin-hunger. No, Brothers and Sisters! You shut that eye against the wicked world. Hah! Don't you take that wicked road on me."

"Preach it, Rev Will."

"That road leads down."

"*Down to the pit!*"

"But I will raise *up* mine eyes. And not those eyes that see and start me grabbing. No, Brothers and Sisters. I'm talking about the eyes down in my heart. The eyes down in the heart of every sinner. Of every yearning sinner on this earth. *Hah!* The eyes that see the Lord in all His radiance, the eyes that are all closed up in those old prophets and kings. And I'm not going to listen with *these* ears. *That* road leads down, too. I'm going to listen with the ears I got in my heart along with them heart-eyes. The ears that are all closed up in those prophets and kings. Cause if I *see* with my heart, and if I *hear* with my heart, you *know* what I'm going to see and hear. Don't you, Brothers and Sisters? *That sweet love!* Lord Almighty! The sweet love of our Savior, Jesus Christ!"

"*Hallelujah!*"

"Open up your hearts, and let that love come on in!" Turned Heavenward, his face shone in the firelight. "Lord, we're a-waiting! We're a-waiting on you now . . . come down upon us! Lord Jesus, we're ready and waiting to go!"

The Negroes sang and shrieked, leaping about. One woman fainted, dropping to the earth in sweating hugeness. She twisted as if seized upon by cholera, alarming me. Until I saw it was a fit of ecstasy.

They raised their arms up, grabbing at the stars.

I could not like their excitability. Yet, joyous they were, and innocent. If the Lord is fair, such faith must count for something.

.   .   .

I SLEPT MIGHTILY after the day's exertions and woke to insect stings on hands and face. My dreams had been of my mother. I barely knew her, for she died when I was small, but I see her in the night at times. Ever kindly she is, and a comfort to me. My scratching opened my eyes too soon, and I sat up with a dreadful sense of loss.

Raines had his boots on. Nearby, our horses waited. Saddled and ready.

"About time you woke up," he said, with a thin affability. Anxious he was to put the place behind him. But there were other things he would not escape. The loss of those we love haunts us forever.

I said my goodbyes to the Reverend Mr. Hitchens, whose teeth were bothered with his breakfast leavings. The gash upon his face looked deep and raw. I almost asked about his criminal history, for the man made me curious. I did not think young Raines a liar, but had to wonder if the tale were true.

The man before me hardly seemed a killer. But such questioning would have been rude and, perhaps, unsafe. I did not fear for me, you understand, but for young Raines. Blameless in himself he may have been, but to these people he was a fountain of misery. With that gray coat. Even Christians have their fits of temper.

"And there is nothing else you wish to tell me?" I asked the parson. "About the killings?" For though I had pieced out a muchness around Captain Barclay, I seemed no closer to solving the murder business. I would ride away not knowing where to go next.

"If I have me another dream, I'll send after you," he said.

I did not reply directly, but told him, "Look you, Mr. Hitchens. I am an old soldier. And this place does not feel safe to me. You must be cautious. There is trouble about, see. We still do not know why those people were killed."

Twas his turn to avoid a straight reply. "Lord, Major Jones, wasn't that a meeting last night? Wasn't that a meeting? Folks just got the Spirit when you stepped in amongst them. You're the first Lincoln soldier any of them seen. Though they had hoped to see you come here garbed in a raiment of blue." He clicked his tongue. "My, my. Wasn't that a jubilation, though?"

Roland and Cupid led us off. Again, they blindfolded us, only to remove my rag the moment they were sure that Raines was sightless. We passed the poor old blind fellow again. He did not accost us regarding his son, since we were riding outward. He only stood and stared with sightless eyes. Perhaps they were the "heart-eyes" of which the preacher had spoken.

When we passed the defile and reached the marsh, Cupid drew his pistol as before. This time, I saw one of the snakes. Huge it was. Not so long as many a Sindhi cobra, but such are thin. The cobra rises up like a mast, his hood a sail. This snake was brown and fat and six feet long. Its path was low. Slithering off a bump of earth, it curved across a pool of standing water. Though the snake kept a long length off, the horses kicked and splashed.

Sightless, Raines turned his head from side to side at the commotion.

Cupid did not fire and the snake swam off. I have no special dread of the creatures, but would not have sought that "moccasin" for closer acquaintance. It looked a deadly thing. I tightened my grip on Rascal's reins, waiting for solid earth beneath his hooves.

I did not know the serpent was a signal. My search was done, and vengeance pounded toward us.

thirteen

We rode in circles, as we had done before. Cupid kept the look-out, while Roland told me humorous tales of a slave named John and his old Master. Somehow, John always proved the cleverer of the two. It is a marvel how these folk can laugh at bondage. I find them much like the Irish. For his part, Raines maintained a perpetual grimace below his blindfold. I felt him seething.

By now, I had a soldier's grip on the terrain. Again and again, we crossed the same wild fields, penetrated the same groves and brushed against the edges of the marsh. We avoided hilltops and roads. To look down at our trail, you would have thought a troop of riders had passed, so often had our horses' hooves slapped the same dust. The Negroes laughed, and now and then I chuckled at their merrymaking. But I only lent one ear to Roland's tales. I scratched my bites and thought on harder things.

Look you. I had learned much, but not about the murders. It seemed I was no closer to the guilty. Had my task been to shame this Captain Barclay, I might have done that well enough. But who had done the killing I could not say. I fought to think, but the mind is a stubborn machine and will not go until it has got ready.

When I recalled the murder site and all I had been told, it seemed there were but two possible constructions. Either the forty—forty-one—Negroes had been surrounded by a force superior in numbers, preventing the escape of more than one . . . or they had trusted those come to kill them and found themselves betrayed and slain like sheep. Which had it been? And what could be the motive? Or the sense?

Again, I felt the answer perching on my shoulders, there for every eye to see but mine. The truth danced behind me like a teasing boy, making faces. It tapped me and ran off. I am not made for matters of investigation, see. I am too slow. I trust more than I should. I read, but am no educated man. My hands are trained far better than my head.

How I longed to speak with my Mary Myfanwy, who always saw what her stumbling husband could not! Oh, I will tell you: A good wife is the best of earthly gifts. We do our women wrong to slight them. They possess a wonderful muchness that might help more than we allow. Of course, I speak of intellect and talents, and not of self-control or steady character, in which they are not equal to a man.

At last, we turned from our familiar path. Cupid led the way along a treeline. I glimpsed a road below us. Cautiously, our guides turned us into the woods. Heading downward. Our horses wound between slender trunks and fits of briars. The day had warmed, and the air smelled thick with life. But where life reigns, death lurks. Roland told us no more stories now. Both Negroes held their pistols at the ready.

We halted near the bottom of the slope, just above the road. Ocher dust showed through the trees and I glimpsed ruts cut by wagon wheels. Roland eased his horse ahead until a flowering tangle blocked the animal. Slipping to the ground, he soothed his mount then pressed ahead, picking his way through the undergrowth.

Suddenly, he dropped out of sight.

A minute later, the Negro reappeared. Climbing up an embankment toward us. He waved his pistol at Cupid.

Our guard undid the blindfold from poor Raines. The boy blinked at the force of the light through the trees, wiping invisible veils from his eyes.

Roland trudged back toward us.

"That road down there," Cupid said. "You go on down and point yourselfs yonder." He gestured to the left with his pistol. "You'll get on to someplace soon enough."

Raines looked sour as a Delhi pickle.

I thanked our guides, then led the way, afraid that Raines was about to start a quarrel. He followed me quietly, if sullenly. I veered to the side to avoid the worst of the undergrowth and waved a last time to the pair of Negroes. Rascal took the bank before I was ready and I nearly pitched head over onto the road.

That got a laugh from Raines, if but a small and cruel one. By the time I had myself back in order, our guides had disappeared.

We sat our mounts in the middle of the track. With Raines giving me a vinegar stare. Twisting his mouth, he clucked his horse to a walk. I followed along in the hardening sunlight. We went perhaps a mile before he spoke, and then he spoke abruptly:

"You think I don't know we were riding rings around ourselves? Or that they took off your blindfold the minute mine went on? You think I don't know where we were?"

"I did not think on the matter at all," I told him, which was true. For I had other thoughts enough to busy me.

A butterfly strayed from a bush, yellow as saffron in a heathen market. It was a yellow day, all sun and dust.

Raines rode with his eyes to the fore like a lancer on parade. Wounded in his pride, he was. Affronted. For though he was a decent sort, twas clear his treatment by the Negroes had humiliated him. Their own long shame could be no consolation. The son of a prince may condescend, but does so at his pleasure.

"I've hunted this country since I was a boy," Raines continued, tart as cress. "Every year. I know these hills. And every damned field. Every creek." Young and thin-skinned in his self-regard, he turned his face toward me. "We're not five miles from that nigger camp right now. I know those Indian mounds. I could lead you right to the damned place in under an hour. 'Beersheba,' " he said in a tone most men reserve for fallen women. "It's nothing but a lair for thieves and killers."

"Will you betray them, then? Is that your intention, Lieutenant?"

He rode on with that bitter, scalded look. Then he straightened his back and rose up in the stirrups. Scanning the country ahead.

A lone rider dropped down a long slope toward us. It was not hard to recognize Mr. Barnaby.

"You think old Mr. B. hasn't been watching over us the whole time? You think he doesn't know where they're lying out?"

I reined in my mount. "He would not tell."

Raines cast a disdainful glance down at my person and thrust his right hand into his pocket. "Oh, wouldn't he now? Well, maybe I will. That Martin's Will should've hung a dozen times. The man's a murderer. A white-man killer. And the rest of them are nothing but runaways and wanted men. Holding back information about fugitive slaves is against the law in this state."

And would you see them chained to soothe your pride? I almost asked. But gulf enough there was between us now.

He swapped his interest back to Mr. B., whose poor mount struggled closer under its burden.

"We're lucky they didn't cut our throats," Raines added. He fumbled through his pockets, one after the other, with increasing urgency. I did not understand what he was after, but his fingers scrambled under the cloth like a man who is missing his money. Pockets explored, he patted down his uniform. With a look of panic.

"Lieutenant Raines," I began, "I know I am not part of your society. And perhaps this Mr. Hitchens was, indeed, a killer. I cannot say, but—"

My escort unleashed a volley of curses unworthy of the lowest Christian man. Or heathen, for that matter. I had not heard such language from his mouth. Or from the mouths of many other men, save cooks and drillmasters.

The first word that he spoke that I can share was:

"*Locket.*"

"Those niggers took my damned locket," he repeated. "They must've gone through my pockets while I was sleeping. "The worthless—"

I will spare you his imaginative employment of the English language. Suffice to say the boy was killing mad. He even reached for his side, instinctively, to where his holster would have been had he not been deprived of arms for our journey.

Barnaby spurred his mount when he heard the shouting. He come up with a question on his face.

Raines was in a vicious child's rage. A regular tantrum it was.

"Master Francis?" Barnaby asked, in wonder.

Raines would look at me no longer. Twas as if I had stolen his treasure. He steadied his eyes on his servant, saying, "They stole my locket. The damned—"

I saw that Barnaby held a bundle in his hand. Prepared he was to pass it to young Raines. It was the lieutenant's pistol belt. With his revolver's grip protruding from the holster.

I nudged my horse between master and man. Clumsily, I will admit.

"Wait you," I said. "Lieutenant Raines, listen to me. I will retrieve your locket. It is my fault, see."

"They should be whipped and hanged," he snarled.

His anger might have frightened slaves. But it only brought my own spleen up within me. I do not like a tantrum in a man, and my patience is not endless.

"You're behaving like a child," I said. Not without some heat.

Raines went silent. Lips parted, as if seized up in midword. I wonder if anyone had ever been so blunt with him. Harvard learned or not, he had not studied humility or met defiance. His face put me in mind of the white-bearded officer I had shot point-blank at Shiloh. Amazed the man had been that the world would cross him. I saw the kinship twixt Raines and Barclay now. It was no band of blood, but one of iron. The South grew richer crops of pride than cotton. And pride is not the least of the deadly sins.

"If one of them took your locket," I said in my old sergeant's voice, "and if you did not lose it as a result of your own doings, Lieutenant, I will retrieve it for you. If you will but wait here with Mr. Barnaby, I will fetch it back, and no harm done."

Raines hated me in that moment. "You in league with those coons, Jones?"

"No, I am not. And you know that I am not." I turned to Barnaby. "Mr. Barnaby, would you calm him down, then? Reason with him, would you? I will fetch him his locket."

"You've got three hours," Raines said, reaching into his waistcoat for his watch to time me. But the watch was missing, too, along with its chain.

"And I will fetch your watch and chain, besides," I said. "And anything else that was taken."

I tugged the reins to steer my horse about.

Twas curious. Finding himself bereft of more than just the locket calmed Raines a little. As if a general theft were less acute than the specific one. But under the brim of his hat, his face shone crimson.

"You know the way, sir?" Barnaby asked me.

"I will know it from up there." I gestured toward the long, low ridge from which we and then Barnaby had descended.

"Right you are, sir, right you are. Hardly Piccadilly to Pall Mall."

Rascal wanted to be off, as if he sensed the urgency of the matter himself.

Look you. I did not want Raines doing something foolish. Such as confronting the Negroes in his pride. For then there would be killing, I was sure.

I was about to give Rascal a kick, the way I had seen better riders do, when Raines stretched out his hand. Twas not a proffer of reconciliation, but a plea for attention.

He could not reach me. The hand remained suspended in the dusty air between us, as our horses danced.

His anger had blown over like a summer rainstorm and something near despair annoyed his eyes.

"I ask you . . ." he said, ". . . Major, I ask you, as a gentleman, not to look inside the locket. If you can reclaim it . . ."

I nodded in agreement. For I already knew whose portrait lay therein.

Mr. Barnaby said, "Careful of the marsh, sir, it ain't pleasant. The snakes kept me awake most of the night." He flipped his thumb over his shoulder. "There's a smithy at the crossroads just ahead, sir. Master Francis and meself will be there waiting."

.   .   .

RAINES HAD INSTRUCTED me never to cling to the saddle, but to let the horse's motion aid my balance. Well, I clutched that saddle tighter than I would my immortal soul. All the way to the marsh I held on to the leather lip ahead of my groin. Then, as Rascal began to splash among the reeds, I strengthened my grip to the utmost.

I did not see another great serpent, though two smaller snakes disturbed the water's stillness. The wetland smelled of cucumbers and rot.

The Reverend Mr. Hitchens had not heeded me. No guards were posted by those Indian mounds or above the defile. No one watched at all. Unless you count the blind man, Uncle Toby. He plunged toward me, testing the air with his hand.

"You seen my boy?" he begged.

My swift return excited all the camp. Hitchens himself had been at his ablutions and come toward me naked above the belt. He had a look of strength larded by age. His chest, too, bore a slash. But more commanding were the vines of scar that crept over his shoulders from his back and around his thickening sides.

Would I have killed the man who whipped me thus? I have killed men for less beneath a flag.

The preacher pulled on a frock coat over his flesh. His face was marked with questions for the ages.

"You there," I called to a fellow in a shapeless cap and a faded, florid waistcoat, "hold my horse."

The fellow jumped at my command, accustomed. His freedom was forgotten in a moment.

I dropped down hard on my bad leg.

Hitchens parted his lips on a word, but I cut him off. "We must speak, sir." I glanced around at the curious African faces. "Privately."

"What's wrong, Brother? Are the soldiers coming?"

"Walk with me, if you please, sir. Walk with me and I will tell you."

He shooed the others off us and we strolled. They kept away but trailed us with their eyes. Full of foreboding they were, and not without reason.

Hitchens steered us back into the pines. Toward the log that had supported our first conversation. I did not wait to reach our destination, but explained my purpose as soon as we left the camp.

He shook his head. " 'Thou shalt not steal.' Lord, I'm sorry to hear of such doings." His dismay was authentic, yet I could not say he was shocked. "Folks here still aren't used to living decent," he went on. "Takes a piece of time to put them right. After all the troubles been forced on them." He stopped and stood, a penitent, before me. "But I am ashamed, Major. Ashamed and troubled."

"Can you get them back? He won't be calmed, see. And might yet do a thing worth the regretting."

"Oh, yes, Brother. Surely. I'll collect his things, all right. And it was a kindness of you not to shame me in front of my congregation. Or any of them in front of me. That was a true Christian kindness."

"Time there is little," I warned him.

"You just wait up by the sitting log. I'll get what needs to be got and come on back."

I strolled ahead and sat me down. The morning had turned to noon and the forest hummed. Busy as a city, that is nature. With every creature industrious.

Yet, it was a peaceful place, for all the buzzing. I tried to use that peace to think things through. I do believe we are guided by His hand. What had been the purpose in my return? Was it only a matter of petty theft, or had I been given a second chance to ask what I had been too dull to ask before? At least since yester-eve, a thing had gnawed me. And yet I could not say what that thing was.

I waited in the shade, grazing my fingernails across my bites. Insect and ant had tasted Abel Jones here in the Southland, and serpents lurked. It seemed as mean a place as Rajasthan, though green and watered.

The Reverend Mr. Hitchens returned with promptitude, a smile cleft into the deeper cleft of his wound. It was a smile of shame stirred with success. He closed on me and held out a big hand.

I took the locket, watch and chain, and dropped them into my pocket.

"Thank you, Mr. Hitchens," I said. "You are a good shepherd."

He shook his head, smile graven with sorrow. "Mine's the thanking duty, Brother. You like to kept a trouble off Beersheba. A trouble and a tribulation."

"Would you sit beside me for a moment?" I asked him. "I have some more questions, see. It will not take long."

He blessed the log with his ampleness. Hasty he had been about his doings and sweat enriched his faded coat of black.

"Mr. Hitchens . . . I am told you are a wanted murderer."

He nodded. "I figured that young fellow had his eye on me. Surely. Others marked it, too. Some of the hard ones didn't want to let him go off with all his knowings."

"I do not know what he will do, see. Perhaps the time has come for you to leave here."

He shook his head. With finality. "I done run enough."

"It's not just you. The others are in danger if he talks."

"I know. I know that, too. I'll pray on it. I'll pray for him to see the light."

"And I will pray, as well. But not all prayers receive a prompt reception."

"You *do* believe in redemption, Major? You do believe in that blessing, don't you?"

Oh, there is a question with which I was familiar. Redemption was the only hope I had.

"I believe in the redemption of the soul," I told him. "Here below . . . the law will have its way. Caesar will have his renderings."

"Don't you believe a man can repent? Start over again?"

I drew marks in the dirt with the tip of my cane. Erasing marks I had made the day before. "A man can repent." I nodded slowly. At a thing I knew. "And a man can change, sir. I believe that is in our power. But we may not escape the judgement of our neighbors."

"The Good Book says, 'Judge not, lest ye be judged.' "

"The Bible says a muchness of things by which men won't abide. That is a thing you know yourself, Mr. Hitchens. Better than me, I expect."

He made a sound so deep in his throat it seemed to rise from his heart. "I believe a man can lift himself up."

"And he can fall down again," I answered, thinking of myself on the field of battle. "To be a good man is a daily struggle. A battle it is that only ends at the grave. If it ends there."

"I shall not fall again," the preacher said. "I do not know if I will rise, but know I will not fall."

I wished that I might say that of myself, and with as much conviction.

He stared down at the earth. Staring under it, perhaps. "Brother, I killed that man who called himself my master. After he sold off the woman I had taken to me. As she had taken me to her. She would not lie with him. Not smiling and giving. So he stripped her to the waist at the whupping post and took a rod to her. With his own hands, and with plenty of folks looking on. They kept me tied up through all that, for they were rightly fearing what might happen. Wagon done carried her off to Memphis, to the slave pens. Don't expect she fetched much, all broken up the way she was." He tapped his fingers, once, upon his knee. "Soon as they let me free of the tying up, I took a hatchet to that man and burned his house. I never could track on Darly, bless her heart. But they were surely tracking on me. Yes, sir. Dogs and all. Brought out the militia, cause a white man's death is worth something. I struck north. With hatred in my bosom."

He sighed. "Time come and I married again. Married proper that time. That was across in Indiana. But they had the persistence of Satan, those slave-catchers. Out for bounty money. They wouldn't quit cause of no river. Not the Ohio, nor the Jordan. And there were mean folks up North there to help them, too. Pointed them on their way, and glad to do it. Well, when those slave-catchers weren't quick enough to take me, they nailed the doors and shutters of my cabin closed. With my Treesa and our baby child inside. And they burned that cabin down, sir."

He closed his eyes until he had gathered himself. "I didn't kill all three of those men like folks say. But I killed two. And even now . . . though I have repented . . . although I would not do those deeds again . . . I cannot forgive them. There is sorrow in my heart for my doings, Brother. And I forgive the men who scarred my face and whipped me til the bone showed out. But I cannot forgive what was done to those I loved." He almost smiled. "I pray on it til my knees hurt up through my shoulders, but I cannot forgive them."

Before I could speak and mutter an empty comfort, he laid his hand upon my shoulder. His touch raised a small cloud of dust. "I tell myself repentance is a start. That forgiveness is bound to follow. I shall not fall again, Brother. I shall not fall. But, tell you true, I may not rise no higher. Perhaps a man's only got so much Christian in him."

He withdrew his hand, and I felt the loss of it. The wounds we hide are more in want of comfort than the wounds we show.

"You go on, now," Hitchens told me. " 'Seek and ye shall find.' "

I rose to go, weary of a sudden, and with a hot and choking ride before me. But then I turned again, just as the reverend fellow labored to his feet. His jaw had dropped with the effort and his eyes swelled. He put me in mind of men whose hearts betray them. In the medical sense, I mean.

He must have seen the despair I carried with me.

"What is it, Brother?" he asked. "What's so mighty? Pressing down on those shoulders?"

I could have told the man a thousand things, but I was sent to question, not to blabber. "My thoughts will not come straight, see. About this killing business. It chews at me, but I cannot get it clear." I looked into his gouged and kindly face. Into a killer's kindly face, Man's own. "You said this slave fellow . . . the one who returned to lead his brethren to freedom, this Hesiod . . . you said he claimed he had a revelation?"

"Surely," Mr. Hitchens said. "Must've been a powerful one, too. When he passed through here a-preaching and gathering folks up, he wouldn't even answer to his right name no more. Told everybody they was to call him 'Angel.' "

.   .   .

I GALLOPED. Clinging to saddle and mane. Rascal and I splashed through the marsh, and serpents be damned, if you will pardon me. I gave the horse his head up on the good ground. He flew like a very Pegasus.

I had it now. I had it from the front end to the back. And had to get me back to Sherman and Grant, to warn them before Lott could kill again.

Lott and his Judas band of killing madmen.

When I reached the low ridge, I followed its crest for speed. Time seemed everything to me in those moments. As if I might gallop all the way to our Union lines without stopping. Yet, the flesh is weak. I mean not mine, though that is weak enough. I saw that Rascal was sheathed in sweat, a shining creature. Foam minstreled his lips. Game the animal was, and had given me all that he could. I did not want to ruin him, so I slowed us to a walk.

I had hoped to judge a straight descent to the spot where the forge must lay, but fell a bit short in my calculations. I had expected a column of smoke to guide me, but the sky was an unstained blue. We ambled down a meadow to the road. Twas then I saw the peddler, a Hebrew fellow, sweating worse than Rascal as he went. Too poor for horse and cart, he pushed a barrow through the countryside. Dust encased his trousers to the thigh.

As I rode up, he set his burden down. Taking off his topper, he wiped his forehead. Judging whether I might be a danger.

It struck me then, as oft it did in India, how life plods on. For me, Lott's evil seemed large enough to drown the world in excitement. And greater still, a scorching war had come. But the peddler had his business to conduct, as others had loaves to bake, or infants to suckle. The toiler must address his fields if he will eat through winter. It is as when a man is broken-hearted. Around him, life continues without pause, although he knows the world is at an end.

"Your pardon, sir," I said. "There is a smith, I believe, just down this road? In that direction?"

"*Einen Schmied suchen Sie?* A blacksmith?"

"Just so."

He pointed, confirming my direction. "*Es ist nicht weit.* It is not far."

"Thank you, sir."

"Mister?"

I looked down at him from my saddle throne.

"I shoes a horse *besser* than the lazy man up the road."

"The horse is fine. It is an appointed meeting place, see."

"There is something else you need? The medicine? *Ein Heilmittel?* A salve to make the healing?"

There were no salves to heal where I was sore. I shook my head and gave him disappointment, wishing him good day. When I looked back, his hat was back on his head and he had picked up the handles of his barrow, pushing through a country slashed by war.

Twas not far at all to the smith's, not half a mile, as I would shortly learn. But my journey met with another interruption. A figure, near-familiar, traipsed over a field. A woman it was, or a girl, coming to intersect my route.

When I come up to where she stood, I found Paddycakes. Dirtier than usual. As if she had been rolling in ashes.

She looked at me with a mix of anxiousness and hesitation. She had been warned, of course, that Yankees eat their fellow humans.

"Are you all right, Paddycakes?"

She put her fingers to her lips and smiled, body swaying. Blackened in patches, her straw hat shadowed her eyes but let me see their glow.

"I seen the devil," she said. "I really seen him. Tell Marse Drake."

I patted the horse's rump behind my saddle. "You can tell him yourself, girl. He's just ahead. With Mr. Barnaby. Now get you up, for time there is little."

She took a step backward, smile fleeing. "I ain't getting on no Yankee horse."

"Well . . . then just go along this road. And you will find him." Rascal would need a bit of rest at the smithy's. And slow watering he would want. I had been cautioned not to let him gulp. The girl might catch us easily enough. "Go you, now."

She shook her head ferociously. "No, sir, Marse Yankee. I'se hiding," she said, from the sunburned edge of the road.

"First of all, girl, I'm not anybody's 'marse.' And what on earth are you hiding from?"

"The devil."

"Well, I'm sure Lieutenant Raines and Mr. Barnaby will protect you."

"Not from no devil. Bridie tole me all about that."

"And exactly where did you see this devil, Paddycakes?"

"At Shady Grove," she said. "Bridie say it all belong to her now."

.   .   .

THE BLACKSMITH'S SHOP WAS A HOVEL, infested with children and fleas. The hearth was out, which explained why I could not mark the location from the high ground. The smithy and his helper sat in the shadow of the doorway, carving sticks. As if they did not care whether business appeared. The South is different, if not a different country.

Raines and Barnaby occupied a bench in the shade.

I handed Raines his trinkets. The watch and chain hardly mattered to him, but he clutched the locket to his heart as if it were his stolen love returned. And then I tried to tell them about Lott, forgetting Paddycakes entirely. For the girl was simple and I never could understand her properly.

Barnaby listened sober-faced, for he had seen much of the world. But Raines made faces like a restless boy. At last, he said:

"I'd be glad enough to see Micah Lott hang, no matter who owned the rope. But you're saying he's taken to killing Negroes to liberate them? Because he thinks he's carrying out the *Book of Revelation*?" He was so perturbed he could not keep his seat, but rolled to his feet and headed for the water barrel. Dipping himself a drink, he asked me, "That old coon preacher put that in your head? Your murderer friend?"

"No, Lieutenant. He only helped me see what had long been

spread before me. And I cannot say exactly what is in Lott's mind, though mad enough it seems to me. Whether he believes the sacrifice of some Negroes to trigger a crusade is a fair price, or whether he is convinced he is God's appointed avenger . . . or if he believes he can bring on the Judgement Day through his own doings . . . that I cannot tell you. But he is taken with the *Book of Revelation,* that is certain. A man does not brand his own hand with seven stars in a fit of fancy. I should have thought on it long before. For Lott believes the book and this war join. Beyond that, I can only tell you that he and his men killed the forty Negroes. Who were betrayed by a Judas of their own, a man with a different madness."

"You sound a little sun-bothered yourself."

I longed to ride on, to return to my own kind and leave this self-cursed land behind me. But my horse needed time, and Raines still wanted persuading.

"Well," I tried again, "war is a madness. And love, too, is a madness. Of more variety than there are kinds of fishes in the sea. There is madness in plenty in this world, and likely I have my share. But Lott is a killer who needs stopping now."

The mind is queer. I thought, just in that instant, of Mr. Shakespeare's sad old king pleading to the heavens to save him from madness. Perhaps our ceaseless prayer should be: "Oh, Lord, spare me the madness to which I am born."

"Master Francis?" Barnaby said, fanning himself with his hat. "It don't matter a bit, these revvy-lations. That's what Barnaby B. Barnaby has to say. What matters is that Lott's come up the killer. He's right on that business, the major is. And there's a fine pheasant to flush, as me governor liked to put it."

"But where's the proof?" Raines demanded. He made his voice theatrical. "For God's sake, look at it! Suddenly, the great, bloody-handed champion of abolition is a slave-killer himself?" He turned to me, so troubled by this world. He looked for sense and stumbled over mankind. "I trusted you," he told me. "And I'm beginning to feel a fool because of it. This doesn't make a peck of sense, not any of it."

"Do not look for sense," I told him. "Look for belief. Lott is the killer, and I will stake my life on it."

He dropped back down on the bench. Hard enough to jar his spine. "Will you?" he asked, in an oddly resigned voice. "*Will* you stake your life on it? Or is there something going on that you won't tell us? Some Yankee scheme? The way you go creeping around . . ."

"Master Francis," Barnaby tried again, cajoling a moody child, "begging your pardon, but it seems to me the major here's done a proper job, he has. It's wicked what all comes out when the questions are put right. A proper fellow, the major is. And ain't it a pleasure to think that Lott's the guilty party? And not none of you what wears the gray coat of honor? Ain't it come out as good as it could come?"

Now, you will say, "This Raines boy wanted spanking. For boy he was, though long past twenty-one." But I will tell you: He had learned things that no man wants to know, about his friend and the woman whom he loved, about his teetering world and about himself. He was not cruel, but only disappointed. And fearful. For what one man may do, so might we all. And, despite his taste of battle and of heartbreak, his life had been a sheltered one. There is no harsher master than reality.

"Oh," I said, "I near forgot. I saw the girl, Paddycakes, up the road. I thought she might come after."

Raines waved that problem off. "She knows her way home. She'll come around when she gets hungry enough."

"It ain't far, sir," Mr. Barnaby assured me. "Shady Grove's not four miles down the pike. Why, it ain't a half-dozen miles from there across country to the Negro camp, for that matter. If a fellow goes straight and proper. It's a small world, as me governor used to say, when a gent ain't playing ring around the rosey." He glanced back around the corner, to where a scrofulous lad was tending Rascal. The high afternoon condensed the Englishman's shadow. "I think your horse is ready for a trot, sir." He clapped his hands, thinking, perhaps, of a pending dinner. "Shall we go then, gentlemen? Off we go then, friendly as bacon and eggs!"

As we rode away, the peddler rounded the bend behind us, sweating his way into his chosen country.

. . .

As soon as he had assured himself that Raines and I would not resort to pistols, Barnaby dropped behind us, chewing on strips that looked like ruined leather. The afternoon's warmth was sufficient to call for opened buttons and we rode easily. Although my heart longed to gallop all the way to Union headquarters, my head knew that the journey would last at least another day, and likely two. For we must go first to Corinth, to tell the Confederates all that we had learned. Only then would I be granted safe passage.

I thought of Lott, of how I had not liked the man. Scripture hurled about is Scripture fouled.

Raines had strapped on his pistol, but still his hand lay buried in a pocket, clutching the charm I had retrieved. Perhaps it soothed him, for when he spoke again his voice was milder.

"Micah Lott?" he said, clucking his tongue.

"Still in doubt, Lieutenant?"

"No," he admitted. "I was only riled. You've figured out just about everything else in the state of Mississippi, so why not that?"

I thought on his meaning, then said:

"I will not pass on Captain Barclay's secrets."

"No. I suppose not."

"Or anyone else's," I promised him.

"Except Lott's."

"That is different. And you, Lieutenant? May I ask you to keep the secret of the Negroes in the woods? They do no harm that I can see."

"Your preacher friend is a known murderer."

"I have killed more men with less cause myself."

He looked at me with eyes as narrow as razor cuts. I did not mean the statement as a brag, but perhaps he took it as one. Our words are awkward things to tell our meaning. And though we had dealt with a band of clumsy highwaymen, he had no way of knowing my service history. Nor would I tell him my tale, for the past is present enough without our chatter. Likely, he saw a bobbing little man, attempting to fit himself into seven-league boots. But let that bide.

"Let them be," I said. "There'll be no harm beyond some stolen chickens."

He did not answer, and I did not press him. We would have time when he was calmer still.

Rascal snorted. The shiver passed along his neck and back. Then he settled again. The day had slowed beyond helping, although I longed to gallop. I thought again of things that Lott had said to me. Trying to remember chapter and verse.

" 'Thrust in thy sickle and reap,' " I recited aloud, " 'for the time is come for thee to reap; for the harvest of the earth is ripe.' "

Raines glanced at me.

"*Revelation,*" I told him. The sky glowed gilded blue.

"I know," he said. Of course, he knew. The spoiled theologian, the Harvard man.

"The preacher, Hitchens, said something that struck me," I told him. "Yesterday evening it was. He said he dreaded the *Book of Revelation.* That was the very word he used. 'Dread.' Now you will think it strange, but I will tell you, Lieutenant: I knew exactly what the fellow meant. It is a hard book, that one, hard and cruel. It does not follow rightly after the Gospels, and I have wondered why the Lord had need of it, why he had to put it in the Book."

"God didn't put it in," Raines said. "Men did. Men like Micah Lott."

I was about to defend the sanctity of the entire Holy Writ, and sorry I was for the liberty of my speech, when I noticed wisps of smoke above a grove. A soldier gets to know each kind of smoke. This rose from dwindled fires, from burned remnants. It was not much, just smudges on the blue.

I pointed up the road. "There has been a fire," I said. "See there? The smoke?"

A mask of wonder covered the lad's face. He whipped his horse and shouted:

"That's Shady Grove!"

fourteen

 ever believe that strong men do not weep. That is a theme for hypocrites and fools. Young Raines was strong. I speak here of the strength that matters, and not of clumsy force or loud bravado. Even in Mick Tyrone's medicine, the heart is the ultimate muscle. Strong arms falter, but stout hearts last. Raines had more heart than he could yet master, and the tempest in his soul left him bewildered. He sat and wept, as if remembering Zion.

I recall it clearly, how he thrashed his hat upon the ground then sat with his legs drawn up and his face dropped toward his knees. He quivered as if wracked with enteric fever, and his sobs were gasps of despair. I have wept thus myself, once, in distant India. But that is my story, and this day's sorrow was his, and I must not be selfish in my tellings.

I recall the sound of his weeping, and the fidgeting of our horses, and the whisper of the ashes. Barnaby's footsteps crunched amid the ruins, then stilled. He, too, wore a baffled, broken look. Tears wet his eyes, but I did not think they were for the master of Shady Grove. Myself, I stood there, helpless as a child.

Crows had gathered, cawing in the trees or dipping through the final ghosts of smoke. In India, some heathens worship fire and expose their dead to the elements. Black birds assemble for the feast, as they congregated here. Perhaps it is all the same, this world, like but for climate and costume. Perhaps our mortal differences are dreams. Perhaps that final battle from the Book is here and now, and every single day.

But let that bide.

We found three bodies. Charred and showing bone. Barnaby identified two of them as Samson, the old servant, and his wife. He recognized them by familiar properties, for nothing like a face remained to greet us.

We all knew Barclay. Where once the porch had been, a legless dummy, shaped of ash, lay by the tipped-over skeleton of a roll-chair. A blackened pistol touched the mitten that had been a hand.

America burns differently. In India, you torch the thatch of roofs, or light the adornments of a palace and let them sear the marble of the walls. But here, where wood is abundant, fires level. Only a few blackened braces stand, whittled down by the blaze that failed to consume them. Foundation brick cracks from the heat, but holds. Our ruins are a jumble like a battlefield, where you can read a life from tattered remnants.

An ember flared and black smoke puffed.

I began to poke in the ruins, with no more sense than a widow who walks in her sleep. Oh, it is odd how fire works. It burns the robe of silk and spares the rag. The room where I had found Barclay in his midnight despair, amid the hundred gowns, had collapsed down into the library, then all had fallen to the burnt earth below, for there was no cellar to the house. Metal buttons and clasps gripped scraps of cloth. Strings of melted beads gleamed like queer snakes. Amid the black and walnut of destruction, flakes of color teased the eye. Books had burnt to rectangles of coal. And then I found one, small and thick, with hardly a scar upon it. A candle might have brushed it for the slight damage it wore. The title shone gold. Twas foreign. I carried it to where young Raines sat crying.

"Look you," I said, in a meager voice, "I found this. Perhaps you should keep it? To remember?"

"Go to Hell," Raines said, without looking up. "You can all just go to Hell."

"I'm sorry, see . . ."

Oh, he looked up then. Eyes wild and fierce. "Is this how you all make war? Is this . . . it? Your noble crusade for the Union?" He face was wrecked with tears, and raw, and swollen.

I did not know what to say. But I knew what I needed to do.

I had to get back to our lines, to reach Sherman or Grant. Or Halleck, if he was the great chief now. I had to reach someone, anyone, who could stop Lott and his murderers.

I just held out the book to Raines. For I was bereft of words.

He brushed it away. But his sobbing spell had been broken.

I did not retract the book, but nudged it closer. Almost forcing it on him. At last, he grasped it in his hand. Absently examining the title.

He smiled. Twas as if the sun had pierced dark clouds.

The smile faded quickly, and he thrust the book back at me.

"Here," he said. "You take it." His eyes followed the outline of my person, down to my feet and back again, and I could not figure his changed tone of voice. "I have all I ever wanted from Shady Grove. You take the book."

I accepted it. For the moment, you understand. A book is a precious thing and must not be discarded. Unless it is immoral and lascivious. I would put it in my saddlebag and offer it to him later, when he had calmed. Surely, he would want a small memento of his friend and fallen rival.

I turned the book in my hand to read the spine again. *Don Quixote*. Miguel de Cervantes. At least that was not French, I did not think.

I flipped it open and saw English words.

"Take it," Raines said, in a cooled voice, "and read it. It suits you."

Now that he seemed in better order, I was about to raise the business of Lott and my need to move expeditiously, but Mr. Barnaby crunched his way toward us, stepping with care across the desolation.

"Begging your pardon, sir," he said to Raines, "I'll try to find us a shovel down in the shanties." He glanced up at the crows. "We'll be wanting to bury the three of them before we go."

A new voice at my back corrected the manservant:

"You'll have to bury four."

I turned and come up facing Captain Wylie. The pistol in his hand was aimed at me.

.   .   .

"He's a damned liar and a dirty little coward," Wylie said, speaking of me. His voice was distraught and the pistol not a yard from my nose. He would not miss. "Him and Lott been working together all along, Drake."

He thumbed the hammer back. One click, then another. Twas a forty-four caliber Colt, just like my own.

Believe me, Wylie had my strict attention. But from the corner of my eye I caught a movement.

Barnaby had drawn his pistol, too. I thought they meant to shoot me from both sides. But the Englishman said:

"Pull that trigger, Captain, and you'll be dead as old King William and Prince Albert."

Wylie had no yellow in him. His weapon did not waver. Nor did his eyes.

"Kill me then, you fat sumbitch. What do I care? My wife's dead. Even my dogs. And my house burnt down around them. All cause of this runt Yankee."

Raines had barely moved. He sat upon the earth, as if to rise were futile. But he said, "Wasn't him, Buck. Honest to God. He's no more siding with Lott than you or me."

"Then why'd they do it? Why kill them a woman like that?

Burn a man's house?" For the first time, his eyes moved off me. To scour the ruins of Shady Grove with a glance. "Why do *this?*"

I had a great deal to say, for I saw the terrible end laid out before me. And time there was little to stop it. Good men would die, and murderers would reign. But I had experience enough to know that if I said a word he would pull that trigger.

"It's a war, Buck," Raines told him. "And war seems to be about the best excuse that's come along yet for meanness."

"That ain't war. That's not even Yankee war."

"It's war for some folks," Raines insisted. "Men like Lott."

"Captain Wylie," Barnaby said, "begging your pardon, sir, but I'd be delighted not to kill you. And I can attest to the major's innocence, I can. He's the one come up with proof how Lott's behind them slave murders. And plenty else besides, if you ask Barnaby B. Barnaby. Now if you'd be a right gent and lower that cannon, we might discuss this decent and civil like."

Wylie looked at me with the perfect hatred I had seen on the face of the sepoys and holy men we executed in the wake of the Mutiny. But he lowered his Colt. He did not release the hammer, though, and he held the weapon ready at his side.

"They killed Ada?" Raines asked him, in a gentled tone. He knew it already, of course, for Wylie had just told us. But there are questions to be asked in sympathy, the repetition soothing as a liturgy.

Tears swelled in the warrior's eyes, though Wylie fought them back. "They killed everything they could kill," he said. "And burnt what they couldn't. I was off patrolling, with just two of the boys left back. Killed them, too."

"I'm sorry, Buck."

"I reckon I'll do me some killing hereafter." His eyes stabbed into me again. Glistening. "See what comes of it."

I had an urgency in me, for I had much to say. I had it all now, every single bit. But there was fear in me, too, I will tell you truly. For Wylie was a man who would kill you in a calm mood. Excited, he would tear you into bits. I hesitated until I could no longer hold my peace and still think myself a man.

"If you want to finish Lott," I told him, eyes upon his gun, "I can help you. But there is little time and we must hurry."

. . .

"WHAT THE DEVIL'S HE GRUNTING ON ABOUT?" Wylie asked Raines. After I had tried to explain what was coming.

"Bunch of niggers lying out in the woods," the lieutenant said. "Set themselves up a couple of lean-tos and declared it the Kingdom of God."

"Sounds like niggers," Wylie said. Every time he looked at me his nostrils flared. And the gun remained cocked in his hand.

"Martin's Will is with them. Leading them. Claims he's seen the light."

"Well, help us, Jesus. A rope's all he needs to see. You sure it was him, Drake?"

Raines nodded. "Ask our Yankee."

Wylie whistled. "Well, wouldn't that be something? Micah Lott up against Martin's Will. I might just ride out there to watch." Then he considered. "You don't think they're together in this some-ways?"

"They are not," I said, impatient. I would have to watch my tone. But Martin's Will, or the Reverend Mr. Hitchens, was not the point. "Don't you see?" I asked. "There's a pattern. It's clear as day." I looked, warily, at the broadness and bigness that was Wylie. "First, Lott attacked your farm. Then he struck here. I'm not in league with him, as God is my witness, man. But he's following wherever I go. And killing wherever I leave."

"Sounds like you might be his pointer dog," Wylie said, digging the thumb of his left hand into his pistol belt.

"I fear he has been using me as such." Twas something to regret a life long.

"Then you're in with him, after all." Wylie's pistol nudged higher.

"Captain Wylie, you are fond of hounds," I said. "Would you kill your best pointer? I have done much for Lott—without intent—but he would kill me sure, given the chance. And he will see to it that the chance comes soon. For his pointer knows too much and is set to bark. He will see that."

Wylie snorted. "And this is all over some preacher nonsense? All hellfire and hoors of Babylon?"

"It's twisted in his head. But the doings are clear. He thinks he is a messiah with fire and sword. And his vengeance follows after me, like plague does a summer campaign. Now he will kill the Negroes at Beersheba."

"The ones in the woods," Raines explained.

"So . . . instead of killing you," Wylie said, "you want me to ride off and rescue a passel of coons who run away to sing hymns and steal for their supper?"

"No, Captain Wylie. I want you to help me stop Lott."

"Jones," Raines interrupted, "for God's sake. You're the one who's not thinking clearly. It's not half a dozen miles from here to that camp. And it isn't hidden worth a damn. If he burned Shady Grove this morning, Lott's been there and gone." He got to his feet. Dried tears stained his face under rumpled hair. He picked up his hat and dusted it against his leg. "In fact, I'm surprised he wasn't already there when you went back. You were lucky."

I was as frantic as a child who has seen a house afire but will not be believed. I wanted to draw out my timepiece, but feared Wylie would think I was reaching for my Colt. The afternoon had begun to wane. We still had time, but not much.

"No," I insisted. "Don't you see? Lott may be Bedlam mad, but he knows the killing business. He'll wait for their evening meeting. When all are gathered to pray. That way he doesn't have to collect them, or chase them. He won't miss a one. He'll trap them like he did the forty others, and butcher them the same. I think the setting takes his fancy, too. For he would rather kill a man at prayer. It steeps the vengeance." I looked from man to man. Each had lost much. "I *beg* you, gentlemen. We still have time to save them. And stop Lott."

Wylie turned to Raines, who glanced up through the wisps of smoke. Judging the light we had left. Sunbeams speared between the trees, killing the day.

"Think there's anything to this, Drake?" Wylie asked. "Don't think it's some kind of trap, do you?"

"We'll have to ride hard," Raines said in response.

"And there ain't but four of us," Wylie said. "If it is some Yankee bushwhack."

"Surprise ain't to be sniffed at, as me governor's governor always said, or so they tell me," Barnaby said. "And that was him what fought with the Iron Duke. No, they won't be looking for Barnaby B. Barnaby and his mates, they won't. Begging your pardon, gentlemen." He drew himself up like the soldier he once had been, stomach thrust out mighty and magnificent. "It *do* sound like the matter needs attention, don't it?"

He wheeled toward me, still on muster parade, though his face was newly troubled. "I should have mentioned it before, I should. But I didn't think it jolly well signified. I sees it now, though, now I sees it clear."

"What's that, Mr. Barnaby?" I asked. Near frantic with impatience I was, but unwilling to spurn an ally through discourtesy.

"The Indian," Barnaby said. "Now don't all this explain the Red Indian I laid me peepers on last night? By the Negro camp, it was. He was prowling like a Welshman out of work. Begging your pardon, Major. That weren't but a figger of speech. No, I thought the devil was scavenging for victuals. Foraging, like a tinker after dark. And here he was off on a scout for Lott himself!"

"Dammit, Mr. B.," Raines said, "you should've told us. Lott's known to have an Indian riding with him."

I should have told them several things myself. About a certain

Indian and his visits. But I did not. For that would only have raised new doubts about me, deserved though they might have been on that single count. And now the hour was past for all disputes. Twas time to act. And little time was left.

"How did you know he was an Indian?" I asked, though. For I wanted to be sure of the matter. I thought he would mention the ribbons in Broke Stick's hair.

"Oh, it was how the bugger moved, begging your pardon. A white man has a clumsy way when he's sneaking about, and the Negro a furtive one in his doings. But your Indian's simply going about his business, and clever, too. I saw him in the moonlight, creeping low. Dressed like a white man he was, but no less of an Indian."

"Please, gentleman," I said. "Shall we go?"

"What the hell," Wylie said. "I'm in a killing enough mood. You, Drake?"

"Yes," the young man said, staring at the wasteland that had been so much a part of his life. "Some killing sounds about right."

"Then we're decided," Mr. Barnaby announced. "The burying can wait for the sake of the living."

The faithful servant moved for his horse. Trying to start us all going. You see, there was great justice in that man. He might want vengeance, too, but in his heart he wanted to save the Negroes more. I will believe that to my dying day.

He almost made me think well of the English.

Before we could mount, a figure burst out of the woods. Shriveled and ragged she come, the slave named Bridie. Her turban was gone and her hair sprang wizard wild. She bore a little satchel in her hands, and her features were lunatic.

"Git, white folks," she cried, approaching us the way a rabid creature will. "You *git*. I buried mah black cat bone, buried it deep down, now all this place be mines."

She thrust a hand into her sack and drew out a fattened fist. Her walk was twisted worse than mine when I went caneless, and she was bent. But grinning. Oh, grinning like the very bride of Lucifer she was. She scrambled, as a crab might do, for Wylie.

"Blessed are the dead!" she yelped, hurling dust over his uniform.

Before he could react, she came for me, digging in her little bag again.

And then she froze. Not five feet from me. Hand raised ready with her witch's baptism. She stopped as if a spirit blocked her way, as if a dreadful veil had been drawn between us.

Terror strained her features. She seemed to be struggling to see me. Then her jaw dropped, and brown stumps showed where teeth should have been. Her eyes bulged madly from her pockmarked face.

Her fist dropped and loosened. Dust sieved through twitching fingers, trailing down her skirt.

And then she bolted. Scrambling for the woods as if pursued.

I never claimed to be a handsome man.

.　　.　　.

WE RODE THROUGH MILD LIGHT and fading heat. Our pace was brisk, but gallop we did not. I was learning about the horse, see. Just like a man, it cannot run at a full effort without blowing itself. Its spunk must be husbanded for the moment of need. I had seen cavalry charges in India, canter and trot, the ranks beginning to waver as gaps appeared and *sirdars* barked for the men to close up, then the lowering of the lances and the bugle calling horse and rider to rush, the shouts and crashing as they met the foe. I had thought the measured gains in speed were tactics. Now I saw the animal counted, too.

Our hoofbeats made a rumpus in the landscape, while the countless creatures that drowse by day told the world of their waking. The sun's decline spread beauty over paucity and even stunted pines were gilded things. Four raw men rode through paradise, spiting its peace. We rode to kill, and that inflames a man as mercy won't.

Wylie was a masterful rider and his mount a splendid beast. But he had ridden long and hard, and now he set the pace, for his horse was worn. It angered him more, that need to show restraint. He thirsted after blood and could not get there quick enough to slake him. Once decided upon a course, his set face showed no second thoughts at all.

Raines was thorough-bred, just like his horse. Light as air, he glided over the earth. I worried he would die. For fineness is a thing men cannot bear. In battle, they can sense a better spirit and strain to slay it though their lives be spent in the act. His light brown hair streamed behind him, and the falling sun thrilled in his eyes. If fear was in him, hatred was its master. The boy would kill for all he had endured. He would kill for the sake of Barclay's death, and then for Barclay's theft of his youthful love. He would kill because the world had disappointed him, because the silver of his faith had tarnished. He would kill because it is a pleasing thing, though we pretend otherwise. He would kill because it is a way of dying. I saw him clearly as the miles passed. He would pull the trigger twice or thrice after his pistol had emptied. Furious that his will could not forge powder and ball out of thin air.

Barnaby wore the face of a veteran soldier. All aplomb. He knew what killing was, and meant to do it. To him, it was a job that must be done, but he would take no joy from it.

I think he was a better man than me.

As we rode, the servant spoke solicitously to Wylie. As if the rougher fellow had become his charge and wanted comforting. Barnaby warned him to be cautious, not to risk himself. I could not understand it. I half thought he would ask Wylie to turn back from the danger ahead. Now, Barnaby's worry seemed a bit queer to me. For there was barely a tie twixt him and Wylie, and his attentions should, by right, have gone to Raines.

Wylie waved him away like a pesky fly.

As we traced the ridge, I edged up to the new widower myself. For I had a question gnawing me within.

"Captain Wylie?" I asked. My voice was careful as a guard on forward picket.

He turned a killer's eyes in my direction. The falling sun painted his face red as gore.

"You said . . . that Lott's men killed two fellows you left behind. By any chance, was—"

"Dai Evans?" Hatred for all mankind poisoned his voice. "First they shot him down. Then they cut him up like a hog." He leaned from the saddle and spat into the grass. "Kept you alive, Dai did. Every time the boys got set to hang you, he'd make 'em laugh until they let you be." He snorted, turning away. "Old Dai got thanked right pretty for it."

I would not think upon such matters now.

We entered the valley. The pines. With the marsh beyond. The light fell golden on the ridge and smoky blue below.

We rode down into silence.

Listening, I was. For the first shot. And the spurt of fire that would follow. The volleys and the screams. I did not know how far the sounds would carry, for the earth is strange in the ways it tells its tale. I have been half a mile from a bloody skirmish and not known there was fighting anywhere near. Regiments have marched past dying comrades, unaware the fellows were in need. And then you hear a battle a day's march away, carried through the air clear as a good choir, and you quicken your step in a hopeless try at succor.

I heard nothing. Nothing but the fresh dusk sounds, the calling of rested birds.

The marsh loomed. In long shadows. I would not want to go through there in the dark.

Our guns were out. But not for serpents.

Single file we rode. Spaced apart, so we could break if fired upon.

I jumped, but twas only a greeting bird. I know not its name, but it sounded like a loon.

The splashing of the hooves seemed loud as ocean waves. If Lott had placed men on watch while he did his business, they could kill at least a pair of us from the shadows before we spotted them.

I did not see the snake till I was near past it. Coiled as thick as rope on the deck of a ship. An arm's length from Rascal's legs.

It did not strike, but watched us with steady eyes. Nor did it slither off. This was its hour.

In India, I hated night patrols. Look you. I have no special fear of snakes. Not as I do of horses. But when you must ply the gulleys and the ditches, or crawl across a field toward a hut, you do not worry about the enemy's bullets half so much as you fear the cobra's fangs. When your path is errant, they rise up all around you like spring toys. Once, on the worst of nights before Delhi, two died screaming of ten men who went out with me.

I did not want to think about that now. No more than I would think of poor Dai Evans. It is bad luck to remember old dangers and failures before you go into battle. You must think better thoughts. Or, best of all, you should not think at all.

At the far end of that vale of reeds and water, Barnaby nudged forward, raising his hand to halt us. The light was soft as velvet, but rich enough to let you hit your mark.

We stopped. Grouped too closely for my taste. Even as Barnaby spoke, we scanned around us. The rocks. The mounds ahead. The winding path.

God's oblivious creatures filled the ear.

Maybe I was wrong, I thought. Perhaps Lott had not come for them at all. What if I read him wrong, and he had not killed the Negroes? What if his fight against slavery was sincere? What if his killing, cruel though it was, had been confined to white flesh, Wylie's family and the heir of Shady Grove? With the servants accidental victims? What if his hand had not torched the plantation?

What if Abel Jones was but a fool, too swift in his conclusions, as he had been in the midst of the Fowler affair? What if Lott was far away and I was only blasting the hopes of Mr. Hitchens, leading yet another Rebel to Beersheba?

Barnaby whispered his knowledge: Tracking Raines and myself the day before, he had discovered an overlook back of the camp. The slope was gentle on both sides. If we worked our way behind the mounds, between them and the marsh, we might avoid the rocky defile and descend into the camp without a warning.

A dark bird swooped. Perhaps it was a bat.

"I got me a devil feel," Wylie said. He sounded uneasy. I had not expected that.

"The cautious come to rights," Barnaby told him, with concern flecking his eyes. "That's what me governor always said, and he lived to be fifty. Careful is clever, and clever is careful, Captain Wylie."

Barnaby gave his mount a tap with the reins and we followed him into the gloaming.

The air felt cooler of a sudden. Perhaps it was the night drift off the swamp.

What if we rode smack into Lott's command? Well, at least the Reverend Mr. Hitchens and his people would have some warning.

I knew I was riding with men who would fight. But the Colt in my hand felt like my only friend. The Colt, and the Testament thick in my pocket. My bloodied souvenir of Philadelphia.

Then I heard it.

Not a sound. But the absence of sound.

Nature reads man well.

The world had gone still as the grave.

Twas a world of eyes.

All watching.

The others sensed it, too. I felt them tighten.

The trees opened a little and I tried to sense our position. If I was right, the camp was just to our left, behind a rise. But shadows trick us. And we had ridden into a shadowed world.

The air was cool, but I was sweating a torrent. As I had done before a dozen battles and half a hundred nameless scraps in India. Twas hatefully familiar. I felt what I had prayed I might leave behind: The ready hand of Abel Jones the Killer.

Suddenly, a wonder pierced the evening. Twas voices raised in song, a sturdy hymn. As beautiful as Heaven on a Sunday it was. With harmonies as glorious as love.

The firing started but a moment later. The shooting and the shouting and the screams. We had no bugle, but we turned as one. And charged into the Valley of the Shadow.

fifteen

The Indian shot Wylie down the moment we broke from the trees. But it was the reflex of a man surprised, not an ambush. Broke Stick had failed in his task. He failed to hear our coming.

Perched too close to the doings the Indian was, amid the wild alarm of the massacre, the howling and the gunfire, the hoof-thumps and whinnies, and the crackling of burning shacks. Perhaps he sensed no threat that night and relaxed his vigilance. Or perhaps he was tired from his midnight gadabouts. In any case, a fatal choice it was, that slackening of attention, and the Indian knew it the instant he saw us. A look of surprise spoiled his face as we burst from the darkness. There was death in his firelit eyes, and the death was his own. It made him seem a man like you or me.

He barely saw us in time to raise his revolver and fire. But shoot he did, before any of us could aim. He fired and barked a warning that went unheard in the bloody madness, doing his sentry's duty at the last.

Wylie, who rode closest to the Indian, paid the price for us all.

Backward the captain fell, pistol spinning off as he clutched his face. His hat sailed away and blood plumed from his head. Even had I not seen the spew of gore, I would have known him dead by the way he tumbled. Lifeless men are rag dolls stuffed with lead. Wylie crashed to earth beside a shanty. Flames painted the walls and lit the captain's features. His horse charged onward into the mêlée.

Broke Stick smiled.

For an instant he smiled, but no longer. Barnaby and Raines both gunned him down, the young man wheeling to fire a second time into the crumpled figure. A wall collapsed and flames reached for the Indian. A ribbon in Broke Stick's hair took fire, then the hair itself lit up. But he was burning elsewhere now, among the damned, and did not even twitch as the fire explored him.

All these were the acts of crumpled seconds. The speed of violence slays the man untrained, the heart unready. For every shot that I report, a dozen more were fired. For every scream set down, a hundred sounded.

"*Get off the horses,*" I shouted. "*Get down, for God's sake.*"

I swung out of the saddle, a clumsy pendulum, trying to stop my horse from rushing onward. I had the measure of the doings, see, although the details blurred. Beyond the burning huts the preaching ground had become a killing ground, as I foresaw. I did not know how many men Lott had with him, since some had fallen across the weeks and might not have been replaced. Still, there could be as many as a dozen.

I saw only three on horseback, herding the Negroes. The rest had dismounted to butcher with a method. For the cavalry will give you a fright, but the infantry does the killing. A pistol discharged from the saddle will not strike half so true as the one fired by a man with his heels planted. As long as we stayed on horseback, we were no more than targets on offer. And some of Lott's disciples had seen us now.

Amid the tortured Negroes, amid the fallen and falling, Lott stood out. Hat off and hair awry, his beard waved and his stony features glistened. A pistol stretched his left hand, while a cutlass in his right hacked into man-meat. Wherever he went, blood rained. He slashed at praying hands and fleeing backs. His lips moved, but the noise destroyed his words. It looked as though no human could withstand him.

If this was not the end of days, it was a hint of Hell.

Alone of all his men, Lott cared nothing for us. Slaughter was his purpose on this earth. But the others saw us clearly now, for the fires drew our outlines. While they were creatures flirting through the shadows, too far and faint and quick for our revolvers.

"Get down!" I screamed as loudly as I could. Barnaby was out of the saddle and scampering. He, too, saw things with a survivor's eyes. But young Raines was at risk, with his fine horse rearing up as he wasted bullets avenging a fallen friend.

Perhaps, for that one moment, death enticed him.

The shifts of combat come as quick as lightning. Of a sudden, we were at a disadvantage. Momentum had been on our side when we flashed out of the trees, but the Indian had blunted the shock before it had any effect. Three men in a muddle was all we were now.

We had not made a plan, see. I like a plan, like any proper soldier, but there are times, and this was one, when all you can do is go forward and trust your arm. It is a dangerous course, but not all battle fits into a staff tent. And I know how to do it, how to hit an enemy from behind and cut into him. But losing Wylie broke our charge, and Raines was new to fighting. If Shiloh had been his first real scrap, it only would have confused him. It is in your second or third fight that you start to learn.

Raines would not see another fight if he did not dismount. Rifles turned toward him, willing to interrupt their Negro-killing with a gray coat on offer.

A white man darted from the trees, running to where Raines strained in his saddle. The attacker held a pistol in each hand.

I shot low, beneath the rearing belly of the horse. I saw the wince of the hip, the stutter of the leg, and the man went down. I let go of my mount and ran for Raines, for I realized he could not hear me. I am not sure he would have heard any man. He looked the cavalier, he did, valiant on his stallion. But such men die for nothing. And I needed him.

His horse nearly trampled me, though I had plenty of ginger in my step. I tugged the boy's spur then grabbed his boot. His wild face turned toward me. He almost shot me, finger tightening on his trigger, before he realized who I was.

"Get down!" I shouted. "You're naught but a target, boy."

Then I ran for the shadows, as fast as my bad leg could go. Along the way, I put another bullet into the man I had brought down. He was armed and alive, see, until my bullet bit into his spine. I snatched up one of his pistols, the one in his left hand. For he had led with his right as he ran toward us. The pistol from his left hand would be the richer, by one round at least, perhaps by more, for some men will fire the gun in their favored hand empty before they remember the other paw is armed.

I felt a presence behind me, as soldiers do, and turned to fire.

Twas Raines. Following me obediently. Behind his back, his horse pranced off and settled.

I could not see Barnaby, but knew he could handle himself. A man popped up with a rifle and I fired at him quickly, without aiming. I could not hit him at the range he offered, but I wanted to unsettle his own aim. And when he saw the pistol flame, he faltered, cringing for cover. Just long enough to get us into the darkness of the undergrowth.

Some Negroes ran. I saw them. Breaking through the cordon we had spoiled. Some would be saved. We had done that, at least. But I could not get a clear look at our situation. For the flaming shacks had filled my eyes too long. Though my back was turned toward the fires, they still burned in my vision. There is a rule of fighting in the dark, see. You never look toward the source of light. But time had been the fiercest of our enemies, and the flames had been our guide unto our enemies. Now the darkness trapped me like a cave. I needed time to heal my eyes. And Raines would, too.

Twas odd. All others blurred, but I saw Lott. He stood in the very center of the preaching ground, a musket shot from where we crouched in the brush. His cutlass rose, and then the blade descended. With a machine's regularity. Now and then the blade caught in flesh and bone, and his shoulders turned to wrench the metal free. He splashed the fresh blue night with stars of blood. Despite the range and my dazzled eyes, I would have fired on him. But trapped and wounded Negroes surged between us, running to and fro, crying horridly. My round would not hit Lott, but might hit them.

Seconds. All this happened in seconds.

"What do we do?" Raines asked me.

"Don't look toward the flames. Just follow after." I dashed, if so I may describe my blundering scuttle, deeper into the trees. The young man's footfalls crashed at my heels. Bullets chased us.

The world flickered and raged.

Lott's men were good killers. But they were not good soldiers. They did not shout out messages of cooperation. Some hunted for us, but others turned back to the Negroes, each man to his chosen delight.

Then I saw one tumble from a horse. I thought Barnaby had dropped him. But Cupid rushed from the shadows, his old dragoon pistol a great chop in his hand. He used it to beat the fallen rider to death, then wrenched a revolver from his victim's grip.

He charged into the maelstrom. Twas all wrong. He ran for Lott, blasting at others as he went, not counting his rounds, surely unaware of how many bullets remained in the captured gun. He brought a rifleman down and leapt the body. Heading straight for Lott. Fighting off the clutch of his wounded fellows, shoving all flesh from his path, trampling the dead and the dying.

He raised the pistol.

Lott saw him late. Cupid's pistol almost touched his head. I could not see the Negro's fingers, but felt him pull the trigger.

Then he stopped cold. Astounded at the failure of the gun.

Before the Negro moved again, Lott shot him. Muzzle to his torso. Cupid staggered backward. He almost tripped at a corpse, but kept himself upright. Fighting to steady himself. Amazed at what had happened to his body, he stared down at the hand clapped below his heart.

Lott's cutlass flashed. It met the base of the Negro's neck and hewed deep into his collar. One dark hand closed over the steel, then went limp. When Cupid fell, he took the blade down with him. Lott had to bend over and place a boot on the fellow's chest to retrieve it.

All of Lott's men had dismounted now. Or perhaps the horsemen had fallen to those Negroes who fought back. My vision was returning, but battle always keeps its share of secrets. I could not place or number all our enemies. And Mr. Barnaby had gone missing.

Seconds sprawled and minutes widened. A woman with her arms hacked to stumps staggered off with her babe in her teeth as a cat will. Blood covered all, luminous as ice. Children thought they could hide in the near, afraid to stray too far from dying parents. Lott's men cleared the brush of them with Bowie knives. They might have been the innocents of Bethlehem. Negro men, and women, too, fought back. But bare fists are no match for blades and bullets.

I had not seen the Reverend Mr. Hitchens.

Then Lott's men made a mistake. The riflemen nearest us turned back from the hunt to resume the killing of Negroes. Perhaps they thought that we were dead or running. I never will know.

"Keep you from me so we are not one target," I told Raines, as I prepared to rise and plunge into the stew of it. "And do not shoot until close enough to hit."

Even then, I thought our plight near hopeless. But I could not watch more of such a slaughter. Not without one last attempt at justice.

I knew the boy would come, for he had heart.

We charged out of the dark. The enemy's eyes suffered from the firelight now. When they turned again to meet us, it was too late. I killed one man a body length away, before he could swing his rifle for my head. My bullet sought his heart, if heart he had. And Raines brought down the man who blocked his path, shooting him between the hips, then clubbing his skull with the pistol's butt.

How many were left? I saw but three white faces on that field, not counting Lott or Raines. And Lott was no longer white, but painted crimson. His face and beard were seared with blood, and his hands were crusted brown. Flames blazed in his endless depth of eyes.

I heard a different scream. It come from Raines. Shrieking like a banshee he was. Twas the cry we all would come to know, that Rebel yell.

He had surpassed my progress. I could not match the pace of his good legs.

He ran for Lott.

But he could not clear his aim. Limb-robbed bodies, sculpted by the Devil, collided with the boy, smearing him with blood. Others wraithed across his line of fire.

I glimpsed another fellow, a white man with a hatchet, rushing to take Raines from behind. Then another of Lott's men appeared.

I had a clean line on the second man and put him down.

But Raines was running to his death. I saw it clearly. I shouted to him. But he was gone beyond my here and now.

I saw it as a soldier sees. Friends have died as I watched, nearby and helpless.

The fellow with the hatchet loomed at his back.

Raines wheeled with perfect instinct and pulled the trigger.

His gun was as empty as Cupid's pistol had been.

Raines shoved the muzzle into the bearded face, stabbing the barrel at the fellow's eyes. With his left hand he sought and grasped the wrist that guided the hatchet. But anyone could see Lott's man was stronger. He looked as if he would break his opponent's back at any moment. Raines fought desperately, but his feet lost purchase as his spine arched rearward. I saw his gritted face in profile. There was no hunger for death in him now, but a famished appetite for life.

I lurched to the side, trying to get in a shot, and collided with a child. The little fellow screamed as we both went down.

Still, I am quick, if clumsy of leg nowadays. I come up fast and aiming.

Wonder filled the hatchet wielder's face. The tool dropped from his grasp and he collapsed, heavily, into Raines's embrace.

Barnaby must have shot him, I thought. Or else one of the Negroes had armed himself.

Then I saw Lott. Lifting his revolver toward Raines. With a steady hand and nothing to block his aim.

I could not have gotten a clean line of fire in time to stop him. But I saw something else in that last second.

Lott's son appeared, close by, in the human wreckage.

I shouted out his name:

"Isaac!"

The boy turned and I shot him. Twice. The first shot tore him, and the second slew him.

Lott had faltered when I called that name. As I had known he would. He swung about in time to see his son die.

He did not even try to take revenge. I never heard a man scream as he did. Twas a lamentation mighty as plagues and floods. Lott dropped his cutlass and his pistol, plunging toward the boy. Howling he was, until you thought shreds of lung must spit from his mouth.

His face summed up the torments of this earth.

The shooting stopped, although the shrieks continued, the calls of pain, of loss, of mortal dread.

Lott fell to his knees before his son. The light from the fires lapped his blood-caked face. He might have been in hell or a burning slaughterhouse. A shriveling creature, he knelt among the slain. Clutching his boy by the shoulders, meaning to lift him. But a corpse is a selfish thing and will not help. Lott bent over the boy, all blood and agony. The burning shanties no longer lit his eyes. Now it was the heart's inferno that made them glow so hugely, consuming him from within. Wailing, he gathered up the boy and pulled the heaviness to him. Drawing his son against his chest, he set to howling like the maddest dog.

He raised his tear-racked face toward the stars.

Lott found no ready Bible verses now. Only an animal's bellow to summon God.

There was naught else under Heaven. Only his son. He held him as though he might squeeze life back into the body.

The boy's head lolled, white-eyed, and his arms poked out like sticks.

Lott drew him up for a father's kiss and stroked his hair as he buried the boy in his shoulder.

I saw Raines walk toward him. Slowly. Eyes hunting for the pistol or cutlass the old man had dropped.

I did not want Raines to have that deed in his memory. So I stepped forward and lifted my captured gun, my own Colt long shot empty.

But I would not have Lott on my conscience, either. Although the memory of the son is worse.

Cupid rose from the dead. His shirt was bibbed with gore and he made slow progress, staggering, almost as if he were blind and smelling his way. Raines shied off instantly, for his body understood deep matters that his brain could not. Cupid's left arm dangled and his cloven shoulder drooped. But a Bowie knife gleamed in his strong right hand.

He moved as if guided by devils. Perhaps he was already dead, returned to earth to drag Lott down to Hell. His face did not look of this world at all. Twas cleansed of all the things that make us human.

Lott rocked his dead son in his arms and wept.

Cupid paused above him, blocking the firelight and casting Lott into the shadows. He raised the knife. Breathing hugely, fueling himself for the blow. Blood throbbed from his barely living carcass.

The blade swept down.

The first strike nearly severed Lott's head. The second chop finished the business.

Wheezing blood, Cupid bent over. Swaying, he clutched Lott's beard, then straightened his dying body one last time. He waved the head above him like a banner, spraying blood across the soil of Beersheba. Lott's blood and his own. He opened his mouth to shout, but no sound emerged. The part of him that made words had already perished. There was naught left but a human wreck triumphant, signalling his victory to the world.

Cupid swung the head down hard. Pounding it against the earth. Smashing it down to make it deader still. Then he fell to his knees and took up his knife again. And he hacked Lott and his son. In a slowing madness.

We all pulled back as the air drenched with their blood. Then Cupid gasped and crumpled. But he refused to die. He buried his face in his enemy's flesh and rent him with his teeth. Until his own flesh slowed to a quiver then stopped.

Raines stood watching, empty pistol hanging at his side. Standing amid the carnage of a small affair at the far edge of a great war. I wished that the boy had gone to be a preacher, that his study of theology had held him, and that he had never raised a hand against his fellow man. I knew by his look he would never forget what he had seen.

I limped over and tugged him away. For I saw what he did not. The Negroes who had survived, intact or wounded, were having their revenge on those of Lott's men who were not yet dead. It was no place for us.

.   .   .

ABRUPTLY, RAINES AWOKE to another concern.

"Where's Mr. B.?" he said. Twas almost a cry. The fear of loss in his voice was a child's for a father.

I quickened, too, for I had not thought on Barnaby since the tide turned. Now I feared that he had fallen wounded, if not dead. What if the Negroes mistook him for one of Lott's pack?

But Barnaby was a splendid gentleman's gentleman, and would not keep his master waiting long. As if he sensed our worry, the Englishman materialized from the shadows. And a great deal of materializing that was, I must say, with his globe of girth all stained with gore and powder, his Derby hat lost and his hair in disarray. He come limping along almost comical. At first I thought he was mocking my manner of walking.

Roland, the Negro who was unsound on the origins of Jesus, pranced at his side. Oh, Barnaby knew more of the Negroes than ever he told to us. There was a story there, as yet unfinished. But let that bide, for this tale is enough.

When the Englishman's steps grew troubled, Roland helped him. As the two men closed toward us, I marked the woe on Barnaby's face. His features were entranced by pain, and though he sought his master anxiously, his eyes would not stay fixed on any spot.

He had been shot. Sweat jeweled his forehead, streaking through the smear, and he looked faint.

We rushed toward him, but he sought to dismiss our alarm. Assured that Raines was well, he only shook his head and said:

"Poor Wylie . . ."

"Mr. B.?" Raines begged. "Where are you wounded? Where's—"

Again, the Englishman refused our proffered aid. He even stepped free of Roland's grip. A fellow of aplomb and stirring appetites he was, drawing strength from the presence of kindred souls. Though dirtied by the combat, he seemed a very Falstaff in his prime, lit by some English hearth, not burning shanties. Twisting to see behind him, he sighed and said:

"I fears I ain't been mindful, Master Francis. Grazed me atop the walking muscles, the fellow did."

He danced to get a look at himself, turning in the cast of the dwindling flames. The bullet had entered the Englishman's mass at a spot that wants no telling. Suffice to say, he would not ride or sit nicely for some time.

"It ain't gallant," he cried out, near despair at his sharpened knowledge of the location of his wound. "Oh, ain't it a wicked shame?" But another theme soon set his head to shaking. "Poor Wylie," he said. "I tried me best to warn him, Master Francis. But the fates won't mind us for a golden guinea, as me governor always said. That Bridie should be whipped, and I'll say no more. Marking a fellow for death what done her no harm. A mix of goofer dust, no doubt, though Barnaby says no more."

I looked at the fellow in wonder. "Surely, you don't believe—"

"Indeed, I do, indeed! Deadly, deadly. Voodoo's a right science of the darkness."

"Sir," I said, in genuine Christian alarm, "you surprise me."

"You ain't been to New Orleans," he told me. "Proper folks get haunted twice a day." Then he winced severely and grew quiet. We helped the English titan to the earth. With him muttering all the while that he wanted no fuss, and what would his governor's governor think, the one who fought with Wellington and Pakenham?

I was the one who saw the devil. The evil man among the evil men. The Judas.

He dashed from the grove and threw himself atop Raines's horse.

Hesiod. Known as Angel.

I raised my captured pistol to shoot, but Raines struck at my hand. Loyal to his horse, protecting the animal. He did not understand what he was seeing.

Angel fired back at us. Not aiming. Only trying to deflect our aims. Then he kicked the horse to life.

"You fool," I told Raines. "He's the one—"

Raines was an intelligent man. Realization crossed his face, then shame.

"I'll bring him down," he said.

Twas then I struck the poor boy on the jaw. Putting him out cold.

"Sorry, Mr. Barnaby," I called, already scuttling for the horses clustered behind the smoldering ruins. "He'd only get himself killed, and I'll not have it."

The big man waved me on. He understood.

"I'm coming on along, too," Roland declared. "I wants me a slice of that nigger."

I let him come, and welcomed his assistance.

Now, you will say, "Why did he take the Negro and not Raines?" And I will tell you: Young Raines would have out-ridden me, and Angel would have killed him. For Raines was brave, but he was not yet skilled. Or hardened as you have to be for some things. And he had seen things that would render him unsteady for some days to come. But Roland had been a slave, and would be steeled to much.

Seconds, only seconds we had.

A limping little man, I was, foundering among the horses. Yet, I found Rascal quickly enough. As if the horse found me. Usually, I had a time getting up on his back, but I'd got vinegar in my blood and fair vaulted into the saddle.

I had to bring this Angel down to earth.

I thought I knew my way, but it was dark. In but a moment, Roland took the lead. We galloped out the way I first had come into the camp.

If Angel was skilled as a rider, we might not catch him. For Raines's mount was splendid, as such creatures go. And Rascal may have been a marvelous horse, but I was a bobbing fool set in his saddle.

Ahead, we heard a whinny, then a shot. And another whinny. Hoofbeats and hoofbeats, resounding.

The moon was young as we come to nature's gate. Old Toby lay across the path in the light. Gone to his reunion with his son.

A horse has a certain tone when a whinny becomes a shriek.

Such it was that we heard up ahead. Shrieking and stomping and curses.

Twas then I kenned it. Raines's horse was his master's horse, indeed. Angel had met difficulty managing him, despite the way he had with other horses, for the beast would have no stranger on his back.

"Come on," I barked, as much to myself as to Roland.

"Goin' to kill that nigger dead," my companion swore. "Kill him dead, if it takes a month of Sundays."

If he did not kill us. I remembered the giant muscles of the man, displayed in the wrestling match with the Swede at Shiloh. If Angel shot as well as he scrapped, there might be trouble waiting.

We thundered down the glen made by the mounds, with the trail snaking between moon-washed boulders.

I had no idea if I had any bullets left. I knew my Colt was empty in its holster. Did the pistol I had captured have any rounds in its cylinder? I had counted four shots as I fired my captured weapon in the scrap, but knew not if the man from whom I had taken it had fired the rest away. Always check your ammunition. It is a fundamental matter, see. Yet, I had thought the killing done and neglected a duty the youngest soldier learns.

I chose to believe I had one shot left. If I had none, then that was God's decree.

My shoe scraped on a rock-face as we rode. It sparked. My bad leg would be bruised the worse come morning.

Twas all I could do to stay atop the horse.

Our path tended downward. You felt the decline by night as you did not by day. Heading toward the marsh.

We had gained upon our quarry. As we burst from the defile, I saw a maddened oddity ahead, a creature newly forged of man and horse. Black in the moonlight. Black, but clear of outline. Splashing into the wet ground.

Angel raised his hand and brought it down. I heard the cut of leather on living hide.

I clutched the pistol in my hand, thumb upon the hammer.

The stolen horse would not obey its rider. Refusing to go on, it bucked and reared. Spiteful of the whip, the beast had spirit. Its hooves threw silver water in the moonlight. Angel damned the animal with shouts, and beat it madly.

"Don't shoot until you're sure of your mark," I called to Roland. Uncertain if he even had a gun. "His aim's worthless while the horse is like that."

We plunged on through the shadows.

Then Angel fell. I saw him tumble backward. The horse dashed onward.

I pulled ahead of Roland, better-horsed. But Rascal, too, shied at the edge of the swamp. I was about to do some whipping myself, when I saw a wonder. By the pallor of the moon.

Angel sprang up from the marsh. But he was a transformed creature. He had gathered up a dozen ropes and, as he rose, he swung them left and right. They lashed from his limbs and torso.

He was screaming.

Snakes. Maddened, they had fanged so deep they fastened to him. He must have tumbled into a very congregation of serpents.

He tried to run. Some of the creatures dropped away. But others lashed and twisted around him. He stumbled. Dropped to his knees, he rolled backward, over-burdened. When he come up for the last time, a fat rope flew through the moonlight and struck his chest. He trailed a writhing arm as he sank down.

"*I* ain't going in there," Roland told me.

.　　.　　.

BACK AT THE CAMP, Raines stood guard over Barnaby. In case the thirst for blood had not been slaked.

But I could read the air. The danger was past. Now all was sorrow. Armed with torches, the Negroes searched for their loved ones. Sudden cries marked hard discoveries. As long as the torches moved, their light meant hope. But when one paused, then stopped, it marked a loss.

To hear those plaintive calls wrenching the night was to shed all doubt of the African's humanity. He loves as we do, and his heart feels loss. I am not one to speak of revolutions, for I dislike disorder of all kinds, but slavery must be banished from our soil.

A thing had changed in me, see. For though I never wished ill to the Negro, I had felt no special care toward his plight. I pitied from a distance, but did nothing, with Christian lips, but not a Christian heart. Now things were altered, deep within, the way that never quite fits into words. I had become an abolitionist, I suppose, although I value quiet and circumspection, and would not have upheaval in the streets.

I just like things done fair.

No matter what the generals said, the war was over slavery. And slavery was all that caused the war. It was the plague upon our golden land. Twas clear. And the rest was blather.

Now, do not think me radical or wild, for I am not. I would not set the Negro on a pedestal. But I would make a little room at the table for the fellow, and give him honest work for his two hands. I would not give him more than I would you. But, fellow Christians, dare we give him less?

Let that bide.

The shacks were little more than embers now. The torches flickered on, scorching the dark. Barnaby sat in the light of red-veined logs and sparks.

"Mr. Barnaby?" I asked, "have you had a great deal of bleeding, then?"

"Well-staunched, I'm well-staunched, sir. All done proper, and little harm to come of it," the game fellow said. "But ain't it a beastly shame? That's what I calls it. For scar it will, and where the sun don't shine."

"It will be an honorable scar," I assured him.

He looked at me, with rueful eyes aglow. "But what if I was to marry again, I ask you? Not that I plans it just at the moment, sir. I don't. But what if it come to that, what if it did? No proper wife would think such marks was got honorable. Sooner or later she'd see it and think I went running. And Barnaby B. Barnaby ain't never run a step. And I'm vain enough to say it, that I am." He quivered like a jelly made of sorrow. "Oh, the shame of it is more than a man can bear, sir. For see it the lady will, though the soul of modesty. It all comes out in the wash, as me governor always said. And seeing is believing, is what *I* says, and seeing that will set her mind to working."

"First get the wife," I advised him, "then worry."

.   .   .

THEY BROUGHT THEIR DEAD OUT of the preaching ground, lighting the way with torches. They carried the bodies in ragged quilts and canvas scraps that had survived the fires, for few of the corpses were whole enough to loft over a shoulder. All were placed in a shed that had not burned. The quilts and scraps soon turned to blood-dark sops. Barnaby, Raines and I kept off to the side, near our horses. We would not move on until the morning, but this was not our business. We watched the Negroes at their labors, their women crying and the menfolk grim.

As always, there were mothers loathe to part with children's bodies, insisting they were sleeping and not dead. It is among the commonest sights of war, whether here or off in distant India.

In the morning, we would bury Wylie.

The tethered horses shuffled. Raines closed his eyes, pretending that he slept. I did not blame the boy, nor think him weak. He had so much to bear, and he was young.

The embers became ashes.

I thought that all the bodies had been gathered, for the Negroes who could walk formed ceremoniously, all but one who had gone raving mad. Expecting them to improvise a service, I clambered to

310 / Owen Parry

my feet out of respect. Instead, they started for the preaching ground, in somber procession.

When they returned for the last time, they bore a single body on their shoulders. I saw a gashed face by the torchlight. The Negroes wept and sang.

Their hymn told of a stranger, travelling through a world of woe. Going home, he was, to see his loved ones, who had made the journey over Jordan before him. It was a simple tune and crudely sung, but not unmoving.

As they passed, I reached to doff my hat and realized I had lost it. I bowed my head and prayed as best I could. I, too, wished to go home, but to my wife and son. And I was not certain all the Jordan's waters would wash me clean.

We must have faith, and go through.

They placed the Reverend Mr. Hitchens in the hut with their other dead. Then they set their torches to the shanty.

I could not bear the smell after a while. I have had my fill of burning flesh.

Kicking Raines on the heel, I told him to stay alert.

"You leaving?" he asked, in a voice come out of a drowse. And I heard fear. It is the minor things that trip our nerves.

"I am going for a little walk," I said, then added, "to take the air," for that was how a gentleman would put it.

But I had not gone far before I heard footsteps, and not familiar ones. I turned, hand on my pistol. Every chamber held fresh powder and ball.

Twas Roland, come to bid a last goodbye. Pale as milk in the moonlight he was.

"Guess we'll be going on north after all," he said. "Go call on Mr. Lincoln." He smiled. And isn't that a wonder and a blessing? You chain a man all his life, and still he smiles. "Tell him how come Jesus was a Negro."

Now, Mr. Lincoln liked a humorous tale, but this was irreverent.

"It is a long way to Washington," was all I said, though. I could not find it in me to be stern.

"Major?" His smile faded. "What's it like to be free up there?"

I opened my mouth to say a hundred things, to warn him against high expectations, to tell him men were never truly free, no matter the hue of their skin, that freedom was a matter of degree and a gift that asked responsible behavior, to explain that our armies found Negroes an encumbrance, to speak of faith as our only true liberation . . . but those were things that he would learn himself, and now he needed hope and not a lecture. I only said:

"Freedom is a great deal of work."

My answer nonplussed him for a moment, but soon his smile rekindled. "Well, I guess I'd rather work for a piece of that than for nothing. The way I been doing."

And then he shook my hand and walked away.

When I steeled myself to return to the smell of the bodies, the last of the Negroes had gone. Leaving only ashes. I sat me down by Raines and Barnaby, resting my back against a tree. There was no more to say. Not in the dark. We waited for the dawn, each man alone, and even the horses fell somber.

Yes. We must have faith. And go through.

In the grayness, at the first pure hint of light, a spirit appeared. Floating down out of the trees in her pale raiment.

I recognized a familiar lope. And the outline of a tattered hat. When she stepped up close, her dress was torn and soiled.

Twas Paddycakes, the simple girl. She swayed above us, thumb between her teeth, bare feet planted just before young Raines.

"See, Marse Drake?" she said. "I tole you there was devils."

epilog

He led me to the river. We passed the last Confederate pickets and halted on a bluff above the Tennessee. The water ran brown and quick, dividing a green world.

Our horses tapped the earth, impatient with their masters. One path wound south along the river's edge. My course, like the current, led north.

I had put on my uniform again.

"Stay close to the river," Raines told me. "Your people are a few miles along. There's an outpost where the trail forks."

The morning cool was frail and the day would burn. The birds had taken asylum in the trees, leaving the sky an unmarred blue, deep and clean. I remember the river and the sky, and the leaves heavy with a month's rain and sun.

Raines had eyes as pure as that sky, though they were brown not blue. But there was a different quality to his look now. Twas slight, but you would know it. He bore the taint of someone who has seen more than the common run of men. By the end of the war, many would carry that look. Or a worse one. But let that bide.

He was not ready to part from me, for the heart wants resolution. We like a proper ending to our stories, although the wonder is how we continue.

"I trust you will greet Mr. Barnaby for me," I said. The Englishman was recovering from his wound in a country house renowned for the wealth of its larder.

Raines nodded. A lone bird called and careened. Swooping over the river. My companion sighed.

We all lack words to say the things we mean.

"Look after yourself, you hear?" he said. Staring across the river, not at me.

"And you," I answered. "Do not confuse foolishness and duty."

He looked down to where his hands reposed on leather. "I don't like thinking of you . . . over there." His fingers struck me as peculiarly delicate that morning. Gesturing northward, he said, "It's a troubling business, this war."

"As all wars are, Lieutenant." I reached into the pocket of my tunic and brought out my little Testament. His old friend's book was still in my saddlebag, see. This *Donkey Hotie,* as it is pronounced. Raines would not take it, and I dared not abandon it, though it was a novel and dubious. For books are jewels far finer than the diamond. So, I would make us even, and still more.

I held out my present to him. Twas stained, but the words were pure.

"Look you," I said. "Take this for good luck."

He weighed it in his hand. Young and lovely foolish he was. For he valued the gesture more than the Scripture itself. But he would have time to see his way, if war did not consume him.

"Thank you," he said, with a smile. "I'll keep it by."

He thought my spirit simple. Well, if it is, I count that as a blessing. I would be simpler still, if only I could.

Twas hard to part. A great war stretched before us, and soon it would close between us again.

We spent another moment judging the river. Past a bend, above the treetops, black smoke stained the day.

"One of your gunboats, no doubt," Raines said, tucking the Testament in a pocket. "We're a good ways from the Jordan."

I held out my hand. He buttoned the book away and leaned toward me. His grip was fine, but firm.

"Perhaps, it isn't very far at all," I told him. "If only we had sense enough to see." I broke our handshake, for duty must be done. "Now I must go and give them my report. General Halleck will want to know as much as your Beauregard."

"After the war, then. You come on down here. As my guest."

It was his way of saying, "Do not die."

"I am a bad penny," I assured him, "and will turn up. You look to your safety, Lieutenant Raines. Remember that rashness profits no man."

I thought he would ride off. Instead, he reached inside his tunic and drew out a letter. Twas neatly folded and sealed.

Holding it toward me, he said, "Please. Take this." A smile he wore, but a wistful thing it was. "I wish you could deliver it in person, but I suppose that's unlikely. She needs to know about Billy. Send it on to her. Please. When you get back North. I give you my word there are no military secrets in—"

I raised my hand to tut him. Above the muddy river, the smoke thickened.

"I will see it is delivered," I said. "Now go on with you. Before the gunboat comes and makes a fuss."

"I'm beholden to you, Major."

"We are all beholden."

He smiled, all youth and warmth and possibility. Bright as the day of a sudden. The look of him would have softened Caesar's heart and turned a very Hector from his spear.

With a snapped salute, Raines tore off his hat then turned his horse and slapped it. He galloped off. A smile lingered where the dust had risen. Approaching a grove, he waved a last time and let out a "Rebel yell."

I turned northward, singing out a hymn.

.   .   .

THE MEMORY OF THE PORTRAIT let me spot her. Playing at mallets and balls she was, upon a lawn that led down to the sea. She looked a chastised queen, like Scottish Mary. The balls she tapped might have been worlds she ruled.

I called to her from the edge of the game, but the breeze was brisk and northern. It rinsed my words with salt and swept them off. So I intruded, though with great reluctance. Young swells, who should have been in their country's uniform, shot me looks they might have given a beggar. Newport drew the gentry, see. And though the mansion where she stayed was not so grand as those that would rise later, twas fine enough to mock all thoughts of equality.

At first she seemed to think I was a servant, my uniform a livery. I will admit I do not look distinguished, although I keep my buttons polished up.

When I made her understand I bore a letter from Raines she paled. Lifting a hand to her mouth. The wind robbed her hair of its order, teasing her eyes. Wide they were, and blue with a hint of purple. Have you ever seen a girl with lilac eyes?

She took the letter. At first, she held it gingerly. As if it were alive and threatened harm. Then she mumbled a pardon—she who was so proud and clear of speech—and hurried off. Unsteady she went, and it wasn't the wind that swayed her. Waving off inquiring looks, she hastened to a bench above the sea. Twas on a little bluff. I thought of Shiloh. Although this was a thousand miles away, and cool, and orderly, as better folk insist.

I took me off a little ways to a painted iron chair beneath an arbor. It was a welcoming place to sit, with the smell of the sea all clean and flowers for sweetening. I meant no further intrusion upon her, but felt that I must linger. In case poor Mrs. Barclay had a question. For she was made a widow unexpected, and well I know how little letters tell. She might be anguished over a trifle that could be explained in a word. I had come far, and might bide half an hour.

I sat on the chair and watched the gulls and the boats out in the chop. It was a bracing place after the Southland. Twas a world I understood. Despite the wealth about me, I knew the rules. I am a Northern man, see.

White sails scooped the wind and hulls danced over the gray-green sea. I watched them until I was half mesmerized. But I could no more escape my memories than could the young woman with the letter in her hands.

Halleck had been harsh and, I thought, foolish. If you will permit my judgement of a superior officer. He asked me questions then answered them himself. He did not listen. But glad enough the general seemed that all had been resolved, saving him the need to make decisions. He scorned the South in each regard, and had no taste at all for Negro matters.

Grant was subdued and sad. Halleck paid him no respect. I felt Grant's service might be at an end.

Sherman raged that Micah Lott had fooled him. And that the world was not as it should be. Born to fight, he was. And fight he would. Who could see how far that rage would take him? Or that he would break slavery's back himself?

I did not see my dear friend Mick Tyrone, for he was sent with patients to St. Louis. I left a letter.

Washington had been squalid with the Spring. McClellan promised a great campaign in Virginia, all flanking maneuvers by sea and strategic lines, but Mr. Lincoln feared it would come to nothing. My friends were glad to see me and I them, although dear Mrs. Schutzengel was dismayed that her revered *Herr* Marx did not think the time yet ripe for the convention she had proposed. Now she was unlike to go to London to change the world. Of course, she had a boarding house to run and pies to bake. I still doubted Molloy's fitness for marriage, but I stood up by his side and didn't he grin? I did it for Annie Fitzgerald's sake, you understand.

I hoped I might go back to my clerking duties in the War Department. It was the one thing I was fit to do. But first I begged a parole of Mr. Nicolay, Mr. Lincoln's private secretary, to take the letter north to Mrs. Barclay.

On the way, I snatched a Sunday with my beloved in Pottsville. One day with her is a decade with Helen of Troy. Although I won't compare her with a pagan, for she's a chapel woman to the bone. My only sadness was my little son. Oh, John was in fine health and walking proud, and he had his mother's intelligence. But he was growing up in his father's absence and I seemed queer to him. It nearly broke my heart. War breeds cruelties far from the fields of battle.

Other matters prospered. I bought a few more shares of railroad stock. Already, there were gains on my initial purchases. Evans the Bags at the bank was pleased as punch. For a Welshman does not mind a tidy profit. And he had developed beneficial relations with a correspondent on the Philadelphia exchange out of the business. The collieries prospered under the war's demands, though the Irish miners were truculent, and my Mary Myfanwy's dressmaking venture drew so much society trade she could not answer it all, but must hire on a girl fresh over from Galway. The lass was clever and clean.

I had one golden day at home. And a silver night fit for polishing in the memory. Nor do I mean that indecently.

Monday morning, seated in the railroad car, I read a newspaper to staunch my tears. Officers must not weep before the public, see. For there are those who would not understand. Before the train reached Hamburg, I found sorrow in a society report.

Olympia Cawber, the young wife of Mr. Matthew Cawber, industrialist and financier of Philadelphia, had departed this earth. Her illness was unspecified, for high folk think the flesh a shameful thing, and she come of a great family. I recalled Cawber's letter and its mention of an indisposition. Who can foresee the moment after next? The poor man loved his wife with great ferocity.

Let that bide.

At last, I got me to Newport. It seemed a splendid place to me, although its glory days were just beginning. Naval fellows were on the town like lice, but the Good Lord put serpents in Eden and we must learn to take the good with the bad. I had learned through telegraphic communications that Mrs. Barclay had gone to her summering early, see. I had not hinted at the note I carried or the sorrowful matters I had witnessed. Her family assumed I was pursuing a legal matter to do with her ill-starred marriage. And I suppose I was.

Now I sat and waited. White clouds rolled in and pressed down on the gulls. I filled my lungs. But my eyes kept returning to Mrs. Emily Barclay. She sat with the iron posture of a sergeant. Staring off across the inlet. As if awaiting a verdict. And yet I knew the verdict had been returned.

She did not fuss. Nor act the least bit unseemly. I was too far away to read her features, but sensed that her weeping had been brief. She looked as controlled as a well-drilled company. Utterly unmatched to the Southron temper she was.

What had she dreamed would come of such a marriage?

I felt a man's impulse to go to her. But that would have been the impertinence of a peasant tugging at the elbow of an empress.

I sat and waited.

The game on the lawn broke up. It held no allure for the players once their queen was gone. Indeed, the other women seemed her handmaidens. And the men were as slight as the cloth of their summer suits. I caught one fellow looking back toward her. But even he knew better than to approach. She sat with the letter clutched at her waist, staring into the past. Or the future.

Twas then I realized I had been forgotten. I am the sort of man her kind forget.

I would have slipped away, leaving behind a note with the name of my inn, had the commotion not erupted.

A fellow in a Navy uniform come racing through the gardens. Now I must tell you: Such folk do not run. They dress up finely, sailing officers do, and barely lift a finger. As if they were aristocrats commissioned. But this fellow was fair galloping on his pins. Hat waving in his hands like a signal flag. And shouting he was like a madman.

Then I heard his first distinctive words.

"Major Jones," he shouted. "Major Abel Jones . . . can anyone tell me—"

This would never do. It was indecorous. And we must leave the widow to her grief.

I got me up and waved my cane, prepared to bark him down if he failed to see me.

Barking my name again he was, when his eyes found me at last. It took him long enough, and I pitied the crew at sea when he kept the watch. An enemy ship would be on him before he noticed.

He hushed, for which I was grateful, and slowed from a run to a trot. Closing on me, his pace broke to a walk. Red and out of breath he was, for sailors don't like effort.

"Major Abel Jones?" he asked. Looking down at me doubtfully. I do not aspire to naval elegance, see.

Up the lawn, by the covered porch, the leisured folk had paused to watch our doings. For a rich woman is as curious as a peddler's wife.

"I am Major Jones, sir," I assured the fellow.

"Thank God," he said. Now that is another thing. These sailing folk have no proper religion and use the Lord's name vainly without cease. And I hear tell they have improper habits.

Nor did I know what to call the fellow, for naval ranks are queer and I can't read them. The braided devil neglected to introduce himself, but only said:

"I have a telegraphic message for you. From . . . it's from the President's office. I had to get my code book out." The fellow was fair cooking with excitement. "We're to sail at once. My ship's at your disposal . . . England . . ."

"May I see the message, sir?"

That flustered him the worse. He blundered through his pockets. Fishing the paper out at last, he placed it in my hand.

Twas from good John Nicolay, Mr. Lincoln's secretary:

aj. Report immed C. F. Adams U. S. minister London. USS Hammond your disposal. Waste no moment. Agents murdered unknown hands. Confed involvement feared. Conspiracy. Danger. jn.

The adventures of Abel Jones will continue in:

Honor's Kingdom

---

history & thanks

All authors owe more debts than they can recompense, but an immediate payment in prose is due to Fred Chiaventone, former cavalryman and author of two fine novels of the American frontier, *A Road We Do Not Know* and *Moon of Bitter Cold*. Although we share the experience of soldiering and an interest in the human realities of our national past, Fred's abundant knowledge shames mine. His critical reading of this novel—especially of Abel's description of Shiloh—gave the tale a generous burnishing. The tarnish that remains is mine alone.

As for that national history of ours, I am a fundamentalist. I believe the Civil War formed the America we know, modernizing our country and destroying the imperial legacies of human bondage and a landed aristocracy. The cause of the war was slavery. And the sin of slavery haunts us to this day. I hope our new century will, at last, finalize the justice a great war enabled and a spoiled peace delayed. Our progress has been mighty over these last decades. But our journey is not finished. The Jordan is in sight, yet we cannot reach its banks without our brothers.